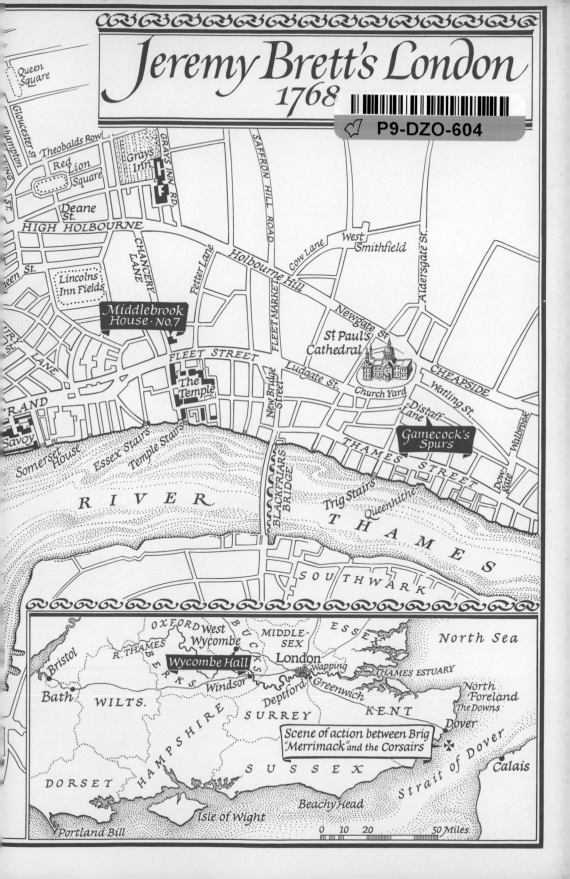

F. van Wyck Mason

by F. van Wyck Mason

Brimstone Club

Brimstone Club

F. van Wyck Mason

Illustrated with sketches by John Alan Maxwell

LITTLE, BROWN AND COMPANY · BOSTON · TORONTO

LIBRARY OF CONGRESS CATALOG CARD NO. 76-143707

T03/71

FIRST EDITION

Published simultaneously in Canada
by Little, Brown & Company (Canada) Limited

PRINTED IN THE UNITED STATES OF AMERICA

This book is for
Arthur and Dorothy Thornhill
with deep appreciation
of a generous and loyal friendship

Foreword

IN presenting this tale I have striven to describe a fascinating period in the history of Anglo-American relations — that one which immediately preceded the outbreak of the War for American Independence.

It has proved as challenging as it has been intricate to attempt to re-create a society possessed of ideas and values as foreign to present-day Anglo-American tenets as those of ancient Egypt.

England, 1768, was basking in an unprecedented prosperity. Her armed forces were flushed with brilliant victories won all over the globe. Conquests had been effected which laid the foundations for the greatest and most beneficent empire the world has yet beheld. Her commerce for the first time outstripped that of her principal competitors, France and Spain. As a result, a few classes gained enormous wealth with which, admirably, they encouraged the arts in all directions: literature, painting, architecture and sciences — to name only a few. Such was the brilliant side of the era.

On the grim side there was only sordid, grinding poverty and oppression through incredibly brutal laws and little or no hope for social or financial advancement; such was the lot of the common British and American Colonial subject. On both sides of the Atlantic these sturdy people stubbornly refused to surrender inalienable rights inherent to all freeborn Englishmen.

At this time, George III, well-meaning but weak and not too intelligent, ruled Britain through Ministers many of whom were corrupt and diabolically clever profligates and debauchees. These came very close to destroying an empire, in fact, but not in name.

It has proved difficult in the extreme to select representative events, characters and scenes from the vast amount of research acquired through voluminous study. I can only hope that I will be proven successful in my choices.

First of all I must explain that the "Brimstone Club" was a fraternity known at that time as the infamous "Hellfire Club." I did not select the true name for the title because for reasons of space it became necessary to elide certain scenes and events from the times they actually occurred during the activities of the Hellfire Club.

Nevertheless, descriptions of West Wycombe and the Caverns of St. Lawrence are authentic. Some of the orgies are described as they actually happened; others are the product of my imagination but at the same time typical of that day and society.

All the principal characters are fictitious, including the Brett family, the Constables, Lord Middlebrook, Peregrine Falconer, Henri Breboeuf, Dolly Lawton, Mrs. Stanhope and the rest of her "girls."

However, John Wilkes, Benjamin Franklin, the Chevalier d'Éon, Colonel Barré and Lord Sandwich are historic — subject, of course, to my interpretation.

It is my hope that I have, without undue emphasis on the rampant eroticism of that day, described a lusty, callous and fateful period.

I am greatly indebted to the cheerful patience and ability of those secretaries who have contributed so much towards the creation of this book. They are: Jeanne-Louis Mason, editor and research; Nancy Middlebrook; and Enid C. Ball.

My sincere thanks also go to Miss Margaret Franklin, researcher in the records of the British Museum. Her efforts in the Colonial Records Office were of first importance.

Much recognition also is due to the assistance of many of the staff of the Boston Athenaeum.

F. van Wyck Mason

"Hampton Head"
Southampton
Bermuda

Contents

Contents

Brimstone Club

I

Fog off Dover

BY THE PALE AND WATERY LIGHT of a winter's sun a Third Rate ship-of-the-line sighted around noontime remained a towering black outline on the oil-smooth sea.

The Channel continued so completely windless that at a distance of some two miles the man-of-war appeared to be patiently awaiting engulfment by a dirty gray bank of fog creeping sullenly in from the French coast. Although this Third Rate had passed too far to leeward to permit identification, Captain Amos Buckler opined that likely she was outward bound for duty in the Mediterranean.

Jeremy Dabney Brett used a short telescope to study her from the poop of the merchant brig *Merrimack*, 270 tons, experienced a burning impatience that, even after six interminable hours, Father's vessel still should be making no perceptible headway — and already she was a week overdue, thanks to a howling winter gale which for two days had mauled the ship off the Lizard. The *Merrimack* hadn't traveled fast or far since, hampered as she was by a stumpy jury foremast inexpertly contrived out of a spare mainyard.

What rendered the situation worse was that *Merrimack* was old, very old. She'd already been a leaky veteran of the Siege of Louisburg in 1747 when, nearly bankrupt, Silas Brett of Portsmouth, New Hampshire, had used the last of his resources to buy her, dirt cheap.

3

By now the brig's fabric had become so rotten and worm-eaten Jeremy preferred not to think about it more than was absolutely necessary. Lord, how his heart had sunk on boarding this pitiful remnant of S. Brett & Son's once-proud fleet of sturdy merchantmen which, for two generations, had showed the family's scarlet-and-blue house flag from West Africa's steaming coasts to the Orient, not to mention the West Indies and Scandinavia.

Poor Pa! He'd taken it mighty hard when one Brett vessel after another had been captured or otherwise lost during that accursed war with the French and Indians which had lasted for seven ruinous years.

What really had come near to breaking sturdy old Silas Brett was that hurricane which had sunk the *Avon*, his last remaining vessel, a fine, high-sided bark, with the loss of all hands. Now only the weary old *Merrimack* remained to show the Brett house flag and keep alive the firm's hopes for recovery.

Jeremy Brett collapsed his glass and stuffed it under an arm, then, his mood as gray as sea and sky, took a turn along the windward rail. Unseeingly he peered over this strangely placid Channel at the chalk cliffs near Dover seen as a dim white line rimming the northwestern horizon. Um. Yonder lay the Mother Country from which the Bretts of South Devon had for time out of mind sallied forth against Dutch, Turks, Spaniards, sea rovers, or anyone else attempting interference with free use of the seas.

How was he going to fare on his mission to this fabled and well-loved but wholly unfamiliar Old Country? No telling. Anyhow, before long he'd be making first moves to restore the family fortunes. No use stewing over possibilities he couldn't begin to anticipate. Suddenly restless, he abandoned further speculation and, following an established practice, stripped off his coat, tossed it with his skullcap of muskrat fur onto a transom, then commenced lightheartedly to skip and shadowbox about the deck.

During a long ten minutes the tall young fellow, curly, dark-brown and collar-length hair flying, ducked, crouched, swung and punched the empty air again and again with startling rapidity.

From the poopdeck Jeremy Brett's maneuvers were casually being observed by copper-skinned Henri Breboeuf whose high-cheekboned features remained expressionless; he disdained the supercargo's preference for fists in place of a sword. *Quel malheur!* Such amazing

4

speed and agility applied to the use of a blade should prove of infinitely more value to young Monsieur Brett amid the complicated and probably perilous world into which the pair of them were about to venture — if, indeed, this wretched tub ever reached London. *Dieu!* She rode sullenly as any of those log ships which, every summer, sailed for English ports from the Piscataqua's delta. "Ungainly" was the best that could be said about such a curious contrivance which, consisting of tall mast trees and massive yardarms heavily chained together, created a very rough replica of a ship's hull.

On such timber rafts two masts would be stepped and supported by unusually stout rigging. Next, a crude deckhouse designed to shelter a small crew would be constructed before canvas was set to catch prevailing westerlies and start the logship lumbering, half awash, across the Atlantic. If the weather held and the crew proved capable, a tedious voyage could earn Colonial timber merchants a mighty tidy profit.

Henri Breboeuf was one of numerous grandsons sired by that hardy empire-builder, the Baron Jean Vincent l'Abadie St. Castin, on a wide selection of copper-skinned maidens, usually complaisant daughters of useful sagamores, sachems and local kings. For diplomatic reasons the lusty baron had espoused quite a few savage bedmates.

Henri Breboeuf's nose was hooked, thin and high-bridged; he had a smooth, olive-bronze complexion and wore coarse, blue-black hair braided into a thick queue clubbed over the nape of his neck. His bright black, deep-set eyes were never still, always flickering about so restless that, from the start, they'd always put Jeremy Brett in mind of a boar wolverine's.

In the direction of the foredeck suddenly arose a series of strident discordant groans followed by squealing, shrill trills and arpeggios as, with infernal clarity, a set of bagpipes began warming up for the benefit of a squad of hairy, wild-eyed time-expired veterans of the Black Watch who, having fought, starved, suffered and frozen amidst the wilds of Lower Canada, at long last were being returned to the Highlands.

Ever since the chalk cliffs had been sighted these Scots had been singing endless, unintelligible wild ballads and circulating pannikins of red Jamaican rum. Sometimes they tussled roughly but happily

5

amongst themselves and swore fearsome oaths never again to desert Caledonia's misty crags.

Breathing quickly, Jeremy pulled on his jacket and, body yielding to the *Merrimack*'s monotonous rolling, went forward to watch these dark, bearded men commence still another violent war dance.

He grinned. More power to these "Tug-Muttons," or "Frozen Asses," as New England troops termed those wild Highlanders they admired for incredible endurance and efficient ferocity in battle almost as much as they dreaded the Scots' cunning lawlessness between campaigns.

The Highlanders were collecting about a leathery, one-eyed piper who, having inflated his bag, already was extracting experimental trills and chords from his chanter. Eagerly they drained wooden drinking cups before commencing to stamp and skip about on feet enclosed in Indian moccasins.

Losh, would it no' be wonderfu' to be shut o' Canada's endless gloomy forests and the broad North Atlantic's heaving, icy wastes? True, yonder lay only England which wasna' home but 'twouldna' be long ere they'd be across the Tweed — back in God's own country and free to indulge in such familiar pastimes as feuding, fornicating and cattle-lifting.

When the piper commenced an ear-piercing war song, "The Battle of Killikrankie," they leaped about in a wild, up-spring dance and singing:

> *Clavers and his Highlandmen*
> *Came down upon the raw, man*
> *Who being stout, gave mony a clout.*
> *The lads began to claw, then*
> *Wi' sword and targe to hand,*
> *Wi' which they were na slow, man*
> *Wi' many a fearfu' heavy sigh,*
> *The lads began to claw, then.*

Jeremy Brett noticed rheumy-eyed old Captain Buckler appear on deck. Now he was steadying a tarnished and verdigris-speckled brass spyglass against the mainmast's base. Following the direction of the skipper's inspection, Jeremy noticed a bank of mist out of which was

6

materializing a pair of small, low-sided, single-masted vessels, also becalmed about two miles distant.

"Dun't like the look of 'em," Captain Buckler grunted, snapping shut the brass lens cover to his spyglass. He then swayed so stiffly to the brig's motion and looked altogether so decrepit that Jeremy again lamented that Pa, teetering on the edge of insolvency and forced to economize, had entrusted his last remaining vessel to this frail and ineffectual dodderer.

"Dun't like it," repeated the old man, wiping tearing eyes on a greasy cuff.

"Don't like what, sir?"

"Dun't like, neither, the way that fog bank is rollin' in from east'ard. Least of all do I fancy the look o' them two luggers out yonder."

Jeremy raised short straight brows a trifle. "What about them? Likely they're ordinary fishing craft or maybe smugglers working in-shore to land after dark."

"Mayhap. Still, dun't like their rangy lines; might be a brace o' corsairs cruisin' out o' Brittany."

" 'Corsairs'?"

" 'Tis the French name for the pirates of Barbary, like 'picaroons' and 'buccaneers' in the Caribbean."

Thickly dressed against the raw atmosphere, the two peered across the slowly heaving lead-hued Channel.

Jeremy narrowed small, dark-brown eyes. "How can those be pirates? Surely His Majesty's cruisers must keep the Channel free of such vermin?"

Amos Buckler's thin, brown-mottled features tightened. Through gapped and rotting teeth he squirted a long arc of tobacco juice far out over the rail. "Used to, but that was afore the King's Friends corrupted the Admiralty out o' all recognition.

"I could puke when I think of the stout officers and seamen they've cheated of pay and promotion to make way for court dandies who can't tell a windlass from a marlinspike. Aye, and for the fine, stout ships their greed is ruinin' right now. Someday, England will pay a terrible price for inferior construction, starvation, wages, rotten food and —"

Captain Buckler broke off, releveled his glass. "Mr. Brett! Them

7

luggers *are* corsairs! See! they're running out sweeps! Pray God this fog thickens afore they can close in."

Young Brett, heartbeat quickening, watched twenty-foot sweeps, six to a side on each vessel, start to swing and splash till over-long bowsprits pointed straight at the becalmed brig. Then, perceptibly, the luggers commenced to advance, with the winter sun's revealing flashes of steel on their decks.

Henri Breboeuf, gripping the main shrouds, swung lightly onto the use-scarred rail. Blessed with uncommon fine vision he first noted that well astern of the strangers a puff of wind was darkening the Channel's oily slate-gray surface.

Sacrée Dame! The strangers would benefit first. No part of a seaman, the dark young mixed-blood nevertheless foresaw that should this breeze continue to blow as at present the fog bank might advance fast enough to overtake the luggers and conceal the weary old *Merrimack.*

Word spread. Soon the brig's company from cabin boy to owner's son lined the bulwarks. Obligingly the wind increased till the outlines of those rakish craft became lost amid slowly moving gray strata.

"Now God be praised," coughed Tom Jott, the *Merrimack*'s purple-nosed mate. "If only we'd a few sweeps aboard we'd soon be out o' this pickle."

Captain Buckler ran an eye over the brig's stained and idly slatting canvas, half-heard the rattle of a loose block banging rhythmically above. "Don't much favor this settin' 'round waitin' for the axe to drop like a Christmas goose in a fattenin' pen."

Thanks to red rum warming their bowels the Scots on the foredeck quickly resumed dancing and bawling unintelligible Gaelic ballads.

Henri Breboeuf meanwhile eased a stout but gracefully designed campaign sword from its sheath and commenced a series of remarkably swift patterns of cuts, thrusts and parries. Accustomed as they were to this brooding furriner's exercises the crew paid Breboeuf little heed.

Once dark billows of fog commenced drifting over the bulwarks Jeremy Brett figured it safe to seek his supercargo's cramped quarters just forward of the main cabin. The eternal *swish-bump! swish-*

clunk! of bilge pumps served to remind him of the *Merrimack's* rotten state.

From under his bunk he pulled a brass-mounted traveling desk and decided for Pa's information to add to his chronology of the *Merrimack's* miserable crossing.

Ye 9th March, 1768

RESPECKTED SIR:

With a vast Sence of Releef wee did, with the first Light of Morning this day, raise the Coast of England. Yet to-day the Brig has crawelled along untill before midday the Wind died out Compleat.

So bad have the Leaks groan Pumps are kept going around the Clock thirty Strokes to the Minute.

Conseekwence the crewe is much Fatigeed. So poore is the Vessel's state Cap't Buckler prays wee shall Encounter no hard Winds ere wee enter Thames River for in Storm off the Lizzard the Foremast broke off so close to ye Deck only a short Stump remains to support a weake littel Jury Mast.

Our time-expired Highlanders are growing mighty Drunk. Trust they will not cause trubbel. Captain Buckler appears littel capable of curbing these cursed Froze-Asses!

Brett dipped his quill into a leaden ink bottle, at the same time became aware that the bagpipe's wails were dying out amid a babble of strident voices.

I must Confess, Honoured Sir, I grow much Apprehensive over Prospeckts towards mending our firm's Fortunes in England. From all I have learn'd London Town is vast and a confusing place to a Unknowledgable Colonist like y'r dutiful son; altogether a strange and a dangerous Place. However I am Determin'd to Remain Wary and Exercise every Precaution uppon arrival.

Following y'r Instrucktions my first Intent is to wait uppon y'r agents and persuade Messers Mason & Sampson to Obtain high Prices for y'r Cargo.

Once said Merchandize is dispos'd of I shall attempt to gain favour of the Board of Procurement and Advance our Applickation for Contracks covering construcktion of supply Shippes for His Royal

9

Majesty's Navy. I confess, y'r only Son is much at a loss as how to proceed in London all will be so strange, so confused.

Lord God! How *did* a raw Provincial go about soliciting contracts from His Majesty's Government?

One of my earliest projects, Sir, will be to locate y'r Daughter and my Sister. Possibly Perdita's husband possesses Influence at Court which may Attrackt the Admiralty's Favourable Attention. How very unfortunate I possess no knowledge of Lady Constable's whereabouts.

Boots came clumping down the companion ladder in such a hurry Brett put down his quill, hurriedly sanded, and shoved the letter into the portable desk.

The boatswain, a toothless old fellow one of whose eyes was white with cataract, appeared, dabbing at a bleeding bruise on his cheek with a filthy bandanna. "Mr. Brett! Cap'n says come on deck quick! Quick!"

On gaining the fog-shrouded deck he was greeted by a burst of extra-loud and discordant skirling. Peering through dank fumes, when he made out the old Captain's meager outlines and realized he was shaking with rage. Beside him hovered the Mate, as anxious and equally ineffectual.

Beyond them swayed Henri Breboeuf leaning against the taffrail, a half-smile on his features.

"What's amiss?" Jeremy queried.

Captain Buckler shook a gnarled fist at the foredeck. "I ordered them damned tug-muttons to pipe down but they're crazy-drunk and won't heed. One even drew a dirk on me, the Captain! Were I but ten years younger I'd ha' stretched him instanter! Listen to that screeching."

> *There was a Cameronian cat*
> *Was hunting for a prey,*
> *And in the house she catched a mouse,*
> *Upon a Sabbath day.*
> *The Presbyter, being offended*
> *At such an act profane*

Laid by his book, the cat he took,
And bound her in a chain.
And straight to execution
Poor baudrons she was drawn
And high hang'd up on a tree;
Mess' John he sang a psalm, sang he.

"They *are* making an unholy racket," Jeremy admitted, "but what real harm are they doing?"

The old Captain's ragged gray beard quivered amid the ghostly mist and he waved arms in futile outrage. " 'Harm'? God above! They're like to lose me the ship and get us our throats cut into the bargain."

Jeremy queried sharply, "How so?"

"In a dead calm pea-souper like this least noise carries far over water; if them luggers we spied truly *are* corsairs this racket will guide them villains straight to us, fog or no fog." His cracked voice grew querulous. "When them ijits forrad quit caterwaulin' to catch breath I heard the noise of sweeps — and not far off!"

Young Brett was shaken. Why hadn't he been smart enough to foresee that, lacking Highland music, the luggers could have had no idea of which direction to row? Pa long since would have stopped the racket and got ready to repel boarders.

How effective a defense could be improvised? Not much. In Portsmouth, Pa'd been able to sign on only four able-bodied seamen among the *Merrimack*'s ten-man crew; the rest either ancients or pimply youths lacking experience, strength or self-confidence.

"Please, Mr. Brett," Buckler pleaded, "*can't* you make 'em damn Scots shut up?"

Jeremy cast loose buttons on a frayed blue pea jacket and groped forward through blankets of slowly eddying fog.

Once the blear-eyed Scots spied the owner's son they only sang louder.

"Stop this racket! Stop it, I say!"

Sergeant Lachlan MacPhee, beetle-browed and bandy-legged as any ape, heaved himself erect, bearded jaw truculently outthrust. "Mon dear, we be only ainly amusing oursel's as is our right!"

"I said *stop that noise!*"

11

"An' did ye so? Well, ye miserable Yankee pup, I'll ha'e ye ken ——"

The Sergeant's kilts swayed when, leaping forward, he ran into a right to the stomach which doubled him up and sent him staggering aside. Brett punched the bagpipes out of his embrace.

Sergeant MacPhee, on recovering balance, emitted a roar and, crouching, gripped the handle of a skean dhu protruding from his stocking's top. Before the Scot could free his weapon Jeremy's fist smacked the point of his bearded jaw and he dropped inert among his befuddled countrymen.

"Quiet!" Brett rasped. "French pirates are closing in."

Hissing Gaelic curses, the Highlanders attempted to stand but froze into inaction when Henri Breboeuf's clipped accents bit into the situation. He swung his sword in a slow arc. "Do not move, anyone."

Snarls arose but the shadowy figures made no overt move.

"Stay still and listen to Mr. Brett."

Jeremy Brett made an impressive figure, with the fog magnifying his six-foot stature.

"Seems you Scots are aching for a bicker. Very well — wait and you'll soon get your guts full of fighting. An you don't believe me, harken! Hear those splashings, or are you deaf as adders?"

Above the soft lapping of waves alongside could be recognized the rhythmic *swish! tunk! splash! swish! tunk! splash!* of sweeps not far away.

Sergeant MacPhee swayed to his feet and, dazedly shaking a disheveled head, rasped, "Muster-r Brett, mayhap ye're right, but I'll yet settle wi' ye for that soncy knock."

"I'm looking forward to it. Now sober up and ready your men."

Called Captain Buckler's reedy voice: "Quick! For yer lives cast loose the guns." Which sounded brave enough except that the *Merrimack*'s "guns" consisted of four worn-out six-pound carronades.

Heretofore the efficiency of His Majesty's cruisers had obviated a merchantman's crew learning the use of carriage guns. Still, if he roared orders the corsairs just might be bluffed and hesitate to close in.

Recalling a brush with picaroons off Cuba, Jeremy Brett ran aft, gripped the Master's bony shoulder. "After the first discharge there's

12

small profit trying to reload guns, men will only fall over themselves; order pikes and cutlasses broken out."

Admittedly, he'd overlooked much of vital importance but why hadn't he at least inspected the brig's ordnance?

Brett returned to Sergeant MacPhee. "Any of your men know how to serve swivel guns?"

The Highlander, gingerly testing his jaw, gave a surly nod. "Aye."

"Say 'Aye, *sir!*' — damn you!"

"Aye, sir-r. Some may know the use of such." He swung on Captain Buckler. "Ha'e ye any blunderbusses? Such are unco' handy for repelling boarders."

"Nary a damn one," admitted the ship's Master. "Only a few pistols and muskets. I reckon we'll have to depend on the swivels."

2

Corsairs

⌐~~~~~~~⌐

T HE SCOTS, unsuccessfully trying to sober up in a hurry, clumped about buckling on claymores and selecting rust-speckled muskets from an arms chest hurriedly hauled from the Captain's cabin.

Slinging on cartouche boxes they lurched about and, hit-or-miss, succeeded in charging the brig's four swivel guns before ramming home dangerously heavy charges of musket balls and buckshot.

The scrawny, one-eyed Bosun's manner appeared anything but confident while removing padlocks from the *Merrimack*'s small-arms chest and then dealing out clumsy brass-mounted boarding pistols. Pikes and a handful of dull-looking cutlasses were issued to scared-looking men and boys.

While jamming a second pistol into a wide leather belt Jeremy Brett peered about, miserably uncertain about the course to follow since Captain Buckler was issuing no commands; only dithering about leaving the Bosun and Sergeant MacPhee to supervise loading of two little carronades mounted along the starboard beam.

Gunports, hinges stiffened by rust and warping, could only be forced open with frantic use of handspikes.

The fog remained as damp and impenetrable as ever when the mixed-breed Canadian ran on deck wearing a loose-fitting hunting shirt adorned by elaborate beadwork across its back and breast. In addition to his sword Breboeuf was armed with a spike-backed toma-hawk stuck into his belt; straight, blue-black hair dangled like a mane beneath a leather skullcap adorned by a stiff fish-hawk feather. But for a lack of war paint, his European breeches and footgear Baron Castin's grandson might readily have been taken for a Penob-scot brave.

Gaze restless, he ran up to Brett. "What shall I do, *mon ami?*"

"Ask Captain Buckler."

Breboeuf's strong white teeth glinted in a taut grin. "The old man is much confused."

Jeremy drew a quick breath, tapped a reservoir of unsuspected self-confidence. "Take the command of those 'tug-muttons' on the bow. When the enemy tries to board wait for my order then tell 'em to loose the swivels. After that they're to use small arms, then better use bayonets and claymores."

In contempt tempered with pity the supercargo lingered at Cap-tain Buckler's side as he stood gripping the tiller which, for lack of steerageway, yawed without effect.

Lord, how soggily the *Merrimack* was rolling with loose gear rat-tling and thumping about.

Amid an eerie silence broken only by the slatting of idle sails, the dull *thud-thud* of pumps working below, successive billows of chill, silver-gray mist kept rolling over the bulwarks. Imperceptibly, these grew less dense until Jeremy became able to glimpse hands on the forecastle charging a long-snouted swivel gun. Presently the *Merri-mack*'s crew heard an ominous *swish-clunk! swish-clunk!* made by sweeps working in from starboard.

When indistinct voices could be heard the Mate fingered a brass-mounted boarding pistol. "God send this scum attacks us along a single beam."

"Amen to that." The Captain's mottled, brown hand wiped sil-very beads of moisture from his beard. "We be much too few to defend both rails."

Cupping an ear to sounds of quickened rowing, Jeremy judged the luggers could not be over a hundred yards away. Then, inexplicably, the rhythmic splash of oars ceased and a faint mewing of gulls wheel-ing about the becalmed brig became audible.

Under a faint breeze commencing to blow out of the southwest

the fog dissipated and the luggers became discernible, dark and low on the sea.

Cold hands wrung Jeremy's bowels; swarms of indistinct figures were lining the luggers' rails. Why had Ma held out so long 'gainst Pa's sending their only son to sea save for a single trading cruise to Jamaica, Antigua and Barbados?

Glancing sidewise, he was shaken to find the Captain with jaw sagging, staring at the enemy. Was this maundering ancient deciding whether to open fire right now and maybe scare off the luggers, or to wait till they rowed so close they'd offer unmissable targets for the *Merrimack*'s raw gunners?

It stood to reason when the pinch came only the Scottish veterans might be depended upon; if only they weren't so few and drink-dazed.

If the *Merrimack* was lost with her would go any possibility of S. Brett & Son regaining ships and solvency; it was conceivable also that soon he might get killed or be so badly wounded he'd be incapable of accomplishing anything even if he lived to reach London.

On all sides sounded curses on the Royal Navy which should have been patrolling such a vulnerable stretch of the Channel.

It was compounding ill-fortune that Amos Buckler was proving so utterly ineffectual.

While adjusting the set of a new flint gripped between the jaws of his pistol's cock, young Brett watched the luggers close in; spray flew high and white from sweep blades swung to a cadence set by what sounded like caulking mallets pounded on empty kegs.

The two vessels, rowing some fifty yards apart and almost abreast, looked to be sixty feet overall and showed little freeboard.

Bitter fluids welled into Jeremy's mouth when fog thinned and revealed dark knots of men crowding the corsairs' rails. At a quick estimate he judged there must be between twenty and thirty men aboard each of them. They must be heavily armed since the sun, beginning to pierce the vapors, was drawing steely flashes about the decks.

When Captain Buckler suddenly emitted a curious, gasping cry Jeremy turned and saw the Master's rheumy eyes fly wide open; his head jerked spasmodically backwards and he swayed an instant before collapsing with the suddenness of a marionette whose strings had been cut. Mouth sagging open, he lay awkwardly sprawled, well-patched cowhide boots a-spraddle. Amid the confusion no one save the helmsman seemed to have noticed the old man's fall.

Brett lifted Buckler's head; one look into those fixed and vacant eyes told him the old man was as dead as Julius Caesar.

Sergeant MacPhee, the black-and-yellow stumps of his teeth revealed in a savage smile, trotted up and cast the body only a cursory glance. "Yon rogues soon will be alongside. What's to be done, sir-r?"

"Take over the bow swivel and musketmen on the foc'sle. I'll captain the carronades. I'll open fire when I figure we can rake their decks to best effect, so wait till the pirates are bunched and getting ready to board, then touch off your swivel and blast 'em with musket and pistol fire."

Suddenly, inexplicably calm, he yelled at Henri Breboeuf. "Take charge of the after swivel and men on the poop!" and then repeated MacPhee's instructions.

The Canadian nodded and, deep-set jet eyes agleam, trotted over to the foot of the jury foremast where the Mate hurriedly was passing out pikes and cutlasses.

Brett's voice rang the length of the entire cluttered deck. "Everybody to his post! Keep calm, aim carefully and we'll win out of this!"

Howls and high-pitched yells continued to beat across the water; sounded very near.

Moses, the Negro cook, ran out of the galley, white-eyed and lugging a bucket of sand which he started scattering about the fog-dampened decking. He must have seen action before to have learned that spilt blood can render men's footing dangerously uncertain.

Sight of that shiny black countenance brought Jeremy a recollection from his one cruise to the West Indies. Someone aboard Pa's brigantine *Housatonic* — Pa always named his ships after American rivers — had described an effective defense against Cuban picaroons.

"Come here, Moses! Listen careful-like, then do what I tell you."

"Yassuh?"

"Go stir up the galley fire fastest you can."

Moses ducked a fuzzy, bullet-shaped head. "Yassuh. What do I do den?"

"Get your two biggest iron pots ready. When you hear me holler, 'Up, *Merrimacks!*' fill those kettles with hot coals and fetch 'em to me fast as you can."

18

"Yassuh, but what fo' ah do that?"

"Never mind!" Brett blazed so savagely the other flung up a warding arm and stepped back. "Just fill those kettles with coals and bring 'em when I want 'em!"

"Yassuh! Ah does that real quick!"

On gaining the waist Brett was encouraged to find the Boatswain and the few able seamen blowing on slow matches just as if they'd done so before. He hoped so. Everything depended on the one-and-only discharge of carronades charged to the muzzles with musket balls and scrap iron.

The Highlanders still somewhat unsteady from rum lined the rail, raised eldritch war cries and shook bony fists at those over-long and slender bowsprits now boring in like a brace of titanic lances.

Just when should the carronades be touched off to cause the greatest possible havoc?

Jeremy flung the Captain's crumpled body a furious glance then glared about desperate for guidance. The only people seeming to retain any semblance of self-possession were Henri Breboeuf and whiskey, terrier-like Sergeant MacPhee.

By now fog had dissipated completely and revealed the luggers' rakish hulls in full detail. Their crews were busy striking useless brown sails.

Face after anxious face was swinging questioningly in the supercargo's direction. An unfamiliar ringing quality in his voice Jeremy shouted, "Now listen well! Mr. Breboeuf commands on the poop; Sergeant MacPhee commands forrad. All hands will obey my orders as acting captain."

To his astonishment the ragtag and bobtail defenders raised a wavering cheer.

The attackers answered with deep-throated yells and, brandishing all manner of weapons, set up a menacing clamor something like that raised by hounds closing in on a stag brought to bay.

On the *Merrimack*'s deck rose hearty cursing over the absence of a King's ship.

Oarsmen in both luggers now speeded up their beat and came surging forward for the kill. Fifty yards short of the helplessly wallowing brig the corsairs pulled extra hard for a few strokes, then, allowing sweeps secured by lanyards to trail alongside, closed in together, caught up weapons, and came rushing forward, howling in half a dozen languages.

Leaving the Mate at the helm, Brett, gulping down a sense of panic, shouted, "Don't fire yet! Let 'em come closer. Let ——"

A terrified young sailor serving the forward carronade panicked and convulsively jammed the ruby-red tip of his match on the little cannon's touchhole. A small streak of dazzling flame shot upwards then the piece roared and belched a whirling cloud of brown-gray smoke. Like a high-strung colt suddenly spurred the gun carriage recoiled against its breechings.

Most of the swivel's shot flew high but judging by a scattering of shrieks and screams a few musket balls must have found marks among dark shapes swarming about the luggers' bows.

Sergeant MacPhee spouted Highland oaths but waited to fire his swivel. "Bluidy fool's wasted a fine chance to hurt 'em bad!"

The attackers replied with a ragged volley of small arms fire.

Like huge and angry wasps musket balls hummed past Brett's ears as, leveling a pike, he bounded over to the unfired carronade. "Quit that!" he snarled at a wild-eyed seaman who, cheeks ballooned, had begun to blow on his match.

Even as the smoke-veiled gap separating the vessels narrowed to nothing, seamen among the brig's crew became aware that under a barely perceptible breath of wind out of the southwest the *Merri-mack*'s main boom had creaked, had started to swing very slowly towards the lee bulwarks but no more attention was paid once the Bosun yelled, "*Look out!*"

The tip of a lugger's bowsprit was thrusting over the bulwark and probing the main shrouds like a cyclopean forefinger.

Brett drew a deep breath, bellowed, "Swivel gunners! Wait till they start to board!"

A few pistols cracked, corsair clamor swelled, then above the rail appeared a succession of heads in stained, varicolored bandannas or outlandish hats.

The Scots grouped about their swivels waited although firearms were banging in all directions.

"Fire! Fire Number One carronade! Damn it, *fire!*" Brett shouted then saw that for all its gunner was grinding a smoking match into its touchhole the piece refused to go off; undoubtedly its priming charge had become sodden by fog.

Brett was grabbing a quill filled with FFFFg powder from the priming box when a thick-bodied corsair thudded onto the deck and, leveling a pike, leaped forward, but somewhere amid the drifting fumes of gunsmoke a pistol banged and shattered the outlaw's head.

Reeling sideways, Jeremy recovered balance in time to duck beneath the thrust of another pike and to snatch a pistol from his belt. He jammed the weapon against his assailant's belly and nearly blew him apart; a reek of scorched flesh and burnt hair assured that, for the first time, he'd killed a man.

More boarders in shrieking fury swarmed over the old brig's rail.

The gunner whose carronade had misfired took a ball in the belly and fell, raising unearthly shrieks while flopping and writhing about the *Merrimack*'s thinly sanded deck.

The length of the bulwarks became crested by dark and menacing outlines.

Above the rising tumult Brett barely heard MacPhee's shout: "Shall we loose, sir-r?"

"Fire! For God's sake, fire!"

First MacPhee's, then Brebocuf's swivel gun thundered, adding whirling clouds of choking gray fumes to the confusion.

Vision limited to arm's length Jeremy peered confusedly through eddying smoke hopeful that the swivels had accomplished significant damage, but when the fumes drifted aside he glimpsed Scots on the foredeck scrambling to reload. Apparently they had missed the main body of corsairs jumping onto the *Merrimack*'s deck.

When his crew, their firearms emptied too soon, started to fall back Jeremy snatched up a stray cutlass and used the flat of its blade to make them halt. No use. White-eyed with terror they scattered and ran below gibbering.

On the foredeck Breboeuf, hatless, was shouting in a high, thin voice: "Stand fast! Reload quick! Second craft's alongside!"

A dull, grinding noise sounded as another bowsprit poked almost leisurely over the rail.

The Highlanders managed to fire a second time, but the charge they'd rammed down their swivel's bore proved too light and accomplished little to discourage boarders from the second lugger who, screaming curses, hurdled fallen bodies to charge the *Merrimack*'s hopelessly confused defenders.

Panting, wild-eyed, Brett brandished his cutlass, tried to rally the few crew members still on deck. "Stand, you bloody cowards! Damn it, stand or get your throats slit! Come on!"

A few seamen heard and started uncertainly after him.

The Highlanders abandoned their still-smoking swivels, grabbed up bayoneted muskets, and howling war cries fired a ragged volley into the boarders then set themselves behind their bayonets and plunged into the melee.

More by instinct than anything else Jeremy jerked free the pistol remaining in his belt, peered breathlessly about until, through a gap in the smoke he noticed a lean, leather-featured fellow using a hatchet to direct the attack. Barely in time Jeremy remembered to squeeze, and not pull, the trigger. Whether he hit or not he never knew for sure so dense remained billows of the choking, rotten-smelling smoke, but a burst of shouting in French, Breton and Portuguese suggested he'd done damage of importance.

The bumping, crackling noises made by vessels colliding and grinding against each other grew louder, then the wind had increased and carried away most of the battle smoke.

Panting like a hard-run racehorse, Jeremy glared about, realized that the Mate had grabbed the tiller and was attempting to utilize barely perceptible headway.

He also perceived that the *Merrimack*'s deck amidships had become strewn with dead and wounded.

Shooting had died away to only an occasional report; by now most weapons had been discharged and there'd been no opportunity to reload.

Amidships, a knot of fighters swayed back and forth, slashing, hacking, jabbing.

Emitting hoarse shouts, Brett, quite unaware that a bullet had severed a lock of hair, backed into a clear space and glimpsed corsairs from the second lugger swinging over the bulwarks. Brett pointed with his cutlass's blood-dimmed blade. "MacPhee! Get those—"

Howling, a quartet of shaggy, bareheaded Highlanders headed by the Sergeant collected and, plying bayonets in unison, succeeded at the cost of two men in driving the pirates back aboard their own craft.

The Sergeant though bleeding freely from a scalp wound had driven the razor-edged head of an espontoon into the breast of a scarlet-shirted giant whose huge beard had been plaited into two braids and secured by pretty baby-blue bows.

"Now! Now!" Jeremy waved forward a pair of seamen hesitating by the tiller, then hurled himself at a knot of screaming boarders so effectively that, to his surprise, his blade lopped off an attacker's sword arm and sent the dark-faced fellow lurching aside howling and clutching futilely at spurting arteries.

Faintly the Mate's voice penetrated the din. "Wind's rising. Hang on and drive 'em back!"

Defenders took courage but their rally proved only partially successful; the boarders were too many, so that for a space the struggle continued to hang in the balance.

In the center of a ring of assailants for the most part wearing heavy jackets or jerkins of leather, Henri Breboeuf was no longer allowed opportunity to deliver well-timed cuts and thrusts. Hard pressed, he could only strike to fend off destruction until his sword, struck by some stout weapon, broke off close to its guard. Nothing remained but to leap backwards over a tangle of fallen men; screeching like a trapped lynx, the Canadian jerked the war hatchet from his belt.

Screaming an Etchemin warcry, Breboeuf at once hurled himself at a pair of snarling, heavy-bearded corsairs. One he brained but the other fled before he could get to him.

Gripping his tomahawk Henri Breboeuf charged and again raising his warcry drove back the disconcerted boarders a few paces.

Catching a glimpse of sable features and white-rimmed eyes peering from the galley's doorway, Jeremy Brett remembered, shouted, "Up, *Merrimacks!* Up, *Merrimacks!*"

The Negro lurched out lugging a pair of iron beanpots abrim with glowing coals. These he put down before promptly taking to his heels.

Brett yelled to a lanky and heavily-freckled seaman who, armed with a reddened pike, appeared to be keeping his head. He indicated the smaller pot. "Carry this and follow me!"

By holding his cutlass between his teeth Jeremy was able to grip a pot in one hand and use the other to swing up onto the main shrouds and find himself looking down on a lugger's bow. He saw that both luggers, their bowsprits still entangled in the brig's rigging, were now lying close together at right angles to the *Merrimack*'s beam.

Despite a pistol ball's rapping him smartly on the shoulder,

23

Jeremy concentrated on a dark rectangle of an open hatch in the nearer lugger's cluttered deck. A powerful heave sent his fire pot arching downwards. It landed a trifle short but bounced once and spilt coals in all directions before vanishing below.

Furiously assailed from two sides he was forced to launch the second pot in the far lugger's general direction but then got so busy defending himself he'd no time to learn what that cast might have accomplished. Ducking under a hard-swung blade, he half-tripped over a fallen musket which he clubbed and flailed frantically about him.

The Mate, who'd taken refuge behind the tiller to keep eyes on the mainsail's worn canvas, sang out: "Don't quit! Wind's risin'! Drive 'em back!"

The weary old vessel shuddered, slowed its sullen rolling and very reluctantly responded to the Mate's weight on the tiller handle. One of those over-long bowsprits looming above the bulwarks very gradually began to move aft. The other, however, remained firmly entangled in the jury mast's rigging. Scrabbling crabwise across the deck, the Bosun hauled hard on the mainsheet.

Dazedly, Jeremy Brett crouched near the main hatch attempting to estimate the situation. Across bodies lying about the deck in awkward, improbable attitudes, he made out a trio of panting, scarlet-faced Highlanders using clubbed muskets to beat off a swarm of assailants.

Breboeuf was swinging his tomahawk in powerful, wide arcs which kept a ring of enemies at a distance. Abruptly a sharp explosion sounded from beyond the brig's bulwarks.

Taking a fresh grip on his musket's barrel, Jeremy started forward; then a shaft of grayish smoke pierced by a streak of dazzling flame shot up from beyond the rail. Disconcerted, the corsairs fell back and men who'd remained on the luggers raised panic-stricken wails. The attackers made for the rail; amazingly soon not a corsair able to run, limp or crawl remained aboard the *Merrimack*.

Her blocks and tackles rattling as her canvas commenced to fill, the *Merrimack* began to pull away and free herself from the larger lugger which, amidships, had begun to belch smoke streaked by flame. The effort to separate ended in failure since the bowsprit had become inextricably entangled with the jury mast's shrouds.

In vain Brett raced about, yelling to his handful of followers to use axes, hatchets, cutlasses, anything to cut free. Their frantic, disorganized efforts accomplished nothing.

The defenders soon were forced to retreat before sheets of flame which with appalling speed leaped the bulwarks, and hungrily fed upon the old vessel's weatherbeaten fabric.

The crackle and roar made by clouds of blinding, whirling hot smoke and gases quickly rendered the *Merrimack*'s foredeck untenable.

The Mate ran up, gray whiskers singed and eyes streaming. "Sir, better abandon ship in a hurry afore fire reaches the cargo. Remember, 'tis mostly turpentine, tar and rum! Nothin' burns better!"

For a despairing moment Brett glared helplessly through blinding clouds of sparks and smoke. The Mate was right; no hope remained of saving Silas Brett's last vessel. In agony he bellowed, "All hands stand by to abandon ship!"

3

H.B.M.S. *Nereid*

—————⌣—————

A HANDFUL OF THE BRIG'S COMPANY, headed by the Mate, ignored frantic pleas from disabled shipmates and though half-suffocated by whirlwinds of spark-laden smoke managed to lower the longboat unnoticed by Jeremy Brett and the men collecting on the *Merrimack*'s stern to launch her gig.

From among shifting fumes ran Henri Breboeuf with jacket smoking and sable hair and brows singed into grotesque patterns. Nonetheless he turned aside to help Sergeant MacPhee limp aft. Apparently the Scot had taken a ball through his lower thigh; blood kept dripping from the hem of his kilt.

For the first time Brett saw the longboat pulling away under a rain of sparks and brands and felt overwhelming relief. "Got any wounded aboard?"

"No," called back the Mate. "No time for 'em! Hurry, save yerselves."

"Come back, you bloody cowards!" But the longboat's oarsmen merely increased their efforts to win clear.

Jeremy winced when someone gripped him by his wounded shoulder and yelled over the crackling roar, "Look, sir. Look yonder!" He pointed at the indistinct outline of a ship in the act of emerging from a distant fog bank. Judging by her unusually tall masts, long yard-arms and narrow beam she might be a small man-of-war.

Among agonized screams from men not quite dead amid sheets of fire which precluded any attempt at rescue, Brett, Breboeuf, the cook, MacPhee, another Scot and one of the ship's boys freed the gig's falls and lowered her to the surface. Then Jeremy remembered. "Get aboard but don't shove off. Must get ship's papers — back in a minute."

"We'll wait," snapped the Canadian, "but not for long."

Wheezing, Brett plunged into the Captain's cabin, swept chronometer, sextant, compass, log, manifest and other precious documents onto a blanket on the Captain's bunk, then hurriedly knotted it into an ungainly bundle.

Coughing furiously, he groped into his hutch of a cabin and all but strangled while struggling to unlock a heavy padlock securing the ship's money box to a stanchion.

By the time he regained the deck a series of loud explosions sounded from the main hold; fire had reached tar and turpentine barrels. A whirling geyser of dense black smoke gushed skyward when the main hatch was blown off.

Through streaming eyes he glimpsed the second lugger backing away from her flaming consort in a frantic hurry. Apparently the corsairs also had sighted the man-of-war's dim outlines.

He found the gig bumping under the stern. The Boatswain and the cook were manning oars, so he dropped his bulging bundle into it, and, clutching the brass-bound mahogany money box to him, jumped and landed on the ship's boy, knocking his wind out.

Breboeuf, gasping with pain from blistered hands, grabbed an oar and pulled hard.

The gig had barely started to pull from under the stern when a terrific explosion made the *Merrimack*'s hull shudder, sent flaming debris soaring above the maintop. Panting, blackened and half-dazed, Brett found an oar, helped to row the dinghy any which way, away from those scorching whirlwinds.

Fumes from the burning vessels followed and concealed not only the longboat but the presumed ship of war.

Thanks to the Boatswain's inspired cursing the gig's oarsmen finally pulled together and rowed to windward.

Then came the *boom-m!* of a carriage gun fired amid the murk.

Soon a slant of a rising breeze cleared away smoke and fog to disclose a sloop-of-war flying the Blue Ensign. She was crowding on sail in pursuit of the surviving corsair whose consort, spouting great sheets of flame, had almost burned to the water's edge.

Although the longboat's crew kept hailing, the warship paid no attention, only continued in pursuit. Thanks to the freshening wind not much time was required for the sloop, ignoring a white flag, to start reducing the corsair to sinking wreckage.

Darkness was descending by the time H.B.M.S. *Nereid*, cruising under easy canvas returned to pick up the *Merrimack*'s boats.

4

Off Deptford Dockyard

FOLLOWING A TEDIOUS TRIP up the Thames estuary, Lieutenant Archibald Turnbull of the Royal Navy, portly, choleric and middle-aged, ordered H.B.M.S. *Nereid*'s anchor dropped off Deptford Dockyard amid a heterogeneous scattering of shipping anchored or moored in the great, dun-colored river.

All visible wharves and wet and drydocks were occupied by a variety of warships ranging from huge, 100-gun line-of-battle ships to lesser men-of-war of widely varying tonnage and design; present also were tubby transports, victualers, ungainly mast rafts out of Scandinavia and New England, and merchantmen from the Hanseatic Ports, Russia, Holland and France.

Ashore, hammers thudded, saws rasped, tackles creaked, horns moaned, bells jangled, all creating a discordant yet vital undertone.

Deeply impressed if not awed, Breboeuf reflected much of Jeremy's own reaction by observing in very faintly accented English, "Surely, *mon vieux*, half the ships in Creation must lie here?"

In various yards and slips farther upstream showed the raw yellow skeletons of vessels under construction or undergoing extensive repair. Beyond these towered great mounds of lumber, weathering for at least twelve months before use.

Long, low and narrow roofs indicated the presence of ropewalks cutting ruler-straight through congestions of dingy brick or stone warehouses, sail-lofts and arsenals. Smoke from innumerable chimneys climbed sullenly into the cold gray sky.

Bumboats soon appeared alongside manned by gravel-voiced watermen offering food, fuel and liquor; others solicited the favors of painted, aging and shrill-voiced whores.

Gripped by deepening anxiety and depression, Jeremy tested the wound smarting in his right shoulder. The *Merrimack* and her cargo had been lost and, worst of all, covered by not a penny's worth of insurance — Silas Brett & Son had been too hard up to afford even partial coverage.

This March afternoon although overcast and raw was a welcome change from the North Atlantic's furious, frigid blasts.

Jeremy and the young Canadian seated themselves on damp canvas covering the *Nereid*'s main hatch and continued to view Deptford Dockyard while awaiting a summons to sup in *Nereid*'s gun room mess.

Already their stomachs quailed over the prospect of more greasy stewed pork and watery, tasteless potatoes and onions dumped onto battered tin plates. The worst food of all, they'd discovered, was the ship's biscuit; iron-hard, it remained so alive with maggots only a starving man could consider it fit to eat. A grizzled gunner's mate had said: "An ye *must* eat these, first do this."

He'd rapped a biscuit's edge against the table's edge until numbers of white, slowly wriggling weevils fell out. "*This* is what our fat-cat Lords of Admiralty deem good enough for the likes of us!"

When a blunt-bowed bumboat pulled up offering fresh fruit and vegetables Breboeuf sought the side, then called, "Fellow's offering fresh oranges."

Before a red-jacketed marine on deck duty could prevent, the Canadian dropped a threepenny bit into a bucket held up by the vendor who then tossed a half-dozen small oranges over the bulwarks.

"Want one?" Jeremy called in an undertone; the sentry glanced furtively about before stuffing an orange into his pocket. "Thank 'e kindly, sir."

Cor! Such might serve to firm up scurvy-loosened teeth. The marine shouldered his musket and tramped off, muttering, "God bless, sir, but don't leave no peels abaht — don't want to be kissed by 'e bosun's daughter!"

While oranges didn't make much of a supper they offered considerable improvement on Navy rations.

They were licking fingers when, from the Captain's cabin, liquor-heated voices were raised so loudly it became obvious that the brig's Captain, overage Lieutenant Turnbull, was cursing the day he elected to make a career of the Royal Navy.

While hooking watch cloaks against an ever-rawer night wind, both Colonials heard the Captain's plaint: "Aye. Damme, after near twenty years of faithful, faultless service why was I, for no reason, reduced from sailing master of a fine, fast frigate to command this blasted cockleshell? And that after I'd been deluded into believing I was to win a post captain's commission and command of a Fourth Rate. Is this just? Hell's fire, *no!* And who got my appointment? None but the pox-ridden by-blow of a noble lord, one of the so-called King's Friends!"

His companion, also a superannuated lieutenant, rasped, "Aye, sir, being passed over like this adds but another outrage to too many."

Glasses clinked in the Great Cabin below. "Here's to swift downfall to the King's Friends ere they ruin the King's Navy, complete — 'Jemmy Twitcher' first of all."

"Who's 'Jemmy Twitcher'?" Jeremy queried of the dark.

Behind the two Colonials a voice quietly informed, "The Fourth Lord Sandwich, a rakehell named John Montagu. To England's eternal shame not long ago he was a Lord of the Admiralty."

The speaker proved to be the Officer of the Deck, Ensign Lightfoot, a planter's son from the Tidewater of Virginia.

Mr. Lightfoot continued in bitter undertones: "If you imagine advancement in the Royal Navy is difficult for home-grown Englishmen, imagine what it's like for Colonials!"

"I can imagine," Jeremy admitted before changing the subject. "Mr. Lightfoot, what is likely to happen tomorrow? I'm most anxious to find my firm's agents to report what's occurred."

The Virginian shrugged. "As I understand it, you and your men will be set ashore during the morning, possibly near the Customs House, in Wapping or somewhere near London Bridge."

Turning away, he paused. "Oh, by the by, another of your men died a while back — oldish with a bald head; and the surgeon claims the Scottish sergeant's been taken with bad blood and ain't likely to last the night. Too bad."

31

Mr. Lightfoot then readjusted an enormous muffler about his throat; the wind really was growing keen.

"What about my papers and navigating instruments?"

"All properly boxed up; you can claim them from the Purser.

"Good luck to you with your agents — you'll need it. They're an uncommon hard lot of rascals, the most of 'em.

"By the by, an you stand in need of a cheap, clean room, try the Bengal Tavern. 'Tis on the waterfront hard by Fryingpan Stairs." The Virginian strode off, shouting some order to the anchor watch.

5

Concerning Henri St. Castin Breboeuf

$$\smile$$

S UCKING WETLY ON A PIPE — he'd left his tinderbox below — Henri Breboeuf swung arms a few times to warm up, "*Alors*, my friend. If you've not more money in your chest than I imagine, we find ourselves in a rare, fine pickle, do we not?

"As for me, those *sacré* flames spread into my quarters so early I could not save a damned thing save this old suit — a hunting shirt's no use in London — so I have not a *sou* with which to bless myself — if I wanted to."

Grimacing, he touched his hip. "What I hate most of all is not wearing a sword. Lacking one, I feel more naked than if I were without breeches!"

Brett was reminded of his grazed shoulder when he gathered his boat cloak and considered his companion through the gloom. To his surprise the Canadian didn't appear so Indian-like in this half-light. "Tell me something, friend Henri. How come you speak English so handily?"

Breboeuf laughed softly. "Grace to my father's good sense. After the fall of New France he decided to let bygones be bygones and engaged in business with our English conquerors."

"Business? What kind?"

"As a son of the famous Baron St. Castin, even though he was only half-white, my father became an important factor in the fur trade with what is now called Nova Scotia and New Brunswick.

"To further his ambitions, my father married himself to the half-English daughter of a Swiss officer in a mercenary regiment on garrison duty in Louisburg.

"So you see, *mon ami*, I am redskin by only a quarter — on the surface, at least," he added quietly.

Jeremy asked, "Your mother's father was there during which siege?"

"The first one, in 1745; the one conducted by the Bostonnais army."

Restlessly Breboeuf gathered his cloak tighter, then sat forward, elbows on knees. "Surely it must have come as an astonishment to the English Government that Provincial militia lacking aid from even a squad of British Regulars could, by themselves, overcome so strong a fortress as the 'Gibraltar of America,' as Louisburg once was termed."

A measure of Jeremy's depression lifted. "You can lay to that! Ever figure our present troubles with the Crown stem from the fact that, after us poor Provincials had lost so many lives and spent, for us, a great fortune to take Louisburg — the Treaty of — of Aix-something —"

"Aix-la-Chapelle?"

"Aye, the British Government, without a by-your-leave to us Provincials, *returned* Louisburg to the French, so from Louisburg countless Indian raids again were sent against New England, and it also served as a haven for pirates and privateers which preyed upon our ships!"

He broke off. "Sorry, I got carried away; you were talking about yourself."

The mixed-blood sighed, stared through the darkness at clumps of light dimly seen on the Thames's south bank. "A matter of small importance. My most important ancestor was, as I have related, the illustrious Justin, Baron St. Castin — you have heard of him?"

"Who in north New England hasn't? Wasn't he the one who established a great trucking station on Penobscot Bay round 1690, then ruled the region like a king?"

"The same," admitted the Canadian. "By all accounts my grandsire was a lusty, capable individual who really understood Indians

34

and always dealt honestly with them. Yes. My grandsire ruled his barony in the Maine district of Massachusetts with a heavy hand — always fairly.

"He even built truck houses in Acadia and the province now known as New Brunswick."

"Aye, Pa used to trade in that direction, too."

A flat smile curving lean lips, Breboeuf continued, "To further his ambition, the Sieur St. Castin deemed it politic to marry — more or less casually, one suspects — daughters of sachems ruling tribes powerful enough to be courted for allies.

"Grandmother Lin-kini, a Beothuk, was the last of his Indian wives. The Baron married her when a very old man."

In the near distance arose the wailing notes of a wherryman's bugle soliciting passengers.

Breboeuf went to the rail, spoke over his shoulder. "From that union my father was born. In due time the youth was sent to the Recollet Fathers of Louisburg, then on to Quebec for further education; finally, for a little while he attended the Sorbonne University."

"Where's that?"

"In Paris. Afterwards, he acted more white than red, and because he bore a noble name Papa purchased a sub-lieutenant's commission in the Regiment of Béarn then returned to Cape Breton and Louisburg.

"He served in the siege of '58 and, on capitulation to General Wolfe, was taken prisoner.

"When exchanged, my Papa managed to make his way back to Penobscot Bay but the old Baron had died recently — a very old man.

"As I already have told, Papa then married my mother, the half-English daughter of a Swiss mercenary officer, and then because an older brother — also a mixed-blood — had taken over the Baron's business and holdings, Lucien St. Castin changed his name to Breboeuf and formed a trading company of his own. He built his station near St. George's Fort on St. Andrew's Bay."

A gurgling of water about the *Nereid*'s anchor cable became noticeable in a brief silence.

"I proved to be the only child, for after I was born *Maman* became barren.

"*Je vous n'ennuie pas, mon ami?*" Curiously, since they were getting to know one another better, Breboeuf spoke increasingly in French. "I do not fatigue you?"

"Since we're about to become guileless Provincials stranded in London, go on — especially about your family."

"Papa was so occupied with trading among the tribes, *Maman* sent me for instruction among the Benedictine Fathers of Québec — the Recollet Friars' Lycée in Louisburg, you must understand, had been destroyed by the English conquerors at the same time they blew up the Citadel of St. Louis and destroyed all fortifications."

Even white teeth glinted briefly amid the gloom. "The good Fathers taught me a little French history — distorted, you may be sure — simple mathematics and a little Latin. Soon these pious men gave up any attempt to make a convinced Catholic of Henri Breboeuf and sent me home.

"After that, *Maman* persuaded Papa that since Canada had become an English possession and very likely would remain that way it might be wise for their child to learn English, their way of thinking, rules of waging war and, most important of all, their methods of trading.

"To start with, I was made to study under a succession of English schoolmasters. For the most part they were intelligent, liberal men who had found themselves, who disagreed with the puritanical ways of *les Bostonnais*. — As you no doubt are aware, we call all New Englanders 'Bostonnais.' "

"Your instructors must have been good," remarked Brett. "Your grammar and diction are fine and you use French sparingly. All along, I've been puzzled how you picked up such an elegant turn of speech."

The Canadian created a rattling noise in his empty pipe, laughed softly. "Peter Keighley, my final tutor, claimed to be, and I think indeed he was, the second son to a baronet of ancient lineage who had held a number of high posts at the Court of Saint James's.

"Peter Keighley, who also became my close friend, was educated at Harrow and reared in Court circles. He took up with fashionable society and used the last of his inheritance to gamble. Bankrupt, he was forced to flee to America to avoid a debtor's prison.

"From him I learned some things concerning British high society and their curious amusements and standards of morality. Perhaps

37

some of this knowledge, limited though it is, may prove of use in our precarious circumstances. *Qui vivra, verra.*"

A marine, on his way to relieve a sentry posted before the Captain's door, snuffled and blew his nose with his fingers as he tramped by muttering, "Good night, gents."

"You were saying?" prompted Jeremy.

"I was recalled from a visit to a cousin in Brittany with whom my father did much business, when news came that an epidemic of virulent smallpox had nearly wiped out my father's trading station at Pénébesque on Penobscot Bay.

"When I returned to Pénébesque, it was to discover that my parents, his Scottish factor, several *habitants* and many Indian and half-Indian relatives had perished."

Breboeuf spread wiry brown hands in an inimitably Gallic gesture. "By a miracle, since I had not been inoculated, I escaped the disease which still was raging along the coast."

The mixed-blood fell silent while visualizing hardwoods among dark evergreen forests around Pénébesque showing timid flashes of green under promise of spring; endlessly shifting skeins of ducks, geese and other migratory fowl literally darkening the sky; the Penobscot River, dotted with outgoing ice, flowing crisply past all too many log cabins above which no longer arose plumes of smoke; beached canoes, pirogues and bateaux still filled with melting snows, looking desperately forlorn among festoons of rotting fishnets.

Jeremy's shadowy head inclined. "Remember folks saying the 'pox was especially potent last winter. How many survived in Pénébesque?"

"A very few, mostly half-whites." His shoulders lifted under a borrowed watch coat. "Strange, but we part-whites appear to survive better than full-blooded Indians."

"What did you do?"

"For all I was not yet twenty, I attempted last spring to keep up my father's trade with the Penobscots, Wewenocs, Montagnais, Beothuks, Micmacs and other tribes along the seacoast.

"I wasn't doing badly when one of my father's half-brothers, Jules, came sailing down from Port Royal in a big schooner. He had aboard a few cannon and a big crew of former privateersmen, pirates, *coureurs de bois* and such riffraff.

"Jules claimed the post at Pénébesque as his. *Enfin,* he occupied my village, the dock and truck house, then stole all my freight canoes and coasting shallops."

Viciously, Henri Breboeuf spat over the side. "Graciously, this creature, Jules de Tremblay, consented that should I depart peaceably he would allow me a canoe, a few weapons — my sword among them — a single slave and a few louis d'or. Generous, was he not?

"When I swore to return and lift his scalp Jules only sneered —" a grim tone entered the Canadian's voice — "which someday he will regret.

"All that summer and into early fall I made my way southward along the coast selling my sword and services to anyone who could pay, white, red or mixed-blood, no matter what they wanted done, and so I made a living of sorts, mostly by bush fighting."

Henri Breboeuf drew a slow, deep breath. "Eventually, it became evident I was too often risking my life and not making much money or gaining much prestige.

"So last winter I determined to return to Europe and discover whether a light conscience, plus sharp wits and a well-handled sword could not accomplish more towards advancing the fortunes of one Henri St. Castin Breboeuf."

The ship's bell sounded six dull, chill-sounding notes and was answered aboard several nearby vessels.

"Concerning your wits, my friend, I've not yet had time to form an opinion," Brett remarked, "but the way you handled your blade aboard the *Merrimack* really *shone!* Wherever did you learn to handle a sword so handy-like?"

"While at school in Québec there were many hungry but expert fencing masters. Ah, *mon ami!* the hours I've spent strengthening my wrists through swinging a heavy *casse-tête* — that is an Indian war club which carries a big, round stone bound to one end."

"Wrists, you said?"

"*Oui.* My father, who in his own right was an accomplished fencer, held that the left hand of an expert duelist must be as well trained as his right; on occasion this lends a generally unsuspected advantage."

"Aye. I guess it would, at that."

39

6

Concerning the Brett Family

—◡—

JEREMY DABNEY BRETT shoved the last crescent of orange between his lips, then sought the rail, long gray boat cloak curling under the increasingly cold breeze beating downriver. For a moment he viewed the impressive glow created by myriad lights in London, then reseated himself on the hatch cover.

"And now, *mon ami*, will you tell me something concerning yourself?"

"Seeing's you've just obliged, 'tis only fair I say something about us Bretts.

"Soon after King Charles the First lost his head Sir Lionel Brett, my great-grandfather, who'd been a devoted Royalist, had to flee for life to Massachusetts Bay with a pack of Covenanters snapping at his heels.

"First he settled in Newbury Port but soon discovered he couldn't stomach dour and self-righteous Puritans there any better than he had in England.

"Still single, he moved northward till he reached the Hampshire Grants on the Piscataqua River where he bought considerable land on John Mason's original trading grant and settled near where Portsmouth Town now stands."

The Brett family for generations, explained Jeremy, had lived in

Devonshire, mostly seafarers who'd sailed under Hawkins, Drake and Anson, and sometimes managed to win riches — old Sir Lionel had set up one of the earliest shipyards in New England.

"Well, what with knowledge gained in the Royal Navy and plenty of prime timber standing right at hand Sir Lionel prospered; built for himself merchants vessels so fine and fast that when the Restoration came along his reputation was so good Contract Commissioners from the Admiralty gave him orders to build supply ships for the Royal Navy."

Jeremy's discourse was interrupted by the arrival alongside of a wherry-load of drunken officers who'd mistaken *Nereid*'s identity. Once they'd been directed to a huge three-decker, Jeremy resumed.

"George Brett, Grandsire Lionel's heir, proved shrewd and above the average and for a song bought title to thousands of acres of fine timberland along the Piscataqua and its tributaries."

Jeremy Brett paused, visualizing scenes familiar since childhood. Along the Piscataqua lay booms of log-and-chain impounding huge brown logs eventually to be shaped by Brett's Shipyard into towering masts and sturdy lower yards. He could see again in the distance and guarding the Piscataqua's entrance the outlines of a small gray fort named in honor of King William and Queen Mary.

He could picture himself as a gawky, pink-cheeked lad who never could tan like other boys, exploring, barefoot, the cove below Pa's comfortable mansion. Screamed at by terns and gulls, he'd picked a course among glacier-smoothed stones whitened by barnacles and streaked with tattered strands of yellow rock weed.

"And then?" softly prompted the Canadian.

"Grandpa George, by all accounts, was uncommon venturesome and lusty. 'Tis said he begot the Lord only knows how many 'woodscolts' along the coast. On account of Injun attacks and sickness only my Pa, Silas, lived to grow up and get handy on the cornhusks like his Pa.

"Anyhow, whilst he was still a youngster he went along on Sir William Phips's expedition down to the Bahamas to hunt Spanish treasure lost in a great plate fleet wrecked during a terrible tempest.

"As you've maybe heard, friend Henri, Sir William Phips's venture proved vastly successful. Our share proved considerable — leastways by New England standards.

"Back home he added onto his boatyard and built himself a fleet of merchantmen and started trading timber, horses, tar, pitch and turpentine and stockfish to Barbados and Jamaica in exchange for rum, sugar and maybe now and then a parcel of black slaves for the Virginia plantations.

"Pa had finished the big brick house I was born in when during a trading trip to Boston he courted and straightaway married Lady Lucinda Dabney, recently arrived from the Old Country.

" 'Dabney'?" Breboeuf's cool voice queried out of the darkness.

"Yes. Mother once told me her ancestors came over from Brittany a way back and spelt their name 'D'Aubigny.' " He chuckled. "So you see, Henri, I too have French blood in me for all I reckon it must ha' become considerable thinned out by now.

"Over the centuries the Dabneys," Jeremy continued, "were a hard-living West Country family; sometimes they exercised real influence at the Court of St. James's."

Naturally, Jeremy failed to mention a legend that his exquisitely lovely mother had been hurriedly packed off to America as the result of girlish indiscretions with a Royal Duke twice her age. Her banishment, his family believed, had been engineered by a brother who, faced with debtor's prison, desperately had needed the sizable fortune the Lady Lucinda was on the point of inheriting.

Nobody had been able to understand at the time why, besieged by rich and well-connected suitors as she had been from the moment of landing, this sprightly English beauty had been won by Silas Brett, fresh down from the Hampshire Grants. Admittedly, he'd been a rising man, but coarse-spoken and socially awkward — only recently had he become well-to-do.

On the other hand, neither could Silas's friends and associates grasp what he saw in this flighty, affected creature who dressed, talked and acted like aristocracy and referred in an intimate way to the King's Friends who, in effect, were ruling England in the name of that dull-as-ditchwater Hanoverian, George the Third.

Nor did the former Lucinda Dabney's son mention that her first baby had arrived, full-term, three months earlier than it should have. Luckily perhaps for all concerned the infant had died shortly after birth, which surprised nobody; few babies were able to survive for more than a few weeks the frigid blasts of a New England winter.

Following birth of the Bretts' second child — a daughter who received the currently fashionable name of Perdita — Silas's high-spirited young wife had made valiant but ineffectual efforts to adapt herself to the drab existence of frontier life.

Pa, Jeremy stated, had perceived his best interests lay in learning from his wife what she knew about corruption in the Home Government.

Uncommonly farsighted for a Colonial, Silas Brett had commenced maneuvers to evade the hotly protested Stamp Act of 1765 — in all truth a justifiable effort to extract from the North American Colonies monies to help pay in part for protecting them during the war of 1756–1763; resulting as it did at long last in permanent security from attack and ever-increasing prosperity.

The first signs of revolt, Jeremy explained, had come during the summer of 1765 when a Boston mob burned Vice-Admiralty Court records, had looted the home of the Comptroller of the Currency and finally had forced Chief Stamp Agent Andrew Oliver to resign.

"Maybe you've heard, Henri, the Ministry *did* backtrack a couple of years ago and repealed the Stamp Act but then Lord Townshend got new and similar tax laws passed; things have gone from bad to worse."

Henri Breboeuf chafed chilled hands. "I do not understand these politics but did I not just before we sailed hear that New Hampshire alone of the Colonies refused to join in an embargo on British goods?"

"True, but without shipbuilding and the mast trade we'd soon starve. By a long shot, New Hampshire's the poorest Colony in New England."

Patently losing interest, Breboeuf heaved himself erect, peered down on his companion. "You were your parents' last child?"

"Aye, I came along pretty soon after my sister, Perdita." Brett described how Lucinda Dabney Brett had determined to bring up her children as if inhabiting an English manor house.

Jeremy explained most of their clothes had been imported from abroad and, because Silas Brett could afford such an extravagance, vivacious Mistress Brett had imported a succession of "distressed gentlewomen" to serve as governesses.

Jeremy recalled his mother as tall above the average and, though well-rounded, very lithe in her movements. Her face he described as heart-shaped, dominated by large, dark-blue eyes and a small Vshaped mouth set off by fugitive dimples which men from all walks of life had deemed irresistible.

Jeremy admitted his education by a number of tutors had been haphazard.

Over discordant singing rising from the Captain's cabin he continued: "Can't say my early years were altogether happy, because Mother insisted that wherever I went I must be well-dressed, washed and combed. Imagine having to go about in shoes and stockings and English-cut clothes when luckier lads went about in homespun, shock-haired and barefoot!"

Jeremy's tone grew bitter. "Worst of all, I was cursed with this damned 'peaches-and-cream' skin.

"Why I can't tan I'll never know; used to play in the summer sun till I turned redder than a boiled lobster and would blister pretty bad; but afterwards, I'd only peel till I looked like I'd been skinned alive. A few days later I'd have back this cursed pink-satin complexion."

A harsh laugh escaped him. "Soon as a boy near my age spied me he'd begin yelling, 'Yah! Yah! Little Lord Brett's come to town! Yah! Yah! Dandy!' 'Was yer Lordship's bawth heated just right this morning?' 'Come now, Sir Jeremy, air ye too proud to shake hands wi' commoners like us?'

"When I tried to shake they'd pull me down and though I fought like a trapped lynx they'd pummel the hell out of me and tear those damned English-made clothes.

"Pa never interfered; allowed I'd better learn to fend for myself; when I got bigger he taught me how to use my fists. Soon's I'd licked a few bullies bigger 'n me the rest laid off and I even made some friends.

"While Pa never encouraged me to use a sword, claiming skill with a blade often led to foolish duels, he taught me to use firearms and swing a cutlass pretty pert. When with a long rifle I could, at twenty paces, split a shingle stuck edgewise in the ground there were no more taunts about 'Little Lord Brett.' "

The most memorable event of his adolescent years, Jeremy admitted, had been that memorable voyage to Jamaica and Barbados in the *Androscoggin,* on which he'd discovered, cautiously, grown-up delights such as wine and women, with song running a poor third.

Jeremy smiled. "On my return from sea I briefly attended Harvard College — that's in Cambridge, a place near Boston ——"

" 'Briefly'?"

"Aye. I got caught, *flagrante delicto*, entangled with a proctor's lustful wife."

"And then what?" Breboeuf demanded, interest returning.

"Pa was madder that I'd been stupid enough to get caught than over having to forfeit my tuition money.

"Soon after my return in disgrace, poor Mother perished slowly and painfully from what Boston physicians termed a 'decay of breast.' "

Following the former Lady Lucinda Dabney's demise, Jeremy continued, he and Pa had come to a better understanding, possibly because he'd discovered that Silas Brett, still hale and hearty in his middle fifties, wasn't the pillar of moral rectitude folks around Piscataqua had thought.

"One day," Jeremy explained, "I was experimenting in the stable hayloft with a young miss named Esther who was visiting neighbors. Hair full of hay dust and clothes twisted every which way, we froze when in a box stall below I recognized Pa's voice and our maidservant's halfhearted protests.

"Through a crack in the loft's floor we could see what was going on; I vow there was nothing inexpert about the way my Pa flipped up our dark-haired kitchen wench's petticoats, pushed her onto a pile of fodder and went to work."

Henri Breboeuf chuckled.

"Likely Pa spied Esther and me sneaking out of the stable later on — must ha' figured his frolic hadn't gone unwitnessed for from that time on we talked pretty free about what delightful botherations females are and how best to handle 'em."

In the darkness Breboeuf grinned, recalling his own initiation into the lists of love. He'd been fishing for speckled trout at the mouth of a brook feeding a birch-shaded pool in which he used to swim whenever mosquitoes or black flies didn't make it inadvisable.

Comfortably naked he'd been reveling in the sun's caresses when a pair of broad-hipped Acadian girls cutting willow withes had emerged giggling from the underbrush — they must have been watching him because before long they'd welcomed his not inconsiderable offering into the roseate realms of Venus.

Reluctantly, Breboeuf returned to the present in time to hear his companion saying, "Out of sheer bad luck, Pa one way or another lost five out of his six merchantmen during the last French War. By the time peace was made Pa had taken to heavy drinking and often flew into rages which cost him friends at a time when he needed all the help he could get."

Henri placed a hand on Jeremy's forearm. "A most sad account. I grieve, *mon ami*, especially that his last vessel and cargo has been lost and without insurance." He peered momentarily at sleepy, yellow-red lights across the water then said quietly, "About your needs, *mon ami*, I do not know, but Henri Breboeuf must bed a woman tomorrow night. Seven weeks at sea have created formidable pressures in his loins."

Jeremy joined him. "If there's anything left in the *Merrimack*'s cash box once the men have been paid off, we'll take a look about, by God. I, too, feel ready for a foot race, a fight or a fuck — preferably the last. Even a toothless old squaw would look inviting."

"Aye, *mon ami*," chuckled the Canadian, "London's the place! From all I hear 'tis a vast gambling hell and bordello."

7

King's Shilling

JEREMY BRETT swung legs out of a hammock slung in the gunner's mess and, after visiting H.B.M.S. *Nereid's* foul-smelling
head, went on deck to shiver under a piercing wind beating up the
lead-hued Thames. Well, only one thing was certain — this must
prove a decisive day in his life.

Never before had he felt so aware of friendlessness and lack of
experience as in this frighteningly huge and forbidding city. How
should he go about approaching Pa's agents, Messrs. Mason & Sampson, an old and prosperous concern heading the Navy Board's list of
Contract Commissioners for Jamaica and North America?

What sort of a reception would be accorded a green young Colonial who'd just managed to make a total loss of Brett & Son's ultimate vessel?

Morosely he watched Henri Breboeuf, still yawning cavernously,
emerge from the companionway with almost feline grace.

Without warning a violent commotion broke out on the foredeck;
despairing yells went up mingled with curses and bellowed
commands. Mutiny? Such wasn't impossible. Nowadays, it was rumored not a few Navy crews were resorting to desperate means to
escape the brutal fate of men serving in His Majesty's ships of war.

Jeremy made his way forward to find Moses, the *Merrimack's*

Negro cook, bleeding at the mouth and with eyes white-ringed in terror, backed up against the bulwarks. With huge fists he was lashing out at a squad of scarlet-jacketed marines.

Once he saw the former supercargo Moses dove through the marines and, flinging himself onto his knees, convulsively grabbed Jeremy's legs, gibbering, "Save me, Baas! I tells 'em I born in Noo Yawk but they tryin' to 'press me just the same."

"Stand back, damn you!" Jeremy clenched fists and shifted balance onto the balls of his feet.

The marines, red-faced, stood their ground. One man closed in brandishing a pair of handcuffs, another leveled a bell-mouthed brass blunderbuss.

The marine Sergeant ran up snarling, "Stand aside, ye bleedin' Yankee! Try to stop this nigger from taking the King's shillin' at yer peril."

Pa always had drilled into him the value of self-control in tight moments yet to practice restraint was a touch-and-go matter. For all such impressment was highly illegal — under the American Act of 1746 which forbade the Royal Navy to impress Colonial-born subjects — wherein lay the sense of facing hopeless odds — especially in this foreign place?

Tumult rising in the gun deck argued that other members of the *Merrimack*'s crew were being beaten into submission.

Came Henri Breboeuf's acid comment once the struggling Negro had been dragged below, "Such admirable restraint should carry you far in London Town."

"Ah-h, the hell you preach!" Pink features flaming, Brett shouldered past the marine on guard before the Great Cabin's entrance and found Lieutenant Turnbull in a rumpled dressing gown, still unshaven, wolfing kippers, tea and porridge.

Mouth too full to permit speech, *Nereid*'s captain merely reared back, bloodshot eyes hardening.

"I protest, sir! I most vigorously protest this outrage!"

H.B.M.S. *Nereid*'s master jumped up, wiped lips on a stained napkin knotted about his thick, short neck. "Damn you for a curs'd Provincial whelp! How dare you to address me lacking permission?"

"I dare, sir, because members of my crew are being illegally impressed! Under the American Act of '46 they are exempt from —"

The *Nereid*'s commander went purple. "Blast and damn the

American Act! When I'm shorthanded I'll 'press whomsoever I please!"

A marine corporal came running in with espontoon leveled. Jeremy swung to confront him.

Lieutenant Turnbull roared, "Lay a finger on that Jolly and I'll impress you, too, so help me God!"

Again, Pa's training made him pause, fist cocked. "Sir! I protest! Such action *is* illegal!"

"A fig for your American Act!" snarled the Englishman. "Peters! Conduct this insolent rogue out of my sight before I lose my temper. Straightaway set Mr. Brett and his passenger ashore, together with any of his crew unfit to take the King's shilling!"

8

Mason & Sampson, Agents

⌒⌢⌒

COULDN'T *anything* be done about the *Merrimack*'s men manacled in H.B.M.S. *Nereid*'s orlop? With whom could he lodge protest? Where could he turn? Jeremy Brett could find no answer. How could a body feel so utterly bewildered, so miserably impotent?

Shoulders hunching against a thin, cold drizzle Jeremy clumped away from the Bengal Tavern. His boots, squelching over the waterfront's greasy and well-worn flint cobbles, took him past a seemingly endless succession of wharves above which the stark black outlines of masts and yards were so thick they reminded him of a fire-ravaged forest back home.

He skirted the carcass of a big farm dog which must have lain where it had died for a considerable time — mud on it was so thick.

Before long the battered and weathered Bengal Tavern's swingboard sign became obscured by a heavily loaded, high-sided wain creaking past, iron tires rasping over the cobbles. A hangdog drover in a dirty smock was leading by the bridle the first of three horses pulling in single file; apparently many streets in this area were too narrow to permit the passage of a pair of draft horses hitched abreast. So immersed in misery was Brett, he almost got himself knocked down.

"Watch out, ye bloody stupid bastard! Be ye blind as a bat?" The driver suddenly cracked a whip he'd held curled in his hand and caused a report loud as a pistol shot that echoed down the narrow street.

While the vehicle was rumbling by, Brett noticed the number 45 scrawled in chalk across a tarpaulin protecting the load. Even when he noticed in dull disinterest the same "45" painted, scratched or otherwise displayed in a number of places, he didn't pay any attention.

Elsewhere there were crude graffiti reading "Wilkes and Liberty!" "Up John Wilkes!" "To Hell with the King's Friends!" and sometimes, "Lordly Bloodsuckers!"

A lucky thing the Bengal Tavern where Henri Breboeuf had been left in charge of a pitiful sum remaining in the *Merrimack*'s strongbox had turned out to be situated at no great distance from Messrs. Mason & Sampson's warehouses and their handsome red-brick countinghouse on Great Hermitage Street.

A grimy, rag-clad urchin sidled up, extended a claw-like hand, whining, "Fer the luv o' God, Guv'nor, bestow a ha'penny, only a little ha'penny! Ain't tasted a morsel o' bait in two days."

When Jeremy mechanically reached for a pocket swarms of pinch-faced brats suddenly appeared from nowhere clamoring shrilly and with menacing undertones. God above! He'd never imagined such vicious small creatures could exist with wild-streaming hair matted into grotesque elflocks. Filthy scabrous patches of skin were visible under nondescript draperies of noisome rags and tatters. He'd never come across creatures the like of these among the worst stews along Boston's waterfront.

More urchins swarmed out of alley mouths, left off combing heaps of refuse to converge upon this fool who actually had made a charitable gesture.

Waving a billet of firewood snatched from a passing cart Jeremy attempted to scare off the encircling mendicants but, yammering, they only circled around him like wolves about to pull down a sick deer. Abruptly, he appreciated why most pedestrians in this vast and awesome city carried a stout staff or heavy cudgel.

Finally he had to lay hard about him before these predatory guttersnipes began to retreat, shrilling unintelligible obscenities.

Passersby merely laughed or paid no attention until a carter bent from his seat and slashed the ragamuffins with his whip.

Presently Brett spied a weathered sign reading "Great Hermitage Street" and a moment later he sighted a handsome brick building trimmed in gleaming white towering above its dingy surroundings. Across its front ran a wide panel with "Mason & Sampson, Shipping Ag'ts" lettered in gold upon a black background. Apprehensively, he made for it.

Jeremy Brett roused from abysmal misery on recognizing the Bengal's faded swing-board. Bracing himself he entered a grimy little bedroom rented soon after H.B.M.S. *Nereid*'s boat had dumped Henri Breboeuf, himself and pitifully scant baggage at the foot of Trig Stairs, a landing at no great distance from the soaring dome of St. Paul's Cathedral.

He found the swarthy young Canadian, of all things, placidly sipping a pewter mug of steaming tea laced with Jamaica rum — if the aroma meant anything.

Breboeuf sprang lightly to his feet, dark eyes narrowing abruptly at Jeremy Brett's expression. Nevertheless he attempted a light tone while decanting the teapot's amber contents into an earthenware cup lacking its handle. "Enter, *mon ami*, and sample this brew before it cools. I promise it will wipe away your grim look."

Mechanically, Jeremy accepted the cup and emptied it at a single gulp before sinking heavily onto the side of a sagging, sour-smelling double bed.

After a brief interval, Breboeuf queried softly, "I take it the interview with your agents did not progress favorably?"

"Hell's fire, no! Even after I sent in my name and business I was kept freezing above an hour in a damn drafty anteroom. Finally a fellow named Bland, a mere quill-driver and a snotty fat-cat of no importance, sent for me."

Breboeuf invited quietly, "I do not wish to distress you unnecessarily, my friend, but will you relate exactly what chanced *chez* Messrs. Mason & Sampson?"

Slowly, then more rapidly as his voice deepened with rancor, Jeremy Brett spoke out.

"At first this pursy pop-eyed fellow accorded me a sort of ill-favored courtesy till I came to telling about the *Merrimack*'s loss. This swine then adopted an impatient patronizing tone he reserves for what he terms 'beastly Colonials.'

" 'I take it your cargo was lost complete?' says he.

"Said I, 'There wasn't time to save anything beyond the navigating instruments and ship's papers.'

" 'Such as?'

" 'The log, the manifest and bills of lading,' I told him.

" 'No cash?'

"If this Bland bastard had been less obnoxious I might have told him the truth but I told him 'no.' "

Mechanically Jeremy's gaze sought the *Merrimack*'s brass-bound strongbox set beside the bed but failed to notice Henri Breboeuf's sudden coloring.

Shoulders sagging, Jeremy went on: "I tried to remind that contemptuous stuffed shirt that for well over twenty years Silas Brett and Mason & Sampson had done business and together had made a packet of money. When I asked for credits to charter a vessel and purchase cargo Mr. Bland only pursed his fat mouth and looked at me down his nose as if I'd sprouted an extra head.

" 'Past history, my lad, pays no dividends,' he observed. 'Let us face facts. Your firm's last ship and cargo were lost *uninsured*, so your father faces bankruptcy. Unfortunately, as I judge, he's far too old to start afresh.'

" 'That's not so!' I raged. 'Mr. Brett is just as brisk as ever.' Then I calmed down, saying, 'Pray tell me who at the Board of Construction I should address to learn the terms and procedures by which vessels for the Navy are built in New England yards.'

"That moon-faced bastard only sneered, told me that without influence in high places I'd get nowhere, especially being but a raw Provincial. Then he had me hustled out before I could plead any further."

"Then you accomplished nothing to the advantage of Brett & Son?"

Jeremy trembled with a recurrence of outrage. "On the contrary, Mr. Bland — there's a misnomer for you! — refused to surrender either the brig's papers or navigating instruments and reminded me that Pa is heavily indebted to Mason & Sampson for cargo collected in anticipation of the *Merrimack*'s return to Portsmouth."

"And so, *mon pauvre ami*, you find yourself at a loss as to where to turn."

Helplessly Jeremy glared about their dark and miserable little bedroom. "That's putting it mildly. Curs'd if I can even begin to see my way; London's too big, ugly and confusing. I've nowhere to turn."

"You describe the greatest city in the world very aptly but consider another view. Already enormously rich and powerful, London is capital of a great and swift-expanding empire. Its upper classes grow richer and more powerful each day. Here, as nowhere else, one hears great fortunes can be made without delay."

Breboeuf forced a spuriously confident smile to dark and narrow features. "In and about London live many of the foremost painters, architects, poets and writers of our time because they are encouraged by rich patrons."

"To hell with all that! What will this failure do to Pa?"

Breboeuf shot him a quick half-smile. "Mr. Brett cannot learn of your misfortune for some weeks; possibly, if you will accept my assistance, he may avoid bankruptcy and recoup at least a part of his business."

" 'Recoup'! And what have I to go on? Twenty-seven pounds, gold, in yonder strongbox — damned lucky I took your advice and didn't fetch it to the agents!"

Teeth faintly agleam the Canadian held up a hand. "A correction, *mon ami*; not even a half of that sum remains in your money chest."

Jeremy stiffened, dark eyes narrowing. "If this is a jest, Mr. Breboeuf, 'tis poorly timed."

"I am not joking," said he in a suddenly steely voice, "but before you attack listen to what I have to say."

Henri Breboeuf crossed to a rude wardrobe, then faced about. "When we parted this morning, for some reason I foresaw most clearly exactly what would occur once you arrived at the counting house of Mason & Sampson. I took steps, sensible ones I trust, in order to preserve us from disaster; I hope you will agree I have not thrown away the last of your money."

He brought out a navy-blue, long-skirted jacket cut on military lines with turned-up yellow lapels and deep cuffs, and adorned with large silvered buttons. Also he produced breeches of yellow nankeen, white silk stockings and a pair of elegant shoes buckled in pewter. Excitement breaking into his voice, Breboeuf said, "Are these not tasteful? And this?" He produced a small black tricorne hat bound in bright but slightly frayed silver lace.

Amazed, fuming and incredulous, Jeremy snarled, "What the hell

56

have you been up to? How dare you throw away the last of my hard money, you goddamn treacherous mongrel!"

Copper hues in Breboeuf's lean cheeks deepened but he ignored the insult, cried, "Calm yourself and believe I gamble to win salvation for us both. Look at this."

From the depths of the wardrobe he produced a slender walking sword sheathed in black morocco leather ornamented by an elaborate ferrule of richly gilded brass. "This, *mon ami,* was the finest of bargains! The hook-nosed pawnbroker I dealt with had no idea of this beautiful weapon's true value. Look well at it!"

Sullenly Jeremy accepted Henri's purchase, but couldn't help admire its guard shaped in the form of a mermaid voluptuously feminine in every finely-sculptured detail. One delicate little hand held a comb to gracefully flowing locks while the other poised a hand mirror set with a tiny diamond.

"Lovely, is it not?"

"Yes. But how dare you steal from my strongbox to buy us a useless plaything like this!"

"Useless! *Nom de Dieu! Useless?* When you see how 'useless' it proves in our interest you will eat your reproach!"

Fists balled, Jeremy in red-eyed fury surged forward but the young Canadian leaped backwards and in a flicker unsheathed the sword and leveled its point at Brett's eyes.

"*Tiens!* You are but too impetuous! If you do not believe in me then confide what plans you have for the future."

That Henri could remain so icily self-possessed was infuriating but again Pa's wise voice sounded at the back of Jeremy's mind and his rage began to ebb, leaving him breathless, buffeted in a mental rapids in which he could find nothing firm to cling to while rallying his wits.

Harshly he demanded, "What in hell can you offer in exchange for stealing Pa's money?"

Narrow black eyes intent on his red-faced companion's wide-set brown ones, Henri Breboeuf returned the slender strip of steel to its scabbard. "First, I did not *steal* the money," said he sharply. "I *borrowed* it only to make a good investment — just as would an honest tradesman from a banker."

"Possibly."

"I have discovered that not far away lies a tavern called the Gamecock's Spurs. From what I can learn its gambling rooms are less than fashionable but well patronized. One suspects the players there are adventurers, professional gamblers and gentlemen who, having lost heavily in some fashionable club, dream of recouping and resuming their place in Society.

"In such a spot provided Lady Fortune smiles and," he smiled thinly, "my hands and judgment do not falter, it may be possible to win enough money to gain *entrée* into a smart gaming club where large sums can be won."

"Or lost."

"Or lost, which is possible since Henri Breboeuf never will cheat till he must to survive. Tell me, *mon cher ami*, at this moment, how much money do we stand to lose?"

"Very little, and that's the plain truth."

9

The Way to Distaff Street

━━━━━⌣━━━━━

N OT EASILY did Jeremy Brett fight down resentment over the matter of the *Merrimack*'s money box. In the end however native common sense made him realize nothing was to be gained through antagonizing his companion; in all this vast and confusing metropolis wasn't Henri Breboeuf the only person he could turn to?

What hell it was to find himself so friendless and completely at sea; better cool down and remember that Henri must be nearly as disoriented as himself.

After draining the last of the teapot's lukewarm contents he went over to offer his hand. "All right, Henri, grant you meant for the best."

Jet eyes suddenly overflowing, the other tightly gripped his hand. "*Jesu*, Jeremy, never will you regret those words."

"Hope not." He forced a smile. "Now that that's settled, what's the next move?"

"*Bon!* I will confide a plan." Laying the sword across his lap the Canadian sank onto a rush-seated stool, peered up at his companion. "Is it not most urgent to obtain in London contracts covering construction of vessels in the shipyard of your father?"

" 'Urgent' ain't the word; I've goddamn well *got* to or Pa's ruined."

"Understood, but to accomplish this you first must secure support from influential officials which in these times can only come through bribery, blackmail or conspiracy. The use of honest materials and skilled craftsmanship no longer carry weight with the Board of Construction."

A rasping laugh escaped Silas Brett's only son. "Expect you're correct. Everyone says the Admiralty's riddled with graft and corruption. You noticed conditions aboard the *Nereid?*"

When a scuffle broke out in the Bengal's taproom below Breboeuf waited till it ended amid volleys of curses and a crashing of furniture. "First must be discovered which officials can be approached, and then how you are to reach them."

"True. Reckon such introductions would call for a deal of money."

A Gallic shrug elevated the lean-faced young man's shoulders. "Unfortunately, that is but too true, *mon ami.*"

"And where is such money to be found?"

"Who knows? When one commences a journey one must always take the first step."

"That's sense. How do I — er, we make this step?"

Breboeuf laughed. "To begin with, clean up the best you can. Straighten your stockings, brush dirt from your shoes and breeches; meanwhile I will rub the brass buttons on your watch coat till they shine like those of a successful sea captain.

"First — " Henri Breboeuf produced a comb lacking several teeth and not without effort tugged Jeremy's wavy, dark-brown hair into some sort of order, then braided it and secured the resultant queue with a length of black ribbon fished from his new jacket's pocket.

"And now for my transformation!" Laughing softly, the Canadian donned the military-appearing navy-blue jacket which fitted him surprisingly well; white thread stockings then were rolled up and gartered above the knees of the tight-fitting yellow nankeen breeches, bearing a few faint stains to betray previous usage.

Already, Henri had shaved and had clubbed blue-black hair into a neat queue. Once he'd donned the silver-bound black tricorne, he offered his wide-eyed companion an elegant court bow.

Then he buckled on his sword. Affectionately he passed fingers over its handsome hilt. "And now, *mon ami*, before it grows dark let us seek out the Goddess Fortuna and invite her to nod at us."

"Where we going?"

"To the gaming rooms I mentioned at the Gamecock's Spurs." He grimaced while adjusting his sword belt. "One suspects it will prove a shabby place with low-limit table stakes which is well; we have so little to risk."

"And how much can we hazard?" Jeremy couldn't restrain emphasizing the "we."

Coins gleamed briefly on the pinkish palm of a long, muscular hand. "Four gold guineas and exactly one dozen pine tree shillings."

While they were descending to the inn's noisy taproom Breboeuf said, "Considering our circumstances you may deem me crazy but I am paying a spit-boy a penny to conduct us to the Gamecock's Spurs. I understand it lies some distance away."

"A whole penny!"

"When navigating dangerous and unfamiliar waters do you not hire a pilot? In this vast place we would lose our way within a very few minutes and likely get our throats cut into the bargain."

Jeremy nodded glumly when a gaunt lad of ten or twelve appeared, ragged and runny-nosed. "Gents, ye'd best take along one o' them, costs but a farthing." He pointed a dirty finger at a clump of cudgels standing in a barrel.

"Here is a halfpenny," Breboeuf said. "You will get another when we safely reach the Gamecock's Spurs."

"Gawd bless yer ludship!" The urchin made a swift grab for the little copper then for want of a pocket, tucked it into his cheek.

To his last hour Jeremy Brett never quite forgot their journey to the Gamecock's Spurs. Never had he imagined creatures wearing human form could exist amid such squalor; although he'd explored sordid areas along Ship and Lynn streets on Boston's waterfront these by comparison had appeared clean and decent.

On entering a narrow street or alley they generally were forced to swing clubs to escape swarms of importunate beggars, pimps, and hideous drabs who shrilly offered their favors for tuppence or even a ha'penny.

Wrecks of ancient buildings sagged towards one another along stinking, garbage-littered passageways often not five feet wide.

They followed the spit-boy along a succession of crooked, dark and narrow thoroughfares in which mud, swill, and human and animal excrement lay inches deep. Seldom did they encounter real paving;

loose rocks had been tossed only into the deeper potholes and kennels ran abrim with slimy green fluids.

Through necessity Jeremy and his companion learned that a yell of "Stand clear!" served as belated warning for passersby to hug the nearest wall and shield their faces lest they get drenched by festering contents of a slop jar or chamberpot.

Nauseated, the Provincials pinched noses and kept cudgels ready. Small wonder the spit-boy had remarked that anybody having the price should travel in a public sedan chair which, roofed and enclosed, protected a passenger from the worst hazards of travel on foot in London Town.

In a rather wide street a tumult was beginning about a private sedan chair being carried by a pair of brawny, beetle-browed chairmen in livery. Apparently they had been forced to halt by an overturned barrow.

Wide-eyed, Jeremy Brett watched its occupant, a hatchet-faced woman, powdered and painted like a caricature, lower a side window to screech incomprehensible orders at her chair-bearers.

A half-grown youth — apparently a butcher's apprentice because of the bloodied apron he wore — pointed, yelled, "Lawks! If 'tain't 'er Gryce, the Duchess of Bilgewater. Let's salute 'er proper-like!" — then heaved a bucketful of offal through the sedan's open window.

Delighted jeers arose when the passenger, a successful madam judging by her feathered headdress and tawdry finery, tried to scrape festoons of slimy, pink-gray entrails from her gown. At the same time she vented such a typhoon of filthy invectives that the crowd quieted in admiration.

Breboeuf clutched his companion's shoulder, hissed, "Come, whilst this *canaille* still is occupied."

To the Provincials' vast relief the spit-boy at last reached Distaff Street and pointed to a swing-board sign dangling from an iron crane let into the façade of a brick-fronted structure three stories high. "Yon's yer mark, so, please yer ludships, I'll 'ave t'other ha'penny."

Once the Canadian had dropped the coin into his grimy paw the urchin cocked his head to one side and winked. "Mind yer don't try findin' yer way back to 'e Bengal alone. Best 'ire a brace o' stout rascals to escort yer. 'S Gawd's trewth."

The spit-boy vanished with the ease of an eel darting into a weed bed.

Jeremy noticed that whoever had painted the tavern's sign must have had a measure of talent; a brass-back gamecock complete with short-cropped comb and exaggeratedly long spurs glared arrogantly across a small cobbled square fronting the establishment.

The signboard's paint, Breboeuf concluded, had only remained colorful because it hung suspended well above a muddy tidemark created by the splattering made by wheels and the hooves of saddle horses.

To leap the garbage-oozing kennel in Distaff Street's center and so gain the Gamecock's smoky taproom proved unspeakable relief.

10

At the Gamecock's Spurs

⌒

THE GAMECOCK'S SPURS proved to be considerably more commodi-
ous than when viewed from the little square it fronted. Despite
meretricious efforts at elegant ornamentation it remained obvious
that in the not-very-distant past, this in all probability had been a
sizable farmhouse to the rear of which had been attached a roomy
barn and carriage house.

Street noises, Jeremy noted with pleasure, were muted by a heavy,
white-painted double door.

The two young Colonials peered cautiously about and discovered,
no doubt because the hour was early, this taproom wasn't in the least
crowded. A few patrons seated on banquettes behind narrow tables
and in bored fashion were drawing on foul-smelling clay pipes while
sipping ale, porter or beer from battered pewter cups and tankards.

Breboeuf, gazing down his nose with a supercilious air, led the way
to a corner banquette. He smiled thinly. *"Mon ami,* in a place like
this, always remember to keep *two* walls to your back whenever possible." He smiled nervously as they settled — in fact, barricaded —
themselves behind a stout and well-scarred oak table.

"Wot's you gents' pleasure?" demanded a burly waiter wearing a
none-too-clean apron over what once must have been an expensive
livery of mulberry velvet.

Jeremy started to order beer but Henri nudged him and loudly ordered two dry — very dry sherries thereby attracting the attention of patrons who, seen through a haze of pipe smoke, suggested a salmagundi of characters of all ages and conditions.

Among them, looking ill-at-ease, were a pair of subalterns from some Royal Guards regiment; white waistcoats and the bright-blue revers on their scarlet tunics stood out among seedy and generally somber civilian costumes.

Present also was a party of ungainly, roughly dressed fellows with healthy pink-brown country complexions. They were blustering at waiters in an attempt to disguise unfamiliarity with such surroundings.

The Provincials presently noticed hung to a handsomely carved door a small sign reading, "Gaming Rooms Open at 7.00. Close at Sunrize."

Soon other patrons began to enter; some arrogant and self-assured, some furtive; the majority appeared pasty-faced, jaded and none-too cleanly. Many individuals wearing well-cut but sadly dilapidated garments peered superciliously about as if trying to patronize an establishment of such low *ton.*

Quickly Henri pointed out what he took to be professional gamblers; for the most part these restless-eyed fellows affected short swords, more or less neat tie-wigs and coats with enormously deep cuffs. It gave Jeremy pause to note how many gaudy, brocaded waistcoats betrayed the outlines of a pocket pistol.

A few ran speculative eyes over him and his companion. More fervently than ever Jeremy cursed his milkmaid's complexion when an effeminate creature in an elaborate blond wig winked and quirked a brow in open invitation.

The moment a big brass mantel clock began to strike the hour of seven a Negro boy wearing a huge silk turban of yellow topped by a soiled white ostrich plume began beating a gong whereupon stout double doors leading to the Gamecock's gaming rooms were opened.

At once patrons bawled for drink bills, paid them in dreadful eagerness, and made for the entrance. Within a few moments the taproom was all but deserted save for a few discouraged-looking individuals who morosely delayed finishing drinks as if apprehensive over parting with the last of their funds.

A jolly-looking, red-faced young fellow paused before the Colonials, drawling, "See ye're fresh fish. An you wish to find seats at a good table ye'd best make haste; house is likely to be full up to-night."

Delicately Breboeuf drained the last golden drop of his sherry, then arose and half-bowed. "Our thanks. And the best of luck to you, sir."

Once they'd entered the main gaming room the Canadian warned, "Whilst I play, stand very close behind me lest some sharper tries to signal my cards." White teeth shone in his lean dark features. "And for luck, hold your left ball tight."

Right now Jeremy Brett lamented an almost complete unfamiliarity with cards or of gambling of any sort for that matter. True, Mother had tried to instruct him in the rudiments of whist, pharo and loo till her patience had worn thin; somehow, he'd never taken a fancy to cards. 'Twas far better sport to box, wrestle, pitch horseshoes, or go hunting or fishing. Criminently! What would people back home make of such confusion?

Following a careful survey of the gaming rooms — there were two of them — Breboeuf elected to sit at a pharo table at which the maximum wager permitted was a modest half-guinea. Without difficulty, he identified by their shamed expressions several ex-members of smart clubs where it was commonplace to risk hundreds if not thousands of pounds on a single play. While turning back soiled lace on their cuffs these gamesters stared at fellow players in open contempt.

After a while Jeremy's anxiety commenced to evaporate, became supplanted by a curious sense of anticipation when players methodically stacked in little ranks crowns, half-crowns, shillings and sixpences. Excitedly he watched Breboeuf covertly assess the character of other gamesters encircling a green pharo table to the surface of which a complete suit in spades had been glued and then varnished over.

The atmosphere betrayed no trace of joviality; was only tense and grim. An almost toothless and saturnine old fellow bought the bank and prepared to deal; the players' expressions hardened. All at once Jeremy was reminded of a pack of timber wolves he'd once seen edging in on a cow moose exhausted through struggles to escape a massive snowdrift.

More patrons from various walks of life appeared until both card rooms were crowded and increasingly hot and ill-smelling.

Over his shoulder Henri warned, " 'Ware pickpockets." Beyond a doubt such were already at work even though they knew that if detected they'd inevitably get their necks stretched on Tyburn Tree.

Jeremy began to sweat from more than the heat when Henri's narrow brown hand reached out to place a silver shilling on the six and another on the knave stuck to the table — two coins less in the slender reserve. Jeremy remembered enough of his mother's instructions to know that the matching of a suit didn't matter: any six or knave turned by the dealer would win.

Players rapidly placed bets about the board, sometimes with a flourish but more often uncertainly, until the layout became speckled by dully glinting coins. Everyone fell silent and onlookers, now two-deep about the players, watched the banker's bony fingers, adorned with jeweled rings of dubious value, expertly riffle a fresh deck. Then, without looking up, he passed the cards to his right-hand neighbor for cutting.

Emitting a soft sigh the dealer faced a card to his left — this was the "soda" which, for some obscure reason, had no bearing on the bets.

Henri Breboeuf went rigid under his new coat as the gaunt banker faced a card to his right and called out, "The ten of hearts loses!" because the first card faced always lost. Deftly the banker then collected all coins resting on the ten of spades and added them to the modest stacks before him.

A third card was turned and placed to cover the "soda." This completed a "turn," the Canadian explained without turning his dark and narrow head.

"A four of clubs," intoned the dealer, who then counted out even money on all bets covering the four of spades.

All other bets, Henri's included, remained on the layout for another turn. More money clinked onto the layout and the banker announced, "Next turn!"

While fresh wagers were placed a tall, hairy fellow standing to Jeremy's left reached to place a penny on the florin he'd wagered on the queen.

"Why'd you do that?" Jeremy asked involuntarily.

"Just copperin' me bet," the hairy man explained gruffly. "Women bein' fickle creatures, I figger my queen is about to lose, so I suspends me wager."

On the third turn a six was turned and when Breboeuf was paid, Jeremy breathed easier but sweat still cascaded down his back.

Breboeuf let his knave ride and used his winnings to cover the nine.

For a good while the Canadian, playing an icily calm game, won steadily; then his luck changed and the coins stacked on the stained green baize before him commenced to diminish.

Jeremy experienced panic. Great God! What if Henri got cleaned out?

Several gamblers, their last penny gone, quitted their seats loudly cursing foul luck or slinking off in crushed silence.

Apparently unperturbed, Henri turned, managed a smile over a navy-blue shoulder. "You still are warming that left ball?"

"Sorry. I forgot." Jeremy delved into his breeches pocket.

Incredibly, the luck altered so that by the end of another hour's play the sinewy Canadian had more than trebled his original stake. Dazzling possibilities presented themselves, blinding Jeremy to the realization that his friend had become the focus of coldly calculating eyes.

After losing three modest wagers in succession Breboeuf unostentatiously passed Jeremy a handful of coins, then distributed the balance among inside pockets.

"Why quit now?"

"*Mon ami*, it does not pay to stroke Lady Luck's pretty bottom too long so let us seek a bit of food. I feel so hungry I could eat a horse then chase its rider."

After helping themselves extensively to an assortment of bread, cheeses and pickled pigs' feet stacked any which way on a sideboard they mingled with patrons moving towards a door on the gaming room's far side. Through it had sounded whistles, yells and bursts of excitement and applause.

They entered a lofty carriage house dimly lit by clusters of smoky torches and pervaded by the faintly erotic smell of leather harnesses and the ammoniac reek of horse urine.

A throng of shadowy onlookers stood before a row of box stalls, others perched on a chariot, a phaeton and a huge mail coach lining the farther wall. Others of the noisy crowd occupied a ladder leading to a loft, wisely cleared of hay, serving as a gallery.

Politeness proving futile, Jeremy kept hands tightly closed over the coins in his pockets, shouldered a way through the crowd until with Henri close behind they gained the perimeter of a boxing ring corded off by double strands of stout ropes secured to heavy posts driven into a floor of hard-packed dirt. In it a pair of panting, half-naked and blood-streaked boxers were slugging, toe-to-toe.

"Ten to five bob on 'e Turk!" yelled someone.

"Done! Five back at yer on 'e Wagoner!"

They gained the ringside barely in time to see a tall, gaunt fighter land a crashing bare-knuckled blow on his opponent's blood-smeared jaw. A gale of cheers, whistles, catcalls made the carriage house resound and the crowd clamored like foxhounds making a kill. "Hit him again! Wagoner's done!"

The winner, meager chest heaving, raised fists above his head and grinned, exposing widely gapped teeth. To Jeremy it looked as if he'd broken a hand.

Loudly a referee clanged a brass dinner bell, bawled, "Turk Tanner wins by a knockout."

The wild-haired winner danced a little jig, then gasped, "Let thems wot deems Turk Tanner's best days are by think again. Me, I can beat any middleweight in Holbourne, Cheapside or Wappin' to a pulp!"

After using the heel of his undamaged hand to rub blood from a badly swollen eye, he spat contemptuously on his foe's slowly squirming body, then blinked about the smoke-clouded coach house. "Nah, then; any gemmun 'ere want to spar so's 'e can boast he's fought 'e famous Turk? Five shillin' says yer can 'ave a honest go at me; for ten I'll tyke a dive so's yer can boast ye knocked me down."

A well-set-up but rather pasty-faced young fellow raised a hand. "Done, friend! I will try a round or two with you on the understanding you're not to take a dive! An I knock you down, fair and square, Turk, you'll earn a pound and five if *you* flatten me."

"Orl right sir; at yer service, Sir 'Arry."

"Hell," Jeremy muttered in Breboeuf's ear, "that's a nasty bet. Turk's left is near to useless."

The young rake — Henri took him to be such by the elegance of his clothes — peeled off a long-skirted coat of dark-blue velour and a waistcoat of brocaded silk, then rolled up his sleeves and undid a lace-trimmed neckcloth. The challenger glanced about, his garments dangling over a forearm, saw Jeremy, and half smiled. "You've an

69

honest look about you, friend. Guard these garments and I'll stand you all you can drink."

Delaying only to kick off buckled pumps, the challenger ducked agilely between the ropes, braced stockinged feet wide apart, then went into a half-crouch and raised bare fists in the accepted stance.

Turk Tanner blinked. "Does yer mean wot yer says, Sir 'Arry? Ye'll *really* pay five quid an I knocks yer flat?"

"To be sure," laughed the man called Sir Harry. "Come, Jarvis, sound your damn bell and let's start."

Within instants Jeremy arrived at several conclusions: first, from the practiced and easy way this challenger moved here was no mere blowhard; second, Tanner's misshapen left remained dangerous — it must have been broken long ago — third the professional wasn't nearly as tired as he was pretending — he must have put away the Wagoner in short order.

The crowd, sensing the unusual, yelped, "A sovereign on Sir Harry — even money." "Take yer!" "A guinea, two to one, on 'e Turk!"

To start with, aside from Tanner's injured hand, Jeremy wouldn't have granted the lightly built challenger much of a chance; the professional looked tougher than tripe and powerful as an ox but quicker and more intelligent.

Dare he risk precious shillings on Turk Tanner's chances? He started to sing out but native New England caution kept him quiet.

Quickly he was glad he'd kept his lips buttoned. The challenger proved very light on his feet and could block and deliver punches with the speed of a striking rattlesnake, but how long could the lighter man maintain his agility? Sir Harry appeared wan as a ghost, in anything but good condition.

Sure enough, after he'd been tagged by a series of glancing blows, Sir Harry smiled in a sickly way and appeared to slow down, whereupon Turk Tanner, lowering his shaggy head and roaring like a bull, charged.

Sir Harry, however, neatly sidestepped the professional's charge and putting full weight behind his shoulder delivered an uppercut so vicious it caught his opponent flush on the jaw and sent him reeling off balance, eyes rolling and hairy arms flying apart. Immediately the challenger sprang in, drove a terrific punch into Turk Tanner's midriff which doubled him over and dropped him in breathless agony to the straw-strewn ground.

Ignoring resounding applause, the winner, scarcely breathing hard, coldly scanned the crowd. "And that being that, I stand ready to take on anyone for three rounds — was up a bit late last night — and pay ten gold guineas provided he can knock me down."

To his astonishment Jeremy Brett heard his voice calling, "Done, sir! And five pounds to you if you can fell me!"

While the crowd yammered, the winner offered a derisive half-bow. "That's uncommon sporting for one of your sort," he declared staring at this unfashionably dressed and pink-faced young fellow. "By your accent you're Colonial. Sure you can pay?"

Angrily Jeremy called, "Where I hail from, mister, we don't risk money 'less we can make good, so it's ten if I knock you down — five to you if I fail."

Breboeuf hissed, clutched his elbow. "Don't be a fool, he'll likely trick you!"

"Let him try," was all Jeremy Brett said while unbuttoning his coat.

Quickly news of the bout spread to the gaming rooms and would-be spectators appeared until the ring's ropes sagged inwards, materially reducing the space within.

On entering the ring Jeremy Brett made frantic efforts to forget he'd been a great fool to risk five precious pounds. Still, from what he'd seen he *should* be able to absorb harder knocks than his opponent now getting rid of a lace-trimmed shirt and exposing a well-muscled torso.

Once Jeremy followed suit his deplorably smooth, pink-and-white skin evoked whistles and cries. "Lor' love us, ain't 'e the pretty one!" "A real cupid." "'Urry and tyke 'im apart, Sir 'Arry, afore 'is nanny comes to fetch 'im home." "Knows of a Greek gent who'd pay a mint for such a lovely lad." "Is peaches and cream all ye eat, dearie?"

Once the referee, a bandy-legged, lop-eared and broken-nosed ex-prizefighter had clanged a hand bell until the onlookers quieted, the antagonists squared off, fists raised, knuckles gleaming white.

Turk Tanner, having sufficiently recovered to squat outside a corner of the ring, called, "You, 'e ruddy Colonial, watch 'is left! Keep yer guard 'igher."

Immediately Jeremy raised hands, bare knuckles catching rays from storm lanterns slung to rough-hewn beams above, and dancing lightly on the balls of his feet retreated as far as the ropes permitted, feint-

71

ing, feeling out the other's speed and timing. If only the crowd would quieten! Such uproar was confusing, nothing like fighting a match in some neighbor's hay barn.

Later on, he was able to recall the sequence of events after he recovered from a flurry of quick, stinging blows; he could remember skipping sidewise, giving ground, then going into a defensive crouch despite yells and jeers to stand and fight.

He remembered, also, Sir Harry's first effective punch, which landed on his short ribs and sent a shower of white-hot needles shooting through his side and magically shortening his breath.

Tempted to counterattack, Jeremy recalled the ten pounds at hazard, so kept eyes on his opponent's and remained on the defensive. Still lightfooted, he ducked, weaved and sidestepped until the weight of Sir Harry's punches began to slacken and his truly remarkable timing showed signs of deteriorating.

The instant he sensed rather than saw bleeding knuckles on Sir Harry's left hand lowered from its usual leading position he gathered, put his entire weight behind a tremendous punch at the top of the other's heaving, sweat-bright stomach.

Before he could quite realize it, the Englishman, eyes rolling, was writhing and making futile little motions on the dirty bloodstained canvas, gasping, "Uh, uh, uh."

The referee came up. "What's yer name, cully?"

The Canadian glared, grabbed his sword hilt. "Be respectful."

"To a damned Provincial? What for?"

"Because he's a gentleman!"

Before the cold menace in Breboeuf's expression the referee fell back a step, said sullenly, "To settle 'e bets I got to give 'e winner's name!"

"Jerry," snapped Breboeuf, then, on inspiration added, "among sporting circles in America he's known as 'Boston Jerry'!"

"A bleeding American? Now wot about that!"

Observed a quiet voice, "Well, well, we live and sometimes we learn. Till now I've believed Americans could fight only with scalping knives and tomahawks. Seems I've been misled."

The speaker's finely chiseled but slightly puffy features were dominated by rather small and very bright black eyes. He'd a long, ruler-thin nose, a slightly receding chin and a wide mouth about which hovered lines indicative of humor — tiny crow's-feet radiating from the corners of this heavyset dandy's eyes seemed to confirm this.

"I take it, Boston Jerry, you come from our possessions in North America?"

At the other's condescending tone, Jeremy started to bristle. "Correct," he panted. "I am from Portsmouth."

"Portsmouth! Is there a Portsmouth in America?"

"Aye, sir, Portsmouth is the finest port in the Hampshire Grants."

"In that case, young sir, pray accept my card. An you care to present yourself at this address such a courtesy under certain conditions may serve to mutual advantage.

"A very pretty bout, may I say, sir, and against a worthy opponent. I am not unacquainted with Sir Harry's skill in the ring."

Jeremy's numbed fingers closed on the rectangle of pasteboard.

THE MARQUESS OF MIDDLEBROOK
MIDDLEBROOK HOUSE
NUMBER 7 CHANCERY LANE

II

" 'Ware Mohocks!"

S IR HARRY, who appeared to bear no ill will over his defeat, advised, "Take care on your way home — bands of Mohocks are said to be abroad tonight."

"Mohawks? In London!" Since childhood Henri Breboeuf believed Mohawks were the tribe most dreaded of the Six Nations, not that the Oneidas, Cayugas, Senecas, Onondagas, Tuscaroras — the newest members of the Iroquois Confederacy — were any bargain.

The Six Nations, allied to the Crown of England since time immemorial, were relentless enemies to Hurons, Montagnais, Beothuks, Micmacs or any tribe owing allegiance to the King of France.

"Ah, yes," said Sir Harry. "Here, we spell the name 'Mohocks' to designate gangs of well-bred rakehells who roam the streets at night and amuse themselves by committing acts of violence such as assault, arson, rape and even murder now and then."

The nobleman, enjoying his role, then explained that in London after dark only a semblance of law and order was maintained by a handful of privately employed usually superannuated constables and night watchmen. Inevitably, such were favored targets for reckless young gentlemen terrorizing the streets with little fear of retribution.

Casually, Sir Harry described how, earlier this week, he'd joined a band of Mohocks in the popular sport of "boxing the watch"

—which consisted of nailing shut the door to an unwary watchman's shelter and rolling it down a slope at the cost of broken bones and possibly the wretched fellow's life.

"Caught a Tartar last Tuesday, though," laughed Sir Harry, rubbing his bruised jaw. "Picked a watchman younger and stouter than we'd expected. Fellow drew his sword and laid about him so well he nicked two of our number whom he captured and dragged before a magistrate."

"What happened to them?" Jeremy wanted to know.

Sir Harry grinned. "My blueblood friends got fined two-and-six apiece; after which the magistrate severely reprimanded the watchman for having 'interfered with the young gentlemen's fun'!"

Sir Harry arose, nodded pleasantly to Jeremy and the Canadian. "Trust we shall meet again, Boston Jerry, in the ring or out. Adieu, I'm off to try my luck at cards — possibly I'll fare better."

Thanks to a short spell at the pharo table more coins became added to the collection distending Breboeuf's pockets.

Quitting the gaming room, Henri Breboeuf led the way to an evil-smelling privy where he thrust a clutch of coins into Jeremy's swollen and dully aching hand. "In case something separates us before we reach the Bengal."

Jeremy nodded. "All right, but we'll stick to one another like death to a dead nigger. Wish to hell our lodging were closer."

Various steeple bells sonorously had commenced to dispute the exact instant of two o'clock when Sir Harry checked them near the door. "Since you're from abroad I'd best warn that the fact you carry considerable winnings ain't gone unnoticed. Better hire yourselves a linkboy and a brace of bullies to see you on your way — don't hesitate to use that." He tapped the hilt of Breboeuf's sword. "I'd escort you myself, lads, but, alas, tender moments await me in another direction!"

Smoking torches carried by importunate linkmen revealed outside the Gamecock's Spurs a throng of beggars, idlers, whores, pimps and public chair porters. Sir Harry selected a scrawny, rag-clad youth holding an unusually bright torch, then beckoned a pair of burly fellows swinging hawthorn clubs from thongs secured about thick wrists. He gave them instructions, dickered.

Jeremy wanted to know, "How much will they cost?"

"Six shillings, more than the going rate, but 'tis wise to be generous. Likely they'll see you safe to the Bengal. Good luck to you!"

His flaring torch held on high, the linkboy started without hesitation. The bully boys slunk along at the wayfarers' heels. After half an hour's tramping along lightless, narrow and twisting alleys, Breboeuf, treading warily as a cat, muttered, "Stand ready; this damn boy is cozening us; should have reached the tavern before now."

Jeremy's grip tightened on his cudgel. "That's right. He's slowing his pace and —"

He got no further; the linkboy suddenly had plunged his torch into a deep puddle in the alley's cobbled paving. Darkness closed in like a smothering, foul-smelling blanket.

The Canadian's sword hissed from its scabbard even as Jeremy wheeled and struck hard at the nearest bully boy. Emitting a hoarse scream the fellow reeled backwards. Under the menace of Henri's sword point the other had started to take to his heels when out of the shadows charged a swarm of half-seen vagabonds expecting the linkboy's betrayal.

Stung by Breboeuf's blade, someone screeched, then fell heavily onto the muddy cobbles, but other shadowy figures continued to close in.

Need of preserving the all-important winnings made Jeremy lay furiously, blindly about him. Exhilaration seized him whenever his club evoked ear-piercing howls of pain.

Too soon the cudgel was wrenched away. He balled fists and, bellowing like an angry bull, charged the shifting crowd of enemies. Sticks and fists impacted. Gasping for breath, Jeremy punched, ducked and butted.

Breboeuf, too, began breathing hard. His sword arm ached like an exposed nerve, yet he so handled his blade that his assailants gave ground.

Somewhere up the alley a warning arose, " 'Ware Mohocks! 'Ware Mohocks!"

In stooping under the sweep of a quarterstaff Jeremy tripped on a fallen man and staggered off balance, dimly aware that the Canadian, having spitted someone, was having trouble in disengaging his blade.

"Mohocks! Mohocks!"

Vaguely Jeremy heard feet pounding down the alley and voices shouting incomprehensible slogans; at that same moment a footpad behind Silas Brett's son brought a club down on the crown of his head. White-hot sparks spun in Jeremy Dabney Brett's eyeballs. Darkness descended.

12

Captain Antonius

A T THE IDENTICAL INSTANT the vagabond clubbed Jeremy into insensibility Henri Breboeuf backed into a doorway and, right wrist tiring, shifted his weapon to the left — kept on thrusting and slashing at the shifting pattern of shadowy figures.

Shouts of "Mohocks! — 'Ware Mohocks!" sounded closer when a hard-flung cobblestone dealt him a shrewd blow in his side but he managed a short cut which laid open the cheek of a big assailant. Howling, he disappeared down the alley.

The approaching Mohocks were so slow coming up the Canadian retreated, slashing and stabbing, into a doorway, but no sooner had his back touched its mud-splashed white panels than it gave way and he was yanked indoors. The door banged closed and promptly was barred muffling baffled curses which suddenly changed to yelping cries of terror. A gang of elegant, half-drunk Mohocks had gained the scene, swords ready or brandishing iron-shod staves.

Shaking and bathed in sweat, the dark-faced young Canadian grabbed the back of a chair and, sword point level, peered through sable hair streaming over his face and discovered himself to be in a small sitting room lit by a number of candles; they must have been spermaceti, for they burned brightly and gave off hardly any smoke at all. Opposite him a tiny fireplace was glowing cheerily.

"They say any port in a storm is better than none," observed a crisp voice.

Quick as a startled buck Breboeuf wheeled and faced a spare, lean-faced, middle-aged individual who, Italian rapier in hand, was clad in a paisley-patterned silk banyan or dressing gown. A loose-wound turban of brilliant blue silk protected what seemed to be a completely bald pate.

"*Pardon!* My most earnest thanks to you, sir," panted the Canadian. "Rabble really was pressing hard. Could not have withstood them much longer."

"So one observed," commented the other, returning his rapier to a soft sheath of orange velvet and placing the weapon on an inlaid card table. "Put away your sword, young sir, you'll not require it in here."

His benefactor, Breboeuf perceived, approximated his own stature and build, though he must be somewhat senior in years. He in the flowing dressing gown had penetrating clear, light-gray eyes; a cruel, pale-pink crease of a mouth; the chin was long, strong and narrow while ears lying flat to the skull were so sharply pointed as to suggest those on an ancient faun.

He offered a curt head-bow, then informed in a not unpleasant voice, "Permit me to introduce myself. I am Mark Antonius, late Captain in His Neapolitan Majesty's Dragoon Guards."

Henri remembered manners and with a flourish raised his new sword in salute. "Sir, Henri St. Castin Brebouef of Pénébesque in the Eastern Province of Massachusetts, at your service."

"Ah, a Provincial? Amazing, I watched you just now handle your blade with skill."

"I was trying to stay alive. By your name, sir, I take it you are an Italian?"

"Wrong. I was born in England and, for a period, served with the Royal Life Guards."

"You were a captain, sir?"

"No," came the suddenly taut reply. "Only a half-starved, penniless and therefore friendless cornet in the Blues."

While they conversed, Henri's jet eyes flickered, busied themselves with the surroundings. Judging by the gracefully designed furniture and the good pieces of silver and bric-a-brac in evidence this was no ordinary middle-class lodging; rather a *pied-à-terre* such as

he'd heard were furnished by wealthy and influential gentlemen for the accommodation of some particularly satisfactory mistress.

Confirming this impression the Canadian noted on the mantelpiece a gold-mounted tortoiseshell comb and the foot of a pink silk stocking escaping from under cushions on a gilded French love seat.

As he calmed down and his breathing leveled, he recognized the titillating odors of scented hair powder, sense-stinging perfume and an aroma of liqueurs.

"Your pardon, Captain," Breboeuf said, picking up his sword and starting for the entrance, "but I have a good friend out there. If you have no objection, I would like to step outside to find out how he has fared. The fighting appears to have ceased."

Captain Antonius's hard gray eyes flashed as he snapped, "Certainly not! Many persons remain in the street outside. Listen."

From beyond heavily shuttered windows sounded subdued voices and the soft shuffling of feet.

"Probably ruffians are waiting flat to the wall to either side of my doorway. While I respect commendable concern for a friend, the door must remain locked and barred till daylight."

"I understand, sir." The Canadian heaved a lingering sigh, then used supple fingers to rake strands of hair from his eyes. "To say that I am most profoundly grateful to you is not sufficient, but please *Monsieur le Capitaine*, why did you rescue me?"

Before making reply the spare figure in the banyan helped himself to a pinch of snuff. "Watching the melee from yonder window, I became impressed by the way you managed point and edge, even when hard-pressed."

Gradually Captain Antonius's colorless slash of mouth widened, softened his expression. "Since your swordsmanship appeared too fine to be spoiled by a pack of rogues I decided to preserve your skill.

"And now, my young valiant, your name — authentic or a *nom de guerre* — it does not matter."

Breboeuf, mud-smeared and disheveled, offered a not ungraceful half-bow, said evenly, "Your pardon, sir; my name once more is Henri St. Castin Breboeuf."

" 'Breboeuf,' eh? We may get on. You, like me, evidently are of foreign descent. In my case my father was Italian and a celebrated architect-builder who many years ago left Pisa, and was brought here to design and construct great country manors, town houses and even a ducal palace. My mother being English, I was born in the County of Essex."

Captain Antonius indicated a sideboard and invited his haggard guest over to sample a Cheshire cheese swathed in a clean white cloth and flanked by a tray of biscuits and a brace of small black bottles marked "porteau" in flowing script.

The two munched for a time, quite openly took one another's measure amid a silence which permitted hearing a sound of giggles, followed by a patter of light feet. Down a narrow, winding staircase materialized an enormous gray Persian cat supporting impressively flaring white whiskers. With graceful elegance the creature was flourishing its plumed tail.

Amusedly, Captain Antonius's pale eyes flickered to a mantel clock showing the hour at three. "Ah. The inventive sisters Holcomb grow impatient, ever alert for a fight, a foot race or a frolic."

Employing the upturned toe of a red-leather Turkish slipper, the host stirred the hearth into a blaze. "Evening's still but a pup; I'll soon summon the little darlings below. Meantime pray inform me concerning yourself."

Somewhat restored, Henri obliged, described the loss of the *Merrimack*, his and Jeremy's all-but-destitute arrival in London, and concluded with a brief account of recent events at the Gamecock's Spurs.

Impassive, Captain Antonius sipped from a fragile stemmed glass. " 'Tis an ill-famed establishment at best, my young friend. Small wonder you were misled and assaulted. Let us hope your friend escaped serious harm."

"I pray so," Breboeuf said earnestly. "Likely he has — he knows how to use his fists."

Seated before a chimneypiece of well-carved marble Captain Antonius considered his guest. "Since you come fresh from the American Colonies can you tell me whether your people really are on the brink of revolt?"

Breboeuf shook his lean head. "That would be going too far, *Monsieur le Capitaine*."

"Call me simply 'sir' — and a word to the wise, around London, or anywhere in England for that matter, spare use of a foreign language; nowadays *all* foreigners are viewed with suspicion, as well as Colonials, Roman Catholics, Scots and Irish."

13

Rosy Interlude

CAPTAIN ANTONIUS sought the foot of a narrow staircase, then called up in a soft but carrying voice, "Jenny! Descend straightaway to the powdering room. Fetch my spare dressing gown, slippers, towels, a comb and a jug of hot water."

Briefly Breboeuf went to inspect himself before a full-length pier glass gleaming at the hallway's end; he grimaced. Lord! What with his coarse, blue-black hair streaming in wild disorder over his rumpled neckcloth he looked an utter mess: bluish stubble was darkening his chin while a large purple bruise had caused his jaw to swell on one side.

Worse still, the new blue coat was mud-splattered and ripped across a shoulder and his waistcoat had lost several of its brass buttons; but thank God his and Jeremy's winnings remained safe within his waistcoat.

If only he'd the least notion about what had become of Jeremy!

Before Captain Antonius could anticipate, he darted over, wrenched open the front door and peered into the stinking gloom. No bodies lay in the trampled muck, no figures lurked among the shadows. All was quiet save for a drunken man shouting and reeling along the kennel.

Quickly he rebolted the portal and turned to face his host's coldly furious glare. "How dare you? Never, you unlicked puppy, ever again dare defy Mark Antonius!"

With mercurial speed the host's menacing expression relaxed into what appeared to be a genuine smile. "Forgive me, my young friend, I fear I've overlooked how much you must have endured this evening. Come and Mistress Jenny will repair your appearance in the powdering room to save a climb upstairs. Later, we shall dine and otherwise amuse ourselves — provided you're not too fatigued."

"Oh, I'm not, sir, please believe that!" Oddly enough, despite the day's harrowing succession of events, Henri Breboeuf felt no more than slightly fatigued.

Captain Antonius then indicated his establishment's powdering room — a closet cleverly let into wainscoting beneath the staircase. Its apple-green walls and the floor were white-speckled by layers of hair powder and a conical powdering mask with twin eyeholes stood to one side of a dresser cluttered with little boxes and bottles of cosmetics. On a shelf above was a row of blockheads supporting wigs of various lengths and styles.

A short but supple and dark-haired young woman with round, rosy features, luminous bright-blue eyes and a saucy upturned snub of a nose quit pouring steaming water into a copper basin and laughing said, "Please sir, me name is Jenny, and I'm at your service — entire-like. Why d'you goggle so? You must have encountered many a prettier maid."

"Not so!" Henri blurted. Such cleanly beauty after all the ugliness endured of late! A far cry, this, from those awkward bush wenches and sinewy, tawny-skinned squaws he'd mounted granted half a chance. Not for nothing was he descended from the fecund Baron St. Castin — a fact discovered at the age of twelve.

By candlelight Jenny's rosy complexion appeared unmarred; her mouth was luscious, slightly pouting. In calculated confusion tight little red-gold ringlets escaped from a crisp, lace-edged mobcap.

"Pray seat yourself, sir, and be comfortable. You've naught to concern you now."

Blinking, the Canadian settled into a small armchair and barely stifled a groan; someone must have fetched him a shrewd kick on the rump.

Able to view this pretty attendant in a triptych mirror set before him, he quickly perceived that Jenny was entirely nude beneath a fairly transparent peignoir of powder-blue voile belted in pink satin. Flagging spirits commenced to stir and rise.

"Would your Honor like me to sing a little song to soothe nerves and restore your vigor?"

"Aye, that's just what's needed."

In a rich contralto she lifted her voice:

> *The licensed by the law do't,*
> *Forbidden folk and a' do't,*
> > *And priest and nun*
> > *Enjoy the fun,*
> *And never once say "nay" to't.*
> > *For they a' do't.*

> *The goulocks an' the snails do't*
> *The cushie doos and quails do't,*
> > *The dogs, the cats,*
> > *The mice, the rats,*
> *E'en elephants an' whales do't.*
> > *For they a' do't.*

> *The wee bit cocks an' hens do't,*
> *The robins an' the wrens do't,*
> > *The grizzly bears,*
> > *The toads an' hares,*
> *The puddocks in the fens do't.*
> > *For they a' do't.*

Jenny passed a damp napkin over his forehead, wiped away a layer of dingy perspiration. "Ah! Jenny, that's better, vastly better. Am I mistook or didn't I hear someone singing in company with you a while back?"

She nodded pertly. "Aye, sir, me sister, Jill. For all she's a year my junior we so much resemble we're oft mistook for twins." A shadow flitted across her clear pink features. "Like true twins we're close-bound; always together we face life's hardships and pleasures."

She winked. "And 'tis a worthwhile bond, sir. Fine gentlemen find rare enjoyment in entertaining the pair of us and gladly loosen purse strings according."

Sighing, Breboeuf half-closed his eyes, watched Jenny hang his weskit and its heavy burden beside his ruined coat; if she noticed its remarkable weight it wasn't apparent save for momentary hesitation before she settled it on a peg.

Jenny knelt to remove slime-smeared shoes and stockings and then to ease off his breeches, and in so doing, perhaps accidentally brushed the swelling between his thighs.

Humming, Jenny next sponged his wiry brown neck and almost hairless chest and was about to lower the target when Captain Antonius called, "Hurry up in there! Mr. Breboeuf must be famished. I know I am!"

Humming melodiously, Jenny removed the mixed-blood's small clothes, quickly sponged legs and thighs, helped him into a dark blue-and-yellow banyan, then knelt to slip on heeled slippers.

"Feeling restored, your Honor?" Teasingly she laced hands behind his neck and raised satiny-red lips. "Kiss me for a tip — Ah! That's fine and a fair start —"

Jenny conducted him to a small but elegantly furnished dining room walled in faded yellow brocade and hung with several large mirrors. Two armchairs and a table had been placed before a grate of coals throbbing in a microscopic fireplace. Wineglasses of various sizes glistened before each place.

"I trust Jenny and Jill have managed a satisfactory bit of supper," commented the Captain, freshly combed and wearing a voluminous dressing gown of midnight-blue velvet.

Captain Antonius raised a brimming glass of sherry. "Here's to a lucky chance encounter; may we never find cause to repent it!"

The gray Angora reappeared, coiled leisurely before the hearth, then from round, topaz-hued eyes considered this stranger with an uncompromising intensity before commencing a *toilette intime*.

Breboeuf relaxed instinctive wariness and smiling said, "And to think I've been ready to damn London as the ugliest, most dangerous city one could imagine."

The host's tone became coldly incisive. He scowled. "And so it is! Make no mistake about that. Mistrust everyone. Lower your guard but for an instant, my new friend, and you may never learn what has happened. As in your wildernesses, vigilance is the price of survival.

"Shall we now address ourselves to more agreeable subjects?" Captain Antonius rang a table bell and the pantry door opened.

Although by now becoming inured to surprises, Henri gaped when Jenny entered carrying a wooden bowl of salad and moving with neat, little steps. Close behind appeared a second young woman who might easily have been mistaken for Jenny save for a tooth missing in her lower jaw; like her sister, Jill wore a crisply frilled white cap, high-heeled slippers of black satin, and long white silk stockings effectively gartered in scarlet ribbons — nothing else.

The candle and fire light created a pale rose sheen on generous expanses of ivory-white, smooth bodies.

Commented Captain Antonius, "This, my friend, is what the English of the elegant sort call 'salad served with French dressing'!" He fillipped Jill's round, pink-crested breasts when she bent to offer a silver salver supporting a brace of delicately browned partridges. "Another pair of tender little birds, eh what? But as to these, my friend, pray recall the gourmet's caution: 'Never before the salad course.'"

Chewing, Henri thought, is it possible that this same morning I sat in a filthy bedroom, hungry and near penniless?

Pale-pink bottoms and breasts jiggling, the sisters decanted wine before serving a trifle. All the while they were chattering gay nonsense.

At length Captain Antonius shoved back his chair and lit a yard-of-clay pipe from a paper spill he held over the grate.

Once the table was cleared, Jill, after warming plump buttocks at the fireplace, settled onto Captain Antonius's lap, twined a slim arm about his sinewy neck, then while kissing him on the mouth, groped downwards.

Jenny's heels clicked softly over the parquet floor. Wearing a dreamy smile she approached the young Canadian. "La, sir. Are you so over-weary — ?"

Clear of the disordered table, Breboeuf stretched legs before him then settled back in his chair. "Your opinion, *jolie alouette?*"

"I will decide, sir." Dropping onto his lap, she parted his banyan.

"If all Colonials are so handsome, Jill, I vow we're wasting time in England!"

14

Cadet Ruffler

⌣

THE SUDDEN CLANG of a nearby church bell sounding two resonant strokes caused Henri St. Castin Breboeuf to start up in bed as if so many war whoops had been raised outside his door. He sprang from the covers, blinking dazedly amid bright yellow shafts of sunlight beating through partly drawn curtains.

Where was he? Why was his body one huge ache? Burns suffered aboard the *Merrimack* ached like a bad tooth.

With a taste in his mouth like that of a *habitant*'s winter socks, the Canadian gingerly swung legs out of a wide bed which afforded irrefutable evidence that he had not slept alone.

A minute sound at his bedroom door attracted his attention just as it began to ease open. Wildly he looked for his sword. It was nowhere in sight, which was just as well because it was only the big, sleepy-looking Angora cat making an entrance.

Stark naked, he sprang to a wardrobe which proved empty save for frilly night rail. Panic struck. Hell's roaring bells! What had become of his clothing — of the waistcoat full of winnings! Only the blue velvet banyan he'd worn to supper an aeon ago remained draped over the four-poster's footboard.

Christ Almighty! Tired or not, how could he have been so unwary, so completely taken in? Right now, Henri Breboeuf was destitute of weapons, clothes, and oh, my God! *What* had become of *the winnings?*

Somehow that least common quality called common sense came to his rescue, forced him to subdue furious, shamed rage. What would be accomplished if he flew off the handle and went berserk like some stupid, drunken Indian?

Think, Henri. Think, Henri Breboeuf, calm yourself. At this moment you stand quite unharmed and free to think and then take whatever course you decide on.

Think, Henri, think! *Bon.* Yes, I shall continue to play the stupid, naïve Colonial, but I must not overplay, no, not at all; Captain Antonius is shrewd.

He swayed over to splash his face with handfuls of cold water, then combed his mane of hair into a semblance of order.

Evidently the dear Captain was playing him for a cully, he thought angrily, or was he *really* being cozened? Come to think of it; he'd not been robbed beyond hope of recovery. On the contrary, he'd been rescued from footpads in the nick of time and then had been loved more expertly and ardently than ever before.

Banyan a-flutter, he descended the stairwell on silent feet, then halted to listen. All he could hear was Jenny and Jill conversing in the kitchen. He resumed his descent to discover Captain Antonius standing in a cleared space in the sitting room's center — all the furniture having been pushed aside.

The Captain had stripped to his waist and in stockinged feet was exercising with a heavy rapier. The wiry figure danced lightly back and forth his shimmering blade repeating a complicated series of thrusts and parries.

At length the former Guardsman noticed the Canadian standing at the foot of the stairs with bare toes curled away from the chilly stone floor. The spare figure saluted with his weapon. "Ah, my friend, one observes you have had your sleep out."

Breboeuf tried to smile, but his self-imposed calm abandoned him. "My sword! What has become of my sword? I demand an answer!"

"Tut, tut, young man," the Captain said, "do not disquiet yourself. See? It stands in yonder corner, as you'd have noticed were you more observant."

"I crave your pardon, sir. I am being very rude. But that sword means much to me."

"Yes. Surely a fine weapon is to be cherished like a bride," he smiled, "perhaps more so. It lasts longer and properly handled will never betray you.

"I told Jenny to fetch it down and since it needed cleaning I did it myself. I'll confess to a certain curiosity concerning its history. The guard is so beautifully fashioned and its blade forged of such fine Bilbao steel I cannot but wonder how an impecunious gentleman like yourself managed to acquire it!"

Crossing to warm himself before a dying fire, Henri Breboeuf explained without reservation how he'd "borrowed" from the *Merrimack*'s strongbox for subsequent activities.

Captain Antonius draped a towel about lean, hard-muscled shoulders, then bent, supple as a ballet dancer, to slip on silver-buckled pumps with battered red-lacquered heels. He straightened, smiling.

"No doubt you are worried over the disappearance of your garments? Well, the sisters Holcomb at present are cleaning and repairing them. Believe me, my young friend, they stood in need of attention.

"Incidentally, your money is in a safe place."

"I trust so, particularly because much of it isn't mine."

Irritation hardened the host's aquiline visage. "You *trust* so! Remember your manners. One might take offense over such an implication. Rest assured, your coins will be returned, every penny of them except for a reasonable amount deducted for food, shelter, and er, bed. Set such a sum down as tuition paid on account of remaining alive and winning an initial success in this rich and wonderful, wicked city."

The Canadian shrugged, managed a short laugh. "Your point, sir, is well taken. Trust I shan't disappoint you."

After wiping sweat from face and torso the professional pulled on a shirt flounced down its front by worn but sparkling Flemish lace.

With a resumption of calm, Henri said, "Sir, I stand very deep in your debt. Why are you treating me so uncommon kind?"

While sheathing his rapier, Captain Antonius replied impassively, "Young sir, only because of your outstanding swordplay did I take you in. However, now I know you are from the American Colonies it is possible you can prove useful to me in my — er — profession and at the same time stand to improve your prospects."

91

Captain Antonius, he sensed, must have an interest in the American Colonies. Henri said as much.

"Admittedly, I *am* interested in them, for obscure but practical reasons." A hint of color entered the Captain's gaunt and sallow cheeks. "Have you heard anything about those so-called 'Wilkesite riots' which took place here a few years ago?"

"No. Please, sir, what do you mean by 'Wilkesite'?"

"Ah, then you've never heard about John Wilkes, the pestiferous reformer and even more redoubtable rake?"

Warily, Breboeuf shook his head.

"Surprising!" commented the Captain. "Fancied all you disgruntled Colonists would know of their English champion in Parliament who was forced to flee abroad."

"Sorry, sir. I fear I am very ill-informed."

"Well, to some John Wilkes is a powerful reformer and a fearless crusader for the rights of the common man; to others he's a blasphemer, a rabble-rouser, a witty but depraved and conscienceless rake of the worst sort. He was one of the leading spirits of the infamous Brimstone Club, about which you will undoubtedly hear a great deal."

Absently Breboeuf rubbed a cold foot against the calf of a hairy leg. "And why did this John Wilkes have to flee England?"

"John Wilkes evaded arrest and fled to the Continent after expulsion from Parliament. Today he is an outlaw. However, 'tis sure he soon will return voluntarily to surrender himself in order to test the validity of that general warrant from which he fled."

"And what, sir, can be a 'general warrant'?"

"A very old and long unused law under which an English subject can be thrown into prison on the complaint of persons unnamed without specific charges being made. 'Tis the same as the *'lettre de cachet'* still used in France; the English public won't stand for such an outrage, as John Wilkes seems about ready to prove."

Breboeuf said, "Come to think on it, since my arrival I *have* noticed 'Wilkes,' 'Liberty' and '45' painted or chalked in all manner of places. Please excuse my ignorance, but to what do such refer?"

"For a short and incomplete explanation," said the Captain, "Number Forty-five indicates the forty-fifth issue of the *North Briton*, a political journal founded and usually edited by John Wilkes himself in refutation of my Lord Sandwich's *Briton*, which that noble earl subsidizes to disguise our present Government's corrupt policies; Tobias Smollett edited it for a while."

Captain Antonius bent, tossed a log onto the embers, then straightened, saying acidly, "In the Number Forty-five issue, Wilkes violently attacked corruption in our Government, which is controlled by the so-called 'King's Friends.' What really got him into trouble was an implication that our present King's mother had been seduced by Lord Bute — then the Prime Minister.

"And then came the matter of a scurrilous poem he'd written called *An Essay on Woman*. Although Wilkes wrote the essay for his own amusement and the benefit of a few friends, his enemies, Lord Sandwich among them, obtained a copy through bribery and published it to the public. The uproar in Parliament was terrific — first Number Forty-five, and then this! It was too much.

"So a general warrant was issued and John Wilkes fled to France only a few jumps ahead of the bailiffs!"

Captain Antonius shrugged, got to his feet, a supple, faintly sinister figure. "This use of a general warrant at once caused howls of outrage in the American press — a free subject of the British Crown had been threatened with imprisonment without specified charges being brought. Another shocking example of royal tyranny!

"Of this, more later, perhaps once we've dined, and I do believe our breakfast is nearly ready for us. I will further explain the situation."

From the back of the house sounded sudden squeals and peals of laughter.

Banyan skirts flapping apart, the host returned, chuckling. "They've prepared a real meal."

Henri smiled gratefully. "Your little darlings must possess second sight; my stomach's been calling up to learn if my throat's been cut."

He hesitated. "Pardon my asking, sir, but I would like to learn the correct name for your profession."

"Variously I am termed a 'fencing master' a 'led-captain' or a 'Master of Arms.' I prefer the last designation. And now to the table!"

Said the Captain once the dishes had been cleared, "After you have dressed, my young friend, I believe the time has come for me to decide whether you are indeed as proficient with a blade as you appeared to be when fighting against odds and under miserable conditions."

From a closet Captain Antonius produced a pair of weapons of a sort new to Henri; these consisted of gradually tapering wooden rods about four feet in length; each had a small basket-guard of wicker-work affixed to its thick end.

"I take it you have never seen singlesticks before? Time you became acquainted with them; they weigh more than a small sword and so strengthen the wrist. Best of all, they afford fine exercise with no danger of accidental wounds. Shall we attempt a few passes?"

Here was no invitation but a command so Henri pulled off his slippers and stood.

"One appreciates you still are weary, my young friend, therefore I will not try you too long." He flourished his wooden weapon a few times, smiled thinly. "An you don't disappoint me, 'tis possible I may set you on a course towards distinction and perhaps considerable wealth."

Breboeuf postponed trying to fathom what was prompting this extraordinary individual's interest, accepted a singlestick, then tested his wooden sword for balance. Next he copied his host by executing a series of lightning thrusts and short, sharp cuts.

Captain Antonius slipped off his shirt, then pulled off his turban exposing a narrow head so closely shaven it appeared bald.

"*En garde!*"

A brief set-to ensued, feet padded softly, rapidly as the hickory rods tapped and clicked against one another. Before long the former Guardsman signaled a halt. "Desist! Your footwork appears superior and your last parry *en tierce* was powerful and well-timed. Were you not quite unfamiliar with these weapons I feel confident my thrust *en quarte* never would have tapped you just now."

Twice more Captain Antonius engaged and quickened his attack but Breboeuf was learning and beyond a stinging rap on the forearm scarcely got touched.

Smiling broadly and nodding to himself the Captain returned the singlesticks to the closet and went over to fill brandy glasses standing ready on a sideboard.

"Good! I think for the present I shall call you 'Henri' — perhaps later it may prove advisable to give you a *nom de guerre* under which you will fight. Now let us drink to Dame Fortune. An she smiles we will make certain purse-proud parvenus, degenerate political dilettantes and spoiled sprigs of the nobility pay through the nose."

"How, may I ask?"

"By being well paid to provoke duels, quite without appearing to, on behalf of politically, amorously or financially-minded patrons."

Henri savored the cognac. "So then money and advancement can be gained through hiring out one's skill?"

Captain Antonius's hairless head inclined. "Yes. But success can only be achieved through observation of very subtle limitations. These you must quickly learn."

"Then one becomes a soldier of fortune?"

The Captain observed stiffly, "I never thought it disgraceful for a gentleman to capitalize on hard-won proficiency. I, Mark Antonius, am the descendant of a long line of *condottiere* native to the town of Pavia in the north of Italy. To be sure, I have killed or crippled many men for pay, but always fairly. I am *not* and never will become a hired assassin!"

He picked up his glass and, frowning, slowly revolved it. "Only when properly approached by a person of rank or possessed of sufficient fortune can I be persuaded, through the use of guile and experience, to provoke some personal or political enemy of my patron into challenging me to a duel. As a rule such is not *à l'outrance* but only intended to incapacitate my opponent from public activity," he smiled thinly, "for a given length of time."

"Because of these troubled times, I find myself considering an unusual number of delicate and therefore lucrative propositions — more than I can conveniently handle and still do justice to those patrons I have decided to serve."

In a purely Latin gesture, he spread hands. "To provoke a challenge at just the right time requires the fine blending of diplomacy and opportunity plus deep knowledge concerning a future opponent's character and background. You follow me?"

Henri listened in rising interest as a succession of dazzling possibilities began presenting themselves. "But naturally, *Maître*. Will you please continue? I am all ears."

Captain Antonius settled back in his chair, still twiddling the empty glass. "For example, let us say that a prominent Whig bigwig — 'Lord White,' for name only — is standing for Parliament and is being bitterly opposed by 'Mr. Black,' a Tory of considerable resources and determination. Obviously Mr. Black must be incapacitated to prevent him from pursuing the campaign. You follow?

"Once financial matters have been settled between me and Lord White, he agrees to circulate in various smart clubs and coffeehouses rumors that Mr. Black is spreading scandalous lies concerning Captain Antonius and otherwise impugning his courage and honor. You perceive how it goes?"

"Yes, sir, but so much has occurred in so short a space of time I can't be sure. I'm, well, a bit rattled."

"A good sign that you admit it," the Master-at-Arms continued in a lighter tone. "As I've already remarked, gentlemen following our profession also are paid to intervene in matters of an amorous nature. For example, let us suppose a wealthy gentleman has become too old to duel — but not to dally — and wishes a rival removed from competition for some lady's favor; in such a case an *espada* — to use Spanish — sometimes wins a double reward. Ladies are given to admiring swordsmen accomplished in more ways than one."

15

My Lord's Town House in Chancery Lane

⌒

FOR A SECOND TIME Jeremy Dabney Brett of Piscataqua and Portsmouth tentatively escaped the nothingness long enough to perceive that he must still be living since he lay in what appeared to be
a real bed. Also he learned that his head, and for that matter his
entire body, was aching dully, that even the slightest movement
threatened such violent nausea he was grateful to relapse into bliss-
ful unconsciousness.

He half-roused on several occasions before he finally succeeded in
retaining consciousness and was sufficiently lucid to marshal his wits.

Peering about cautiously — he still dreaded a bout of nausea — he
discovered the damask curtains of what appeared to be a vast, canopied four-poster. The curtains being only half drawn he made out
that this bedroom had apple-green walls, must be spacious and high-
ceilinged, and very handsomely furnished.

Cautiously he parted the bed curtains a trifle wider whereupon
a pleasant voice commented, "La, young sir, at last you're able
to keep those handsome dark eyes open for longer than a wink.
Praise the dear Lord in His high Heaven. Let be, I'll draw the curtains wide."

Moments later Jeremy found himself peering up into the kindly
gray eyes and the rosy, round features of a female approaching

middle age. When she arose to jerk an embroidered bell-pull he saw she was plump, short and solidly built.

Judging by this apparition's neat, conservative costume and crisp mobcap plus the presence of a collection of keys dangling from a ring at her belt, he reckoned this must be a responsible servant — possibly someone's housekeeper.

"Now then, easy does it, sir," came the brisk admonition. "Coddled eggs, weak tea and a French roll will be up directly. Just lie still, sir. Doctor vows that's a woundy bad knock you've taken on your poll; said your skull must be uncommon thick else 'twould have cracked wide open."

"I — be good — promise." Jeremy batted eyes and tried to summon a smile which effort caused the bedroom to tilt several times before settling onto an even keel.

Aware of the weight of multiple dressings bound about his head he concluded he must be wearing something resembling a papal crown.

"And who, sir, might you be?"

"Jeremy Brett, Esquire, or so I believe." He summoned another feeble smile. "Now you have the 'vantage of me, ma'am."

"Why address me as 'madam'? I'm not quality."

"Excuse — ma'am, but back home any respectable-appearing female can be so addressed and generally is."

"I don't recognize your accent."

"Small wonder. I'm from the North American Colonies."

"Well, I never!"

"Your name, ma'am?" She flushed, then informed him almost primly, "Sir, I am Mrs. Richard Rigby — a widow and manageress of Middlebrook House, the Marquess of Middlebrook's residence in London. For your information, sir, 'tis situated in Chancery Lane."

Briskly, Mrs. Rigby made a pretense of readjusting green satin window draperies which allowed a burst of bright sunlight to beat in, steadying and rallying his wits.

"And who is 'the Marquess'?"

"Why, sir, for nearly a week you've been a guest of George Liscard, Third Marquess of Middlebrook."

"Middlebrook? A pretty name, ma'am. Where is it?"

"Middlebrook County, sir, lies on the Scottish border and almost encloses Luce Bay."

"Then my host is Scottish?"

"Heavens no! The Good Lord preserve us from Scots, Irish and all foreigners! No, sir, Lord Middlebrook's family is one of the most ancient in the north of England." Mrs. Rigby straightened the bed-clothes, informing briskly, "The Liscards greatly extended their holdings through having backed the King's cause at Culloden, back in '46.

"May I make bold to ask, sir, whether your family is connected with the Bretts of Bideford?"

"Probably. The founder of our line in America was of gentle blood and came to Massachusetts from Devonshire around 1670."

Hopefully, the housekeeper smiled. "Then you have the right to wear a crested signet ring?"

Feeling very weak, Jeremy forced a wan smile. "I believe so, although none in my line have ever bothered to wear one. A modest 'Esquire' after our name is the most I can claim since we have lived in New Hampshire ever since my grandsire bought into the Grants."

A frown, framed in crisp gray ringlets, creased Mrs. Rigby's smooth, pink-and-white features. "La, sir, and where might 'New Hampshire' lie?"

"In North America — surely you have heard of it."

Mrs. Rigby colored. "Then, Mr. Brett, I must confess I'm flustered. Somehow I've always fancied our settlers in America paint their faces, wear feathers in their hair and spend their free time scalping one another."

"Fear you're a bit wide of the mark, ma'am, except that some of our frontiersmen do fit your description."

"So, young sir, *you* are an American Colonial, or should I say a 'Provincial'?"

"Take your choice, but more often nowadays we call ourselves simply 'Americans.'"

"Ah, indeed? Lord Middlebrook will be pleased. For some reason of late he has displayed mounting interest in our North American possessions."

An angular maidservant entered, balancing a breakfast tray set with a teapot, a fluffy omelet and delicately browned *croissants*. "Annie, go inform my lord the guest has awakened but remains very weak."

Slipping a firm arm behind his shoulder blades, the housekeeper eased him into a reclining position, affording him a better view of his surroundings which, to his limited experience, appeared nothing short of luxurious.

Once he'd commenced to use hands which still quivered to eat, Mrs. Rigby, standing at the foot of the great four-poster, remarked quietly, "You can't yet appreciate, Mr. Brett, how close you came to being murdered; Dr. Squires says 'twas a very chancy matter. 'Twas him set your broken finger and stitched together the gash which runs clear across the top of your head."

A fugitive smile quirked the housekeeper's pale-pink lips. "Begging your pardon, sir, your skull must be uncommon thick!"

"Well, ma'am, reckon 'twon't be the last time you'll hear tell of 'hardheaded Yankees.' "

He tried to protest when she reached out and smeared a *croissant* with honey. "Don't baby me, ma'am. Ain't used to it."

"Tuts, Mr. Brett. Just give in and let me spoil you a day or so more; 'twon't harm you."

"Guess not — earnest thanks." Mrs. Rigby certainly was proving the kindest human being he'd encountered in a 'coon's age.

After wiping lips on a lace-edged napkin, Jeremy allowed his head under its mountainous application of bandages to ease onto a bolster. "Please, ma'am, just how did I come here?"

"I gather, Mr. Brett, my lord watched you prizefight with a black-leg in some tavern — never did catch its name. Being a fancier of the sport — he's no mean boxer himself — my lord appreciated the pretty fashion you handled your fists."

Her bright gray eyes sought his, narrowed themselves. "It's my guess Lord Middlebrook figures someday to win, at long odds, on 'Boston Jerry' — an unknown — at White's and Brooks's."

" 'White's'? 'Brooks's'?"

"They're two of the most exclusive gentlemen's clubs about London or the whole of England for that matter."

He became aware of her penetrating look. "Speaking of such, have you heard mention of 'Brimstone Club'?"

"I've not yet heard of it."

"I fear you soon will." Mrs. Rigby lowered her voice, leaned low over the bed. "A word of warning, young sir, you'll rue it if you have aught to do with that pack of noble scoundrels! Nearly all of them are vastly rich and influential in high places, but clever for all that.

The most of the members are no better than cruel and debauched libertines!"

A rich, even voice interrupted. "Now, that, Mrs. Rigby, is a most captious and unwarranted opinion."

Only then was Jeremy aware that without a sound the bedroom door had swung open to admit George Liscard, Third Marquess of Middlebrook.

16

The Marquess of Middlebrook

━━━━━⌇━━━━━

AT FIRST GLANCE Jeremy judged his host to be nearing his mid-thirties and realized that the Marquess of Middlebrook stood above medium stature, had a small, round belly and sloping shoulders which supported unusually long and muscular arms.

The Marquess's cleft chin somewhat receded beneath a strong Roman nose. His mouth was wide with full, red lips. Large and somewhat protuberant, his eyes, pouched and slightly bloodshot, were dark and strangely penetrating.

Mrs. Rigby noticed her employer had remained dressed for the house in a comfortable dressing gown. Black satin knee-breeches buckled in silver, white silk stockings and red Morocco leather slippers with absurdly exaggerated, upturned toes completed his costume save for a small green-and-gold turban adorned by a single delicately nodding egret feather which must have cost a pretty penny.

Lord Middlebrook's shirt was unbuttoned low enough to disclose a hairy chest decorated, of all things, by a strand of magnificent pearls!

The Marquess of Middlebrook's gait was so quick and fastidious he almost appeared to be executing dance steps in which there was no trace of effeminacy; in fact, the man exuded mature virility.

Lord Middlebrook paused at the four-poster's foot leisurely to survey its occupant; his faintly mottled features relaxed.

"Egad, my young friend, 'tis indeed encouraging to read sense in your gaze and behold traces of color in your cheeks. Although Dr. Squires for a time despaired your recovery I did not; you seem too young and strong to perish before sampling life's pleasures."

While speaking in rich, clipped accents, the nobleman's gaze never quitted Jeremy, lent an impression he was inspecting some thoroughbred animal with a view towards possible purchase.

Jeremy attempted a smile. "I apologize, sir, for my inability to rise and thank you for undoubtedly having saved my life."

A soft grunt escaped the Marquess. "Pray don't delude yourself; I'd have done no less for anyone as handy with his dukes as 'Boston Jerry' — I believe such was the sobriquet you bore at the Gamecock's Spurs?"

"Yes, sir, but my real name is Jeremy Dabney Brett, Esquire — if it's of any moment." Already he was beginning to perceive how much weight even so insignificant a title carried over here.

"Ah, so? So you *are* gently bred. Bears out what I've thought all along. You can give your lineage later on."

Said he crisply, "Mrs. Rigby, order up a bottle of sherry — the Amontillado '58 will do. Then order my chair for eleven o'clock. Warn Thompson to make sure the chairmen are stone-cold sober; cursed rogues were so tiddly yesterday they damn near spilled me onto cobbles before the George & Vulture."

Mrs. Rigby bobbed a quick curtsy and disappeared.

Once a short and dusty black bottle and a pair of delicate stemmed glasses had been placed upon a candle stand, the host seated himself and almost overwhelmed a dainty little gilded arm-chair upholstered in petit-point, then deftly decanted golden liquid into a glass which he revolved a few times between big-knuckled fingers before sniffing its contents.

" 'Twill do till a superior vintage comes along. Have a dram?"

"Thank you, no, sir —" Jeremy wasn't sure "sir" was the correct form of address but somehow "my lord" didn't come readily. "I'm still a trifle dizzied."

"Anything you would like to know, m'lad?"

"Yes, sir. When I left the tavern, I was in the company of a good friend when we got misled and mobbed."

"Um. Ah, yes, seem to remember a man seconding you during your bout with that ne'er-do-well, Sir Harry Knowles — beware of him, Mr. Brett, Harry's a fine boxer but tricky at cards. Your friend is lean, black-haired and dexterous with his blade. How's he called?"

"Breboeuf. Henri Breboeuf. He's a mixed-blood, part Indian, what New Englanders nowadays call a 'Canadian.' Did he get away?"

"Can't say; when we charged the last I saw of him he was backed into a doorway and defending himself pretty briskly."

"How, sir, did you happen along?"

"On quitting that dreary tavern I joined a party of Mohocks out to raise mischief; recognizing some of 'em I told 'em I'd seen a pair of likely fellows quit the Spurs in dubious company. We followed but by taking some wrong turnings arrived only in time to see you and your friend surrounded by rogues and putting up an uncommon good scrap.

"When the scum saw us, they put up hardly a fight — ran like hares. Once the last of 'em had scattered I looked about for your companion but the fellow appeared to have vanished into thin air.

"Since you were out like the wet torch beside you and bleeding like a stuck pig I hired a public chair and had you brought here." Lord Middlebrook laughed shortly. " 'Twas as simple as that, save I had to fee the chairmen because your gore had drenched their filthy upholstery."

His manner altered, became thoughtful. "I believe you just now told Mrs. Rigby you are a native of New Hampshire, one of the North American Colonies — is that correct?"

So the noble Marquess of Middlebrook wasn't above a bit of eavesdropping? Well, well! Gingerly, Jeremy inclined his massive crown of bandages; he still didn't dare risk abrupt movement. "That's right, sir."

"How fortunate."

"And why, sir, may I ask, do you feel an interest in us?"

Replied Lord Middlebrook while delicately sipping Amontillado, "For the time being, Mr. Brett, that is for me to know and for you to ponder on."

Pleasantly he added, "I say, what makes you so curious about my appearance?"

He must have noticed Jeremy's repeated glances at his half-opened shirt out of which was sprouting tufts of fox-colored hair.

"Ah, I have it! You're intrigued by my necklace?"

Jeremy blinked. "I apologize, sir. I really didn't mean to appear rude but while I've seen many a man wearing earrings I've never before seen a rope of pearls about a male throat."

The Third Marquess of Middlebrook emitted an unmistakably wicked laugh and smirked. "You mayhap will notice quite a few others, an you move in the right circles.

"Each pearl," lightly he tapped his necklace, "represents the defloration of a genuine, unsullied virgin. Ha, you gape? Know then, my young Provincial, that the cracking of as many maidenheads as possible — no matter whose — is the latest rage among the *cognoscenti*.

"Should you feel impressed by the presence of these paltry beads, forget it. 'Old Q' —Lord Queensberry, that is — wears a strand which dangles halfway down his shad's belly.

"Lord Sandwich — damn him — has an even longer one. Brags he now can count seventy-three rapes since bets were placed at White's five months ago on a six months' course."

17

Green Pastures

O N A LATE SPRING AFTERNOON Jeremy Dabney Brett, Esquire, without risking a sickening attack of vertigo, at last became able to move about Middlebrook House, which, though smaller than many similar establishments, nonetheless was most tastefully designed and proportioned.

By now a majority of his bruises had faded and a broken finger was mending well but that long scalp wound, closed by twenty-odd stitches executed in horsehair, still itched and on occasion ached abominably.

Now that strength gradually was returning, Jeremy devised a series of exercises such as shadowboxing, push-ups and skipping rope, which kept him occupied for hours on end, but, come evening, he too often forlornly watched his host's glittering town coach, complete with postilions and coat of arms blazoned brightly on its door panels, roll out of a neat little courtyard beneath his bedchamber's windows.

Mrs. Rigby evinced astonishment when he pleaded for newspapers, gazettes, pamphlets or broadsides — anything which might inform him about what was going on.

An item in the *London Gazette* immediately commanded his attention and in rising excitement he read of increasing lawlessness in Boston; inhabitants of that troublesome port were in a rising ferment because the *Liberty*, a seagoing sloop the property of one John Hancock, a prominent Boston importer and a leading member among the so-called "Sons of Liberty," had made port carrying a considerable consignment of taxable Madeira wine and East India tea.

However, the report stated, said John Hancock had refused to pay what he and many of his compatriots held to be an illegal and tyrannically imposed tax. The sloop's crew, assisted by dock workers, while breaking cargo had confined H.M. Customs officials below decks.

The Captain of H.B.M.S. *Romney*, 50 guns, anchored nearby, upon request from His Majesty's Commissioner of Customs, had dispatched a boarding party to release the imprisoned officers, seize the *Liberty*, and tow her from Long Wharf to lie under the *Romney*'s guns.

Once this action had been carried out a furious mob of rioters had manhandled Customs officials wherever found and then demonstrated threateningly before dwellings occupied by other officials in the service of King George III.

This rebellious conduct, the correspondent in Boston admitted, had been only incompletely suppressed; Customs officials and their families had been driven to seek safety on a number of the islands scattered about Boston Harbor. These unfortunates at present vociferously were demanding the dispatch of Regular troops to enforce law and order.

Irritably, Jeremy rubbed a pink-and-white cheek recently smoothed by the Marquess's personal barber and read on: "It has been reliably reported in the City that His Majesty's Government shortly will despatch two Infantry Regiments of the Line to support the Government's laws and impose His Majesty's authority.

"Touching this matter, it is understood Dr. Benjamin Franklin, Agent for the Massachusetts Bay Colony and presently resident in London, is in communication with Mr. Samuel Adams and Mr. John Dickinson, principal leaders among the so-called 'Sons of Liberty' and other rebellious organizations."

Jeremy stared unseeingly across his pleasant little sitting room.

107

How was Pa reacting to all this? No telling. Even while a wave of furious indignation had swept the American seacoast after imposition of the Stamp Act — the first tax ever levied by Parliament directly on the American Colonies — Pa, like a great many sober and responsible citizens, had kept quiet and loyal to the Crown.

Poor Pa! Perhaps it had been this very loyalty which had cost S. Brett & Son some badly needed shipbuilding orders and had hardened his creditors' demands.

True, the old man had changed his views after Parliament's passage of the Townshend Acts, tyrannical in the Colonists' eyes, which had, without in any way consulting popularly elected Provincial or Colonial governments, said that they were to place import duties — modest enough in all truth — on lead, glass, paints, paper, tea, playing cards, dice and several other commodities.

Pa had cooperated in enforcing Non-Importation Agreements so effectively that soon British shipowners, bankers and merchants felt the pinch and protested in Parliament so effectively that soon the obnoxious Acts were repealed, except for the one on tea — because just possibly certain officials high in the Government held important shares in the East India Company, more familiarly known as "the Honorable John Company."

Too bad he couldn't be with the old man to encourage him and plan what had best be done, with the *Merrimack*'s charred bulk rotting on the bottom of the English Channel.

What could be done? What? If only he weren't so out of his depth in these busy, glittering and confusing surroundings.

Sighing, Jeremy tossed aside the *Gazette*, then went to stand at an open window giving onto Chancery Lane from which was rising a series of street cries: "Fresh gather'd peas, young 'astings!" "Hot spiced gingerbread, smokin' 'ot!" "Small coals!" "Cherries, O! Round and sound." "Sweet lavender, sixteen sprigs a penny!" "Scissors, razors, knives to grind."

Presently a strong and not unmusical female voice dominated the rest:

> *Fine Seville Oranges, fine lemons fine*
> *Round, sound and tender and mine;*
> *A pin's single prick their virtues show.*
> *Fine Seville Oranges you may know!*

A far cry tree-shaded Chancery Lane from the stinking stews and alleys of Wapping which so far had furnished his only impressions of London Town.

Residences in this neighborhood mostly looked new, uniformly were of red brick trimmed with white, classic Graeco-Roman woodwork.

The Lane itself, he'd discovered, was largely used by private equipages, men on horseback, and smart sedan chairs, jolting and swaying towards their destinations.

Below, a woodseller's two-wheeled cart appeared with "Wilkes & Liberty" and "45" crudely daubed on its side and tail gate.

When he commented on this to Mrs. Rigby, who silently had appeared, the housekeeper lost her cheerful demeanor and eyed him warily. "Are you a Wilkesite, Mr. Brett?"

"Hardly. I've heard very little concerning the gentleman. Who is he?"

"John Wilkes," she burst out, "is an ambitious and vulgar political upstart; according to his friends he is also witty, practical and farsighted. In sum, sir, the fellow's a very intelligent rake who annoys or amuses his betters whilst plotting their ultimate downfall."

Guardedly — he was learning fast — "Whose downfall?"

"Why, at the time Mr. Wilkes wrote Number Forty-five it was to expose the Ministry's corrupt administration of the Army and the Navy.

"Aye, at that time 'twas a fine pack of rakehells in control at St. James's, among them Lord le Despencer and the Marquess of Granby." The housekeeper sniffed. "Matters in that direction ain't much better today when Jemmy Twitcher, otherwise Lord Sandwich ——"

" 'Jemmy Twitcher'? How did a noble lord come by so odd a nickname?"

Mrs. Rigby cast him a sidewise glance. "Jemmy Twitcher was a low character in Mr. Gay's *Beggar's Opera*. A few years ago when Lord Sandwich was addressing Parliament he assailed John Wilkes, formerly his boon companion and a fellow member in the Brimstone Club, by reading aloud passages from a scurrilous poem by Mr. Wilkes entitled *An Essay on Woman*. The author leaped to his feet and quoted some lines spoken by Captain MacHeath — a famous highwayman in the *Beggar's Opera*, 'That Jemmy Twitcher should peach me, I own surprises me!'

"Lord Sandwich will never hear the end of that quotation till the end of his days; his fellow members in the Brimstone Club especially enjoy using it."

"You've mentioned this Brimstone Club on another occasion, ma'am. D'you care to inform me about it?"

The housekeeper hesitated, sought the bedroom's door and peered out into the hall. She returned, normally placid features set in hard lines. "You'll hear all about it sooner or later anyway so I'll tell you only what I *know* to be true," she stated in cautious undertones.

"The 'Brotherhood of Saint Francis,' as this infernal order was called to start with, was founded by Sir Francis Dashwood— Lord le Despencer — otherwise known as 'Hellfire Francis.' He established it in a ruined abbey near Medmenham. That was away back in 1752, I believe."

"And who is Sir Francis Dashwood?"

"Lord le Despencer once was Lord of the Exchequer — the worst man ever to hold that great office.

"Another prominent member of the Club was the famous rake Lord William Douglas, now Marquess of Queensberry; also, Sir Francis Whitehead, the present secretary, is another founder of this blasphemous crew who offend God and disgrace Mankind."

In her indignation, Mrs. Rigby's voice rose until it fairly rang out. "In any case these mock-monks, aside from celebrating the Black Mass in various forms twice a year hold 'convocations' — really orgies as complicated as they are debauched.

"John Wilkes for a time was a leading spirit." Mrs. Rigby's round cheeks turned a brilliant shade of red. "Believe me, young sir, there's not a vice, no matter how vile or complicated, that is not encouraged, practiced and improved upon by members of the Brimstone Club. Makes any decent body's toes curl to learn even a part of what takes place."

"At Medmenham?"

"Oh no. I forgot to say that, a number of years ago, to avoid interference Sir Francis transferred the Order's activities to his estate at West Wycombe in Buckinghamshire."

Jeremy returned to his window where sunlight illumined his

bandaged head into a silvered crown. "Is my host and benefactor a member of this club?"

"Yes, more's the pity."

Mrs. Rigby, looking frightened, hurried again to the door and looked out just as neighboring church bells began tolling the hour of six.

"Pray remember this well, young sir, the witty, debauched and fashionable rakehells I've described *are not* the heart and soul of England! In the shires dwell countless thousands of stout, brainy and industrious Englishmen — nobles and commoners — who even now are winning us an empire beyond the seas.

"Credit me, Mr. Brett, there is *nothing* wrong with the core of Great Britain despite these posturing, trifling fops who wallow in fashionable corruption."

Lord Middlebrook's housekeeper might have added, but did not, that she'd been widowed when her husband had been killed fighting the French at Pondicherry in India, that her oldest brother had died in battle before Québec City; that two other siblings presently were serving in the fever-ridden West Indies as officers in the Royal Navy.

Anxiously Mrs. Rigby considered the bandaged figure at the window. "There now! I've let myself get carried away. Please, you'll not mention my remarks to His Lordship?"

"Naturally not, ma'am; thank you for your frankness."

"It's just that you, being new come from abroad, ought to be set right about conditions in England. Under this present Ministry, confused we are, but rotten we are not!"

Following a knock, Mrs. Rigby conversed briefly with a white-wigged footman. "Below, sir, is an individual waiting on His Lordship. The caller I'm told speaks like one from the North American Colonies, and since my lord is out and won't likely return before late mayhap you'd enjoy chatting with a fellow countryman."

Jeremy beamed. "Very thoughtful of you, ma'am. I'd enjoy nothing more but I scarce can appear downstairs in this rig so will you invite the caller up here, please?" — Soon he'd learn to omit the "please"; in these latitudes such a courtesy was not accorded to servants, no matter what their importance.

18

Fellow Colonial

TO JEREMY BRETT the visitor suggested nothing quite so much as an oversized woodchuck unexpertly wearing clothes. His thick hair was red-brown, his eyes were small, round and beady; his short and sturdy legs supported a rotund belly and a wide chest and a heavy round head, with a blunt nose, set upon a nearly invisible neck.

The moment the other spoke Jeremy went warm with pleasure; here was a fellow Yankee. Clad in gray serge garments, plain-cut but of good quality, the caller glanced quickly about before his round, ruddy features relaxed in a flat smile and he advanced thrusting out his fist.

"Elijah Pocock, merchant, born, bred and wed in Noo Haven, Connecticut." He cast a quizzical glance at Jeremy's bandages but asked no question beyond: "And who might I be addressin', young sir?"

Suddenly happy as a dog with two tails, Jeremy informed, then engulfed the other's fist in a grip under which Mr. Pocock winced.

"Wa-al now, I do declare, this *is* uncommon fine, Mr. Brett, to meet someone 'thout having to bow and scrape. Said yer name's Brett? Now, come to think on it, I once did a bit o' business with a feller by that name. Aye, 'twas Silas Brett up in the Hampshire Grants. You related?"

"He's my Pa."

"Well, well, now ain't that *something!*" Briefly Mr. Pocock wrinkled a ruddy forehead. "When did yer Pa last put into Noo Haven? Three — mebbe four years back? Aye, an my memory's not at fault, he was captaining his own vessel, the *Androscoggin*. Trust he's enjoyin' good health?"

"I'm afraid he wasn't when we parted in Portsmouth a few weeks back; rheumatics were stiffening his joints."

Their conversation continued guardedly for quite a while till Elijah Pocock hinted he'd dearly like to know how it had come about that a bunged-up young American Colonist should be living as a pampered guest in Middlebrook House.

"I really can't answer that," Jeremy said, "but it stands to reason that somewhere behind Lord Middlebrook's hospitality there's a reason I've been unable to fathom."

Mr. Pocock, losing some of his easy manner, leaned forward. "Tell me, friend, be you by any chance a Wilkesite?"

Jeremy evaded. "I've only been in England a short while and because of my hurts have had small opportunity to observe local politics."

"Pity. To my way of thinkin' John Wilkes is provin' a real friend. Ain't ye seen his name writ 'most everywhere?"

"Why is he such a hero, in your opinion?"

The man from Connecticut moved closer, began to talk in a hoarse whisper, "Because John Wilkes stands right up for the common man — here and in America. Time and again he's fought for our rights in Parliament.

"He favors the abolition of taxes levied on the Colonies 'thout their havin' a real voice in Parliament." Enthusiasm entered the caller's tone. "I can tell you, sir, Jack Wilkes's popularity is growin' by leaps and bounds all along our coasts."

Although his head had started to ache, Jeremy attempted to marshal his wits. "Do I sense Lord Middlebrook may be sympathetic to Mr. Wilkes and his ideas?"

Mr. Pocock's shoulders lifted. "Could be. I was sent here by — well, by a certain eminent countryman of ours to try to find out why your host seems to be interested in Colonial affairs. Perhaps — ?"

"You came to find out?"

"The notion crossed my mind."

"I scarcely know my host — or what this is all about."

Mr. Pocock hastened to qualify the suggestion. "No rush, young sir, no rush at all. Possibly after you've talked with our eminent countryman — well, we shall see what we shall see."

Through the window beat sounds of distant tumult. "What can that be?" Jeremy wanted to know.

"Why I suspect another mob is welcomin' Mr. Wilkes back from France."

"Then he's to be pardoned?"

"That's doubtful. Before the law John Wilkes is still a criminal and a fugitive from the King's justice."

"Then why has he risked arrest by coming back?"

"That's what I and our distinguished compatriot are attemptin' to figger out."

Mr. Pocock humorously raised a heavy reddish-brown eyebrow. "Wonder could I taste some ale? Been waitin' below some considerable time."

Once tankards had been fetched up, the visitor employed the back of a hairy hand to erase foam from his lips before he queried softly, "Ever hear tell o' the 'Sons of Liberty'?"

"Organizations by that name were springing up when I left Portsmouth. You one?"

"In a small way," admitted the other shortly. "Since I'm a merchant tradin' overseas our Committee of Safety sent me to judge the sincerity of Mr. Wilkes's pro-American sentiments. What we need to know for sure is whether he is really for us or only using us to embarrass the King's Ministers or maybe for some private end."

He sighed. "Everyone over here acts so plagued tricky even when they ain't crooked."

"My host for example?"

Those beady little eyes bored straight into Jeremy's wide-set brown ones. "Any notion how close might be the relationship between Lord Middlebrook and Mr. Wilkes — if any? We know they belong to several of the same clubs."

Jeremy thought, Ah yes, The Brimstone Club among 'em. Bandages shone as he turned palms upward in a gesture denoting helplessness. "Can't answer that. I'm still recovering from such a nasty blow on the head my wits even now are scarcely becoming unscrambled. Besides, my host is hardly likely to confide in a simple Colonial like me.

"On the other hand, please tell me who selected you to approach His Lordship? Just who is our 'distinguished compatriot,' as you term him?"

Mr. Pocock steepled stubby fingers beneath a red round chin, nodded like a mechanical toy.

"Dr. Benjamin Franklin, Postmaster-General for the North American Colonies."

"Why's he called 'Doctor' Franklin — he a sawbones?"

"No. Seems St. Andrews College made him a Doctor of Philosophy or somethin' like that. He's also a member of the Royal Society, for what that's worth."

Having heard talk about the Doctor's experiments with electricity and his invention of the lightning rod Jeremy nodded but, recalling Pa's advice, "A man learns nothing whilst he's talking," he kept quiet, ordered up more ale and was pleased to note that Mr. Pocock relaxed somewhat and comfortably rubbed a rotund little belly.

"And why should Dr. Franklin send you to Lord Middlebrook?"

"Wants an appointment, that's what; account of he's heard about a shipbuilding program the Admiralty's about to authorize."

Jeremy's sense of fatigue evaporated abruptly. "You mean to say the Admiralty is finally getting ready to replace some of its half-rotten vessels?"

"Comes to that, though 'tis not yet general knowledge." Mr. Pocock looked uncomfortable. "Ye'll guard yer tongue, young sir? Shouldn't have been so gabby. Please don't undo me. Dr. Franklin would be wroth."

"Of course. But please tell me more about this replacement program — what does it provide for?"

"As yet we know little save that this measure directs building in British and Colonial yards some twenty vessels of differing rigs and tonnages."

Twenty vessels! Visions of those empty stocks and slipways lining the Piscataqua.

"Dr. Franklin is determined the North American plantations shall build a fair share of these. Lord Middlebrook, he believes, can help bring this about."

Mr. Peregrine Falconer

To JEREMY BRETT's considerable surprise word was sent that Lord Middlebrook requested his presence at supper that evening which suited him fine. Back home no self-respecting man could, for days on end, accept hospitality he'd no means of returning — even in modest style.

Blithely, therefore, he accepted the services of a smirking, dark-featured Italian valet who fetched in, among other garments, a long, handsomely tailored coat of canary-yellow velvet, red satin knee breeches and a blue brocade waistcoat secured by bright silver buttons, all of which fitted him so becomingly their measurements must have been arrived at not quite accidentally.

All at once he found himself standing, deeply embarrassed, bandaged head, hand and all, behind a towering footman who, bowing mechanically, opened the door to a small dining salon illuminated by a galaxy of beeswax candles supported by Venetian crystal sconces flanking a glittering sideboard.

"Mr. Jeremy Brett, m'lord!"

Jeremy became aware of a small, bright fire snapping beneath a mantelpiece of elaborately carved green marble. Lord George was seated in a comfortable wing chair with one foot propped on a taboret and supporting on his lap a small King Charles spaniel. A neat little green bow had been secured to the animal's silky head.

"Ah, Mr. Brett, pray enter. Pardon my not rising but I fear 'twould inconvenience Young Q — a favorite of mine." While gently patting his pet the master of Middlebrook House offered a languid but entirely warm smile. At the same time the weary-looking but expressive dark eyes seemed to light up.

"Now then, Boston Jerry, set yourself at ease. Must own I'm a vast fool not to dine comfortably at home more often, not have to posture, strive and chatter amid throngs of empty-headed macaronis, parvenus, titled bores, and painted whores pretending to be wellborn ladies and ladies conducting themselves like whores."

He beckoned a liveried lackey standing statue-still in the background. "Giles, pour Mr. Brett a measure of champagne.

"Well, my young friend, you appear much mended since last we spoke. You may seat yourself."

Jeremy, however, remained before the fireplace, painfully conscious of bandages swathing his head and hand. Embarrassed color welled into those damnably smooth pink-and-white cheeks. "Sir, I much appreciate this opportunity to speak with you."

Deliberately, Lord Middlebrook's reddish brows elevated themselves. "Indeed. And why?"

Jeremy gulped but said steadily enough, "Sir, for much too long a time I have been an uninvited guest, doctored and lavishly cared for."

"And what of that?"

"Why, sir, 'tis only that at present I lack the means of returning even a small part of your hospitality."

" 'Tis truly a commendable sentiment. Pray continue."

" 'Tis just that I can't go on being — well, being kept like — like, well, some hurt but still valuable animal — like a blooded racehorse," he blurted, flushing.

"Your simile is singularly apt, young sir. Lest I miss my estimate by a wide margin, which doesn't often happen, I'll wager six-to-one you've a decent share of breeding in your veins."

He pointed to a small, tapestried armchair, spoke with such a tone of command that the spaniel opened soulful brown eyes. "Now seat yourself. I wish to learn something of your family and breeding."

Damn! There was that patronizing "breeding" once more. Jeremy said stiffly, "And if I comply?"

"You will have, in part, repaid my trouble over you," drawled Lord Middlebrook. "Possibly, you may win for me a rather sizable sum of money."

"Money, sir?"

"Yes, money. And pray remember for the present to address me as 'my lord.' "

Delving into a side pocket, the thick-bodied nobleman produced a small gilt-edged notebook bound in calfskin. "This, Boston Jerry, is what is known among the *ton* as a betting book; everyone with any claim to fashion carries one."

Powerful fingers riffled its pages. "Ah, yes. Here it is — a bet with Freddy Gascoigne: 'Five hundred pounds that one Jeremy Dabney Brett can be proved to have noble connections.' "

Dear God; five hundred pounds! Such a sum was hard come by in Piscataqua; why, a sizable coaster could be built for that! Jeremy burst out, "But, but, my lord, you scarce know me."

"True," Lord George admitted carelessly. "But 'tis the element of uncertainty lends spice to any sporting wager. You'll soon learn that to bet on a sure thing isn't done — most unmannerly.

"You gave your middle name as 'Dabney'?"

"My mother's family name. Her family for many generations held estates in Oxfordshire. Her father was the Third Marquess of Welford."

"Ah, yes! He died in a duel; long ago, an my memory's not at fault."

The nobleman's heavy red features lit. "So then you're connected with the Dabneys of Welford! Egad! Freddy Gascoigne will be sour — always the graceless loser — 'tis half the fun of winning from him."

Jeremy stared at this solid figure in an elegant lounging costume which negligently exposed a string of pearls glimmering about his muscular throat.

"Shall I proceed about the Dabney family?"

"Pray do."

"Back in New Hampshire there's a good deal about Ma's — er, Mother's — family we don't know."

"Know then the Third Marquess's heir got himself killed in Flanders before he could inherit, so the title passed to a cousin, a Sir Hugh Dabney, who, by all accounts, is a dull dog and a drunkard to boot.

"I fear, Boston Jerry, the Dabney fortunes at present lie close to ruin — you are not aware of this?"

Miserably Jeremy shook his misshapen head, watched George Liscard silently empty his goblet. Without prompting, the footman hurried to replenish it.

"Stands to reason when and if, he's confronted by you Sir Hugh will deny any claim of kinship. Is there not some person of social importance in this realm who can support your assertion?"

"Being but new arrived I fear I can't give you an answer, sir — er, my lord."

For no particular reason the little spaniel roused and, quivering with affection, attempted to lick her master's face. Gently, Lord Middlebrook employed a well-beringed hand to restrain his pet. "Down, Q, down, damn you!" He grimaced. "Must confess only kisses I relish come from bitches of the two-legged variety.

"Come, Boston Jerry, can't you find some sort of answer to my query?"

Jeremy hesitated, then brightened. "Come to think on it, near three years back my older sister Perdita —— "

" 'Perdita,' heh? Now there's a fashionable cognomen. Your pardon — you were saying?"

"Perdita went to England on a visit to my mother's brother who is, or was, a baronet by the name of Sir Anthony Blakeney. You've heard of Sir Anthony?"

"Knew Tony well; attended Christ Church together. Pity; dear fellow broke his neck in the hunting field last autumn; therefore you remain short of a sponsor."

Lord George arose, spilling the spaniel onto a gleaming parquet floor, and went to warm his backside before the flames. "Try again. What's become of your sister? Lost touch, eh?"

"Guess that's about the size of it," Jeremy admitted. "We've heard, roundabout — 'Dita's no letter writer — she married a young nobleman named Constable who hails from near a town called Bath."

"Could have been Sir Guy Constable of Chew Magna," commented Lord George in rising attention. "I believe his estate lies hard by Bath."

"Sir Guy! That's the one!" cried the Colonial. "After 'Dita's marriage, Ma — er, Mother got only one letter from Sis — er, Perdita, so we're pretty much in the dark about what's become of her."

"Said your mother was daughter to the Marquess of Welford?"

"That, sir, is the honest truth. Back in Piscataqua we have papers to prove it."

Diffidently, Jeremy asked, "Sir Guy?"

For the first time George Liscard chuckled. "Guess the fellow's your brother-in-law."

"Is he alive? What's he like?"

"Pleasant enough, from the little I've seen of him durin' last season at Bath. Oh, he's well enough born — comes from a fine old County family and is fairly well off though he won't be much longer an he keeps on gaming; Sir Guy is famous for his inept wagers."

"Your sister is still married to this Sir Guy?"

"Expect so, my lord."

"Ha! Now I recall what I've been tryin' to remember. Sir Guy Constable's sire served as Comptroller of the Navy Board of Ordnance during the Marquess of Granby's tenure of office. Birds of a feather, I venture. The lot of 'em played ducks and drakes with Navy finances, got rich in a hurry."

At the term "Navy Board" Jeremy recalled Mr. Pocock and listened hard without appearing to; his host's piercing little black eyes were fixed upon him. He was hoping Lord Middlebrook would enlarge upon this subject when a footman entered to announce the presence in the waiting room of a Mr. Peregrine Falconer.

Lord Middlebrook smiled thinly and got to his feet. "One of Perry's few virtues lies in being punctual. He will join us for dinner."

"Falconer?" *Had* Dr. Franklin's emissary mentioned such a name? He couldn't be sure; if only his scalp hadn't itched so distractingly during that interview.

When the new arrival appeared it pleased Jeremy to encounter someone nearer his own age, whose long face had ruddy-bronze complexion and whose wiry build suggested considerable time spent outdoors for all lines of dissipation lurked about his eyes and mouth.

Mr. Falconer was wearing a silver-gray *justaucorps* or long-skirted coat above a wine-colored velvet waistcoat and black knee breeches.

His natural ginger-hued hair was secured in a Prussian pigtail by a wide ribbon of green grosgrain.

"Perry, this is my house guest, Jeremy Brett," drawled Lord Middlebrook; then to Jeremy's utter astonishment, added, "Jerry here is from America and is by way of being a distant cousin. Trust you'll help him find his way about Society — and officialdom," he added evenly but with a shade of emphasis.

Peregrine Falconer grinned broadly. "Someone's husband returned unexpectedly?"

"No," explained the Marquess of Middlebrook. "He'd scarce landed than he was set upon by thugs who damned near did him in. As you can see, he's had a hard time since his arrival here."

"Then Mr. Brett stands in dire need of relaxation and, if those well-filled breeches are any indication, of feminine companionship."

Jeremy scarcely heard Falconer's comment. What in thunderation had prompted his host to claim him as a "cousin from America" when his connection with the Dabneys of Welford remained unsubstantiated?

"Jerry and his family have long been in the ship construction business in New England; old established firm."

"And where are your yards?" Mr. Falconer inquired.

Jeremy told him.

"And what types of vessels do you build?"

"Anything from small men-of-war to coasting schooners."

"Of what tonnage were those men-of-war?"

"We've built two brigs — one of four hundred tons and twenty-two guns, another of three hundred and fifty tons and eighteen guns."

Mr. Falconer then turned aside. "I say, George, I am fairly famished. When do we dine?"

Throughout a repast consisting of Colchester oysters followed by a pigeon potpie and cold roast pheasant, the two gentlemen conversed about bets and gossip about which Jeremy could know nothing.

From frequent references to "White's" it appeared that both were members of this — with the possible exception of Brooks's the most fashionably exclusive gentleman's club in London. Said Peregrine Falconer, peering into a glass of tawny Oporto, "I say, George, do I sense that your cousin," delicately he lingered on the designation, "has turned up from the American Plantations at er, well let's say an opportune moment?"

"You might, Perry, you might sense that."

Jeremy flushed. Damn it! What in hell were they taking him for? A bumpkin possessed of only simple intelligence?

"Oh, by the by," Mr. Falconer remarked while nibbling a morsel of Cheshire cheese, "presume you've heard old Dashwood's planning a special convocation of the Order of St. Francis to celebrate Johnny Wilkes's return from exile?"

"To be sure, pimps and madams already are scouring London for a supply of virgins, society 'demi-reps' and accomplished young whores."

A chuckle escaped Lord Middlebrook and he winked with spark-like rapidity. "See to it, Jerry, you commence training for this event as seriously as if you were sparring and shadowboxing. Bound to have persons of influence and ladies turn up at West Wycombe to test your abilities."

Peregrine Falconer quirked a narrow brow. "I say, George, does your cousin understand what you mean by 'abilities'?"

"Perry, d'you imagine I've not noticed Cousin Jerry's endowed with a roger of imposing dimensions? Should create a *deep* impression on the most insatiable inhabitant of the Nunnery.

"Decided on a companion for the Convocation?"

Exuding contentment, Peregrine Falconer inclined a neat ginger-hued head. "Not definitely, but I've an eye on a shapely Italian dancer in the Royal Opera's *corps de ballet*."

Jeremy watched his host sit up so sharply his necklace swayed. "Is she young?"

Mr. Falconer kissed his fingertips. "Very. Delectably so. Two-to-one Adelina ain't above fifteen but older than Eve concerning carnal matters.

"And you, George?"

"No one as yet." The Marquess bent to straighten the bow on the spaniel's glossy head. "In that connection, I've ordered Mother Stanhope to fetch a genuine virgin for inspection after we've dined."

Silas Brett's son was finding it increasingly difficult to credit his hearing; thoughts of empty slipways along the Piscataqua faded. B'God, these long days in bed had charged his body with demands which could only be satisfied in the company of a compliant young female.

Chuckled Falconer, "So Mother Stanhope is providing you with a fresh pearl?"

Lord Middlebrook packed and presently lit a long churchwarden pipe. "Would that were the case: I face a conflict 'twixt desire and expediency. Badly as I need to break another maidenhead, Jemmy Twitcher stands in greater need. Last count his necklace numbers a pearl less than mine."

Momentarily George Liscard's carefree expression vanished, became supplanted by a cold, precise manner. "Therefore I'll not blood Mother Stanhope's neophyte tonight but in due time pass her over to the Rape-Master General. Must rally to a friend in need, eh what, my dear fellow?"

A curious smile curved Peregrine Falconer's full mouth. "Why not? As the Jesuits put it, 'The end justifies the means.' " Lord Middlebrook puffed meditatively. "Makes me feel nobly unselfish."

Peregrine Falconer tossed off still another glass of wine. "Rare sensation, eh?"

The host glanced at Jeremy. "I'm told a distinguished compatriot of yours is expected to attend the Brimstone Club's convocation."

"What's his name?" Falconer queried.

" 'Tis a Dr. Franklin. Heard of him?"

Jeremy flushed. "Everyone in New England does, in the Southern Colonies, too."

"Your pardon, Mr. Brett," Mr. Falconer smoothly interjected. "Have you heard talk of — er — communication between Dr. Franklin and John Wilkes?"

"Nothing, sir; I've not been about much. Since my arrival I've been my lord's guest."

" 'Cousin George's guest,' " corrected the host pleasantly. "But perhaps you can tell us why John Wilkes is so popular in North America?"

"Sorry, my — Cousin George; up our way we haven't heard much about him."

George Liscard's manner underwent a subtle alteration. Casually, he indicated tiny glasses of cognac. "Out upon it! I'm a dull host. Enough of such tiresome subjects. Young blades should consider livelier subjects."

"Hear! Hear!" cried Peregrine Falconer. "And now, George, what about the selection of a companion for West Wycombe?"

"I've some irons in the fire; Madam Betty Camp vows she can produce — for a high price, of course — a ravishingly lovely auburn-haired lass of thirteen whose dam stands ready for a mere forty guineas to offer her darling's maidenhead."

"At forty guineas I'll wager her brat is shrill, ugly and filthy dirty."

"For the fun of it, Perry, how much will you bet that's just what she is?"

"Twenty guineas."

"Done?"

"Done."

Both produced betting books. A sizable diamond flashed on Mr. Falconer's middle finger.

20

Mother Stanhope

A FOOTMAN APPEARED to announce, wooden-faced, that Madam
Stanhope, accompanied by a young female, had arrived and was
soliciting His Lordship's attention.

"'Soliciting'! Mark that, my friends. B'God, Giles, you've rare
wit," he told the footman. "Selected *le mot juste*, as our French
friends put it."

"Thank you, m'lord, thank you," the servant murmured, not having the least comprehension.

"Show the pair of 'em to the library. Well, Perry, Cousin Jerry,
shall we view this filly and decide whether she's qualified for consideration?"

Holding aloft a small candelabrum, Lord Middlebrook led the way
to a small, oak-paneled library lined from floor to ceiling with shelves
of expensively bound books. Celestial and terrestrial globes flanked a
wide marble fireplace in which birch logs flared, cozily illumining the
study in dancing red-gold hues.

"For this pleasurable occasion let us make ourselves comfortable,"
the Marquess of Middlebrook suggested, settling into an armchair
beside the fireplace.

Falconer selected the seat opposite. Following momentary hesitation, Jeremy selected a tapestried occasional chair standing near the

library's stepladder. Gingerly he tucked the injured hand into his shirt front to ease rising pain.

When the door was opened, in waddled a singular apparition. To describe Madam Stanhope as grossly obese would have been a sharp understatement; her bulging form appeared nearly as wide as it was high.

A great parrot's beak of a nose frosted by liberal applications of rice powder jutted from between shrewd gray eyes. She wore a monumental wig, elaborately curled and arranged to support a pair of lofty pink ostrich feathers.

Ponderous as she was, Mrs. Stanhope managed a curtsy of surprising grace, murmuring, "At yer service, m'lud, as usual."

"Then, I'm sure, Mother S., 'twill prove excellent. What quality of merchandise have you fetched this time?"

"The fairest, loveliest innocent I've found in years, m'lud; sixty guineas' worth of the most delicate virgin flesh as ever charmed yer eyes. Aye, Dolly Lawton's well-spoken, demure and dainty."

"Then what are we waiting for, Mother dear? My friends grow as impatient as I."

Mrs. Stanhope's painted lips formed a hideous smile as she called to the hall door. "Now, then ducky, out with you and see you remember yer manners."

In the entrance appeared a slenderly graceful young girl who in Jeremy's opinion could not have watched spring blossoms open more than fifteen or sixteen times.

By the firelight long and gently wavy hair cascading over this near-child's narrow and sloping shoulders gave off rich chestnut hues; her legs were long but a trifle on the thin side as were her waist and hips. The most surprising thing about this medium-tall young female was the incongruous maturity of high-riding and sweetly-rounded breasts.

"Now, then Dolly, step before the fire and do just as His Ludship says. Move!"

The girl went scarlet and as she advanced her large and lively dark-blue eyes sought the floor and clung there, emphasized the amazing length and thickness of silky black lashes.

Languidly, George Liscard crossed silk-sheathed legs. "You take oath Dolly is *virgo intacta?*"

"Lawks, yes m'lud!" Mrs. Stanhope sounded cautiously indignant.

"Else I'd ne'er ha' dared to fetch her here. Me own house doctor has examined her and vows Dolly's clean and new as a golden guinea fresh from the Royal Mint."

Jeremy Brett looked on wide-eyed and increasingly stimulated.

Mr. Falconer moistened his lips, then drew a folding quizzing glass from a waistcoat pocket, snapped it open, then through it unhurriedly inspected the auburn-haired neophyte from toe to crown.

Mother Stanhope's protégée remained facing the flames. Rigidly erect, she had begun to tremble perceptibly, and was staring blankly downwards, with narrow, seductively shaped carmine lips sufficiently parted to reveal fairly regular small and very white teeth.

"Come now, Mother," drawled Lord Middlebrook, "don't that clear, pink complexion betray her for a piece of country cunt?"

"Aye, the girl's sure enough country-bred, but she's of good family; vows her Pa is a parson with a living in Berks."

Eyes traveling deliberately over the slight figure in pale blue lustring, George Liscard inclined his head. "That may be so; your filly's conformation does suggest a strain of hot blood. How came Dolly into your tender clutches?"

"Her Pa, swears Dolly, is a widower and is perishing of consumption. So, on account of there were too many mouths to feed at the parsonage, she runs off to London to better her condition."

"That God's truth?" lisped Mr. Falconer.

The girl commenced trembling more perceptibly and squeezed her eyelids so tight shut two pellucid tears formed at their corners and escaped. Her lips quivered and moved but no sound escaped.

Not unkindly Lord George demanded softly, "Cat got your tongue, my dear?"

But still Dolly could only move her lips.

Mother Stanhope abruptly pulled out a fan and commenced nervously to use it. "La, yer Ludship, Dolly's that frightened over the privilege of meeting a noble lud I added a wee tot of laudanum to her tea ere we left home — only to steady her."

Keeping his gaze on the girl, Mr. Falconer chuckled gently. "Laudanum! Now ain't you the wise old bird about this business."

Jeremy's scalp wound and hurt hand commenced to throb while his excitement mounted. Criminently! He'd never beheld a girl even half so alluring.

Commented Peregrine Falconer: "At least, George, you must

admit 'tis a relief to find a wench who don't prattle her silly head off."

"Aye, 'tis indeed something of a miracle." While toying with his pearls Lord Middlebrook raised a heavy brow in Mother Stanhope's direction. "What did you say is this filly's name?"

"She calls herself Dolly Lawton."

Above the fireplace the portrait of an earlier Lord Middlebrook wearing half-armor appeared to peer appreciatively downwards while his descendant straightened on his chair, also produced a quizzing glass and raised it to a level with his eyes.

"If I'm to pay so stiff a price for this pretty one's hymen I intend fully to inspect its owner and invite opinion on her true value — and possibilities."

"Of course 'tis as yer Ludship wishes."

"I say, Perry, what's your opinion thus far?"

" 'Twould seem she owns a fine complexion, a rare white and satiny skin — and that dimple in her chin and those fascinatin' long eyelashes!"

"Hold hard! Don't attempt to prejudice me."

The corpulent Madam addressed her protégée in unctuous under-tones. "Nah, then, my gel, just remember, careful-like, how I've taught yer to peel down. By the numbers now. One!"

But the near-child only quivered and continued to stare at the floor.

Mother Stanhope, breaking into a string of fashionable oaths, waddled over and employed a folded fan to deal Dolly Lawton a sharp blow across the cheek. "Damn you for a stupid little slut! *This* is the greatest opportunity ye're ever like to meet; please His Ludship and his friends and I warrant within a year ye'll own yer home and go riding about Hyde Park in yer private chariot."

Through a delicious haze Jeremy watched the girl's great eyes open wide, wider as, uncertainly, her hands crept upwards to fumble at and unclasp the cameo pin securing a scarlet silk neckerchief; slowly it slipped down from slim shoulders to settle like a bright puddle on the hearth of gleaming marble.

Impatiently Mother Stanhope clicked her tongue. "Come! Come! Get on with it, you awkward baggage. You must do better than that."

She kept casting anxious glances at Lord Middlebrook. "Have patience, m'lud. Must have poured a bit too much of the laudanum."

"Let us hope so. Right now your country cunny betrays all the grace of a marionette."

"Granted, yer Ludship, but as a rule Dolly is poetry in motion."

Slowly the rigid figure's fingers commenced to undo a set of little bows securing her bodice. The flickering fire tinted gold-white the gradual exposure of smooth, very white, plump and almost mature breasts.

Peregrine Falconer uncrossed legs the better to lean forward and poise his quizzing glass. The host's heavily beringed fingers commenced lightly to drum upon his chair's arms. Jeremy gaped like a stranded codfish.

"Two!" snapped the harridan, casting desperately apologetic glances. "Dolly's still green yet I warrant, m'lud, ye'll be charmed with her on the next occasion."

"An such a thing occurs," sighed Lord Middlebrook. "Gad! Right now, Mother Stanhope, you offer no more than an admittedly pretty but frozen and graceless country wench."

The girl, nervously batting her eyes, continued to stare fearfully, blankly before her; then elevating her chin a trifle, she commenced to untie a frilly apron; when it rippled to the glossy floor Dolly stood delicate and motionless as a porcelain figurine in a bouffant skirt of light-blue lustring.

"Tell her to move directly before the flames — or is she wearing too many petticoats to permit a clear silhouette?"

"Possibly, yer Ludship, but they'll be off in a trice. Get on, Dolly, you ain't to bleed tonight so stop acting like a moonstruck goose. Remember," she hissed, "*this* is the chance of your young life!"

Moving more steadily, Dolly did as she was told and, moving directly before the fireplace in swift succession undid tiestrings securing her skirt and those of a prettily embroidered and flounced "show" petticoat.

"Ah, that's more like it," grunted Lord Middlebrook as outlines below the waist became visible through the girl's under-petticoat of fine cambric. "Legs seem straight, and well enough turned, but just a trifle on the meager side."

Garments already collapsed on the fire-speckled floor were joined by the under-petticoats. Imperceptibly, Dolly's movements became less constrained, even fluid; her dark red lips parted and her eyes

came alive after a fashion when finally she stood wearing only a nearly transparent shift of crisp white lawn.

"Not bad. Not bad at all," drawled Lord Middlebrook, steepling jeweled fingers beneath his chin.

At once Mother Stanhope hissed, "Pick up yer things, dearie, lay 'em on yonder bench and try to be graceful about it. An you don't please His Ludship your backside will smart — if His Ludship be so inclined. He's expert with the rod so don't provoke him."

Jeremy felt blood surging to swell and heat his loins. Criminently! Yonder moved no clumsy and thick-ankled farm wench with straw in her hair and a reek of stale sweat about her.

As if an invisible catch had been released Dolly Lawton came alive, deftly bent silk-covered knees to retrieve her discarded raiment. Then, executing a light half-pirouette on high-heeled slippers she clicked over to the bench with pink-crested breasts riding easily beneath her shift.

Treating the onlookers to a tremulous, uncertain smile, Dolly then returned to the fireplace where, silhouetted through the thin lawn shift, it became inescapable that her body indeed was exquisitely shaped.

Deliberately Lord Middlebrook pursed lips, then commenced to chafe palms. "I say, Perry, d'you think this doe will prove satisfactory to the prestigious crony I've mentioned?"

"Aye. If I know Jemmy, he'll slaver at the mouth over this tidbit — and drool elsewhere."

Mother Stanhope's beak of a nose twitched like that of an apprehensive rabbit. "He will! Even the most choosiest of gentlemen would be delighted to score Dolly's maidenhead."

She snapped the fan loudly against the palm of a pudgy but carefully manicured hand. "Now, dearie, forget ye were raised in a parsonage and try to act seductive!"

Breathing rapidly, Jeremy forgot all about his aching head and hand, was only aware of breeches straining fit to burst and wild throbbings in his privates.

Silence in the library became broken only by the fire's cracklings and the steady *tick-tock* of a French clock on the mantelpiece.

A soft half-sob sounded as Dolly bent until her fingers could grasp her shift's hem. Inch by inch she revealed the perfection of her pink-white body by gradually elevating the garment above her. Nude, she remained motionless a moment before casting it aside, then her head jerked back and she flung arms upwards, effectively elevating the trembling contours of her breasts. Her cheeks flamed redder than the roses of York and firelight created lustrous copper tints in her wavy chestnut hair.

Breathing faster, the Colonial gazed on a vision of surpassing loveliness. His gaze descended from apple-shaped and coral-pointed bosoms to the flat stomach with a neat little navel and came to rest on a triangular tuft of cinnamon-hued curls shading the junction of sleek and creamy thighs.

What chiefly captivated his attention was the unusual texture of Dolly's skin. Just off-white on the pinkish side, it didn't gleam like marble but rather suggested luminous, warm satin.

Patiently Mother Stanhope's recruit held her pose till at length Lord Middlebrook broke into a wide smile. "That will do for the present, poppet."

He directed a glance at his house guest. "Well, Cousin Jerry, often find the likes of such among the frozen forests of America?"

Jeremy blinked, must have sounded foolish as he blurted, "Lord, no, Cousin! Why Miss Dolly's prettier than — than a speckled pup!"

The others exploded with laughter to which Mother Stanhope, ostrich feathers flaunting, added cackling, meaningless noises indicative of mirth.

Languidly, Lord Middlebrook raised a hand, crooked its forefinger. "Come here, buttercup. Stand close before me, then turn slowly about."

Head held high, Dolly Lawton obeyed with a mechanical grimace on her mouth and a few tears sliding down her still-flaming cheeks which seemed only to titillate the roués.

"Now stand straight," directed the beldame, "and shove out yer titties so His Ludship can tell how firm they are. Look at those strawberry-shaped nipples — surpassing neat, ain't they, sir? May be a trifle on the small side but they'll bloom an she's treated right."

"Be still, you old bat!" snapped the master of Middlebrook House. "I said come here, buttercup! Obey, else I'll have a footman horse you for whipping!"

Dolly advanced, concealing her breasts with one hand and with the other attempting to cover that tuft of bronze-hued hair at the base of her flat and silvery belly.

Mr. Falconer noted that for the first time the girl was observing as well as simply seeing her surroundings. A faintly calculating gleam seemed to appear in her heavily fringed eyes.

"As Gad's my life," drawled George Liscard, "what refreshing modesty! Should order even Jemmy's tired pego to attention. Jemmy, y'know, never likes does brazen or crass-talking."

Lord Middlebrook got to his feet and, long coat-skirts whispering, circled the slender nude figure tinted rosy-gold by the firelight.

"Jolly bottom," he commented after treating himself to a pinch so sharp Dolly gasped. "Trifle lean but nicely turned, nonetheless, like the belly button — I trow 'twould frame a diamond right gracefully. Aye, Perry, think here's an uncommon tidy little 'satin-bottom,' as Johnny Wilkes terms 'em."

Placing a finger under Dolly's round, dimpled chin, he peered into delicately oval features with a gentleness as sudden as it was unexpected. He then plucked a lace-trimmed handkerchief from his cuff and used it to dab at Dolly's swimming, dark-blue eyes. "Don't squander unneeded tears, poppet; you'll preserve your chastity till you come to romp with the Friars of Saint Francis."

Mother Stanhope's ample bulk waddled forward. "Yer Ludship finds this gel satisfactory?"

"Obviously," said Lord Middlebrook coldly. "Now, my overblown Venus, you may conduct Dolly below stairs and wait."

Beaming, the beldame bobbed another of her graceful curtsies. "And my sixty guineas, m'lud?"

"You'll get 'em in due course, possibly plus a bonus, since it may be some time before I want Dolly delivered — *virgo intacta*."

He laughed at the crestfallen expression. "Damn it, you old bat. Here's earnest money." Deliberately, he counted ten red-gold sovereigns into the madam's palm.

Peregrine Falconer settled back and with practiced grace helped himself from a gold-and-tortoiseshell snuffbox. Aphrodite's ass? He found himself at a loss how to describe the lustrous quality of Dolly's buttocks when, mother-naked save for gartered stocking and slippers, she trotted out of the library in Mother Stanhope's wake.

George Liscard cast Jeremy a ludicrously mournful look. "Egad, Cousin Jerry, what a pleasure 'twould be right now to add so lovely a pearl to my tally. Damn expediency!"

21

Tir Liscard

ONCE THE HOST HAD DEPARTED on a matter of private concern Mr. Peregrine Falconer turned a blade-sharp countenance to regard his bandaged companion with interest.

"George informs me you're handy with your fists. How is the broken digit mending?"

"Dr. Squires expects to remove the splints tomorrow but he says I must favor it for a while. Why? Are you a boxer?"

Vigorously Falconer shook his head. "I don't enjoy getting bruised and prefer to expend my energies," he chuckled, "in other and gentler directions.

"And how are you at swordplay?" Falconer demanded, deep-set eyes suddenly intent.

"No better than the rest I suppose; don't like cold steel." At the same instant he wondered for the first time in days what could have become of Henri Breboeuf; somehow, he felt confident that granted half a chance the mixed-breed would have survived in this bewildering jungle called London.

"And as to firearms?"

Jeremy shrugged. "Depends on the point of view, sir. Round Portsmouth — New Hampshire," he added quickly, "I'm counted a crack shot — for whatever that's worth in your opinion."

Falconer appeared lost in thoughts below the level of his words. "Had any training in the *code duello?*"

"None. People round our neck o' the woods don't go in for that sort of thing. Howsumever, my father's always held that man should handle a pistol just as spry as a long rifle."

"Um. Interestin', 'pon my word, a most interestin' opinion. Is your — er — cousin aware of your skill in this direction?"

Jeremy's smile was bland, disingenuous. "I doubt it, sir, but please remember I might not prove so able by English standards."

A fleeting smile creased Mr. Falconer's wide mouth, momentarily made him appear younger, not so jaded. "Um. I've a bet in mind, sporting of course, since I've no proof beyond your word that you can hit the broadside of a backhouse with a pistol."

Lord Middlebrook returned to the library followed by a tray of brandy and champagne. After a second glass of the latter, Jeremy Brett commenced to feel finer than silk but still wondered why he should be among such people. Hadn't he only dreamt that scene in the library?

Lord Middlebrook said, small dark eyes darting, "Don't know what you've been up to but Perry wants to bet two hundred guineas that you, er, you can prove yourself skilled in the use of a pistol. That true?"

Jeremy drew a deep breath, began to feel a little lightheaded but enjoyed the moment. " 'Tis a matter of opinion — Cousin," he added with emphasis.

"Give me an opinion that holds weight with you."

"Well, Cousin George, with a rifle I gen'rally can knock the eye out of a squirrel at sixty paces." He made a loose motion. "But with a pistol I —" some imp warned him to appear diffident — "well, I ain't so dependable."

"Ever been in a *tir?*" gently queried Mr. Falconer.

"No. What's a *tir?*"

"A duelists' practicing gallery."

"Never even heard of one."

Various clocks were announcing the hour of two when Lord Middlebrook, flushed now and treading a trifle uncertainly, led the way down to the cellars and along galleries stocked with dusty bottles of more shapes and sizes than Jeremy Brett ever had imagined could exist.

A heavy-eyed lad was lighting a rank of spermaceti candles ranged before a long mirror calculated to double illumination of a long and narrow gallery. Sweet-sour odors from poorly corked wine bottles tinctured the cool, damp atmosphere.

Jeremy blinked and through a valiant effort largely succeeded in clarifying his perceptions sufficiently to determine that this wine-cellar-*cum*-shooting-gallery measured some eighty feet in length by ten wide and that near its entrance stood a long table covered with green baize cloth on which lay several flat, brassbound wooden boxes, molds for casting bullets as well as canisters containing gunpowder of varying fineness.

Perhaps twenty paces distant stood an oblong, white-painted iron plate; on it the silhouette of a man, turned sideways, had been rendered in black; a bright pink heart had been sketched at the proper level and recently had been touched up.

From a handsome olivewood box Lord Middlebrook selected a long-barreled and elaborately ornamented pistol. Chill glints showed in the depths of the nobleman's eyes.

"You are certain, Cousin, you've never before shot in this fashion?"

"That I haven't."

"Then I must instruct you in dueling practice. I will fire as quickly as possible at yonder pink heart on the count of three. Call the count, Perry."

Lord Middlebrook turned sideways, planted pumps on the outlines of feet painted on the stone flooring. Then, drawing himself erect, he slowly raised his weapon to the perpendicular.

"One!" called Mr. Falconer.

"Two!" Evenly, the Marquess of Middlebrook brought his pistol down in line with his target.

"Three!"

There followed a staccato report and the *clang!* of lead impacting on iron, then bitter, eye-stinging smoke billowed about until it disappeared through a grille let into the ceiling.

"Wide! Damme, George," coughed Falconer. "Your mind must be on that delicious little Dolly."

A ragged silvery splash had appeared a good inch to the right of the painted heart.

"You're right, the minx *is* appealing — very," Lord Middlebrook grunted.

Easily Falconer declined an invitation to fire. "Know my limitations on such an occasion. Well, Mr. Brett. Care to try a shot or two?"

The expressions of both the Englishmen tautened when Jeremy accepted a handsome pistol as gingerly as if it had been red-hot.

"Careful," cried the host. "You've a hair trigger on this one. Allow me to set it. Now mind you don't brush the pulling trigger till you're quite ready; the pressure now is set so fine a mere breath will discharge the piece."

"Lordy, never seen so elegant a —" When Lord Middlebrook returned the cocked and loaded pistol, it appeared to slip through the Colonial's fingers, but as it started to fall he, with incredible speed, caught the weapon, which immediately went off; the resounding *clang!* of a bullet striking iron followed.

"Sorry to be so clumsy," he burst out. "As I've said I — I ain't experienced —"

"Look, dammit! *Look*, George!" yelled Peregrine Falconer. "You've lost!"

In the center of the painted heart had appeared a silvery star.

Lord Middlebrook's powerful features turned mottled-red and he glowered on his protégé. "What the devil d'you imagine you're about, you Colonial lout? That you should try to make a fool of me I deem most unfortunate if not unwise for one in your situation."

"But, believe me, sir! That was only a lucky accidental shot. Truly, I'm not used to this kind of target practice. I've never before seen a pistol with a hair trigger."

Amid slowly swirling fumes of gunsmoke the three stood taut.

Finally Peregrine Falconer drawled, "I say, George, why not admit Mr. Brett's declaration as honest?"

For an appreciable second longer the nobleman deliberated, then ended with a curt nod. "Very well. But this shot is not to be counted towards settling our wager."

Falconer, mournful brown eyes sparkling unexpectedly, said, "Of course, George, although I could be a stickler and hold you to the original bet; however in the interests of sportsmanship, I won't." He produced his betting book.

"Shall I refresh your memory? Here is the entry, George: 'PF bets

GL Mr. Brett will nick the heart once with three shots on the practice *tir'* — which he has already done, but since his first shot was — er — accidental," he cast Jeremy a penetrating glance, "we won't count it."

"Fear you gentlemen have made yourselves a chancy bet," came Jeremy's quiet comment. Good God! They'd risked two hundred pounds! Back home people couldn't earn anywhere near that for a year's backbreaking toil. "God's truth, I've never before held on such a target."

"Or on a man?" demanded Lord Middlebrook.

"That's different," said the bandaged figure. "A few weeks back I pistoled two, mayhap three, corsairs from among the pack who boarded my ship in the Channel. Would you consider 'em targets?"

"Hardly," came Lord Middlebrook's terse reply. "You may proceed, Boston Jerry."

The Colonial selected heavy boarding pistols, planted his feet on the marks, then faced the target side-on and sighted so deliberately both gentlemen exchanged puzzled glances.

Following the count, Jeremy's second shot missed the heart by two inches. "I declare," Lord Middlebrook chuckled, "I begin to think your first shot *was* merely a lucky one."

The Colonial's third shot sketched a pale smear barely outside the painted heart.

"No hit!" chortled the host. "B'God, Perry, you've lost after all!"

"Sorry to have lost you your bet, sir. You see, Mr. Falconer, it's as I've said, I'm not experienced in this kind of shooting."

Thoughtfully, Peregrine Falconer rubbed a prominent cheekbone. "A mere bagatelle; don't fret yourself, my friend — I trust that I may count you as such? I was christened Peregrine — damned silly name — so my friends call me Perry."

Recalling that Mr. Falconer was reputed to have connections at the Admiralty there was a genuine enthusiasm in his voice when he said, "I'd be honored to do so, sir."

"You may not count yourself proficient, my friend," came Lord Middlebrook's dry comment, "but had a man been standing in place of yonder silhouette every one of your shots would have proved fatal. Damned if I know what to make of you, Cousin Jerry."

22

Benjamin Franklin, LL.D.

$$\smile$$

I N AN ERA when a man of fifty was considered aged Dr. Benjamin
Franklin, Honorary LL.D. of St. Andrews University (1759) and
Deputy Postmaster-General for the North American Colonies, at the
age of sixty-two might have easily been deemed ten or fifteen years
younger.

Standing five feet nine inches tall, his figure had remained straight
and solid. Only occasionally did an entirely fashionable touch of gout
force the philosopher to limp and remain seated whenever possible.

That his low-pitched voice had remained as clear and forceful as
ever was conceded by friends and critics alike. Light brown hair, already commencing to recede from a dome-like forehead, streamed
freely down to brush his shoulders. When ceremony or occasional
hours of gallant dalliance dictated, it was rumored this distinguished
Colonial would don a handsome tie wig of the same hue.

The Philosopher's steady and somewhat prominent eyes were of a
clear, light gray but it was Dr. Franklin's mouth which most would
interest an acute observer; it was wide, mobile and humorous and
further distinguished by a small but quite perceptible triangle of
flesh descending from the center of his long upper lip.

It was easy enough to believe that this vigorous individual, when
he first had arrived penniless and friendless in London back in 1724,

had increased his meager earnings in a printing house by instructing young sons of the nobility and rich merchants in the arts of natation.

Indeed, whenever the Philosopher's name was mentioned, it still was recalled that he once had swum the Thames from Chelsea all the way down to Blackfriars.

Moreover, his accomplishments in the fields of science, literature and practical inventions — such as the lightning rod and a most efficient stove, which still bears his name — plus a profound depth of knowledge on an amazing variety of subjects had elicited rewards and sincere admiration from celebrated pedants in France, Russia, Italy and Hanover.

For the moment, Benjamin Franklin lingered before a window in the second story of the modestly handsome red-brick dwelling he occupied in Craven Street. Smiling, he contemplated the tree-lined and sun-dappled street below, watched a gaily painted phaeton speed by with varnished yellow wheels giving off cheery flashes; a scattering of horsemen were picking a course among slowly swaying sedan chairs which moved aside to permit the passage of some bigwig's lavishly ornamented coach.

Franklin heaved a small sigh before returning his attention to a broad desk littered with correspondence. Before he resumed work he pulled out a watch of red gold, nearly an inch thick, to note the hour. Um. Within a quarter-hour the guests should appear.

Because red-faced and blue-eyed Colonel Isaac Barré was a veteran who'd served with distinction under General Wolfe at the capture of Québec, Dr. Franklin reckoned that that fiery Irishman would arrive on the dot; there was no point settling down to reading more of the mail which had arrived from America only an hour earlier.

Crossing to the mantelpiece he picked up a harmonica and commenced skillfully to play a scurrilous ditty entitled "The Dollymop's Assets." The big man always had lamented his inability to sing true — a fact which, however, didn't prevent his deep appreciation of music in almost any form.

When a vehicle could be heard pulling up in Craven Street, Franklin slipped the mouth organ into his pocket and peering downwards observed that the first of two expected callers had arrived in the person of the Honourable Grey Cooper, shrewd lawyer, pungent pamphleteer and presently Under Secretary of the Exchequer.

The visitor's hired hackney carriage hardly had moved on than a couple of horsemen clattered into sight. One, obviously a groom, hurriedly dismounted to throw counterweight on Colonel Barré's off stirrup when that powerfully built figure swung down from his saddle.

The Colonel raised a face fiery as a midsummer sunset, flourished his crop at the open window, then used it to beat dust from the skirts of a brief, mulberry-hued riding cloak.

Once Mrs. Stevenson, Dr. Franklin's middle-aged but lively-eyed and still curvaceous housekeeper, had shown the callers up to her employer's study she placed glasses and a bottle of rare old sherry on the desk. Then, smiling discreetly she disappeared.

The Honourable Grey Cooper lost no time in coming to the point. "I say, Doctor, is 't true a dispatch boat from America arrived in the river only yesterday?"

"True." With a brief motion Franklin indicated his littered desk. "I have been perusing communications fetched in her."

The lawyer's pale-blue eyes widened. "They convey good news, I trust?"

"That, my dear sir, depends upon one's point of view," Franklin observed. "And have you received intelligences by that same packet?"

" 'Tis that which brings me to this, your comfortable abode."

Unhurriedly the host faced the red-faced Irishman in time to watch him gulp a second sherry. "And you, friend Isaac, have you received transatlantic news of import?"

"Aye, that I have." Colonel Barré's enunciation was redolent of a fine Irish brogue. "But as the wench said, 'Of that, more later,' my friend. First, let us hear what you've learned, my dear Doctor."

The three pulled chairs up to the table-desk.

The Honourable Grey Cooper frowned. "Damme, Ben, if you ain't full brother to a Sphinx! Can't decide by yer manner how the Government's threat of dispatching troops and men-of-war and to forbid Colonial governments from appealing for relief from direct taxes is being received."

"Why, as to that, my dear friend," Franklin smiled gently, "I can only report that Colonel Barré's predictions about violent resistance to the Stamp Act are about to be realized."

The Philosopher's big, brown-mottled hand closed about square-lensed, steel-rimmed spectacles while he cocked an inquisitive brow at Colonel Barré, who, though not in uniform, was wearing a black-braided gray tunic of military cut which complemented taut, fawn-colored riding breeches and jackboots heeled with well-polished brass spurs.

While adjusting his spectacles, Benjamin Franklin directed a shrewd glance at Grey Cooper. "If you gentlemen have no objection I'd like to review certain passages from Colonel Barré's address to Parliament concerning Lord Charles Townshend's Stamp Acts."

"Proceed," invited Grey Cooper, "but pray remember I'm pressed for time — I've an appointment at the Exchequer which I daren't delay."

In a clear, low voice Franklin read words he could almost recite verbatim: " 'Oppression first planted the Colonists in America. They fled from your tyranny to a then uncultivated, inhospitable country . . . They were nourished by your indulgence! Then grew through your neglect of them . . . They were protected by your arms, but they have nobly taken up arms in your defence and have exerted their valour amidst constant and laborious industry for the defence of a country whose frontier was drenched in blood, while its interior parts yielded all its little savings to your emolument.' "

Dr. Franklin put down his notes, peered over his spectacles. "When first I heard those sentiments expressed in Parliament I deemed them well-taken."

The Honourable Grey Cooper murmured, "Hear! Hear!"

"During your impressive address, Colonel," the Philosopher resumed, "you referred to us Colonists as 'the Sons of Liberty.' Well, sir, that designation has captured the American public's imagination. Today it spreads like wildfire along the coast of North America.

"Much like Mr. John Wilkes you have inspired the admiration of the common American. In fact, some Sons of Liberty have gone so far as to propose naming a village somewhere in the wilds of Pennsylvania 'Wilkes-Barré.' "

Colonel Barré's blunt and shiny red features broke into a huge, pleased grin. "And did they now! Why that's a damned complimentary return for a few words of truth!"

Benjamin Franklin nodded, said gravely, "Concerning American reactions to the Townshend Acts and the Prime Minister's threat of dissolving the New York Assembly while — mark this well — at the same time withholding Royal assent to any legislation passed by said

Assembly, or *any other* Colonial legislature! My countrymen are outraged."

Colonel Barré broke in, "Hold on, Doctor, you are losing me. Wherein lies the taproot to all this turmoil?"

Franklin offered a snuffbox. "Why, my dear Isaac, when the provisions of the Townshend Acts became known last year the New York Assembly convened and prepared what now is termed a 'Circular Letter.' They urged other locally elected Assemblies to respectfully petition the Crown for abolition of 'direct taxes,' which they claim to be illegal and oppressive because the elected representatives of the people have had *no voice* in the levying of said imposts.

"They also have invited their fellow Colonists to unite in forbidding the importation of all dutied goods. This, of course, will deal British merchants a shrewd blow in a region where they are most tender — their moneybags."

Raucous music raised by a band of itinerant performers floated through the open window and grew louder as they descended Craven Street, their music making up in volume for what it lacked in virtuosity.

Benjamin Franklin slightly raised his voice. "In vain I have attempted to persuade Lord Hillsborough, presently Secretary of State for the American Colonies, that the Colonists will never pay taxes levied *without their consent,* no matter how reasonable such duties may be — and undoubtedly they are not excessive."

His lenses gleamed as he eyed Grey Cooper. "I know you will find it hard to credit this, dear friend, but please believe, although for the most part, our Colonials remain loyal and true to the Crown they no longer *think* of themselves as Englishmen."

Colonel Barré started. "Eh? Do they now?"

"They do. At the same time they don't appreciate protection and security as an important part of that Empire the Mother Country now is winning around the globe."

"Sensible on their part," wryly commented the Under Secretary of the Exchequer. "And now, Benjamin, in your opinion, what is to be done?"

"Through the exercise of tact, patience and understanding on both sides, I — and any thinking man — can find no excuse for the Colonies to cry for independence. What particularly galls my countrymen is that, despite all warnings, His Majesty's ministers insist on treating us Colonials as mere peasants holding no rights, meekly subject to their Lordships' fiat legislation.

"On the other hand," stated the tall brown-clad figure, "Americans are, to a reasonable degree, ready to assist in defraying costs of wars incurred in their defense — always provided the Crown recognizes the Colonies' efforts towards victory in the common cause.

"For example, many persons in Britain remain unaware that, back in 1745, the New England Colonies — without the assistance of a single British soldier but ably assisted by the Royal Navy — captured the supposedly impregnable fortress of Louisburg on Cape Breton Island."

"Yes, I know," grunted Colonel Barré. "Was there when we took the fortress for a second time." An indignant snort escaped the red-faced Irishman. "And our Government in its infinite wisdom, by the giveaway Treaty of Aix-la-Chapelle, calmly returned Louisburg to France some three years later."

Franklin removed his spectacles, methodically folded back their bows. "As a result, French and Indian raids against New England were resumed in all their savagery until, as the Colonel's just said, General Wolfe took Louisburg for a second time and razed it to the ground."

Through the half-open door to the hall scampered a roly-poly black-and-white puppy with a curly-haired and remarkably good-looking lad of eight in tumultuous pursuit. The puppy sped between Colonel Barré's glossy boots and vanished under his chair.

Laughing, the Irishman caught the onrushing youngster and tossed him aloft. "Hold hard, young sir! Hold hard! Faith, and yer quarry's gone to ground."

The robust youngster dashed off, halted abruptly, then from the doorway offered an absurdly formal bow in Dr. Franklin's direction. "Crave your pardon, Grandsir; hadn't meant to interrupt." He then bowed to each of the visitors.

Dr. Franklin smilingly retrieved the puppy from under Colonel Barré's armchair. Gray eyes a-twinkle, he explained, "At times my grandson has the lamentable tendency to be a bit headlong — but then, Temple comes by such impetuosity quite naturally."

A brief smile curved the Honourable Grey Cooper's lips since the adverb "naturally" was apt, it being well known about London society that young William Temple Franklin was the illegitimate issue of Dr. Franklin's own bastard son, William, who so ably had over-come his inherited handicap as to become Royal Governor over His Majesty's Colony of New Jersey. Also it was known that Benjamin serenely had acknowledged and legally adopted both of his by-blows.

Blue eyes dancing, Temple clasped the struggling puppy to him and was making for the door when his grandfather restrained him long enough to press a silver sixpence into a chubby hand.

A humorous quirk appeared at the corners of Franklin's wide mouth. "Temple, proceed downstairs, bestow this bribe on the street musicians below, tell them to create their cacophony somewhere out of earshot!"

Soberly he refilled the sherry glasses. "Now then, gentlemen, since you have invited my opinion concerning the probable result of imposing this newly proposed taxation on the Colonies allow me to recount a tale about an eagle and a wildcat. Were this fable bruited about Parliament its point possibly might accomplish something."

Sighed Mr. Cooper, "I doubt it. Too many members are occupied in feathering their nests. Nevertheless, let us hear the fable."

Franklin's pointed upper lip lifted a trifle. "It seems that an eagle, king of the skies, whilst circling the heavens one day, spied, far below, what he took to be a large and tasty brown hare, so he stooped, struck the quarry, and clutched it in merciless talons. The eagle was bearing away his prize aloft when, to his pained surprise, he became aware that 'twas not a hare he'd taken but a lusty wildcat whose claws already had begun to gouge painful wounds in his breast."

Mildly Dr. Franklin regarded his guests as if he were relating some spicy anecdote. "Seeking to rid himself of this troublesome prize, the regal bird opened his talons but the wildcat, realizing the danger of falling to his death, only sank in his claws the deeper. The eagle, grievously pained, had no choice but to return his prey to earth and then release it!"

A twinkle showed behind the Philosopher's steel-rimmed spectacles.

The red-faced Irishman for a moment failed to grasp the fable's import; not so Grey Cooper. "Neatly put," he chuckled, peering into his glass. "If the British eagle becomes so stupid as to mistake an American wildcat for a hare he will suffer much pain and humiliation ere he can rid himself of it."

The Colonel burst out laughing. "Damme if yours ain't an apt and telling parable!"

"I fear," commented Mr. Grey Cooper, "the point of your fable is too subtle to reach most Members of Parliament, but wits at White's, and Brooks's will relish and repeat it, not to mention certain members of the Brimstone Club."

Dr. Franklin cupped an ear; in the direction of Oxford Street a noise was swelling then fading, like sounds of combers beating on a shelving beach.

"Another Wilkesite demonstration," grunted Colonel Barré. "More such riots will really start the King's Friends to shitting their breeches." He arose and looked out of the window. "D'you know, Benjamin, the mob already has forced a gentleman venturing out unattended to shout 'For Wilkes and Liberty!' "

Mr. Grey Cooper pulled on a triple-caped cloak. "Tell me, Doctor, why has that unprincipled lecher Wilkes become so blindly adored in America?"

With a benign smile, Franklin shook his massive head. "I wish *you* would explain, my friend. I don't understand it at all."

Grey Cooper grimaced. "Bosh! You know as well as I the fellow doesn't entertain real love for the American cause any more than Sir Francis Dashwood, Lord North or the rest. They only back Jack Wilkes to embarrass Jemmy Twitcher and other anti-Colonials among the King's Friends."

The Honourable Grey Cooper's hired carriage barely had moved away from Dr. Franklin's residence with Colonel Barré, posting ramrod-stiff beside the hackney, and disappeared down the shady length of Craven Street, than an individual, dressed in decent, dark-blue serge grasped Dr. Franklin's door-pull of gleaming brass.

Promptly a maidservant admitted the visitor. "Good morrow, Mr. Pocock, Doctor's been awaiting your arrival."

"My apologies to your master. Please explain I became entangled in a Wilkesite mob on Oxford Street; town's in a turmoil what with rabble growing ever bolder and more lawless."

Mr. Pocock after brushing dust from his cloak was conducted upstairs to be pleased by the warmth of his host's reception.

Steel-gray eyes probing, Franklin queried softly, "Ah, Mr. Pocock, how did you fare at Middlebrook House today?"

The caller ran a grubby finger along the top of a sweat-darkened neckband. "Well enough. After three attempts I today graciously was accorded an audience with the Marquess.

"I deem my time not wasted however, for while waiting to reach His Lordship's ear I encountered a young Yankee from New Hampshire who, it would appear, is Lord Middlebrook's favored house guest."

Benjamin Franklin's brows climbed his lofty forehead. "An American? Well now, which part is he from?"

"His name is Jeremy Dabney Brett; allows he's from near Portsmouth. Says his family are, or have been, shipbuilders on the Piscataqua."

Franklin motioned his guest to a chair. "You seem to have found this young man of interest."

"That's correct, sir."

"I believe you used the words 'or have been' with regard to the Brett family's business?"

"Aye, sir. He didn't exactly say so, but I gathered their shipyards are starved for work, as it were."

"Um. Tell me more about our compatriot."

Mr. Pocock smoothed russet-red hair and perched his chunky frame on the edge of a ladder-back chair before explaining Brett's situation and his need of obtaining consideration by the Admiralty Board of Contractors.

Thoughtfully, the brown-clad Philosopher joined fingers under his chin and at the same time thrust out sturdy legs encased in white cotton-thread stockings. "Indeed? One might wonder just what a very rich and influential nobleman like Lord Middlebrook could expect to gain through taking our young compatriot under his wing."

Benjamin Franklin picked up the scale model of a lightning rod, stared at it as if he'd never before seen the device.

Mr. Pocock shrugged. "Why, sir, from gossip I overheard while in Middlebrook House one suspects that, to start with at least, Lord Middlebrook extended patronage on a whim. Seems he watched Mr. Brett box and beat a formidable antagonist. Since His Lordship is one of the greatest bettors round London he *may* be planning to make a killing with a fighter unknown in England. Just how powerful a pugilist young Brett will prove remains to be seen."

"My friend, you appear fatigued — care for refreshment?"

"That's main kind, Doctor; I *am* a mite peckish. Ain't tasted nary a bite since early morn."

Carefully Franklin restored his model to its stand. "Am I correct that you've taken a notion that Lord Middlebrook might use this young Colonial to further his own end — or ends?" He emphasized the final word.

Thoughtfully, the woodchuck-like Pennsylvanian picked at a hairy nostril. "By 'useful to his ends' I presume you mean young Mr. Brett might be made useful to Lord Middlebrook in some fashion other than merely pulling off a boxing coup? Say politically?"

Several times, Dr. Franklin's massive head inclined. "A distinct possibility, my dear Pocock — one which may even serve to advance certain of my own plans. I am reliably informed that, like Mr. John Wilkes, the Marquess of Middlebrook harbors deep but well-concealed enmity towards many of the so-called King's Friends in general and Jemmy Twitcher in particular. In fact, I guess nothing would please Lord Middlebrook better than to be able to expose John Montague — Lord Sandwich — in some particularly malodorous piece of corruption."

"Aye, sir. I believe you're right. I've heard that, to bring this about, Lord Middlebrook, Sir Francis Dashwood and others wish to improve already friendly relations with John Wilkes and his following for all that, for the most part, they're an ignorant and dangerous rabble."

Pensively Benjamin Franklin rubbed his pointed lip a few times, observed, "They may be all of that — but remember, these Wilkesites are active and number in the tens of thousands."

23

White's Club

By now Jeremy Dabney Brett, Esq., had begun to appreciate the limitless powers of birth, wealth and influence shamelessly applied at the Court of St. James's and in other high places.

Nothing could have more clearly demonstrated this fact than when he paid a second visit to the countinghouse of Mason & Sampson, those long-established Contractors to the Royal Navy for the Jamaica and North America Station.

A curt and rudely worded communication from Middlebrook House accorded the young Colonial a reception at amazing variance with his first approach to Silas Brett & Son's English agents.

Underlings of all ranks hurried out to bow and scrape while Jeremy dismounted from a nervous bay from the Marquess of Middlebrook's ample mews. Promptly he was ushered into a sumptuous, mahogany-paneled waiting room in which appeared no less a personage than Mr. Adrian Sampson, an acid-appearing young-old individual, all smiles and courtesy.

Shortly Mr. Sampson affirmed that his house stood ready to advance credit to their ever-valued clients, Messrs. Silas Brett & Son, shipbuilders.

Summoning a sphinx-like smile, Mr. Sampson further averred that a suitable merchantman immediately would be found and chartered to convey to Portsmouth, New Hampshire, a cargo of Mr. Brett's selection. "Oh, my, yes; there'll be no difficulty whatsoever; 'twill be a vast pleasure to serve your firm again, sir.

"And by the bye, sir, please offer our sincere apologies to His Lordship for that stupidly ungracious reception accorded you, Mr. Brett, upon the occasion of your initial call."

A clerk entered bearing a water-stained envelope addressed in Silas Brett's distinctive, crabbed script. A surge of relief enveloped him; at least Pa was still alive!

By now Jeremy Brett had learned the value of a cool and patronizing attitude. Said he, looking down his nose, "I will communicate with you within a week's time, Mr. Sampson, concerning the chartering of a vessel — say a brig of two hundred tons burthen — and purchase of a suitable cargo."

Balls! Now wasn't this being over-pompous? But to his relieved surprise, the agent's saturnine features expressed only obsequious pleasure. Lord Middlebrook's wishes were not to be lightly regarded.

Employing less than his customary bone-crushing grip, Jeremy shook Mr. Sampson's hand, then sauntered out into the hallway and made for the mounting block where a cheerful, black-browed Irish groom called Tim Mahoney was holding his saddle horse.

"We'll ride to White's, Mahoney," said he shortly. "Lead the way."

"Yis, yer Honor, that Oi'll do."

Half an hour later Jeremy, confident in the smart cut of a dark blue-green *redingote*, followed Mahoney off Piccadilly to enter the top of St. James's Street. Almost immediately the groom reined in, calling over a shoulder, " 'Tis White's, yer Honor," and, dismounting, ran to secure the Colonial's bridle reins before a handsome doorway flanked by a double pair of simple white Doric columns.

"When ye need me, yer Honor, just tell the hall porter and Oi'll be fetchin' yer baste around in jigtime."

Not long ago Jeremy would have smiled and thanked the groom; now, he merely nodded and passed over the reins before pausing on the sidewalk to consider the narrow façade of this renowned three-storied brick structure.

So this was White's! Criminently! Beyond those portals how many hundreds of thousands of pounds had been wagered? How many outrageous escapades had been planned; how many plots, counterplots and undertakings had been designed which these days were shaping Britain's burgeoning empire?

Think of it! Within a matter of moments Silas Brett's son might rub elbows with Cabinet members, world-famous wits, artists and politicians — not to mention gentlemen of inestimable wealth and power.

Confident Lord Middlebrook's tailor had turned him out at least adequately well, Jeremy drew a deep breath — just as if he were about to plunge into the Piscataqua's always icy waters — and, elevating his chin, forced himself to saunter casually up to the club's entrance.

Once a doorman had bowed and pushed open the door a hall porter with a shiny moon of a face emerged from a cubicle to consider this visitor with *hauteur* bordering on insolence. "Sir, may I inquire your business?"

Jeremy looked down his nose and, mimicking Mr. Falconer's languid drawl, said, "My good man, I have an appointment to meet my cousin, Lord Middlebrook. Has he by any chance already arrived?"

The hall porter's manner underwent sharp alteration; he bowed low. "Thank you, sir. Since m'lord has not yet put in an appearance, sir, would you be so kind as to repair to the Visitor's Room? This way if you please, sir."

Jeremy made no immediate move to follow, only lingered in the lobby to examine a variety of documents affixed to a notice board.

Wishing he'd borrowed a quizzing glass — which he certainly didn't require — he merged brows and scanned one written in a delicate, feminine hand: "The Membership is invited to Bestow their Distinguished Patronage upon Mistress Betsy Fielding who dwells at Number 75 Jermyn Street. Among other accomplishments Mistress Fielding is well versed in Discipline, Humiliation and Employment of the Rod, playing either the Active or Passive part."

Another card informed: "A Pair of Fresh young Sisters, Jane and Jill Owens, are to be discover'd at Number 10½ Garrett Street and have been much Commended for rare Skill in Playing a Pink Piccolo in Unison."

Meanwhile a few members entered carelessly tossing hats and cloaks to a turbaned Negro page. They then disappeared into the depths of the club towards a clicking of billiard balls, a steady hum of masculine voices and occasional bursts of laughter.

Reckoning that he had kept the hall porter waiting long enough, Jeremy sauntered into the Visitor's Room the walls of which were apple-green and lined with all manner of prints and paintings of bull-baiting, boxing, dog fights, cockfighting, shooting and of course fox-hunting.

Left to himself, Jeremy inspected his reflection in a gold-framed bull's-eye mirror, was pleased to note the absence of bandages. Although hair had been shaved and trimmed away from his newly healed scalp wound, Cousin George's Italian *friseur* had managed to disguise the denuded area with a convincing hairpiece.

Despite a seemingly interminable succession of late carousings and a surfeit of rich foods and wines his dark brown eyes had remained clear; his features were unblotched but retained that curséd pink-and-white complexion.

All in all he didn't look too badly, probably thanks to frequent bouts with sparring partners supplied by his patron. Yes, his muscles were hardening and his timing improved, but his wind still wasn't what it should be. Should he abandon the newly acquired and fashionable vice of smoking?

Gingerly, he tested his injured finger. Thank God it had healed well and no longer looked shiny, red and misshapen.

While smoothing his *redingote*'s coattails he felt the outlines of Pa's letter, so sought an armchair beneath a window to read:

May 23, 1768

My Dear Son:

Whilst I Appreciate the Unlikelihood of Receeving a Report from you at this Early Date I nevertheless take Penn in Hand to wish you all Sucksess in disposing of the Merrimack's *Cargo to good Advantage. I am Confidentt unexperienced though you be you will have the Resolution not fall Prey to the Vast Size and Hurly-Burly of London nor fall Victim to its vicius Pleasures. Sucksess in this Matter is* most Urgent! *If Truth be told our Firm totters on the Verge of Bankruptcy — a Disgrace never yet Sufered by Members of our Familly.*

Trust Messrs. Mason & Sampson prove Helpfull in every Respeckt & that by the Time this reeches you you will have suckseeded in Discovering y'r. Sister Perdita's whereabouts.

Not long before y'r Mother Died she said Sir Guy Constable's Familly Exercises Considerable Influence (how I hate *that* word!) at Court. Alas, my Memory, like my Constitution, begins to Falter, but I do believe that y'r Bro.-in-law's Father was an Intimate of Admiral Lord George Anson, that Greatest of England's Sailors, during his Term as First Lord of Admiralty. Mayhap he could be of Asistance?

Shortly after y'r Departure old Absolom Perished of a bloody Flux inspir'd by this Damably Seveer Winter. Therfor I dwell chil and abominably Solitary in this once warm and Lively House which lest our Fortunes mend I will be enforced to Sell.

Wish I could inform you, Jeremy, that I am ridd of that cough I took just prior y'r Sailing.

Taking Advantage of this Uncommon Hard Winter and my Duties as Deputy Surveyor of the King's Woods I ordered an Extra Large *Supply* of tall Masts felled for easy Transport to our Weathering Yard. Wee should have on hand a goodly Supply of prime Timber ready next year to fulfill Contrackts. Pray God you Suckseed in London for, failing Receipt of new Business I must unwilling Dismis skilled Artissans who have Served me Well and Faithfully over the yeares.

In Portsmouth, and indeed throughout all New England Unrest increases over this Levy of Direckt Duties and Taxes by the King's Ministers. There is ever Increesing Determination to Resist same to the Bitter End. From the New York Assembly has come a Circular Letter urging our Assembly and all such elected Bodies in these Colonies to agree on no Importation of British Goods whatsoever.

Governor Wentworth is reported much Opposed to this such Measures as are Several of Influential Merchants. Others are joining the so-called Sons of Liberty. These are not being named by Mee at this Point for wee remain Loyall Subjeckts to our Gracious King and will so Remayne unless Pushed too Far! Why can not His Majesty Discover more Reasonable Ministers to serve Him? I hope and Prey for y'r Sucksess.

Write soon.

Yr. aff't. Father,
S. Brett

Poor Pa! Jeremy sighed and refolded the letter before settling back in a chair mentally to draft a reply. He foresaw such would require considerable thought.

No telling at this point how sincerely Messrs. Mason & Sampson intended to abide by their promises; it would never do to arouse Pa's hopes unduly.

Um. At this time of the year mails might with luck reach Portsmouth within five or six weeks. Yes. Better write Pa about their agents' readiness to extend credit and charter a replacement for the *Merrimack* but he'd surely have to remain vague about details.

By now he knew that for Cousin George to be even approximately punctual for an appointment signified nothing — simply wasn't fashionable nowadays to arrive anywhere near on time.

Another half-hour proved anything but boring for across the hall was an oak-paneled lounge, in which Jeremy could get a clear view of knots of gentlemen attired in the very pinnacle of fashion.

One group had formed a ring of chairs opposite the entrance and, smoking, drinking and gesticulating, were listening to a series of anecdotes retold by a lively young fellow, who by his extravagant costume and affected speech must be termed a "macaroni." No one else would wear so much fine lace at throat and wrists, bluish face powder, extravagantly high scarlet heels on diamond-buckled pumps and jewel-set buttons securing a damask waistcoat.

For all this dandy's airy gestures and languid voice, virility seemed to lie just beneath the surface. Apparently he in the burnt-orange *justaucorps* and tight, sapphire-blue breeches must be a favored raconteur, for when he commenced a story the smoke-streaked room beyond the hallway became relatively quiet save for a clinking of glasses and a scraping of chairs.

Keeping one eye on the club's lobby, Jeremy heard a dissipated-looking, middle-aged buck drawl, "I say, Guy, you promised to tell about that jape 'gainst yerself."

"Now as to that," drawled the macaroni, dipping snuff from a proffered box with practiced grace, "I'll leave it to you, Percy — is this tale 'for' or 'against' me?"

Producing a lace-edged handkerchief from an exaggeratedly deep cuff, the youngish gentleman called Guy indulged in a series of wholehearted sneezes. "Just before I came down to London this time, was in my study rereadin' some amusin' lines from Johnny

Wilkes's 'Essay on Woman' when from below stairs came a hubbub which grew noisier till there was a vast explosion of merriment in the servants' hall."

"What was afoot?" queried someone.

"Well may you ask," laughed the gaudy figure across the hall. "Those titters, belly laughs and guffaws sounded so ribald and wholehearted I rang for Hewson — the Hewsons, y'know, have been our butlers for generations.

"He took plenty of time answerin' my ring. My curiosity was piqued when finally he arrives lookin' more than a little flustered.

" 'Hewson,' say I, 'just what in hell is goin' on below stairs?' "

"Fellow hemmed, turns turkey-red and drops his eyes. 'Why, sir, we're only plying a gyme.'

" 'Well,' I say, 'what sort of a game is it?'

" 'Please, sir, I'd rather not sye.'

" 'I insist, Hewson, speak up else 'twill prove the worse for you.'

"Poor Hewson, lookin' very miserable, mumbles, 'Please, sir, I'm *that* embarrassed, pray don't insist on an explanation.'

" 'I do insist. Tell me the nature of this game or I shall be forced to sack you and turn you out with never a reference.' "

From the rear of White's members appeared, commenced pushing into the lounge.

"Quavers poor Hewson, 'Well, sir, to play this gyme, 'e female servants lines up along one side of the 'all where they're blindfolded by the menservants.'

" 'Well, well,' say I, 'that's fine for a starter — what follows?'

" 'Why, sir, the nature of the gyme is that 'e men servants unbutton and expose their — er, rogers.'

" ' "Rogers"? Damme, talk English, man; you mean their cocks?'

" 'Aye, sir, 'twas their cocks the lads unfurled. A blindfolded maid is supposed to grasp it and try to recognize its owner. An she succeeds, she can claim her reward — er, in bed.'

" 'Egad,' say I, 'what a deuced amusin' game — but what provoked that burst of unseemly merriment I heard just now?'

"Old Hewson turns purple. 'Why, sir, 'ave you noticed Maggie, 'e new upstairs maid?'

" 'She the little strawberry blonde with big eyes and bigger titties?'

" 'Aye, that's the very one, sir!'

" 'You may proceed,' say I sternly. 'What about Maggie?'

" 'Well, the silly girl weren't aware that Andrew, the second footman, is a bit of a jokester. 'Stead of presentin' 'is John Thomas 'e 'olds a rollin' pin before 'im. The minute Maggie lays 'old of it she screams, "Lor' luv me! 'Tis Sir Guy 'imself!" ' "

The story-teller's voice became lost amid laughter and ribald comment; the macaroni became lost to sight.

At the sound of loud voices from St. James's Street Jeremy sought and peered out of a window in time to watch Lord Middlebrook's glittering green-and-gold town coach roll up, armorial bearings bright on its doors. Down its folding steps descended the Third Marquess of Middlebrook followed by a heavily built figure in a claret-red velvet cloak.

Moments later Lord Middlebrook and his companion entered the Visitor's Room and beckoned to Jeremy.

"Sir Francis, I take great pleasure in presenting to you Jeremy Brett, Esquire, ahem, a distant cousin only recently come from our North American Colonies.

"— And this, Cousin Jerry, is Sir Francis Dashwood, otherwise, Lord le Despencer. You'll recall on occasion I've mentioned Lord Dashwood's penchant for singular modes of escaping *accidia* or *ennui?*"

Under a crisp, white, full-bottomed wig Sir Francis's long features appeared fleshy with heavy jowls and mottled white-and-red complexion. The lips to a very wide mouth looked sensual; his slightly protuberant eyes were dark gray, pouched, and heavily bloodshot, but nevertheless deep and intelligent.

So this was the famous Lord le Despencer, rakehell extraordinary, satanist and creator of the blasphemous Brimstone Club! Until recently Sir Francis Dashwood had been Chancellor of the Exchequer and, as Mrs. Rigby had averred, the most corrupt and incompetent Minister ever to hold the seals of that all-important office — which distinction Sir Francis would gaily admit when properly in his cups.

Casually, Lord le Despencer, senior peer of the realm, flicked open a quizzing glass, then with almost insulting deliberation surveyed the North American from head to toe.

However, he ended by suddenly smiling and offering a bejeweled hand. "Pleasure, Mr. Brett," he lisped, "indeed a vast pleasure to meet cousin of old George's. Count on seein' more of you — in more ways than one — hee, hee!"

156

"Hell-Fire Francis," otherwise known to his associates as "the Devil's whoremaster," sauntered out into the hallway and was at once surrounded by openly fawning sycophants.

"Now you've met the Abbot of the Friars of St. Francis; possibly you'll be his guest at West Wycombe."

From the interior of White's arose a heated babble of voices amid which the name of John Wilkes could be recognized.

When the storytelling macaroni appeared wandering vaguely about the hallway, Lord Middlebrook laughed. "Of all coincidences! I say, Cousin Jerry, 'you spy yonder peacock coming out of the Oak Room?"

"Yes; I've been watching him. He's been telling a pretty funny story."

"Know him?"

"Can't say as I do."

"You soon will; he's your brother-in-law."

Jeremy flushed. "Cousin George, you're funning me!"

"Not at all. He *is* Sir Guy Constable, the man you say married your sister. Don't know Constable well — spends much time on his country estates. Don't allow all that foppery to mislead you; I'm told he's a real power in the field."

He passed an arm through Jeremy's. "Come along. 'Tis time you met."

So this elegant, blue-faced popinjay was Perdita's husband! God above! Approaching Sir Guy, Jeremy flushed, momentarily lost new-found assurance, then as quickly recovered. Damn it, wasn't he a freeborn English subject sprung from a family quite as ancient as Sir Guy's?

Copying tones and gestures of recent associates Jeremy Brett bowed stiffly, declared himself pleased to meet Sir Guy Constable.

Sir Guy stated in a strong voice which contrasted with his over-fashionable raiment, "Charmed, I'm sure."

"Glad of that, Sir Guy, since you and Mr. Brett appear to be brothers-in-law."

"Brett!" Sir Guy's blue-tinted features stiffened. "God! You ain't Perdita's brother!"

"For better or for worse, that is the case," drawled Lord Middle-brook, highly entertained and watching the two stare.

Barely restraining a torrent of questions, Jeremy held out his hand, just as he would have done back home; for an instant Sir Guy hesitated over such an uncouth gesture committed, of all places, in White's — then suddenly seized the offered fist in a vise-like grip.

"And how, pray, is my sister?"

"In fine fettle and spry as ever about the bedchamber; been cuttin' a dashin' figure about Bath of late. Society dotes on her sparklin' wit, y'know, admires her be-damned-to-you spirit which nothin' can curb."

By this time Jeremy had noted this powerfully built young fellow's bold, bright-blue eyes, modish periwig and flat, curiously pointed ears unlike any he'd ever seen. What his true complexion might be could only be guessed thanks to that absurd bluish powder he was wearing. There could, however, be no disguising the strength of rather sharp features and a box-like chin furrowed by a deep cleft.

They conversed for a moment then Sir Guy's manner relaxed on learning that this pink-faced but powerful brother-in-law for some time had been visiting Middlebrook House.

He treated Jeremy to a surprisingly winning smile before reassuming macaroni manners. "Frightfully sorry, Mr. Brett, really must dash off — overdue at whist. Hall porter will give you the address of my town house. Must be impatient to see your sister so pray call as early as your engagements permit."

He bowed. "Good day. Servant, my lord."

High, red-painted heels flashing, Sir Guy Constable quickly lost himself amid a throng of clubmen.

24

Dolly Lawton's Diary I

I N THE UNUSUALLY LIGHT AND AIRY BEDROOM she'd been assigned on the third floor back of Madam Stanhope's elaborate establishment the girl calling herself Dolly Lawton — she'd been christened Dorothy Lottimore — removed from a dilapidated "portable box" a new lockable diary in which she'd been keeping a full and faithful account of progress towards that glittering goal she'd set herself.

Yes, come what might, Dolly Lawton someday ere long would inhabit a dwelling of her own, have servants, and drive about town in her private chariot. Before she was done, however, the sixteen-year-old was firmly resolved to wear a wedding band legally bestowed by a gentleman of high quality and great substance.

Again blessing Parson Lottimore's often severe but well-earned strictures and painstaking instruction in penmanship, composition and spelling, Dolly, dipping a goose quill, started her fifth entry:

Tuesday — A clear, sunny Summer's Day. I grow ever more convinc'd Madam Stanhope Entertains true Interest in the Advancement of my Career so Carefully does this Accommodating Protectress preserve me from Letcherous Advances offer'd by Sundry titled and rich patrons of this Establishment. Mostly, she Accomplishes her aim by keeping me hid from Sight.

Today I congratulate Myself on having form'd true Friendships with a pair of pretty Young females recently admitted to work in this place of Pleasure.

One is a dainty, Demure-seeming little Italian ballet dancer fresh Arriv'd from the Continent. She names herself only "Melinda" and is scarce sixteen but very Pretty in a dark Way and is very Spirited. Melinda speaks little English but so artfull are her Gestures and Expressions she readily makes herself understood. Mrs. S. at the Moment is instructing Miss M. in the use of Bawdy Language calculated to rouse passion in future Patrons.

Although nearing my Age Melinda passionately professes to be Virgin! An this proves false so great is Mrs. S.'s skill in such matters that with a Wise Woman's help she can contrive to pass Melinda for an Unspoilt Maiden. She is slim yet shewing prettily rounded "Bubbies" (as bosoms are term'd in this Profession) and her lovely dark Eyes convey such an air of Bashful Innocence Mrs. S. counts on pocketting a great Sum in Exchange for Miss M.'s maidenhead — be it real or counterfeit.

Once Melinda's Confidence is won she proves warm-Hearted and Generous. Today she Instruckted me in a few simple Steps of the Ballet — an Art she says has been practis'd by her Familly for above a Hundred Years! To My surpriz'd Pleasure she praised my Form and Carriage, exclaiming, "Dolly Lawton truly doth possess a natural Grace of Movement."

Through the open window floated strident calls of a barrowman hawking fish and oysters in the alley below. "Buy my new Wall Street Oysters. New flounders! Whitings, eels and mussels! Fresh come from Billingsgate Steps!"

Dolly's pen recommenced to scratch softly:

My other new friend I believe to be Danish-born and professes to Eighteen years of age. I like her best of all our inmates. Henneke has a fine Marble Smooth pink-and-white Skin. She is tall, exceeding Strong and Supple which She explains through having ridden Horses all her Life.

If Henneke's account is to be Credited her Father was Cornet in the Danish Cavalry who lost both Fortune and Life in the Recent Wars.

Miss H. is boisterous but good-Natur'd as a Rule, yet with a single Slap she can floor any Servant, Male or Female, in this Establishment. Her hair is the color of clean Wheat Straw while her great eyes are of the most Brilliant Blue to be Imagin'd.

I expect that soon Henneke will win her Fortune. She makes no Bones that she does Delight in Practising the Arts of Love no matter their Nature! She even boasts of taking Pleasure both in Administering Discipline and in Suffering under the Rod. The other night whilst Henneke was disrobing I chanc'd to see her Back and Posteriors all cruelly strip'd with fresh red Weals!

Happily unaware of the future, Dolly added:

Come what may, I will never Suffer such Humiliation!

Dolly broke off long enough to use a penknife and resharpen her quill's point.

I remain firm in my Resolve not to Barter my Precious Maidenhead save to the greatest Advantage. Not that I intend to Cozen or give false Measure to the Man who pays sufficient to make a Woman of Dolly Lawton. Following my poor Father's preaching I intend always to grant Honest Measure for Measure!

Mrs. S. confided this Morning that the Brimstone Club's next Rout at West Wycombe is to be somewhat delay'd so I shall Retain my fragile hymen (what a curious Word! so close to "hymn") some time longer.

I cannot explain why I find myself thinking on occasion of that tall young Colonial with the pretty pink complexion who, that Fatefull Evening at Middlebrook House appeared so Heated yet Remain'd Restrain'd whilst I was requir'd to Disrobe, Expose Myself and be Apprais'd like a dumb Animal. I yet cannot understand what a youth of his Straightforward Stamp should be doing in the Company of so Accomplish'd a Rake as Lord Middlebrook. Possibly Father Time will Give the Answer?

I close this Scribble in haste for Mrs. S. shrills for me to Accompany her on another Tour of Flower Stalls and Millinery Shops where she recruits Many of her Nymphs.

On the way to Covent Garden Dolly became aware that even normally busy streets today were overflowing and that a curious tension permeated the atmosphere.

Parson Lottimore's daughter was shifting a half-filled flower basket from one arm to the other when, to a deafening outburst of cheering, a handsomely painted town coach turned into Russell Street.

"Wilkes and Liberty!" roared the crowd. "Long live Jack Wilkes, Defender of the Common Man's Rights!"

Out of side streets, from private residences, shops, coffeehouses and taverns ran wildly excited throngs.

When the vehicle turned in their direction Mrs. Stanhope gripped Dolly's wrist. "Quick! An that coach passes near we'll be crushed!" She dragged the wide-eyed girl to partial shelter in the entrance to a stableyard.

"Wilkes! Wilkes! Hurrah for Johnny Wilkes!" The tumult swelled until the coach horses began to rear and paw the air with forefeet.

Just before the vehicle reached the stableyard's entrance the wildly yelling crowd closed in, snatching at the horses' bits and cursing the coachman who, frightened, grabbed a heavy whip from its socket and lashed furiously at the mob.

"Speak! A speech!" howled the crowds.

Almost directly opposite Dolly Lawton and the madam the equipage was forced to halt whereupon a window opened and the face of a very ugly man protruded.

"Huzzah for Wilkes! Speak, speak!"

Surprisingly, the crowd fell back sufficiently for a groom to jump down from behind and quickly unfold a set of steps. Resounding shouts made Russell Street reverberate when he whose name was on countless lips, not only in Great Britain but in the North American Colonies, briskly descended.

Dolly formed an indelible impression of a tall and angular figure, found it difficult to have imagined a more dreadfully ugly face.

John Wilkes emerged to flourish a tricorne hat bearing a huge bright-blue cockade; a color adopted as identification by his adherents.

Long and narrow features were dominated by a sharp, cleaver-shaped beak of a nose, close-set and half-crossed jet eyes; the left one focused sharply inwards.

John Wilkes's jutting chin was both prominent and pointed, his mouth was crooked, slanting sharply downwards to the left creating a sardonic expression enhanced by large ears which, flaring away from a narrow skull, were pointed like those on some ancient satyr.

Dolly decided that John Wilkes's complexion, being both blotched and sallow, was most unattractive. But what about those glittering crow-jack eyes? In them shone a vital quality which attracted, and held a body's attention.

On reaching the street the still outlawed politician pretended to recognize persons among the mob, called out such common names as "Harry," "Toby," "Will" and "Jack."

Dolly saw Wilkes raise his arms to signal for quiet, then heard him call out to a solid-looking, well-dressed gentleman, "Sir! I am about to stand for the Borough of Brentwood in Middlesex. Were you a resident of that constituency would you vote for me?"

The pompous, red-faced figure thus addressed cupped hands and bellowed, "I'd sooner vote for the Devil!"

An angry roar arose but was stilled by John Wilkes's upraised hands. Smiling, he half-bowed in the other's direction. "Your pardon, my dear sir, but if *your* candidate don't run, will you then vote for me?"

Amid ringing laughter Wilkes broke off and was shaking hands with a throng of roughly dressed admirers when his crossed eyes encountered Mrs. Stanhope's formidable bulk and that of the wide-eyed young girl cowering behind her.

"Satan snatch my soul if 'tain't saintly old Mother Stanhope! Out marketing for nubile peaches?"

As he approached, Mrs. Stanhope executed one of her graceful curtsies. "God bless you, Mr. Wilkes! 'Tis wonderful to have ye back! Mayhap this time ye'll succeed in driving moneylenders from the Temple?"

John Wilkes offered a fascinatingly warm smile. "Madam, you compliment me past my deserts by associating me with our Saviour."

His gaze shifted to Dolly who flushed, dropped her eyes and bobbed a curtsy. "I say, Mother, what an uncommon lovely buttercup you have in tow. You may conduct your pretty little baggage to my lodgings this very evening."

"La, sir, 'twould be a pleasure, but I fear Dolly's maidenhead already's been bespoke, and as you know full well, sir, Betty Stanhope ain't never been one to go back on her word!"

"Aye, Mother, your word always has been as good as your bond — possibly even better. Have you on hand other tender, unspoilt offerings? Fresh home, I stand in dire need of some companionship."

"Why, yes, sir. I vow I have in my — er — employ the liveliest Eyetalian blossom as ever danced a ballet. Little Melinda knows how to use her legs in more ways than one, for all she claims to be maiden."

The gaunt figure turned as the crowd lost patience and became boisterous shouting, "Speak to us, Johnny Wilkes, speak to us!"

"Alas, my friends, I remain a proscribed outlaw and daren't speak in public. Aren't you aware the King's Friends don't wish you good people to be led astray by a base versifier and a perverted corrupter of public morals?

"But please, my friends, who indeed are the heart and soul of Old England, vote for me in the coming election that I may again speak out for your rights and those of generations yet unborn which," he added with a leer, "I'm sure you stand or rather lie ready to supply!"

In an undertone he added, "Mrs. S., send around your Italian tonight; don't delay. I intend soon to surrender myself for a period of durance vile in King's Bench Prison!"

25

A Bill of Costs

―――――――⌣―――――――

THROUGH A DIAPER-PANED AND LEADED BOW WINDOW giving upon the
sun-bathed and busy width of Little Hart Street, Captain Mark
Antonius sat comfortably in company with that copper-complex-
ioned and dark-eyed Canadian named Henri Breboeuf, who, at his
mentor's suggestion had adopted the pseudonym of "Captain Henry
Briffault." Their attention, however, was not fixed upon the infinitely varied parade passing without.

They sat, sipping ale from pewter mugs, backs to the wall.
They occupied a banquette so situated it was possible to survey
most of the Mitre Tavern's low-ceilinged and ill-ventilated taproom.

Breboeuf's narrow jet eyes were darting about like swallows over a
pond at evening while the fencing master pointed out this, that and
the other notable figure. Captain Antonius also identified prominent
Members of Parliament, important lawyers, holders of high Government office, pamphleteers and, more interesting, several cold-eyed
but affable led-captains — rivals in his precarious profession.

Now and then arguments ensued, voices were raised, tables
pounded upon and there was considerable waving of hands for here,
as elsewhere, the return of the outlaw John Wilkes was stirring the
city into a turmoil of freely-voiced opinions and often violent reactions.

Captain Antonius leaned sidewise, observed from the side of his mouth, "Henri, mark well that tall gentleman in the plum-colored riding coat who is seating himself at that table by the chimneyplace. He is a Mr. Hubert Barth, a vastly powerful political leader in this borough.

"At his right sits the Honourable Grey Cooper, an assistant Secretary at the Exchequer; remember their faces.

"Also remember the features and shape of that fat, red-faced, sleepy-appearing fellow at present lighting a pipe. He is Sir Hector Bayfield — a Lord Commissioner of the Navy's Victualling Board. Don't he look the part?"

Henri Breboeuf concentrated his perceptions, dipped narrow, blue-black head with each identification, aware that the Master-at-Arms wasn't merely seeking to appear knowledgeable. Should the day come when it became necessary to provoke a duel with any of these men it would be disastrous to affront the wrong man.

Thus far he'd adroitly enough managed to get himself called out by a pair of active Wilkesites. In the dull gray light of dawn in Hyde Park he'd pinked both politicians not fatally but still seriously enough to render them incapable of politicking for weeks to come.

"Now mark that tall, lean-faced fellow wearing steel-rimmed spectacles at the table near the bar. That is Mr. Templeton, a vastly rich merchant who for a long time has been one of Mr. Wilkes's staunchest champions and his principal financial backer. A word to the wise — don't let those spectacles delude you, Henri, Mr. Templeton is one of the finest swordsmen in all the Home Counties."

A commotion arose at the tavern entrance as into the Mitre's taproom sauntered a singular figure. Of moderate stature and lithely built, the new arrival was rouged, painted, patched, frilled and buttoned in the macaroni mode. What immediately captured Henri's attention was the fact that this apparition's bright green jacket seemed unusually well-frilled in that region where one might expect to discern the outlines of female breasts.

Daintily, the dandy minced across the taproom with a business-like rapier canting stiffly behind him like the tail of a well-trained setter on point. There was a subtle but definable foreign air about him, Henri decided.

Captain Antonius muttered *sotto voce*, "Yonder goes the celebrated Chevalier d'Éon — a mysterious individual rumored, quite without proof, to be an agent secretly in the pay of the King of France.

"Note those delicately rounded limbs and soft well-curved lips, the fine wavy hair and a complete lack of beard; his smooth, pink complexion and, most misleading, a tender expression in those large and brilliant dark eyes."

Henri, not diverting his gaze, whispered, "What *is* the Chevalier's sex?"

"Nobody knows for certain although duels have been fought to settle that question. The Chevalier is reputed to have killed several persons attempting to discover the truth by force.

"It *is* known that he holds a bona fide commission of captain in the French Royal Dragoons. Nevertheless, when the whim seizes the Chevalier he adopts female garments and manners and is excessively fond of fine laces, jewelry, perfume, and affects low-cut gowns.

"For a fact, that fellow — if he is one — over there has been courted as a young lady of fashion by members of such aristocratic clubs as White's, Brooks's and Boodle's. Moreover, he reputedly attends meetings of the Brimstone Club."

"And what is, er, his or her full name?"

While the Chevalier advanced lightly towards a round table occupied by half a dozen extravagantly dressed bucks and a pair of Guards officers in scarlet tunics, Captain Antonius murmured, "Credit me, Henri, I'm reliably informed yonder individual's full name and title are: 'Charles (or Charlotte) Geneviève Louis Auguste Timothée d'Éon de Beaumont, Knight of the Royal and Military Order of Saint Louis and Captain in the Royal Dragoon Regiment.' "

"Good God! Is that all?" Narrowly Breboeuf regarded his companion. "What might be your private opinion about the Chevalier's sex?"

Captain Antonius formed a bleak smile. "Why as to that, I have formed none — nor do I care to discover the truth at the expense of crossing swords with so deadly an opponent.

"By the bye, it is important to remember that the Chevalier is a Wilkesite and favorable to the so-called 'cause' of the North American Colonies. Does it not stand to reason King Louis XV would shed very few tears should our Ministry keep blundering long enough to goad the Colonials into armed rebellion?"

While the led-captain still was talking the Chevalier d'Éon formally greeted occupants of the round table, then seated himself, talked animatedly and with a deal of gesturing.

Apparently the Frenchman must be reporting some particularly choice item of scandal, for his companions listened attentively before breaking into snickers.

Presently Captain Antonius twisted his neatly trimmed mustache, then produced a thick gold watch and ostentatiously snapped open its handsomely engraved cover, which he would not have displayed in a coffeehouse less fashionable than the Mitre.

"*Zut!*" he rasped. "The hour approaches one. What can be delaying Major Jackson? Damn it, I will grant the boor another quarter-hour then that precious fellow can stuff his proposition where the monkey shoved the nut!"

The lean-faced Canadian nodded over almost untasted beer — he'd never been fond of brewed drinks — nor of gin, either. "Major Jackson is coming to negotiate a fresh assignment?"

Captain Antonius nodded. "Yes. You should know him, Henri. He's a ruffler in the Earl of Hillsborough's employ; which noble gentleman ranks high among the King's Friends and at present is Secretary of State in charge of North American affairs."

"Please tell me clearly, *mon ami* — are we at present being largely employed in thwarting Wilkesites and assisting the Government's candidates?"

"I would have thought you already had discovered this." The Captain's chill light-gray eyes fixed themselves on his companion. "In my — our profession, political convictions play no part; gold in hand remains gold, no matter who pays it."

The tavern now had become crowded to overflowing; sweat-marked barmaids and starveling potboys struggling among the tables were submitted to crude indignities.

Having paid his "shot," as he called it, Captain Antonius had started to quit his seat when a towering figure wearing the scarlet-and-black uniform of an officer in His Majesty's Brigade of Guards appeared. He drove a path through the Mitre's patrons with the ruthlessness of a plow parting a snowbank.

Henri became aware of heavy features, red as an underdone beefsteak, flaring black mustache, bushy brows of the same hue and a massive blue chin bisected by a strip of sticking plaster.

"Ah, there, Captain Antonius!" he bellowed, then halted before the banquette like a ship-of-the-line rounding to anchor. "Better late than never, eh what?"

Coldly, the Captain remarked, "One moment later, my dear Major, and you'd have found me gone. Even while a cadet I was taught the necessity of punctuality. In the future I trust you will observe that precept."

"Tuts! A led-captain's time ain't all that valuable." Major Jackson peered through tobacco fumes. Bulbous, bloodshot and beer-colored eyes came to rest upon the hawk-faced Canadian. "And what in hell have we here?"

A trace of color invading his usually colorless cheeks, Captain Antonius snapped, "Captain Henry Briffault is an expert swordsman who has become my associate. Let that suffice."

Captain Antonius signaled a waiter to shove a chair beneath Major Jackson's ample backside. "Well, what is it?"

Major Jackson looked startled and stared down his nose. "I will be brief ——"

"A mercy," the Captain cut in. "Get on with it."

"Certain gentlemen occupying important seats in Parliament regard with displeasure and alarm a possibility that that traitorous scoundrel, John Wilkes, may regain his seat in the Commons. They have determined that the rascal shall not be elected."

After fumbling in a breast pocket, he pulled out a sweat-marked piece of paper. "Here is a schedule of prices for anti-Wilkes activities; part of it concerns you, my dear Captain."

For Bespeaking and Collecting a Mob	*20 pounds*
For Several score of Huzza-Men	*40 pounds*
For Several Gallons of punch on Toombstones	*30 pounds*
For Roarers of the word "Outlaw"	*40 pounds*
For Demolishing two Houses	*200 pounds*
For breaking Windows	*20 pounds*
For a set of Notorious Liars	*50 pounds*
For Payments of Fines	*300 pounds*
For "Accidents" to befall Obnoxious Personages to be Named	*500 pounds per head*

Breathing heavily, Major Jackson tossed the paper before Captain Antonius before blowing foam from a tankard of bitter ale. He swallowed a huge gulp, then wiped mustaches on his cuff.

When the others had finished reading he recovered the list and stuffed it away. "This, m'dear Antonius, serves to indicate the scope and importance of the business under consideration. No doubt you have guessed that only one item on the schedule 'Accidents' to 'Obnoxious Personages' concerns you?"

"I did." Captain Antonius narrowed small, steel-gray eyes.

"Two of these 'Obnoxious Personages' need your skillful attentions, friend Antonius. Here are their names." He passed over a scrap of paper.

Henri canted his head to read the scrawled names: Mr. Percival Hanford, Captain John Piggott of the Bucks County Militia, and George Liscard, Third Marquess of Middlebrook. "Captain Forbes will — er — attend to Mr. Hanford."

Captain Antonius whistled softly. " 'Tis a large order this; not easily filled."

The big Guardee jerked a nod, bent over the table, and continued in gruff undertones. "Granted. It is precisely because of your high reputation that I have looked you up again, confident that I couldn't place such responsibility in more capable hands.

"Adopt whatever means you wish, my dear Captain, but any active participation by these gentlemen in the forthcoming election must be prevented at all costs. The first to be disabled must be George Liscard, Marquess of Middlebrook."

Middlebrook? The name echoed faintly at the back of Henri Breboeuf's memory but despite concentrated efforts the connection escaped like quicksilver through one's fingers.

Major Jackson's formidable black brows merged. "What's wrong, Captain? Don't you feel qualified, competent to disable His Lordship — excellent swordsman though he may be?"

Snapped the led-captain, " 'Competent,' yes, but 'qualified,' no. I cannot, as a known *espada,* hope to provoke Lord Middlebrook into fighting me."

"Possibly, possibly. It's no concern of mine whether you or someone else disables the Marquess of Middlebrook; just so 'tis done. Remember, five hundred golden pounds lie at stake. I must have an immediate 'yes' or 'no.' "

Henri Breboeuf caught his breath and wondered if he'd heard aright. Splendid Lord God! Five hundred pounds! Many able Navy and Army officers might earn only a fraction of such a sum through a year's bitter campaigning.

Captain Mark Antonius's lean muscular shoulders squared themselves. Said he stiffly, "I accept. How soon must these gentlemen be 'attended to'?"

"You'll be granted three days to arrange this meeting."

"That will be difficult — very difficult. To arrange such a duel calls for a deal of subtlety and so requires more time for preparation."

"Three days is all you have. Do you accept?"

"Yes," grated the led-captain. "Captain Briffault, here, will undertake the job. Half-payment will be made before the meeting, half afterwards."

The Major's chair scraped back. "Very well. You know where to collect your advance. Only do as well as you have in the past!" Major Jackson heaved himself erect and tramped off apparently unaware that recently he'd raised his voice so much searching looks were being directed at him by the Chevalier d'Éon and his companions.

Captain Antonius spoke softly, "Come, Henri, discussion of this matter requires privacy."

"Then let us seek my *pied à terre* which lies convenient close," urged the mixed-blood. "I invite inspection of its décor and," he added with a half-smile, "of my new 'housekeeper.' "

26

Plots and Plans

⌇

T HE PLAIN RED-BRICK HOUSE Henri Breboeuf was renting lay in Little Walton Street. There was nothing distinctive about the structure's façade and a severely plain entrance yet, scarcely thirty feet in
width, it looked both neat and comfortable.

Pridefully, the mixed-blood used a brass knocker cast in the shape
of a dolphin. Almost immediately the door creaked open to reveal a
tall, dark-haired young woman in a mobcap, frilly apron and neat
blue house gown.

She was handsome with oval features, a wide mouth and lively,
slightly slanting eyes. The Master-at-Arms, European fashion, surveyed this young person working upward from her feet to her face.
Hum. Captain Henry Briffault possessed uncommon good taste in
this direction, it would seem, and must have spent freely to achieve
this much in so short a time.

Once indoors the Canadian queried, "Shall we repair to my
study?" Noting Captain Antonius's amusement, Henri broke out
laughing. "I am pretentious, true enough, but wait till you visit my
next house."

Equably, the guest remarked, "To aim high is no fault but remember, my lad, never rush your jumps or forget that some day you yourself may be disabled. *I* know what that's like."

Some of Henri's elation evaporated. Almost sedately, he beckoned his housekeeper. "Betsy, go brew us a pot of the best Suchow tay."

Once tea had been served by the lissome housekeeper, the host, elaborately nonchalant, tendered a new yard-of-clay pipe to be packed from a leaden casket of bright-yellow Orinokoo-Maryland tobacco. At the same time he probed his memory. Liscard? Now where the devil *had* he heard that name before?

As if reading his host's mind, Captain Antonius expelled a great puff of smoke. "Without difficulty I can, and will, dispose of Captain Piggott. He's rated little better than average but the matter of Lord Middlebrook calls for real concern."

"Why so? Then the Marquess of Middlebrook is an expert on the dueling ground?"

"Yes. Said gentleman is counted more skillful with his sword than with a pistol."

Slowly Henri drained his tea saucer. For the first time his benefactor seemed undecided and ill at ease.

" 'Tis not that I fear his proficiency," glumly observed the led-captain. "He already knows me for an *espada*, the professional I am, so no matter how I insult him, he never would deign to duel with me. More likely he'd have his servants thrash me for impudence."

"Then you've already faced him?"

"No, but I have met him on the field of honor while seconding a fellow *espada* by the name of Forbes who claims to be a colonel in the French Army — but when, some time ago, he called out John Wilkes, his name couldn't be located on Frog-eaters' Army list."

Carefully Captain Antonius relit his pipe, then quirked a brow. "You perceive the nature of my dilemma?"

"I guess so," admitted the younger man. "So what is to be done?"

"As I've indicated, *you* will duel with him. He's never heard of a Captain Henry Briffault."

Quiet reigned in the smoke-filled study until the led-captain resumed: "I will instruct you just how to go about provoking His Lordship into calling you out."

Henri's coppery features lit. "Please be confident I'll never disappoint you, *mon Maître*."

"I hope not, but 'tis wise to face the facts; to date you have fought professionally only twice in defeating slightly better than mediocre swordsmen. This Marquess of Middlebrook is of different caliber —

an experienced duelist. When younger he was a killer. Your chief problem is to discover whether long years of high living have not somewhat slowed Lord Middlebrook's reflexes."

Henri licked thin lips. "And if I win, what will — er —be my fee?"

"Three hundred pounds," came the instant reply. Coldly, Captain Antonius added, "You will need all of that and then some to flee the country should you be unlucky enough to kill your opponent."

No harm in reminding his protégé that while duels had been tolerated they remained highly illegal. Should an encounter result in the death of an important personage the winner, lacking funds or protection, would be run down and condemned to prison; a few friendless duelists actually had gone to the gallows.

Breboeuf pleaded, "Please grant me this opportunity, *mon Maître*. I am deep in debt. An establishment such as this is more expensive than one imagined."

"Very well. Come to my house early tomorrow," said Antonius, briskly tapping dottle from his pipe. "By then I will have decided how a challenge can be engineered. I trust that despite your new interests you have been practicing regularly?"

"I have, *mon Capitaine*, and over long hours."

"Good. Arrange your affairs so that if bad luck attends you, you can ride for a Channel port with no loss of time."

Captain Antonius got to his feet, reached for his cloak. "Oh, one more matter; you must select a second who is *not* a known professional."

"Don't fear, I will find someone suitable. If only I could come up with a friend by the name of Brett. He was with me the night you befriended me."

"Why can this friend not accommodate you?"

"I have no idea what's become of him. Jeremy mayn't even be alive." Henri looked miserably uncertain. "Do you think, *mon Maître*, Peter Godolphin might serve me as second?"

"Possibly. Godolphin is a well-bred, worthless rake and not socially important."

27

Perdita

M ANAGING A WALKING SWORD PASSABLY WELL, thanks to surrepti-
tious practice, Jeremy Brett, Esquire, followed a diminutive
page into a waiting room effectively walled in pink-and-gray striped
brocade.

His guide was a merry, blue-black lad wearing huge gold hoop earrings and, according to the fashion of the day, an Oriental costume
consisting of an orange basque, scarlet pantaloons and an oversized
turban of gold lamé topped by an enormous white ostrich plume.
Teeth flashing, the page indicated a huge armchair. "Be pleased, sar,
be seated; Leddy Constable will be down di-rectly."

Jeremy peered about. Um. While by no means as spacious or luxuriously furnished as Middlebrook House, Sir Guy Constable's town
residence in Deane Street nevertheless appeared elegantly appointed.

Sighing, Jeremy placed a new black tricorne smartly trimmed in
white ostrich on a settee, then wandered over to examine his like-
ness in a baroque, gold-framed mirror.

Lord God! Could this dandified image actually be that of Jeremy
Dabney Brett of Piscataqua? In wry mockery he flicked an imaginary
spot from a jabot of delicate Valenciennes lace. He hadn't yet taken
to the use of cosmetics and doubted if he ever would — mode or no
mode — even to disguise that damned cherubic complexion.

For this reunion he'd turned himself out in a short-skirted coat of turquoise velvet with extravagantly deep lace-trimmed cuffs and lapels turned up in canary-yellow satin, colors calculated to harmonize with his still-bright, dark-brown eyes and wavy hair of the same hue.

Thank God, that sickroom gauntness had departed and his features had filled out.

Still studying his image, he wondered whether his self-respect had suffered permanent damage by accepting Lord Middlebrook's hospitality for so long. Had he really changed? His conscience stirred. Must do something in return or quit Middlebrook House as gracefully as possible. Too often he'd accepted "Cousin George's" more or less subtle hints that the future of Silas Brett & Son depended largely upon contacts established in the Mother Country.

Jeremy was startled from his introspection by the sudden appearance of a tiny, tufted marmoset which, costumed in Oriental garb, leaped onto a console to grab a tangerine from a silver bowl of assorted fruit.

Struck by the abrupt realization that he and yonder monkey had a lot in common, Jeremy burst out laughing. Weren't the pair of 'em natural creatures, cosseted, tricked out in absurd costumes and forced into a foreign way of life?

He thought to recognize Perdita's voice in the distance but couldn't be sure — after all, three years had passed since last he'd heard it. He saw again shifting clouds of fine snow whirling over the sharp, "A" roofs of Portsmouth, eddying about the gangplank of that stuffy little merchantman on which Silas Brett had booked passages for his sprightly daughter and her chaperone, the homeward-bound widow of a naval officer. Both had been swathed into bundles of clothing so shapeless only the deviltry sparkling in Perdita's large and lively dark-brown eyes had identified her.

Light footfalls in the corridor ceased, then retreated, leaving him free to reminisce awhile longer and recall that most of the time he and Perdita had been unusually close for siblings reared in a backwoods seaport.

'Dita's principal fault, he recalled, lay in the girl's persistent efforts to boss him because she happened to be a couple of years older. Somehow, 'Dita never had accepted the fact that, for all her piercing wit and boundless energy, she remained a weak female forever unqualified to order men about.

177

He noted a backgammon board, several dice boxes and a whist table already set up — a far cry from bobbing for apples, blind man's bluff, taffy-pulling, hayrides in the summer, skating and sleigh rides during the interminable winter months ending with steaming bowls of clam chowder.

Without closing his eyes Jeremy could visualize that time 'Dita had skated onto a snow-veiled spring-hole in the Piscataqua to fall in, squalling under the water's paralyzing sting. Although but a gangling twelve-year-old, he nevertheless had retained sufficient sense to spread-eagle himself and crawl out to haul in his blue-lipped sister.

On the other hand there was that time he'd tried jumping a half-broken colt over a hencoop and had been thrown so hard he'd seen a million stars and had his wind knocked out. On coming to he'd found his head on 'Dita's lap while she frantically chafed his wrists and bawled like a calf snagged in a briar patch.

"Well, well," called Perdita's rich voice, "and who may this dandy be?"

Jeremy whirled, forgot new manners and gawked at this tall, golden-blonde young woman lingering in the doorway regarding him with a cool, faintly amused expression that silenced his spontaneous whoop of delight.

"Oh God, Jerry, don't look at me like that!" Lady Perdita Constable began to laugh shakily, then made-up eyes filling, she flung wide her arms and ran forward babbling, "God's love, Jerry, how *wonderful!* How very wonderful!"

They hugged and several times he smacked Lady Constable square on the mouth just as he used to do on those rare occasions back home when spontaneous displays of affection seemed indicated.

Perdita was wearing a low-cut house dress of pale-pink challis over frilly nether garments. He reckoned Sister wasn't about to go out.

They stood a few feet apart frankly searching changes in each other. Jeremy was pleased to find little apparent difference in her aspect. True, she now was wearing naturally buckled honey-hued hair dressed in the height of fashion but, thank the good Lord, at the moment she hadn't caused her torrent of silky locks to be smothered under powder.

Only slight traces of cosmetic tinted her oval, delicately-pointed, slightly tanned features. He was pleased, moreover, to note that those firm yet luscious dark-red lips of hers wore no artificial coloring.

Like a cold douche came Perdita's eager query, "How's Papa? Is he in good health?"

"Moderate to poorly when I sailed. 'Dita, you thoughtless creature, why haven't you written in all this time? The old man's been eating his heart out for news of you."

She made a little *moue*. "Poor Papa! Ever heard mention of a certain Hot Place paved with good intentions? Really, I meant to, Jerry, but in this country Society is so — so damned demanding."

Said he carefully, "I'm beginning to understand, but why haven't you found time to give Pa at least one grandchild? You know how much the old man craves one."

She shook her head. "To begin with Guy and I were too busy enjoying ourselves." The intense brown eyes clouded and a small sigh escaped Lady Constable. "Now that Guy needs and wants an heir we've tried time and again, have attempted all sorts of maneuvers but with no result.

"Perhaps 'tis the result of a fall Guy took in the hunting field; his horse refused and landed him astraddle a post-and-rail fence. He near perished of pain.

"Maybe it's my fault." Her teeth glinted in a curious smile. "Shall I take a lover and find out who's to blame?"

Jeremy was surprised to find himself drawling in a bored tone copied from Peregrine Falconer, "Surely, m'dear 'Dita, in this Society you can't always have remained — well, blameless?"

Angry hues surged into Lady Constable's cheeks. "My word, Jerry dear, you *are* catching on! How long have you been over here?"

"Less than four months — how about answering my question?"

Delightfully she wrinkled a short straight nose at him, much as she had in childhood. "A pox on you for a damned nosey Parker! But since you're my only and therefore my best brother I — well, I will admit to passing dalliances on occasion — but always with discretion."

She laughed. "Oh, damme, Jerry, don't look pious — I warrant you've been no Saint Anthony 'round Middlebrook House — if half one hears about Lord Middlebrook's amusements are true."

"*Touché!*"

Perdita's laughter sent the monkey chittering into the hall. "Oh! Oh! '*Touché!*' cries Jeremy Brett of Piscataqua! Who would have thought we 'rude Colonials' could catch on so readily?"

They talked at length of home and their father. Sir Guy's young wife sobered on learning about the empty slipways and the desperate situation of Silas Brett & Son.

Perdita arose, smooth brow wrinkling. "Jerry, such a situation mustn't continue. Guy's lazy, spoilt and self-indulgent, but he's no fool and he's well-connected here and around Bath.

"Come to think of it, he's M.P. for our Borough though he seldom attends Parliament. Let me think about this."

Sir Guy Constable's wife touched a bell which the Negro pageboy answered so swiftly Jeremy was willing to bet the rascal had been eavesdropping — with what results God only knew. London was like this.

"Ayub, tell Mrs. Lynch chocolate and biscuits are to be served quicker than quick.

"I say, Mr. Brett," she drawled in affected tones, "that's really a dashed handsome pig-sticker you've belted on; have you learned how to manage it? Used to rely on a gun or your fists."

He grinned. "At Cousin George's insistence I've taken up fencing."

"'Cousin George!' The Marquess of Middlebrook? Oh, come now!"

He confided the whole story from the Gamecock's Spurs onwards, concluded by admitting inability to grasp his patron's underlying motives.

Again, Perdita wrinkled her nose. "So, my dear brother is about to become a swordsman?"

He smiled. "Hope so. As a matter of fact tomorrow morning I'll have occasion to find out how useful a one."

The handsome young woman's eyes flew wide open. "God's love, Jerry! You're *not* about to fight a duel!"

He grinned. "Not I, thank God! 'Cousin' George got sufficient drunk last evening at the George & Vulture to allow himself provoked in a piddling duel with some arrogant young whippersnapper; fellow dared accuse the Marquess of fixing a race at Newmarket."

"Sounds fishy." Perdita nibbled her lip. "There's nothing political about this?"

"Not that I know of. At any rate directly I take leave of you I'm to meet Captain Briffault's second at the Mitre to arrange a meeting early tomorrow."

Perdita's small and fairly white teeth gleamed and she sounded like her old self when she urged, "Be careful, Jerry. Whatever you do, *don't* get involved in swordplay. You're still a tyro."

When Jeremy smiled he looked years younger. "Shan't. I know I'm greener than grass with a sword. If only I hadn't lost track of Henri Breboeuf."

"Breboeuf? Who's he?"

"A young Canadian who sailed with me on the *Merrimack*'s last voyage."

While pouring fragrant cocoa Lady Constable considered her pink-faced brother. "Tell me, Jerry, how well do you know Lord Middle-brook?"

"Not so well as I need to, 'Dita. He's so often devious and unpredictable; as a rule he's well restrained but any moment he can become savagely uncontrolled. Can you tell me anything about him?"

Perdita knit flaring brows. "No more than hearsay; neither Guy nor I know him at all well. Howsumever" — Jeremy smiled at the familiar, homely word, — "Guy allows Lord Middlebrook's ambitious and a serious dabbler in politics on the Whig side.

" 'Tis rumored for private reasons he's consumed by hate for several of the King's Friends who once did him out of a post in the Ministry. For all he runs around with Lord Sandwich — they've long romped together about the Brimstone Club — Lord Middlebrook is reported sharpening a political knife for Jemmy Twitcher's benefit when the time comes."

Jeremy half-raised a hand. "On occasion I've heard him voice a deep sympathy for the North American Colonies. My host sounds sincere in protestations of preserving our rights and liberties. Is that so?"

"No telling," Perdita said, no longer the modish lady, "any more than fathoming the real motives of John Wilkes, Sir Francis Dashwood and others in the anti-Ministerial party."

Perdita flung up slender hands. "Why don't you try to sound out Dr. Benjamin Franklin? Ever met him?"

"Not exactly."

"What do you mean 'not exactly'?"

"Well, I've talked with a fellow named Pocock who's an agent of Dr. Franklin's, or so I suspect."

His sister broke off, calling, "Jocko! Jocko! Damn that monkey!

He's getting too squirrelish; never's around when wanted and he shits all over the house!"

Her Society manner returning, Perdita drew a playful finger across his cheek. "Now then, brother dear, what do you make of your brother-in-law?"

"Can't say. I've only met him once and then very briefly."

"On that basis, what d'you think?"

"For my money he's a flagrant macaroni and a small-time man-about-town."

Perdita chuckled. "Seems you deem Guy but a trifling rake?"

"I didn't say that."

"No, but it's a fair description of him for the moment. Guy's lately gone so damn daft over gaming he's neglecting Parliament and his poky job at the Admiralty. Unfortunately, Guy's a shocking poor gambler — most good fox hunters are. Nowadays he's losing a damn sight more than we can afford."

" 'Dita," he demanded quietly, "tell me, is Guy really what Pa might call a 'debauched spendthrift'?"

"Hard terms, Jerry, hard terms! Guy's faults are legion but he's sound at bottom. I've a notion he'll pretty soon quit helling, gambling and whoring about. At heart, I think he's but a country squire.

"In the meantime, Jerry, don't allow my devoted husband to lead you astray." She looked suddenly much older. "Recently he's been introducing me to vices which I've enjoyed for the moment but which I don't wish to repeat — novelty has limitations."

Impulsively, Lady Constable placed a hand over his. "You couldn't come to supper tonight? Just the two of us. Guy will be gaming at Boodle's."

"Can't. Maybe tomorrow, 'Dita. I'm attending a — a well, a rather special dinner given by a certain gentleman whose friendship I wish to enjoy."

" 'Special dinner,' eh? In some fashionable whorehouse I'll warrant! Well, then come tomorrow."

28

Frolicks in the Red Room

O F LATE, Mrs. Stanhope had been increasingly occupied, was
considerably put out by news that the Brimstone Club's convocation at West Wycombe had been somewhat postponed.

"Dear, dear!" grumped the madam when at four of the afternoon
Dolly Lawton, crisp and neat in a new dowlass gown, gracefully entered the beldame's chambers to drink a dish of tea.

"If only I'd foreseen to charge His Ludship interest on the delayed
sacrifice of your maidenhead, dearie, I'd feel better." She fetched a
windy sigh, "But Lord M." — only rarely did she employ a patron's
full name — "is too old a customer.

"Says his heart's set on adding another pearl to a certain Lud's
necklace — though why he don't want your hymen for his own only
God knows."

Mrs. Stanhope pursed painted lips, blew on her saucer of tea, and
fetched another sigh that stirred gray ringlets fringing a frilly boudoir
cap. Next she gazed in something like affection on the lovely young
creature seated so primly across the tea table.

"Trust you'll prove grateful, poppet, that I've devoted so much
time to instruct you in the use of genteel expressions of ardor during
voluptuous moments which costs nothing. Such refinements some-

day may entice a gentleman of substance into making an honest woman of you.

"Believe it or not, ducky, my family was a good one, like yours, and at one time I, too, cherished high ambitions."

Scurrying noises, masculine laughter and high-pitched giggles from down the corridor floated through the half-opened door. Mrs. Stanhope smiled.

"Silly bitches are making a quick three guineas through a matinée with some cavalry subalterns — which is about as high as the most of the girls will ever rise — now and then, a few manage to snare a rich protector and get themselves kept in fine style."

"And which of us, ma'am," Dolly queried, "do you think may fare the best?"

Mrs. Stanhope patted Dolly's hand. "You're that rare young female who knows what she's after. Question is — are you willing to persevere?"

Dolly batted long lashes, stared demurely at the floor. "I am determined to get everything I crave." She checked herself. "Who of my companions stands a chance of success?"

The fat old woman puffed out plump, pink-veined cheeks, then the afternoon having turned warm, jerked loose her neckerchief to reveal the summits of enormous, dough-textured breasts. "Offhand, I say the new girl called Janine. If her tale is to be credited she's the by-blow of a great French nobleman. Be that as it may, Janine's soft-spoken, dances only passably well but sings like a bleeding linnet. Best of all, she's quiet, well-mannered and unless I miss my guess owns a real 'fidgety-fork,' as the Irish put it.

"La! dearie, I go yatting on and on. Now listen to me. This evening I'm going to forward your education by letting you spy on a small and gallant dinner party of six. You well may learn about something of fancy games you'll be expected to play later on."

Venus, Madam Stanhope's huge white Persian cat, wandered in flaunting her plumed tail with the unconscious grace of a Spanish *infanta* managing a fan. To disguise rising excitement Dolly stooped to scratch the beast's silky ears.

"Mr. Tom Treymane — that, of course, ain't his true name — and his wife are to entertain in honor of a gent by the name of Peregrine. He's a dear friend of Lord M.'s" She sniggered. "Oh, damme, I clean forgot! You saw that gent the night we went to Middlebrook House and you so awkwardly exposed your naked charms."

Blushes flooded Dolly's face and neck. "Wasn't there a third man present?" she asked in stifled tones.

"To be sure. Fellow's head was bandaged but you so flustered me I forgot to learn his name." She winked. "Never pass up a possible patron.

"Mr. T. is fetching along his wife, so I've told off Henneke and Janine to complete the party."

Dolly hesitated. "Did I misunderstand, ma'am, or did you say that Mr. Treymane's *wife* is to be present?"

The beldame's cackling laugh rang out. "La, poppet, to be sure. Right now 'tis the latest fad for man and wife to share revels of the intimate sort.

"Mr. Treymane is well traveled and rich beyond belief, so, be you clever as I think, you will this night observe much which should advance your career."

She picked up the Persian and her imposing bulk swayed itself erect. "Nah, then, Dolly, be here at nine sharp."

Dolly dressed carefully and reached Madam Stanhope's chambers on time.

Hours later she unlocked her diary and wrote:

Entry in my journal on this, the 30th day of my Residence within Mrs. S.'s Establishment, which though of Modest Aspect from the Street yet is Surprizing Spacious towards its Back. In this Region is Situated a large private Dining Saloon or "Cabinet Particulier" as Janine terms it.

At the Appointed Hour I took care to wait upon Mrs. S. and Discover'd her in fine Fettle over the Prospeckt of a most Profitable Evening.

She then inform'd me Mr. and Mrs. Treymane and their Guests were below and that, in Addition to Mr. Peregrine the third Gent was none Other than that pleasant young fellow who had Remain'd so Quiet in Middlebrook House whilst my Body was being Exhibited and my Maidenhead bargain'd for.

I was seiz'd with Anticipation to view this Stalwart, strangely pink-skinned Adonis with the curly, dark-brown locks. Softly I en-quir'd, "And what might be this gentleman's name and station?"

She confided naught save that Mister Peregrine had described his Companion as "Boston Jerry," a young gentleman "Recently from the North American Colonies."

Mrs. S. fetch'd a gusty sigh. "Oh, that I were younger by Twenty Years! This Boston Jerry looks a dish prepar'd most exactly to my Tastes!"

Madam S. then said, "When, just a while ago, I beheld this strap-ping young Man again — I scarce had noted him during our Visit to Lord M.'s mansion — I Esteem'd him to be aged only a little beyond Twenty."

Without more ado, Madam S. then Conducted me to a narrow Closet. "I judge this Spy-Place sees Considerable use for 'tis fur-nish'd with a soft Carpet, a small Table for Glasses and a Pair of Comfortable little Armchairs set behind a sort of Grille cleverly conceal'd amidst a Burst of that elaborate Gilded Scrollwork which Ornaments one end of the red-and-gold Dining Chamber, called the Red Room because its walls are done up in crimson Damask whilst its trim is most Tastefully coated with pure Gold leaf — or so my Protectress protests.

I confess my Heart commenc'd to thump like a Recruiting Party's Drummer once I seated myself beside Mrs. S.'s Monumental bulk and peered through grille Work to Obtain a clear View of a table Handsomely set for Six. Candlesticks of well-polished plate Sup-ported a Galaxy of beeswax candles which cast over the Scene a most Agreeable mellow Glow such as is never given off by common tal-low tapers.

Oh, the Contrast of such Luxury with the cold, cramped and ugly Discomforts of that Parsonage which was all I had ever Known till I Resolv'd to run away to London and seek my Future. How wise I was!

I then perceiv'd standing near the Entrance, motionless as a graven image, a short, dark-visaged man Servant nam'd Omar. He was wearing a tight Turban of silvered Cloth with what I took to be a heron's Plume nodding above it. His costume of shimmering silk I imagine was of Oriental design. This Indian, as Mrs. S. term'd him, had Sharp and Sad-looking Features which Remain'd without the least Expression when, Bowing profoundly, he admitted Mr. Trey-

mane and his companions whose Entrance, laughing and chattering, was perfectly Copied in Spacious gold fram'd Mirrors set above Sideboards situated on either side of the Room. Another looking Glass was Affix'd to the Ceiling above a wide divan set opposite our Spy Hole.

Never had I dreamt to behold such Modish Cloathing. As for Janine and Henneke, they were most tastefully trick'd out for the occasion. In simple, both Girls appear'd extreme lovely!

Henneke wore a beautiful Gown of Sky-Blue, which to Perfection set off the Hue of her large and lustrous eyes and Contrasted Agreeably with her Flaxen hair.

Janine's petite dark Beauty was enhanc'd by a coat of Lincoln-green silk and flowing Skirts of Canary-Yellow.

Only then did I Address Attention to the Gentlemen below. Mr. Treymane was Affable, red-fac'd and squab-plump but none-the-less appear'd well-enough proportion'd. And his wife, whose Hair was powder'd and most Fancifully dress'd, was a Wonder to behold. She suggested the very Essence of Voluptuousness, Rich and Ripe. Easily a Decade her Husband's junior, she was fair compleckted with Body curv'd in a most Appetizing Fashion.

Mr. Peregrine I recogniz'd instanter, and then my Heart-beat quicken'd when my Gaze settl'd upon "Boston Jerry," the third and youngest of the Gentlemen below.

I vow, Dear Diary, I became struck as never Before by this Tall young Fellow's Manly Beauty, the delicate perfecktion of his Compleckdion, clean image and Lively Manner.

To Mrs. Stanhope I whisper'd, "Have you ever beheld a Youth so masterly and Enchanting?"

Madam S. hissed for me to hold my Tongue. Indeed, this Colonial enjoyed wide Shoulders, narrow hips and stood Taller than Average. This "Boston Jerry" — as his Companions greeted him — was dashing in a Jacket of Orange Velvet, blue satin knee-Breeches and delicate French lace fairly foam'd about his Throat and Wrists.

How Bitterly I envied Janine Coquetting by his side and wish'd myself rid of this bothersome Maidenhead.

I remain'd Vastly Puzzl'd as to what might Transpire; everyone's conduct seem'd so Polite and Genteel I scarce could credit that the scene below was unfolding in a Brothel, fashionable though it might be.

So thoroughly had Madam S. coach'd Janine and Henneke in Upper Class Airs and Graces they, for the Nonce, Behav'd more demure and Respecktable than many well-born young Ladies I have observ'd Patronizing Fashionable Shops.

Once the Company had seated themselves the Indian manservant called Omar silently circulated a tray of long-stemmed Wine Glasses. Apple-cheek'd Peggy, the Chambermaid-Waitress who usually serves Parties of this Nature, did not once Enter but left the Dinner Trays upon a Table plac'd just Outside the Red Room's door.

"Ah, me," Madam S., beaming, sigh'd softly, and whisper'd "would more of my Patrons Exercis'd such Genteel Restraint: note there is little Vulgar or Coarse about their Talk."

To this I attended with Great Attention that I might employ such a Fair Example to Advance my Ambitions. Could I but foresee the Nature of the Fate Awaiting poor Dolly Lawton at West Wycombe!

The Dinner was silently fetch'd in by Omar and Presently Plentifull Liquid Refreshment mov'd the Party to much Laughter and rallying. Kisses commenced to exchange all around. Mrs. Treymane talk'd Sixty-to-the-Minute and roll'd melting dark eyes at Mr. Peregrine in a most Provocative Manner and call'd him "Pretty Perry."

Her Husband appear'd in particular to Esteem Henneke's rosy-pale Charms — Perhaps because they both speak the Dutch Language.

I shall ever recall that Moment while the Indian Servant was serving the Salad, Perry — (I have discover'd Mr. Falconer is his True Name) — rises to his feet and raising his wine glass, Proposes, "Here's a toast, Gentlemen, to the prettiest, most Perfecktly form'd right Breast in all London." And he bows his glass over in Mrs. T.'s Direcktion whereat that Experienc'd Lorette actually Blushes and Appears Vastly Flatter'd.

Her Husband pleasantly enough then offers grounds for Objecktion. "I fear you appraise my fair Julia's breast too Highly. For my part I esteem Mistress Henneke's snowy Love Apple will prove the more shapely."

My Adonis, the handsome young American Colonial, somewhat Diffidently then Enters the Dispute venturing, "For all I am no Authority, I venture Mistress Janine's right tit surely should be enter'd in competition. Eh, Perry?" Then it seem'd to me he look'd at Mr. P.

as if for Approval, that gentleman then nods and fumbles in his pocket then exhibits a gleaming globe of Gold! Says he, "In the manner of Homer's Paris, I offer this golden Apple to the Winner." The lovely bauble then circulates the Table. I fear Greedy lights shone in the Eyes of Henneke and Janine whilst they fondl'd the Golden Apple.

"Julia, my dear, will you be First to submit to judgment by not one but three Paris-es?" Chuckling he adds, "Not three 'paresis,' let us hope and pray" (Whatever that may mean!).

"But, of course," Mrs. T. smiles archly. "Henneke, my dear, you may attend me." The Statuesque and Beauteous Woman thereupon hurries to her aide and Slips downwards a strip of cloth covering the right top of her hostess's gown then slowly lowers it to expose before the flush'd and heated Company a quivering Globular and snow-white Breast. The neat little pink Nipple crowning it seems to peer Proudly about, quite unabash'd. "There now," drawls Perry, "is not that the fairest of bosoms? Is it not an Ornament any Husband could take Pride in? Boston Jerry, what is your Opinion?"

"To my Mind," says my Adonis in a more Confident Voice, "I hold that before the Award is made the fair Janine's udder shall be Produc'd."

Everyone busts out laughing over the Colonial's country term even while he is slipping an Arm about his companion's slender shoulders clumsily to twitch down her Bodice sufficient to admit View of a softly gleaming little Pear-Shaped Bubbie — as the cant Phrase goes in this House — tipped by a Pert, Up-Turned, Rosy-Brown Nipple delicately ring'd in Beige.

Mrs. T. addresses her Husband. "Now, my Love, ere Drink beclouds fair Judgment, pray serve Henneke in Like Fashion."

In a trice the three ladies sit with splendid right-hand Bosoms expos'd, all a-tremble and golden-white by the Candlelight.

Mr. T., red-faced and sweating Now calls for the Companion Bubbies to be Unveil'd claiming "half-measures are worse than None."

Meanwhile the Indian, expressionless as any Waxen Dummy, continues to Serve the Meal as if nothing in the least Untoward were taking place.

Picture the Scene! The Gentlemen still cloath'd entire, endlessly Toasting their bare breasted Ladies. At length the Gentleman nam'd Perry Requires the fair Contestants, now stripp'd from the Navel

Upwards, to stand before a Mirror. "Philosophers claim Wisdom is gain'd through Reflection. Messers, let each man close his eyes and from behind test the Texture of these lovely Orbs. This done, each will indicate the Wench" — Mrs. T. giggled at this Coarse Term — "he deems most worthy to receive the Golden Apple."

As for myself, dear Diary, I should have been hard-put to select a Winner, for each in Her own Way was deserving of Reward. Mrs. T.'s Bosoms were of ripe, round and perfeckt Proportions. Janine's, saucy in the form of full-blown Pear Fruits. As for Henneke, her rising Hillocks jutted arrogantly and, perfecktly Conform'd, were of a pure, creamy-white hue, lac'd by a faint Tracery of blue Veins.

No doubt to flatter their Host the other Gentlemen name Mrs. T. the Winner. She acts vastly pleased but at once bestows her prise on Henneke while playfully patting that blonde Creature's lovely Bottom.

By way of Consolation Mr. T. then locks about Janine's Wrist a pretty Bracelet of Gold Links for which she Embraces him with wriggling, Voluptuous Abandon.

Her candle, Dolly noted, had burned low and was sputtering, so putting down her quill, she flexed cramped fingers and replaced the taper before crossing to a window giving upon a moonlit courtyard. Right now all was still down there save for a brace of alley cats engaged in screeching courtship.

The bell of a nearby church steeple sounded a single time. Unlacing stays and untying petticoats, Dolly, heated by more than the weather, stripped to her undershift.

Loud laughter and snatches of off-key singing beat up that steep staircase leading to Dolly's bedchamber, suggestive that Mr. Treymane's revel no longer was being conducted in quite so genteel a fashion.

The night had become so sultry that before taking up her pen, Dolly pulled forward her shift's sweat-dampened neck opening and blew down a gentle *val* separating breasts which, while not yet as opulent as any she'd viewed through the grille, lent promise of developing into nacreous symmetries which, with time, might command rewarding attention.

After employing a forefinger to flick perspiration dotting her forehead, Dolly Lawton shoved aside a stray lock before bending over her diary.

Can I be falling sick? Whilst witnessing the Lewd entertainment taking place which was New to Me I became aware of a delicious sudden Warmth between my Thighs such as I have never before Experienc'd.

The Party having resum'd Seats at table with the Ladies lovely, Bright-Eyed and nude to the Waist, the Gentlemen although still fully Cloath'd now indulge in covert Gropings, Ticklings, Pinches and Slappings even whilst a Dessert is being dish'd by the silent and Impassive Indian Servant.

Once coffee and brandy is serv'd Mr. T., in high good Humour, calls across the Table, "Perry, I do believe we've had the Luck to Discover a brace of 'Nuns' qualified to grace the Cloisters at West Wycombe." He then addresses Mr. Peregrine: "I say, are further Trials in Order? What's your Opinion? Mustn't enter unschool'd Fillies in the Sweepstakes of St. Lawrence."

"Since the night is young why be precipitate?" drawls Mr. P. "What say you, Boston Jerry?"

"I dare say yes," avers the handsome Colonial, and gulps Brandy as if Dying of Thirst.

"Well then, let us test these young Beauties' Capabilities further."

My Adonis now markedly more at his Ease begins to laugh loudly then hauls Janine ever-willing onto his Lap and Busses her roundly, "Jesus, Girl," I hear him panting. "You make me feel wonderful."

I vow, Dear Diary, of a sudden I became consum'd with a Fierce Jealousy and yearn'd to pull Janine's long black Hair and scratch out her Eyes!

Mr. T. then commenc'd to bellow for Mrs. S. who Sprang, up Instanter, and hurried me out of the Spy-Hole. She then firmly commanded me to my Room where I now Consider what practical Advantage may be gain'd through my Observations.

It was a crying shame, thought Dolly Lawton, thus to be banished at a moment just when the revelers appeared eager to really frolic in the Red Room.

29

To the Green Park

O BSERVED the Chevalier d'Éon while Lord Middlebrook's phaeton was turning into a dusty country road, "Ees it not a crime, milor', we do not more often enjoy these fresh and silent early hours when Nature lends the air so much life?"

"For an ungodly hour you wax quite poetical, my dear Chevalier," growled the Third Marquess of Middlebrook, slumped onto the confortable rear seat of his vehicle which, drawn by a pair of long-legged grays, was being fairly whirled along to the rendezvous.

"*Mais oui,*" smiled the Frenchman, tugging absently at a pearl swaying from his earlobe. "Ees it not amazin' 'ow abrupt the City geeves way to a sweet-smelling countryside of fields and farms? Always I 'ave noticed thees on my way to the Green Park."

"Ah yes, you've visited these dueling grounds before," George Liscard stated rather than inquired.

"To be exact, four times, *Monsieur le Marquis.*" The Chevalier removed a small, silver-bound tricorne from his softly rounded head, permitting a faint morning breeze to stir fine, light-brown and curling hair.

Now that the cobbles of the city had been left behind the phaeton's iron tires whispered rather than rang over a winding dirt road shaded on both sides by oaks and elms.

On a jump-seat opposite the two passengers lay a black oblong case bound in brass and bearing Lord Middlebrook's crest engraved on its lid. It contained a pair of expertly balanced and decorated *épées de combat* — light small-swords forged in Toledo.

Once the trees thinned and fields opened up red deer ceased browsing, lifted sleek heads, and stared briefly before trotting for the nearest thicket but so unhurriedly they disturbed none of many pheasants also feeding over new-cut hay.

The Chevalier d'Éon daintily reset his jabot of Valenciennes lace before inquiring with transparent casualness, "And 'ow advances our frien' Meester Weelkes's campaign for reelection?"

Lord Middlebrook, who'd been drawing huge gulps of fresh air in hopes of ridding his head of last night's tobacco and liquor, frowned. "Meetin' such opposition — so much of it's bought and paid for — no one's prepared to offer decent odds.

"If only Wilkes weren't outlawed and headed for jail any day! I'm deeply regretful over this because Mr. Wilkes works for many sound causes."

"One of wheech, *Monsieur le Marquis*, ees to 'elp the Colonies of North America to win seats een Parliament. *Non?*"

Both men lurched on their seats and grabbed handholds as the grays shied when a hare darted across the road practically under their feet.

"The question of the North American Colonies may forward hopes that the King's Friends can be lured into adopting a policy so oppressive it will bring about a fall of the Ministry."

Lord Middlebrook batted swollen, pinkish eyelids, glanced curiously at the still-young but heavily painted and powdered face beside him. "In brief, it is the Liberal Opposition's resolve to undo 'Lord Lecher' — John Montagu — and expose corruption in the present Government."

Abruptly he realized he might be revealing a bit more than was prudent.

"It is the aim of Liberals to encourage a rebellious movement in America through lending support to Dr. Benjamin Franklin, Colonel Barré, the Honourable Grey Cooper and, among others in Parliament, Lord North, Sir Edward Hawke and Sir Edmund Burke, into maneuvering the King's Friends into more follies such as quartering troops on the inhabitants in Boston, Philadelphia and New York and the imminent dispatch of Regular Regiments to cow unruly subjects in Boston. This is bound to encourage our native Whigs and already aroused Sons of Liberty in the Massachusetts Bay Colony."

Lord Middlebrook emitted a relieving belch. "Alas, my dear Chevalier, politicking nowadays has become a very costly undertaking."

The Captain of His Christian Majesty's Royal Dragoons the Chevalier Charles Geneviève Louis Auguste Timothée d'Éon's hairless features glowed a coral-pink in the dawn's brightening. He fixed limpid yet subtly cruel dark eyes upon his companion.

"To be sure, *Monsieur le Marquis*, the weenning of political wars ees always expensive — never more so than today. Therefore, should you not object, I weesh to offaire a modest sum to advance Meester Wcclkcs's campaign."

"Your meaning, I take it, is that your Royal Master possibly is prepared — er, to back the Whigs?"

D'Éon froze. "My 'Royal Master'? Not delicately do you put thees, milor'."

"Come, come, Chevalier, 'tis common knowledge you live very comfortably in London principally to advance the King of France's interests. Now wouldn't Louis XV rejoice to see his Cousin George lose his North American Colonies and so regain Canada so recently ceded under the Treaty of Paris?"

Summoning a charming smile, the Chevalier inclined a wind-ruffled head. "Eet stands to reason my Souverain would shed few tears over so pleasing a possibility. And so, *cher Monsieur le Marquis*, the power of gold being eendisputable — you perhaps will consider my offer of asseestance?"

Grimacing, Lord Middlebrook eased the buttons on a plain blue linen waistcoat. His stomach felt taut and full of gas as a balloon. Damnation! He never should have sampled those pickled herrings so late at night.

"If your — er — people stand ready to gamble we will welcome a subscription; many of the King's Friends are by no means paupers — thanks to inherited wealth and a tight grip on lucrative sinecures; the sale of influence and shameless exploitation of India and our North American Colonies."

The epicene Frenchman's manner grew brisk; paint tinting his lips became noticeable during a quick but engaging smile. "Very well, *Monsieur le Marquis*, later today — eef your encounter thees morneeng proves fortunate — I am mos' confident of the outcome — where shall a subscreeption of let us say, ten thousand livres d'or be deposited?"

George Liscard plucked a handkerchief from his sleeve and mopped a brow which, unaccountably, had commenced to perspire. "Coutts's Bank, to the credit of Libertas & Company."

"Consider the matter already accompleeshed, milor'." Casually the Chevalier flicked dust from black satin knee breeches.

Lord Middlebrook nodded, belched again. Feeling somewhat relieved he straightened on the seat, saying, "And now, my dear Chevalier, I have also to offer my sincere thanks for consenting to second me on such miserably short notice. Many apologies are due you, Captain d'Éon. I shall explain."

A skylark hovering high overhead commenced melodious outpourings in salute to this fresh new day.

"*Pardon,* milor', one does not quite understand 'ow you became involved in thees leetle *affaire d'honneur.*"

With a wry grin, George Liscard faced his slightly built companion. "'Twas a silly business and largely my own fault. I'll confess I was imbibing a bit too freely at the George & Vulture when at a nearby table a modishly dressed and well-spoken young fellow implied within my hearing that in the second steeplechase at Newmarket I covertly had substituted a 'ringer' — another horse — for my aging Moonraker and as a result had won handsomely.

"I arose protesting to this personable young gentleman that he was very much in error about the matter, whereat he sprang to his feet calling loudly, 'Sir, as to that, I give you the lie!'

"Being a bit over the nines, I splashed wine into his face and called the fellow out — he gave his name as Captain Henry Briffault. Oddly enough, I'd the impression of having seen him somewhere, in a crowd, probably. As the challenged party, he elected the use of *épées de combat.* Said he'd dispatch his second to meet mine to arrange the time and place for our meeting.

"As you are aware, my dear Chevalier, it was decided we should face one another at daybreak this morning on the Green Park dueling ground."

"And who, milor', might be serving as thees *Capitaine* Briffault's second?" d'Éon queried. When the chariot lurched over a stone he bent forward to push the sword case back into position.

A curt laugh escaped George Liscard. "One Peter Godolphin, the rakehell son of a fellow officer and friend I once served with in Inja; 'twas largely because of this second I consented to this ridiculous duel. However, if this young man's principal is enough for a Godolphin, I expect he's worthy crossing swords with."

"You said the name of the injured party ees — ?"

"Captain Henry Briffault. Must be part French though he don't talk like it. Ever heard of him?"

"*Mais non.* The name ees unknown to me. Thees *Capitaine* Briffault, ees 'e young?"

"Twenty-five or six at the outside — which may contribute to his undoing." Lord Middlebrook yawned and stretched several times. "Some people tend to be deceived by my —" he smiled grimly — "er, substantial waist and hearty complexion but I remain in fair trim save for an occasional shortage of breath."

Delicately the Captain of Royal Dragoons smoothed fine, wavy hair before replacing his tricorne while considering an increasing nacreous glow in the east. "*Monsieur le Marquis,* who was your second who arrange thees matter?" He smiled gently. "May one inquire what 'as become of 'im?"

While the chariot rolled smoothly through a little spinney the Master of Middlebrook House looked uncomfortably at his companion. "Of course. Y'see, for good and sufficient reasons I've been encouragin', nay sponsorin', one Jeremy Brett, a young man fresh come from New Hampshire which is one of our North American Colonies. Chose to treat him as a distant cousin — which he just might be."

"And why ees Monsieur Brett not present?"

"The young fool — at my instigation, I'll admit— roistered till all hours last night in a brothel along with those precious lechers, Tom Treymane and Perry Falconer.

"Young Brett came home so roaring drunk he had to be helped to bed. Obviously he would be of no use this morning. In my extremity, my dear Chevalier, I turned to you and I'll ever be grateful for this assistance."

Then tactlessly he added, "Trust you will allow me to second you next time anyone is sufficient foolish as to question your manliness."

The Chevalier's rosy, heart-shaped features stiffened and his limpid eyes narrowed. Said he sharply, " 'Ave you ever believed me to be other than a man?"

Hastily, George Liscard diverted his gaze from the swelling, well-filled waistcoat beside him. "Never!" he lied with convincing promptness, then grinned wholeheartedly. "I'd bet any amount on that!"

"Quite unnecessary," commented the Chevalier with a gracefully epicene gesture. "Three men 'ave already died on that account."

His manner changed and little crinkles appeared at the corners of his eyes. "Long I 'ave 'eard eet said among the *haut monde* that *le Marquis de* Middlebrook is not only a champion *sur le champ d'honneur* but also een many fashionable boudoirs. May I say I long 'ave admired your taste in female companions and the rumored length of your pearl *collier d'amour*. What a delightful conceit ees thees!"

Glancing downwards, Lord Middlebrook saw that his strand of pearls somehow had escaped his shirt front and carelessly caressed the gleaming jewels before restoring them to their place. He drawled, "You compliment me unduly — Dashwood and Lord Sandwich wear lengthier ones."

The coachman slowed his pair to a walk before turning through a gateway let into a free-stone wall enclosing a wide, recently harvested field.

"Believe we're arrived," commented George Liscard. "Ah, yes. Yonder stands Dr. Vernay waiting 'neath the beeches like a hopeful carrion crow."

Along another country lane coming from the city, a public carriage lurched and rocked toward a level grass patch surrounded by pale-trunked beeches. The vehicle's springs, long ungreased, complained and accomplished little towards easing bone-wrenching jolts caused by potholes and rocks.

Henri Breboeuf, who, on the advice of Captain Mark Antonius, had assumed the identity of Henry Briffault, late Captain in the Duke of Baden's Household Cavalry, attempted to ignore a rising tension and sat bolt upright beside Peter Godolphin, Esq.

The mixed-breed was telling himself he should have taken time to shave lest people suspect his hand hadn't been sufficiently steady. His chin therefore was outlined by strong blue-black shadows, brightening dawn also emphasized unusual copper-brown hues in those high-cheekboned features lately admired by a flattering number of ladies of quality or near-quality. Ah, these London women, so ready, so well washed, so seductively perfumed!

Trailing a cone of dust the hired carriage made good time behind a pair of better-than-average livery stable hacks selected by perpetually bored-looking Peter Godolphin, Esq.

Sidewise, Godolphin covertly considered his principal, perceived that never before had this fellow betrayed his Indian ancestry more markedly.

He wondered why he'd taken so strong a liking to this polite yet predatory and cold-nerved North American.

That Captain Briffault was a new-comer to a risky profession was known — also that his commission in the Duke of Baden's Army, which he exhibited with becoming modesty at times, mightn't be above suspicion. Yes. Curiosity more than any other reason had impelled him to agree to second the Canadian — met at a smart *rindotto* or a private *bal masqué*.

Henry was so courteous, ambitious and consumed with the enjoyment of life he'd taken a fancy to him for all Briffault was but a poorly educated foreigner. By the increasing dawn-light Peter Godolphin's principal seemed commendably calm and composed and even attempted to joke while slowly flexing and massaging muscular wrists.

Henri Breboeuf stared at the misty, softly rounded landscape. A few bearded and heavy-eyed farmers on their way to work rumbled by in heavy two-wheeled carts which reminded him of tumbrils used around Québec and Montreal.

My man must be clever and precise, mused Peter Godolphin; daren't miscalculate a single thrust lest he kill the Marquess of Middlebrook and raise the hue-and-cry after him.

But why worry? Henry would attend to this matter as efficiently as he had two previous duels. Hadn't he, Godolphin, watched this young fellow hour on hour dart with catlike agility about Captain Antonius's salle d'armes, blade flickering swift as a snake's tongue?

He recalled in rising confidence the sensitivity of Briffault's fingers on the grip of a blunted practice épée while countering Captain Antonius's onset. Certainly the saturnine led-captain had introduced his protégé to a staggering variety of uncommon thrusts, cuts, ripostes, feints and artful combinations.

The only disturbing thoughts in Godolphin's mind were recollections of Father's reminiscences about Lieutenant Colonel Liscard — as he'd been known before inheriting the title — as a very strong and resourceful swordsman. Possibly he'd been considered a trifle old-fashioned in some phases of technique but sound, very sound. That this summation had been voiced long years ago, however, lent Peter Godolphin, Esq., considerable confidence.

The hackney rattled past a weatherbeaten finger post indicating that the Green Park dueling ground lay close ahead.

Godolphin turned his head. By cupping an ear the Canadian's second caught the sound of hoofbeats in their rear. Turning his head, he watched Captain Antonius canter into sight leading a fast saddle horse he'd selected in case events took an unlucky turn.

As always when under tension, Henri Breboeuf yawned several times, pretended interest in the movements of a cloud of rooks wheeling about the stark chimney of a ruined cottage.

Quite clearly, he recalled Mark Antonius's final injunction: "Remember this, you are in your prime and an expert swordsman. Also, *I* have trained you so thoroughly you should foil any attack Lord Middlebrook may devise. Remain confident but not too sure of yourself. Think only of a prosperous future awaiting you."

Well, the future was bright. Think of it! He stood to win *three hundred pounds* for only a few minute's swordplay — more than many a man could earn in a lifetime of drudgery. *Nom de Dieu!* Next week he'd been promised twice that sum provided he could render a certain Viscount *hors de combat* for a few weeks.

To think that within only a few months he, Henri Breboeuf, an ignorant mixed-blood from the wilds of North America, had become able to afford a comfortable town house, keep a pretty mistress and fill a wardrobe with elegant clothing!

Like a stream high in the Laurentians his imagination raced onwards. Once he'd banked five thousand pounds — a sum he'd determined on as a true measure of success — he planned to quit this fascinating but precarious profession. If he handled the future cleverly before long he'd marry a female of means and social attainment — possibly the daughter of a rich merchant or of some impoverished minor nobleman.

This accomplished, Henri had decided to take ship for Barbados, Trinidad or Jamaica and, in due course, become a landed gentleman. Should he continue to prosper who knew but that, eventually, he might not win high office in a Government. After all, hadn't that celebrated buccaneer Harry Morgan been knighted and appointed Lord Lieutenant of Jamaica?

Peter Godolphin, Esq., broke in on his dreaming. "I see your challenger's carriage halted by the grounds."

"Who is the tall gentleman in the mulberry riding cloak?"

"Major Sir Ernest Dupuy of the Life Guards. He is to act as president. Chances to be an uncle of mine.

"Now, Henry, brush road dust from your coat and rest easy whilst I go confer with —" He broke off, looked startled. "I say! Who's that about to second Lord Middlebrook? *He's* not the one I arranged this matter with!"

Godolphin then chuckled on identifying that lithe, softly rounded figure with the well-filled tunic front. "Well, bugger me gently! If yonder ain't the notorious Chevalier d'Éon!"

At the same moment the Chevalier, on recognizing Peter Godolphin as an associate of Lord Sandwich, was murmuring to his principal: "*Monsieur le Marquis*, until now I 'ave been attempting to grasp what lies be'ind thees encounter. Can eets *raison d'être* be poleetical?"

Lord Middlebrook straightened among long, bluish shadows cast by nearby beech trees and his eyes brightened. "God's love, what a dull clod I've been! Lay you a hundred to one, my dear Chevalier, the King's Friends' grimy fingers are deep in this unsavory pie. Well, well. Should have smelt the stink of 'em long since."

Methodically he commenced casting loose engraved silver buttons securing his waistcoat.

30

Coup de Jarnac

CAPTAIN MARK ANTONIUS peered from a vantage point amid the clump of white birches in which he'd just finished tethering his mount and the led horse to study the not-too-distant dueling ground.

Odd that he felt tenser than if he himself were waiting on the dewy, even grass while ramrod-backed Major Dupuy gravely conferred with the seconds to advance the prescribed but generally futile plea for a reconciliation.

Strange, mused the Master-of-Arms, how remarkably dissimilar were the figures collected out there. The Chevalier d'Éon, in a light-blue coat, was the shortest; young Peter Godolphin, Esq., looked smart in a jacket of a bottle-green broadcloth. Lean and alert as a crane and standing a half-head taller was gray-haired Major Dupuy with a double-caped mulberry riding cloak dangling loose from wide shoulders.

He watched the seconds open small-sword cases and then carefully compare the length of all four blades. To the onlooker it proved reassuring that these wickedly gleaming strips of steel turned out to be identical in length, permitting each of the duelists to handle a weapon to which he was accustomed.

The led-captain yearned to venture closer to the dueling ground; at such distance it would be difficult to catch subtleties of swordplay,

yet he knew he could not: to move closer — 'twould compromise
Captain Henry Briffault's presumed amateur status in which case
a highly profitable encounter must come to an abrupt and ignominious end.

Carrying unsheathed swords the seconds returned to their princi-
pals at present removing footgear after stripping off coats, waistcoats
and neckcloths. Next, the duelists rolled shirt sleeves tight above the
elbow. Henri's hairy forearm looked copper-brown while the stocky
nobleman's shone pink-red.

Captain Antonius stroked his long, wedge-shaped chin. An unusually lovely morning. Save for the singing of birds and the occasional
snuffling of a horse the scene was incredibly still and peaceful.

Jaws tightening, the led-captain watched the president use his riding crop to scratch a line across the ground.

Meanwhile both duelists flexed blades into shimmering silvery
arcs above their heads, then bent knees to limber them.

In the meantime each second, weapon dully agleam, took position
close on his principal's right, ready to intervene instantly at the first
hint of a foul.

How tall the scabrous-trunked beeches appeared, dwarfing the
duelists now advancing towards the line the president had drawn.

A flight of ground plovers darted by, uttering plaintive cries.

Dr. Vernay, supremely blasé about the whole business, continued
to lay out instruments, pledgets and bandages on a black mantle.

A few shaggy and unshaven farmers in blue smocks appeared to
linger furtively at the glade's far end; they'd no desire to be haled
into court at harvest time as witnesses to an unlawful encounter.

Clearly, Captain Antonius heard the president's call of "Gentlemen, are you ready to commence?"

As one, they inclined heads.

"Very well. By agreement, the first blood drawn will not end this
affair; only when life is endangered will I call a halt to this *combat à
l'outrance!*

"Attention, gentlemen! Engage!"

With a silvery shivering sound like high notes struck on a harp
the blades met.

At first the led-captain fixed attention on Lord Middlebrook when,
following a series of thrusts, cuts and parries, the older, heavier-built
figure — too soon, in Antonius's opinion — assumed the offensive.

The nobleman exhibited power, speed and timing to a degree commanding *maître d'armes*'s anxious admiration.

The Canadian's wrist, powerful but sensitive and flexible, caused a staccato ringing of steel on steel when he parried, then, agility personified, leaped in and out but all the while giving ground.

Gaze unwaveringly fixed on the nobleman's bloodshot dark eyes, Henri Breboeuf experienced growing confidence despite the surprising power, skill and speed of his adversary's attack. Pretty soon he began to sense that Captain Antonius's forecast had been well founded. Although very dangerous, some of Lord Middlebrook's combinations appeared a trifle — but only a trifle — old-fashioned.

The rapidity with which that deadly, star-bright point kept speeding in from unusual angles, the way that blue-white edge flickered here, there and everywhere were impressive. Simply because it was somewhat outmoded rendered the older man's style the more threatening.

On stockinged feet dampened by dew Breboeuf continued to dance lightly backwards. Skillfully, he parried a savage lightning thrust *en tierce*, countered it with a rasping *riposte en quarte* so strong it jarred his wrist and caused the nobleman to curse under his breath.

Coldly, steadily he parried, effectively *remised* to nullify Lord Middlebrook's hard-pressed attack. Gradually confidence burgeoned and the conviction grew that, barring a miracle, Henri Breboeuf soon would earn a glorious three hundred pounds!

Nerves under perfect control, he watched the nobleman's powerful blunt features turn purple-red, saw his lips part wide, wider to permit his gulping great gasps of air.

Foiling a strong attack *en sagoun*, he abruptly sensed that Lord Middlebrook's timing slowly but unmistakably had commenced to falter. A few more passes, then would come his turn to initiate a series of combinations mastered through countless hours under Captain Mark Antonius's exacting tutelage.

The veteran *maître d'armes* hovering in the birch thicket also noted that subtle slowing of the nobleman's cuts, thrusts and parries while his protégé remained agile and untired.

At the same time it bothered Mark Antonius that so experienced a duelist as the Marquess of Middlebrook should have elected to assume the offensive so early when, obviously, the advantages of youth and condition rested with his adversary.

The question remained unanswered because now the dark-featured Canadian had ceased to give ground. Suddenly it became apparent to the led-captain that Breboeuf was only fighting coolly on the defensive until the moment came to pink his adversary in arm or thigh just seriously enough to disable him.

Henri Breboeuf experienced warm confidence flood his being, but remained wary although Lord Middlebrook now was panting harder and his squarish features had become suffused.

Good! Never had his own fingers felt more sensitive or supple while his legs and sword arm remained free from fatigue. He contemplated an attack *en tierce* which, by now, he judged to be the nobleman's least strongly defended quadrant. Keeping his gaze fixed on the older man's congested black eyes, he summoned a provocative, derisive grin.

Coolly alert and with weight expertly distributed between the balls of stockinged feet, both seconds noted that tight little smile and drew closer, ready blades gleaming in the sun's first rays.

Mark Antonius sensed rather than perceived a puzzling acceleration in Lord Middlebrook's movements. The shivering rasp and ring of steel on steel quickened in tempo; he foresaw the nobleman was leading up to a *coup de Jarnac* — a complicated but reliable old-fashioned combination which over recent years had pretty well fallen into disuse among fashionable swordsmen.

"Thank God!" muttered the leathery led-captain. "Middlebrook is attempting it too late; he is too spent and winded to bring off *coup.*"

At the same moment the Canadian was beginning to feel he needn't worry when the older man shifted his attack to an unfamiliar pattern. Yes, the nobleman's eyes were staring and his footwork noticeably less agile.

Tightening the grip on his sword handle he expertly countered a series of thrusts which, delivered *en quarte*, developed into a poorly timed sequence of powerful thrusts and half-cuts which nonetheless forced his defense upwards until his épée's point was twinkling on a level with his own eyes.

He was preparing a savage *riposte* when his adversary's gleaming point started to flash downwards but then quick as a striking viper it changed direction and came flashing upwards.

A pang of indescribable agony lanced the Canadian's chest and amid a roar loud as the thunder of a high waterfall Henri Breboeuf's iridescent dreams exploded. He dropped his *épée* and swayed, dissolving inside.

When Lord Middlebrook's point vanished into Captain Briffault's frilly shirt it reappeared on his far side instantly to become circled by a ring of bright blood.

The Chevalier d'Éon sighed and passed his tongue's tip over what remained of his lip rouge. *Nom de Dieu! Le coup de Jarnac!* Milor' must possess nerves of steel to attempt such a thing in his poor condition!

Peter Godolphin, Esq., rushed forward to thrust arms under his principal's armpits and steady him as he stood swaying, an agonized, incredulous expression contorting his coppery features. He barely was in time to ease the crumpling mixed-blood onto the trampled grass.

Chest heaving, George Liscard, Third Marquess of Middlebrook, dashed a sheen of sweat from his brow before going over to stare down, expressionless, upon his adversary. Mechanically he accepted a pledget from Dr. Vernay and used it to wipe blood from his blade then resumed his survey of the dying man lying with dark and narrow head propped against Peter Godolphin's knee. Bright trickles had begun to wander from the corners of his mouth; an expression of stunned incredulity marked sweat-brightened features.

"Bad luck, m'lad, for you'd the hallmark of an exceptional swordsman." His tone hardened and he glared into young Godolphin's pallid face. "Don't know how you became involved in this sorry affair, Peter, but warn this fellow's patrons never again to send a youth on a man's errand."

George Liscard turned away, stepped into his pumps, then calmly rolled down his sleeves and extended arms to accept the waistcoat the Chevalier was holding ready. He nodded to Major Dupuy at the moment swinging up into his saddle.

"Sincere thanks for your kind offices, Major. Trust there will be no aftermath to this discreditable affair."

"Imagine this matter will be kept in the dark. Good morrow to you!" The Guardee saluted with his crop and trotted off.

"I say, Chevalier, shall we repair to Middlebrook House? I'm famished, ready for a cold pie and a bottle of '58 champagne. You see, m'dear fellow, we need to converse further on projects I bear in mind. Among other things, I must learn who hired that poor young fellow — and why."

31

Vain Repinings

I<small>F</small> Jeremy Dabney Brett, Esq., had ever felt worse he couldn't remember — and didn't try to. Criminently! His head was being
beaten by all the hammers of Hell and spasms of nausea continued
to convulse him although already he'd puked up his guts from the
bumhole. Furthermore, the taste in his mouth was fouler than drop-
pings below a hen-roost.

Seated at a small escritoire in his bedroom he scribbled hurriedly
— no point whatever in concocting fancy phrases to disguise what
had to be said.

M<small>Y</small> D<small>EAR</small> L<small>ORD</small> M<small>IDDLEBROOK</small>:

*No words can express the Profound Shame and Consternation I
feel on having so Miserably Failed you after your ever-Generous Care
and Friendship. I can Offer no Excuse for my Conduct.*

*Saving Myself, none is to Blame. Freely, I confess to Haveing at-
tended Mr. Treymane's Frolick in Hopes of earning Mr. Falconer's
Favourable Opinion.*

*Sir, I am about to take my Leave wearing only the Cloathes I
stand in, fully Determined somehow to regain your good Opinion.*

In deep Contrition, I am, Sir, Your Humble, Obed't Serv't,

J<small>EREMY</small> D<small>ABNEY</small> B<small>RETT</small>

He was sanding the note when a wooden-faced footman knocked, entered, and bowing, said, "Sir, m'lud wishes you to repair immediately to 'is study."

"I'll be down directly." Jeremy lingered long enough to fold and seal his letter with a paper wafer.

He then drew a series of deep breaths before marching out into the hallway and down to disaster. Impossible that this was only mid-afternoon of the day he'd wrecked brilliant prospects.

Clad in a wine-hued banyan, the Third Marquess of Middlebrook sat behind a wide desk of Honduran mahogany supporting glasses and a squat decanter of cognac.

"Good afternoon," he greeted. "Come to help me and Margaret celebrate my success?"

He tilted his head towards a door through which floated a suggestion of perfume and snatches of the song "Gentle Shepherd tell me where" sung in a pleasing contralto. Traces of lip rouge were evident on the nobleman's florid features and a pink silk stocking lay coiled on his settee.

"Nothing more restoring than a bit of dalliance after a trying morning is there? All work and no play, etcetera.

"Between bouts with my fair companion I find time to take up a serious matter." Hard, little black eyes narrowed while bushy brows merged. "Pray, sir, and what have you to say for yourself?"

Jeremy squared shoulders, then in silence placed his letter on the table desk's glowing top. "I believe, my lord, this will express my sentiments far better than speech."

"Wrong! Only fools or cowards put on paper what they dare not say."

He put down his spaniel which had remained invisible on his master's lap. Employing a thumbnail, Lord Middlebrook broke the wafer.

Jeremy, standing ramrod-straight with icy shivers coursing down his spine, watched George Liscard purse lips and casually scan the letter. He ended by grimacing then, settling back in a tall leather armchair, said, "Close yonder door; a sound of singing at this moment is out of place."

Next he stared the Colonial straight in the face, then using precise movements the Marquess of Middlebrook tore the letter into small pieces and dropped them into a wastebasket.

Lord Middlebrook rubbed a chin covered with reddish stubble. "You must pardon me, Boston Jerry, for having forgot how vastly green you are, how untutored you remain concerning conduct amid polite society."

He gestured towards the wastebasket. "In there reposes proof of my opinion. Having committed a grave error, d'you fancy to atone by precipitately departing this house — in effect evading a well-deserved reproof?"

"But, sir, I — I didn't think ——"

"Obviously not. You're still too hung over to think clearly. God's blood! Treymane must have staged a real orgy."

"Oh, please! I'd never dreamed of such — such antics."

An emerald flashed on the hand of George Liscard flung curtly upwards. "You will remain silent. I believe I understand what prompts you to wish to run off, tail between legs."

His bored expression softened. "For all it mayn't seem likely at this time and tide — I well, I suspect I once rather resembled you — impulsive and headstrong, yet intending to honor obligations.

"Sit down, man, sit down." He took a sip of brandy. "Possibly it may help restore a measure of self-confidence were I to confide that, years ago, I was guilty of a very similar lapse. Got too roaring drunk to attend a close friend in a duel — poor fellow got killed — so you're better off than I."

Seated bolt upright on the edge of an armchair, Jeremy riveted his gaze on the older man's ruddy, wearied features.

"Cousin Jerry, in view of my own failings I find it possible to forgive, if not entirely to forget. In no uncertain terms I have requested all witnesses of this unfortunate affair to make no mention of it at any time or place. To Society you shall remain my refreshingly young and delightful American cousin."

Jeremy flushed rich crimson. "Oh, sir! How in hell can you be so tolerant of a stupid, worthless ——"

"Enough! 'Tis undignified to wallow in self-pity. Stop and think; can't you understand there are motives behind my leniency — aside from genuine fondness for you?"

He sighed. "Since for my sins I've no son of my own — to speak of, that is," he added softly, "so it pleases me to — er — further your ambitions along with my own."

Amazed, Jeremy blinked and not knowing what to say felt an utter fool.

George Liscard tugged gently at Young Q's long silky ears. "I have invested considerable time and no small sums of money in your possible future and usefulness."

"I'll do my best not to disappoint you, sir."

"See that you do not! I deduce it is dire necessity to obtain business to occupy your family shipyards. Am I correct?"

"Aye, my lord. I ——"

Lord Middlebrook raised his hand. " 'Tis still 'Cousin George' to you."

"Thank you, Cousin George. Right now our yards are idle; Pa is facing bankruptcy."

"Why? An he's the shrewd businessman you repute him?"

"Loyalty to the King don't always pay off. He lost two fine vessels, letters-of-marque, in battle with the Frog-Eaters during the last war along with three schooners prized by Spaniards. For those losses Pa's never recovered a penny's worth of compensation from the Crown."

"Condolences," came the slightly slurred and weary voice. "Many English shipowners have never been recompensed. Money voted for such purposes seems to vanish into certain pockets — whose, the King's Friends well know.

"For reasons of my own I will continue to lend you support and so, I hazard, will Perry Falconer. Also, an you prove adroit, so will Sir Guy Constable — a fool for the moment but well-connected at Court."

Despite his still cruelly throbbing head Jeremy listened, vowed to remember all that was being said.

"Recently I have been in communication with your firm's agents, Mason & Sampson, have directed 'em to collect a shipload of appropriate merchandise for dispatch to Silas Brett & Son of Portsmouth in New Hampshire —" He smiled thinly. "My God, Cousin, how many of our place-names will you Colonials insist on appropriating? New York, New Jersey, New Hampshire, Braintree, Boston, New London, Lancaster and York, for example."

Jeremy reddened. "If you please, Cousin, let me assure you that for every English place-name we've hundreds if not thousands of Indian names such as Connecticut, Massachusetts, Kentucky, Illinois, Ohio, Alabama, Ontario, Erie, Michigan ——"

"I stand, or rather sit, corrected, so spare me further outlandish noises.

"To repeat — as soon as a proper vessel can be found your merchandise will be sent across the Atlantic."

Jeremy could hardly credit his hearing. Tears brimmed his hot and still swollen eyes. "How can I thank you?"

"That remains to be seen," grunted Lord Middlebrook, gulping brandy.

From behind the cabinet door sounded a patter of light feet. The spaniel briefly cocked an ear when a girl called, "Coming soon, Georgie dear? I grow impatient."

"Be quiet, ye greedy wench. All in good time.

"How many ships could your shipyards build, in say a year's time?"

Gratefully Jeremy returned to practicalities. "All depends on the tonnage, design and the quality of timber to be used. Besides, shipbuilding in New England, on account of our climate is seasonal; can't accomplish much in midwinter — nor is prime, twice-weathered timber easy to come across."

Drawled Lord Middlebrook, "I repeat, how many vessels can you manage at a maximum?"

Wits leveling, Jeremy hovered between workable and suddenly soaring ambitions. "Five, if none of the hulls run over three hundred tons burthen."

"Know beans about shipping, Cousin, but would orders for a pair of vessels relieve your immediate needs?"

"Indeed so! Our shipwrights would be fully occupied." He didn't feel it necessary to add that Mark Hanking's or some other adjacent yard would have to be leased should the Navy Board require completion of more than three vessels at the same time.

Lord Middlebrook appeared to retire within himself, steepled fingers under his ample and colorful nose.

Jeremy ventured, "What rig and hull do the Navy people have in mind?"

To his astonishment the answer came promptly. "Supply ships, brigs or schooners, I understand — craft of around two hundred and eighty tons; capacious, but speedy and well constructed of the best materials."

Hotly Jeremy burst out, "By God, our Brett ships long have been admired for fine design, expert craftsmanship and superior quality of fabric!"

"Such a reputation is most commendable and no doubt hard-earned." His jeweled hand fanned away a nonexistent fly and he peered into space.

"However, it now becomes necessary to accomplish the political ruin of certain gentlemen now running the Navy. To put the matter simply: your firm, under the contemplated contract, will be required to furnish finest quality timber and superior construction but, in fact, will have to substitute materials and workmanship of lesser quality.

"The difference between money appropriated and what actually is paid to your yard will, as usual, disappear into the pockets of certain officials our party intends to expose and drive from office, while at the same time assisting the aims of Mr. Wilkes and the American Sons of Liberty, as well as the economy of the New England Colonies.

"The embezzled sums, which, incidentally, you will never see, will offer damning evidence when traced to the wallets of the King's Friends and similar jackals now fattening to the ruination of our Armed Forces at sea and ashore.

"Do you comprehend what is intended?"

"I think so, sir — I mean, Cousin George — but there is one big catch. Our yard has built its reputation through faithful fulfillment of contract specifications." He suddenly felt sweat breaking out on the backs of his hands. "Pa will never consent to trickery in materials or workmanship!"

Lord Middlebrook heaved himself erect, tired eyes ablaze, rasping, "Then it is up to you to make your worthy parent see it's his sole salvation that he cooperates in this matter. Once again in possession of a flourishing shipyard, he can revert to honest practices whenever he wishes.

"Do I make myself clear? It is of importance that your yard wins these contracts. Therefore, since the influence of Lord Sandwich and his cronies in the Ministry must be won —" absently he fingered his pearl necklace — "Through devious and not always savory means I must have your aid." He added gravely, "I plan for you to figure in my maneuvers, Cousin Jerry."

215

Jeremy's mind became a battlefield. Why, oh, why wasn't he more nimble-witted and supple of conscience? The existence of grim and inescapable facts decided him. "Very well. I'll undertake to further your schemes in every possible way."

"You encourage me; I'd begun to take you for one of those self-righteous Yankees who'd slit his throat before violating outmoded and narrow Puritanical conceptions of morality.

"As I have said," continued the Marquess of Middlebrook, helping himself to a pinch of snuff, "success eventually depends upon regaining the goodwill of my former close friend, Jemmy Twitcher.

"Over a space of time I, therefore, have been plotting to command His Lordship's favorable consideration when the time is ripe. One ploy is to deliever to John Montagu, Dolly Lawton, that luscious young virgin."

He sniggered. "Believe you watched her charms revealed in this very room not many weeks ago."

"Oh, yes." Jeremy gulped. "She was fetched in by Mother Stanhope!"

"Aye. That tasty morsel I'll offer Lord Sandwich as a new pearl to his necklace, thus outnumbering Francis Dashwood and myself by another digit in our race to win the Maidenhead Sweepstakes."

He pushed forward the decanter. "Help yourself, Cousin. Also I contemplate another move in which 'Boston Jerry' will act as a principal."

Jeremy was surprised to hear his voice inquiring, "In what way?"

"I have ascertained that recently Lord Sandwich has been winning large sums on the prowess of a ferocious pug known as the 'Irish Ogre.' When we visit at West Wycombe an all-in match will be arranged between you and said Ogre.

"I intend to wager dazzling sums you'll batter Johnny Montagu's prize-fighter to the ground."

It now became gin-clear why, over the weeks, the master of Middlebrook House had supplied a succession of better-than-average pugilists as sparring partners. "I'll beat him," the Colonial burst out. "Count on it!"

Lord Middlebrook strolled over to a window, clasped hands behind him and peered briefly into his carriage court below. Finally he turned, saying quietly, "You will receive instructions just before the match commences; you may be astonished by their nature."

Abruptly his manner changed and, smiling, he lifted his glass. "Enough of dull care! Shall we join Miss Margaret and discover what arts she can devise to entertain the both of us?"

32

Letter from Piscataqua

WHILE a barrow man's long-drawn chant of "Buy my new Wall Street oysters! New eels and mussels!" arose from the street, Jeremy Brett broke a seal of red wax securing the flap to an envelope just arrived from Boston.

Light was failing on this dull September afternoon so, seeking a window, he eagerly read:

Piscataqua Head,
New Hampshire
August ye 1st

MY DEAR SON,

Experienced vast Relief 'pon Receipt of y'r Letter written from Middlebrook House & Would Much like to Hear how You so Soon are able to Employ so Elegant an Address.

— The Merrimack and Cargo having been lost under the Circumstances You describe I cannot hold this Disaster against You for all it drives us nearer the Verge of Bankruptcy.

Howsumever, an old Friend has been sufficient kind enough to Stave off Ruin by ordering a Coast-Wise Schooner, an Assistance most Welcome during this Dreadful Ebb in my Fortunes.

Alas, this little Commission will scarce Serve to Occupy our Yard till the Onset of Cold Weather.

Am Gratified to read of your finding Perdita and her Husband. How does my Daughter behave as a Woman of Title?

I make Hopefull Note What you write about Sir Guy's supposed Influence with the Navy Board. I am Confident you will Exploit such a Connection to best Advantage. An we secure, in the Near Future! orders for two vessels of say 200 Tons such should go Far towards reviving Credit.

At the Moment Matters here lie in a State of deep Anxiety and Uncertainty. The recent Repeal of the Stamp Act and the Townshend Laws has had a Reassuring effect and unless Further Oppressive Acts or Measures, contrary to our Rights and Liberty, are impos'd I am Confident there will be no Resort to Violence.

Perhaps you can Establish the Truth of a Rumour that ere long the King's Ministers intend to Despatch a body of Troops to Boston to Support His Majesty's Customs Officers in a more Strickt Enforcement of those Illegal and Obnoxious Tariffs which as you well know long have been Ignored or have been only Half-Heartedly Applyed.

I pray this Rumour prove without Foundation. Nothing so Enflames the Sons of Liberty in Partickular and the Publick in General as the Sight of Scarlet Coats parading the Streets of Boston, suggesting that Boston has become a Towne to be Occupied and Policed as if it were Enemy Territory.

Writte me immediately for 'tis monstrous Dull and Gloomy in Piscataqua these Days.

Pray convey Paternal Blessings to Perdita and Instruckt her to sharpen her Pen's point.

God bless and Keep you, my dear and only Son. Writte soon.

Y'r affeck't
FATHER

Jeremy frowned at an expanse of grimy roofs and blackened chimney pots stretching away into the smoke-veiled distance pierced here and there by steeples and nondescript domes and towers. He felt a sudden craving for deep breaths of cold, clean sea air screaming in over rust-brown salt marshes.

How comforting, how steadying it would be to hear the dull

thumping of mauls and axes, the rasping whine of saws at work, the raucous laughter of harbor gulls and the screeching of terns.

Thank God, in a few days he would exchange London for a few days in the country at West Wycombe, country estate of Sir Francis Dashwood, Lord le Despencer and Premier Baron of England.

God alone knew how he should conduct himself amid such glittering surroundings. What blunders of etiquette might he commit in all innocence?

From what Peregrine Falconer, Tom Treymane and the others had let drop, he'd be joining enormously prominent lords and ladies, not to mention a sprinkling of Cabinet ministers and other individuals occupying high office. How many of these could not with a mere nod or a stroke of his pen determine the fate of myriads of peoples inhabiting lands as far separated as India, Canada and other scarce-heard-of territories over which the scarlet tide of British dominion was spreading?

33

Dolly Lawton's Diary II

A NEWLY ACQUIRED CANARY was trilling satisfactorily while Dolly Lawton unlocked her journal and wetted shiny, dark-red lips in concentration before commencing yet another entry.

Mrs. Stanhope and your Humble Virgin are all agog over fresh Arriv'd news. It would Appear my Maidenhead is destin'd for Sacrifice to the Lust of a Great Lord none other than John Montagu, Fourth Earl of Sandwich, Assistant Secretary of State and Postmaster-General!

I shudder to imagine my Fate in Store at the Hands of this Ogre who, in addition to other unflattering Titles privately is term'd "The Rape-Master General."

Alack, I am at my Wit's End to know how best to secure the richest Recompense for the Untying of my Virgin Knot and Advancement towards the Goal I am Determin'd on. Will this terrible Voluptuary tear me apart?

Is this Noble Lord, as Rumour has it, indeed afflickted by the French pox?

Mrs. S. informs that She and I will be Join'd on our Journey to West Wycombe by Henneke and Janine, their Attendance having been Be-spoken.

With us also will travel a thin young child nam'd Daisy who, my Oath on it, is not scarce Fourteen and must have led a hard life. Once her Dame had sold her to Mrs. S. for a mere five Pounds, this Unfortunate was stripp'd and Discover'd to be filthy-dirty and Cover'd with sores, Lice bites and Bruises. Four Baths were requir'd ere the squalling little Creature ceas'd to Stink to High Heaven. When wash'd to Satisfaction Daisy appear'd not badly conform'd, has a marble-white Complecktion and Buckl'd golden Hair which may attrackt favorable Consideration.

Plume tip tucked between lips, Dolly paused, listening to Mrs. Stanhope use some especially colorful obscenities in berating a servant which dutifully she added to a growing vocabulary.

Despite Efforts to Remain Self-contain'd my Preceptress is greedily Excited over Prospeckts of amassing a Fortune at West Wycombe through sale of our Charms and Qualities.

Nowadays this Establishment swarms with a Succession of Milliners, Seamstresses, Ribbon Vendors, Bootmakers and Mantua Makers. Happilly, Mrs. S. (who Daily grows Fatter) Insists my Costumes shall All be of White, Gauzy Material and Decently cut.

Dolly paused long enough to scratch an itchy fleabite before dipping her quill.

Mrs. S. assures there will be in Attendance Gentlemen known to me; among them: Lord M. and Boston Jerry, said to be his distant Cousin, also Sir Francis D., Lord N., and Mr. Falconer, who for some Reason I Detest.

An all goes well some Day soon I will climb up into a fine Coach Mrs. S. has hired. What fate will befall me? A brief spell of High Living ending in Despair or a Life of Ease, or leading towards the Honourable Estate of Matrimony?

Alas, Fortune's face is veil'd!

34

West Wycombe Park

⌒

O N THE DEEP AND COMFORTABLE SEAT of a smart coach hurriedly purchased as an impressive adjunct for their visit to Lord le Despencer's country seat Sir Guy Constable lounged beside his lady. Before her face she poised a traveling mask in hopes of warding off at least a measure of road dust.

To his own span of high-stepping chestnuts had been added a pair of long-limbed and well-matched rented animals which led smartly enough through massive wrought-iron gates hastily swung wide by keepers who ran out of a big brick gatehouse.

Once well behind a high wall enclosing Sir Francis Dashwood's estate Sir Guy brusquely ordered the coachman to pull off into a small clearing lined with copper beeches.

A bandy-legged "tiger" in wine-and-white — the family colors — released hand-grips let into the back of the gleaming body, leaped down, and ran to seize the lead pair's bit handles and steady them.

Smiling, he handed his wife to the ground. "My love, shall we dust off and stretch our legs? Egad! I feel stickier than a whore's night-shift."

He flicked road dust from his sleeves then employed a lace-trimmed handkerchief to pat overheated and slightly bloated features.

Perdita, meantime, tilted up the mirror set inside the lid of a traveling cosmetics case bound in Russian leather. In quick succession she smoothed flaring, slender brows, then employed a rabbit's foot lightly to brush rouge over naturally pink cheeks.

Laughing, she offered the brush. "You can use this to advantage, Guy, and for Christ's sake straighten that cravat! Lord knows you squandered so much on it it had better appear perfection's self."

Sir Guy grinned, beckoned the tiger. "Toby, fetch a bottle of Chablis out of the ice bin; Bucks County dust ain't over-palatable."

Seated on the grass and sipping cool wine, the Constables watched their coachman polish their coat-of-arms newly adorning the coach's doors.

Sir Guy nibbled his nether lip. God's love! Already this visit was proving costly beyond belief. So God send the cards would run favorably but if they didn't — well, he could always sell off a few more acres of woodland inherited not long ago from Aunt Hortense. Although the dear old girl always had been deemed a trifle dotty she'd nevertheless proved amazingly capable in real estate matters.

Full skirts swaying over the hay grass Perdita sauntered into an adjacent field to pick a spray of marguerites which, laughing, she used to discourage an over-inquisitive bumblebee before returning to her cosmetics case. "I vow I'm all a-twitter over the prospect of viewing the sinister Sir Francis Dashwood's lair."

" 'Palace' is nearer right," corrected her husband while fumbling in a side pocket. "Here's a rough plan of Lord le Despencer's humble abode drawn from memory by a member of the Brimstone Club — place is so immense James fancied a sketch could prove useful."

Sir Guy smoothed a roll of paper over the grass. "I take it this gatehouse is the one we just now passed and this is about where we now are."

"James notes: 'The Estate of Wycombe Park covers well over two hundred acres. Wycombe House' — here —" he used an elegantly manicured forefinger to tap the plan — "stands on a rise surrounded on three sides by woods of oak, ash and beech and faces a large artificial pond shaped like a swan.'"

Peering over her husband's shoulder Lady Perdita Brett Constable noted that Wycombe House had been designed by none other than that celebrated architect, Robert Adam; its façade of red brick runs two hundred feet and is decorated by forty Doric pillars.

"I've been informed," Sir Guy added, "that the second story reproduces the façade of an ancient Grecian temple dedicated, appropriately enough, to the worship of that merry old tosspot and lecher, the great god Bacchus.

"From what James said, one scarce can credit the amazing richness of this mansion's appointments. Sir Francis is reported to have squandered God knows how many thousands acquiring erotic art from all over the world —"

Perdita broke in, "Guy, whatever is that odd-looking steeple in the distance? D'you see? What looks like a great gold ball shows halfway up its length."

"Um. Can't be anything but the Church of St. Lawrence, designed and built by Sir Francis himself."

"Church indeed! What's that great ball doing up there?"

"A mystery which, possibly we'll solve before long."

Sir Guy plucked a stalk of grass and chewed on it while staring mildly about. "James said yonder church lies beyond the Wye River and stands on tall, chalk bluffs into which have been tunneled underground caverns designed by Sir Francis to accommodate amusements of the members of the Brimstone Club — otherwise, the Friars of St. Lawrence.

"Speaking of the Club, I understand Lord Middlebrook expects to attend this convocation with Jeremy as his guest." Sir Guy's brow creased and he cast Perdita a penetrating look. "Demmed if I understand why the Marquess should clasp Jeremy so firmly to his bosom; surely it's not on *your* account! Don't know whether I approve of my brother-in-law associating with Liberals and Wilkesites — dangerous company. If I'm to help him, help will have to come through influence from a different quarter."

Perdita frowned. "Frankly, I, too, have been worrying over this. I'll do what I can to influence him, but Bro always has fought shy of my advice."

A doe peered from a nearby thicket, saw the couple reenter their vehicle and hurriedly raise windows before a flock of sheep advancing under a cloud of yellow dust could come near.

Recalling a spate of rumors and gossip concerning the goings-on at West Wycombe, Perdita ordered their coachman to drive at a walk while she and her husband scanned this magnificent estate with the eagerness of country bumpkins.

"Ah," purred Perdita, "this *is* a welcome touch of gallantry from an old married man — always provided he's not absentminded."

Suddenly inspired, Guy had cupped and freed Perdita's nearer breast. She wriggled pleasureably but once he started to feel under her petticoats she slapped away his hands.

"Fie, sir! There's no time now. Besides, what if my husband were to catch us?"

"Right. The fool's so insanely jealous he might call me out."

Husband and wife then relaxed to view a succession of wide lawns opening to either side of an apparently endless graveled driveway. Like smooth green ocean swells lush swards swirled around skillfully trimmed groves of trees.

Laughing like naughty lovers they glimpsed, in a pretty little dell, a marble statue of a long-limbed wood nymph being vigorously raped by a horned and lusty young satyr. The statue stood close enough to the drive to enable the travelers to appreciate the half-pleased, half-apprehensive expression worn by the ravished nymph.

"Damme, 'Dita, you've looked exactly like that many a time!" Sir Guy then treated his companion to a kiss of extra-connubial intensity.

A few rods farther along appeared an exquisitely proportioned Egyptian shrine before which rose a thick phallic shaft realistically sculptured in pink marble.

Emerging from the countryside, Lord le Despencer's driveway straightened to bisect a vast emerald-green lawn on which clusters of white sheep were browsing under the care of bare-legged young boys wearing Grecian chitons.

Soon, details of Robert Adam's masterpiece became disclosed in neoclassic splendor. On the lawn before its main entrance persons in multi-hued clothing were sauntering about viewing a plethora of frankly erotic statuary.

Stimulated, Perdita lapsed into broad New England. "Now, I swan; never have spied the likes of such! Look at those flowerbeds and shrubbery; nary a leaf looks out of place."

"Pick up a smart trot!" Sir Guy called up to his coachman.

He motioned Perdita to sit back. Wouldn't do to arrive at West Wycombe Hall at a walk and gawking about like curious peasants.

Elegantly, the new coach flashed left around a flowered circle to be pulled up before the mansion's lofty, colonnaded entrance.

White-wigged lackeys immediately hurried forward, together with a few pet dogs which ran up to yap noisily and set Sir Guy's high-strung horses to prancing.

Sir Guy's tiger and groom leapt down smartly enough to lower folding steps and open the emblazoned door.

It came as a quite unanticipated compliment that Sir Francis Dashwood himself should appear and unhurriedly descend a set of wide steps in time to make a "leg" when Perdita, prettily flushed, alighted amid a swaying flurry of petticoats.

The acme of courtesy, Sir Francis bent over Perdita's extended hand. "Oh, be welcome, Lady Constable and you, Sir Guy to this, my humble domicile. I trust, ma'am, in Wycombe Hall you will find pleasures — er — agreeable to your tastes."

Sir Guy, while offering a deep bow, decided that Lord le Despencer, elegantly turned out in a yellow *justaucorps* coat and waistcoat of burnt-orange velvet, appeared less jaded than when last seen at Brooks's.

The Senior Baron's pearl necklace, openly displayed, shone when he offered an arm and turned bloodshot blue eyes in bold appraisal of this tall, very beautiful and unfashionably healthy-looking young matron.

"I'm certain, my lord, we shan't suffer a moment's *accidia*."

"Not if it's to be avoided," smiled Sir Francis. "Not for nothing is the motto of this house '*Fay ce que voudras*' — in other words, 'Do whatever you will.' "

35

Lord le Despencer

AROUND NOON the sky clouded over, a cold rain set in and drove swans, peacocks and pheasants to shelter; shepherds in Greek costumes flourished crooks and soon herded their flocks out of sight.

Despite the ever-increasing downpour guests continued to put in an appearance; a few arrived on horseback and trailed water into Wycombe Hall's entranceway. Most travelers rolled up in carriages and coaches of varying degrees of elegance. From one of these alighted Dr. Benjamin Franklin and his woodchuck-like secretary, Mr. Jeremiah Pocock, another delivered Mr. John Wilkes, roaring drunk and accompanied by a pair of noisy and randy-appearing Club members.

Next to reach West Wycombe Hall was greyhound-nosed and long-faced Peregrine Falconer who had tarried long enough to deposit a nervously giggling but pretty and very young blonde at the "Nunnery" — a low, vine-covered and cloistered building set some little distance apart on the banks of the placidly flowing little River Wye.

Female faces appeared at windows of this retreat and through the drizzle viewed the newcomer who, complete with a pair of traveling boxes, alighted from Mr. Falconer's equipage to be fulsomely greeted by Mrs. Elizabeth Roach, a notorious madam designated by Sir

Francis to act as "Abbess" for this Convocation. Gray-haired, lean and ascetic of aspect, Mrs. Roach, being a former actress of note, convincingly played her role.

Barely had Mr. Falconer vanished into Wycombe House than Lord Middlebrook's magnificent six-horse traveling coach rolled into sight through silvery sheets of rain. Bedraggled postillions leaped down to steady the steaming, mud-splashed lead pair.

Jeremy Dabney Brett, Esq., hunched under a rain cloak, emerged first, carrying an attaché case clamped under an arm, just as should a private secretary.

Sir Francis Dashwood greeted his old playmate with unaffected warmth. "Welcome! Welcome as always, dearest George!"

"Glad to get here, Francis. Was lucky to be so near here before the foul weather struck; come another hour the mud will grow inches deep."

"Your suite this time is in the West Wing — trust it will prove adequate. Hope you won't resent my assigning your usual accommodation to an old and mutually dear friend."

Lord Middlebrook smiled like a friendly wolf. "His Grace of Sandwich, I presume?"

"Correct. Reasonableness is one of your most endearing qualities, dear George."

Grunted the Marquess of Middlebrook, "Old Fuddlecups is here?"

"No. Don't expect him till tomorrow." He grinned sardonically, "in time to attend vespers at St. Lawrence's."

"How many Friars d'you expect will turn up?"

"Fifteen, perhaps, plus a few guests." He smiled at Jeremy. "By the bye, George, demmed pleased you've brought along your American cousin. Seems a nice chap."

"Glad," said the Marquess, running an eye over guests thronging the entrance hall. "You'll admire his competence in the ring and bedchamber."

"Ah, yes!" The host stared at Jeremy in abrupt interest. "There'll be that little matter of Jemmy Twitcher's fancy Irish pug to be settled. Trust ye'll enjoy yourself any way you please, Mr. Brett. After all, self-enjoyment is the main excuse for this convocation, aside from —" he lowered his voice —"reassuring Mr. Wilkes that certain Friars stand ready to support his views."

Although accustomed by now to the sometimes *outré* splendors of great town houses of London, Jeremy's eyes widened over an incredible display of wealth.

The "Caligula Suite" reserved for Lord Middlebrook's occupancy consisted of a spacious sitting room, bath, two bedchambers and a powdering closet; all luxurious to the least detail.

"Not bad," drawled the Marquess of Middlebrook, using a quizzing glass on a number of erotic paintings and figurines of couples and trios performing the act of love in intricate fashion.

A wooden-faced footman waited to assist Jervis, the Marquess's valet, in anticipating George Liscard's every need.

"M'lud, the guests are invited for coffee in the Tapestry Room at five o'clock," the servant informed, then, bowing repeatedly, backed out of the Caligula suite.

Lord Middlebrook sighed, ordered his valet first to pull off his traveling boots and then unstrap a traveler's spirits case. In stockinged feet he wandered about sipping a glass of cognac.

"Not bad, Cousin Jerry, not bad. Still, 'tain't quite up to the Priapus Suite I usually occupy. Damn John Montagu!"

He dropped into a massive armchair to thrust feet towards a freshly kindled blaze. "Well, Cousin, let's hope your wardrobe proves adequate and that you'll soon get the feel of things hereabouts."

He cocked a brow. "How did your last sparring matches go?"

"Well enough," grinned Jeremy. "Put away several good partners without even breaking into a sweat. Never have felt in better shape."

"Stay so. No need to warn against overindulgence in any direction."

Lord Middlebrook paid no attention to his valet's silent unpacking — Jervis knew where to place what. Already he'd begun to brush out a variety of wigs and settle them on a row of blocks resembling human heads.

"Best see to your own baggage," directed Lord Middlebrook. "Tell your man where you want things put."

Jeremy nodded, sought his bedroom in which a lively blaze was crackling in a fireplace of ornately carved yellow-and-black marble above which hung a mirror etched with all manner of subtly erotic figures.

The rugs were so soft and deep the Colonial almost could fancy himself walking a mossy glade back home. The furniture, fashioned in that style favored by His Most Christian Majesty, Louis XV of France, looked dangerously delicate.

Rain began to drum even louder against windowpanes so Sir Francis's manservant hurried to draw draperies of dark-blue brocade.

Bath completed, Jeremy was astonished to find a complete set of garments already on his bed — well and good — but when the servant attempted to help him into his drawers he revolted and dismissed the fellow till it came time to arrange a lacy French jabot; he'd need help then, b'God.

He grinned at himself in the mirror. Lordy, lord! Like a small boy he suddenly stuck out his tongue at an incredible array of rouge pots, scent bottles and boxes containing rice powder.

In the powdering closet Jeremy allowed the valet to slip a loose-flowing gown over his new finery before seating himself. He then held over his face a gilded paper cone affixed to a handle to prevent inhaling too much of the hair powder whitening his wavy, dark-brown locks.

Came a rap on the door, then the man designated as his body servant appeared to offer a precisely folded piece of notepaper. "For you, sir."

Lord Middlebrook smiled across the sitting room. "My word! A gallant message already? Your Cupid's complexion is proving a richer asset than you imagine."

"Nothing like that. It's only that Sis — my sister — and Sir Guy want me to stop in to admire their Paphian Suite on my way to the Tapestry Room." To the valet he said, "Please tell Lady Constable I will stop by in a few minutes." Lord Middlebrook winced when Jeremy added, "There's a good fellow."

So Perdita was here! Criminently! *Why* had Sis been invited to Wycombe Hall for this occasion? True, he'd heard rumors that, presumably for thrills, jaded but wellborn ladies were given to participating in revels held by the Brimstone Club where, donning half-masks and scanty costumes, they could mingle incognito with fashionable courtesans, expensive mistresses and pretty whores imported from London's most fashionable bordellos.

Why? He choked over the possibility that Perdita willingly had come to participate in the Brotherhood's orgies. Might Guy have forced her? No. Not if he understood Sister at all, at all! Against her will, wild horses couldn't have dragged her under Sir Francis's roof.

"I say, Cousin Jerry, you *do* cut a rather dashing figure. Pray convey my compliments to your sister and Sir Guy; say I anticipate meeting 'em in the Tapestry Room."

Lord Middlebrook lifted a detaining, well-bejeweled hand. "Oh, by the by. Since there's to be no assembly of Friars tonight I deem it a fine opportunity to present you to some persons of note — remember well their names and titles."

The apparently genuine warmth of his brother-in-law's greeting was surprising. Sir Guy, all smiles, extended both hands and beaming, looked Jeremy squarely in the eye, exclaiming, " 'Pon my word, Jeremy Brett, 'tis a vast pleasure we can have this bit of time together."

Over a shoulder he called, "Dear God, 'Dita, *will* you stop preening? Your brother is here."

Lady Perdita Constable, eyes shining, came running out of her dressing room clutching a rouge pot and looking almighty lovely; her tall, generously curved figure was only sketchily concealed by a loose-fluttering dressing gown.

Jeremy kissed her soundly on the cheek as if they still were youngsters. "By God, Sis, ye're looking prettier than a speckled pup! But why paint yourself up like a Penobscot brave heading for the warpath? You've sufficient good looks without gilding the lily!"

Constable burst out laughing. "Jerry, you've made a point! With the rest of the ladies tinted like Pompeiian frescoes Perdita could draw a deal of attention by not trying to improve on Nature."

"Here *is* a swift switch!" gibed Perdita. "Aren't you always after me to paint and act like the Whore of Babylon?"

Once his wife had retreated to complete her toilette, Sir Guy offered a tortoiseshell snuffbox. On Jeremy's refusal he helped himself, sneezed delicately behind a heavily beringed hand, then flicked a few brown specks from a magnificently arranged jabot of Mechlin lace.

Looking up, he drawled, "Just before we left Town, 'Dita had a letter from home which wasn't too cheerful, I fear."

"Dashed unfortunate," he murmured as if to himself, "especially when a bill before the Navy Board is being considered. It provides for the replacement of naval vessels, wrecked or decayed. I know this is true since I hold a minor post at the Admiralty. Fear I don't often attend meetings — too boring and long-winded.

"Undoubtedly a substantial number of contracts would soon be let for 'plantation' or Colony-built vessels save for certain interested persons who are reviving rumors that New England vessels too often are poorly designed and built of inferior materials."

Recalling a conversation in Lord Middlebrook's study Jeremy reddened, *"That's not true!* By God, ship for ship, our yard and most others we know of can match design, quality and workmanship with the best hulls, spars and rigging British yards can turn out and one hell of a lot cheaper, too! Who's back of these lies?"

Sir Guy returned carelessly, "Damned if I know right now. If you wish, I'll find out what I can. Of course, a fat packet of graft is involved somewhere along the line.

"Ah, here's my exquisite Perdita!"

When Sir Guy again offered snuff Jeremy attempted a light manner, said pleasantly. "No, thanks. As the famous Mr. Wilkes once remarked, 'I have no time for minor vices.' "

"La, Jeremy, you've acquired a modish turn of phrase." Perdita dabbed a stray curl into place. "I say, Guy, has the Champion of Liberty arrived?"

"Yes. Only a short while back," supplied Jeremy.

"Then 'twill prove instructive to be on hand should John Wilkes and your compatriot, Dr. Franklin, discuss matters of political importance." He elevated a slender brow. "I say, Jeremy, d'you know how long Mr. Wilkes intends to linger?"

"Well, Sir Guy ——"

"Just 'Guy'; we're all of a family."

"Guy, then. Lord Middlebrook did remark that Mr. Wilkes intends leaving for London tomorrow morning."

"Why so early?"

"I know he sounds crazy but he intends to surrender at King's Bench Prison to demand imprisonment."

"Why the Devil should he court such an ordeal?" Perdita murmured.

"As I understand it, Mr. Wilkes intends to so embarrass the Government they'll be forced, first, to pardon him and thus end use of such general warrants as the one under which he was arrested a few years ago. This accomplished, they'll have no choice but to allow him to take his elected seat in Parliament."

Sir Guy chuckled. "God's love, that's rich! I'll wager that Whore-master Wilkes won't long remain in durance vile. Once news of his imprisonment gets about you'll see a mighty storm blow up. The mob fair worships the fellow — as do the American Colonists."

"Shouldn't wonder but you're right. At any rate, I hope so," Jeremy said.

He sensed Perdita's thoughts were straying. Wearing a scandal-ously décolleté red dressing gown, she was lolling on a dainty little armchair with a slipper dangling from the toes of a shapely leg slung in unladylike and revealing fashion over her chair's arm.

Dreamily she rolled great dark eyes while over her features spread a definitely libidinous expression foreign to Jeremy's experience. "La! I've heard so many weird and wonderful tales concerning the Friars of St. Lawrence I 'most can't wait for the fun to commence. Who knows, Guy, but we may experience some rare delights and prac-tices?"

The carefully made-up young nobleman — again wearing pale-blue face powder — laughed softly. "Have no doubt on that score, poppet! On our return to Bath we surely shall impress our most jaded playmates in concupiscence with new notions."

For Jeremy to credit his eyesight was proving difficult: could this indolent young sophisticate be the same girl who'd been reared in straitlaced Piscataqua? Good God! Right now golden-haired Perdita Brett seemed ready to commit any indiscretion!

Guy Constable quite unnecessarily went to readjust his lacy jabot before a mirror, drawling, " 'Tis predicted Lord Sandwich, among others, will provide very original entertainment at tomorrow eve-ning's convocation."

Perdita invited, "Is it true his *collier d'amour* numbers close on seventy pearls?"

"Aye. He's posted another thousand pounds at Brooks's they'll count a hundred before the New Year."

A throaty chuckle escaped Jeremy's sister. "Then 'tis likely a goodly supply of virgins are arriving in West Wycombe."

Laughed Sir Guy, "The more the merrier! Might even discover a couple for Jerry and my own good self."

36

Significant Interlude

⌒

LONG BEFORE A BELL in St. Lawrence's curious church steeple had struck two sonorous notes many of Sir Francis Dashwood's guests had offered sometimes amusing or transparent excuses to disappear in the direction of their sleeping quarters; a majority really were exhausted by travel or a surfeit of food and drink.

Those white-wigged gentlemen who remained downstairs, smoking, drinking, and conversing in Sir Francis Dashwood's oak-paneled library, displayed amazing vitality.

Lord le Despencer and Lord Middlebrook appeared as spry as if fresh-risen after a good night's slumber. Mr. Peregrine Falconer, more than ever resembling a heartbroken greyhound, remained in the background quietly observant and puffing on a short-stemmed clay pipe.

In dark brown Dr. Benjamin Franklin's broad and muscular form for the moment occupied a huge armchair to one side of the fireplace in which the blaze had been allowed to resolve into a rosy heap of coals. The Philosopher's eyes continued to shine clear, gray and steady behind rectangular lenses mounted in steel frames.

Opposite and facing him squarely sat John Wilkes. What with his abominable squint, misshapen lantern jaw and long yellow beak of a nose the politician, Jeremy long since had decided, was about as ugly as any man could be — a veritable human gargoyle.

So how was it possible for John Wilkes to be reputed almost irresistible to females of all ages and conditions? That this celebrated libertine once had won the almost immediate surrender of "la Charpillion," a famous beauty who firmly had repulsed the persuasive wooing of no less a champion seducer than Signor Giacomo Casanova de Seingalt, seemed utterly incredible.

Yet, despite his repulsive aspect, there was an indescribable and almost hypnotic attraction about John Wilkes.

At this late hour most of the company had relaxed and eased tight waistcoats, jabots and neckcloths; some even had doffed hot and heavy wigs. As for Dr. Franklin, he heaved a small sigh of relief after unbuttoning a turkey-red vest restraining his rotund little belly.

Soft-footed lackeys drifted about the smoke-veiled library pouring wines and brandy and exhibited astonishing memories about each guest's preferences; other servants deftly replaced guttering candles.

The company was adjusting themselves to a period of significant conversation when a slight commotion arose at the library's door. Heads swung about to witness the dramatic entrance of Charles Geneviève Louis Auguste Timothée Marie d'Éon de Beaumont, Chevalier of St. Louis and Captain of the French Royal Dragoons.

The slight figure's pearl-gray traveling cloak was marked by dark splashes of rain.

Raddled and vice-seamed features lighting, Sir Francis sprang up. "*Nom de Dieu!* If 'tain't the gallant Chevalier! Quite a surprise, *mon cher ami.* You really must be mad to travel after dark in such weather. Nevertheless, *soyez le bienvenu!*"

To many of the company, Peregrine Falconer, Lord Middlebrook, and Colonel Barré among others, this vivacious quick-gestured figure lightly advancing on high scarlet heels, for years had been fashionable Society's favorite, fascinating and so far insoluble enigma.

For once the Chevalier had left scant but fine and wavy light-brown hair unpowdered and drawn back and tied above the nape of his slender, dead-white neck. Devoid of facial hair, the Frenchman's skin shone so pink, fresh and glistening Jeremy experienced immediate sympathy.

He realized that the new arrival's dark eyes were brilliant and per ceptive without appearing to be. His voice sounded melodious and feminine.

The Chevalier d'Éon bowed respectfully to Dr. Franklin and Colonel Isaac Barré who had occupied a seat at the Philosopher's left.

The Frenchman greeted Lord Middlebrook warmly yet with a diplomatic detachment which implied no intimacy, then treated Mr. Falconer to a shrewd glance and an enigmatic quick smile before offering a hand to Jeremy, standing a few feet behind Middlebrook's chair. His aristocratically slender fingers closed in a grip powerful beyond belief.

Next the Chevalier greeted Lord Tilton, a towering, square-jawed and heavy-featured individual whose garments were rich but definitely passé in cut. "Country Gentleman" was written all over him.

Various guests deemed it wise to interrupt games of chess, backgammon or piquet to come forward and greet this unique apparition with varying degrees of sincerity. To Jeremy's dismay Sir Guy, obviously well into his cups, stifled a yawn, belched and, face heated with perspiration, prepared to take leave of his host. "Thousand thanks, Sir Francis — lavish hospitality. Mus' go now an' see if m' wife's lonesome or who the lucky fellow is she's got for comp'ny."

Other guests seized the opportunity to offer similar excuses and departed unsteadily towards that vast staircase leading to the second floor.

Geoffrey, Viscount Tilton of Denesmouth, ruddy, weatherbeaten features aglow from frequent visits to a bowl of arrack punch, stumped over to address Dr. Franklin. Said he in gruff but by no means offensive tones: "Doctor, deem it a pleasure — haw! — finally to meet a learned gentleman who though but a Colonial has achieved distinction in many directions. Haw!"

Franklin's pink, triangular-shaped and long-lipped mouth gradually parted. "You flatter me, my lord, beyond my just deserts. Do I sense a desire to discuss some topic?"

"Haw! Indeed so," boomed Lord Tilton. "I invite — haw! — your opinions concerning the Stamp Act's effect on our Colonies and the wisdom of its recent cowardly repeal. Eh?"

John Wilkes, standing before the mantelpiece beside his host lifted a Mephistophelian brow.

In no great hurry Dr. Franklin's clear gray eyes sought John

Wilkes's. Then said he equably, "My lord, it may come as a surprise to hear me state that, in my opinion, the Stamp Act and the Quartering Act both were entirely *legal* expressions of the Crown's sovereign authority." Slowly he inclined his massive head. "Yes, my lord, said laws were written and passed within the powers of Parliament. And yet, however legal their passage, a burning question remains — were these *wise* measures?"

Guests quit gaming tables to collect in a loose semicircle about the fireplace.

"Any erudite and reputable lawyer, my lord, will advise a client *not* what he is empowered to do but rather what humanity, reason and justice indicates he *ought* to do."

John Wilkes, grinning like a death's head, joined in, "Aye, Lord Tilton, if the exercise of sovereignty and the liberties of a people cannot be reconciled, then what course will a people of our own blood pursue if there is no hope of relief?

"Beyond doubt, they will defy sovereignty, however legal, to take up arms. Surely, my lord, no man of English blood or heritage can be coerced into accepting slavery!"

"Hear! Hear!" Sir Francis Dashwood accepted still another brandy from a footman perpetually hovering at his elbow and spoke with amazing force and clarity. "My dear Geoffrey, as my friend Dr. Franklin has pointed out on several occasions this so-called 'American Problem' arises chiefly from a conflict between fact and theory, which I venture lies near the roots of so many social upheavals."

Although other guests gradually closed in on the group before the fireplace Peregrine Falconer and the Chevalier d'Éon lingered in the background listening attentively.

Dr. Franklin resumed in soft but effective accents, "Please credit, Lord Tilton, no one can be more eager than I, nay more anxious, to effect a sincere reconciliation between the present Ministry and the North American Colonies."

Voice sharpening, he looked Lord Tilton straight in the eye and said not unpleasantly. "Any move towards America's demanding *independence* from the Mother Country to me is as abhorrent as it is unnecessary!"

Lord Tilton's shaggy brows elevated themselves. "Since you hold such views — haw! — what course do you recommend?"

Benjamin Franklin's gaze shifted to coals throbbing sleepily on the hearth; following a momentary pause, he said slowly, "My lord, if America is to remain under the sovereign sway of the Motherland, some appropriate mode of imperial organization will have to be devised to effect equitable conciliation of conflicting claims and dedicated to the advancement of rights and liberties dear to all Englishmen.

"Indeed, sir, I fear there *is* grave danger that in the near future the cold hand of legalism may freeze the blood of brotherly communication. Eh, Mr. Wilkes?"

A satanic twinkle appeared in the politician's straddled eyes. "Aptly put, Doctor, very aptly put! 'The cold hand of legalism may freeze the blood of brotherly communication.' Wish to God *I* had conceived so telling a phrase!"

The host lifted his glass and seemed to look through it at Colonel Barré — he whose name before long would, coupled with that of John Wilkes, be chosen for the name of a raw village growing on Pennsylvania's frontier.

"Tell me, Colonel," drawled Sir Francis, "ain't it true that thus far, at least, the Colonists have suffered *no* really grievous or unjust suppression at the hands of the Ministry?"

"In a strict sense I daresay not," admitted that lean-featured Irishman who had served with distinction as General Wolfe's Adjutant General at the Siege of Québec. "Nevertheless, my lord, I feel the Americans have just grounds for complaint in that their interests continually are being subordinated to those of English merchants trading with or in the New World."

Colonel Barré cast Benjamin Franklin a quick, sidewise look before continuing, "May I inform you, Lord Tilton, that, in 1760, British exports to the American Colonies were valued at two million pounds and that British merchants carried some four million pounds' worth of American debts on their books?

"Is it not obvious, therefore, that British tradesmen must *intimately* be concerned with our present Government's commercial policies towards the Colonists?"

Looking as if somewhere he had lost the thread of the conversation, Lord Tilton mopped heated, scarlet features. "Haw! The English landed gentry grow weary of paying, unassisted, for the recent war with France. Damme, why shouldn't the Americans bear at least

a part of that expense? Haw! After all, 'twas *their* frontiers and *their* security we were defending, eh what?"

His voice swelled. "Are you aware, Colonel, that the British public debt at present weighs to the extent of *eighteen pounds* per head per year on English taxpayers whilst only *eighteen shillings* per head per year is levied on Colonials? Indeed, we landowners consider ourselves the most grossly overtaxed people in all the world! I'm sure Lord Middlebrook and others present will agree to that. Haw!"

In a quick aside to Mr. Falconer the Chevalier murmured, "Apparently 'is Lordship 'as 'eard nothing about the eensufferable taxes paid by peasants and *petit bourgeois* een France!"

For a space the conversation degenerated into a number of still well-controlled disputes. In the heated atmosphere tinctured by tobacco smoke, wig powder, snuff, perspiration and perfumes candles burned dimly, created a penumbra which bathed the spacious, oak-paneled library in suffused amber tones.

Jeremy overheard Dr. Franklin saying, "What most arouses Americans is the Crown's forbidding them to print paper money of their own." He gazed mildly about, domed forehead faintly gleaming. "You can readily appreciate, gentlemen, that this prohibition of a freely circulating currency plus the threat of more and higher taxes furnishes radical leaders in America their strongest argument for immediate action."

Sir Francis, having lost much of his languid air, took a pinch of snuff before inquiring of the Postmaster General of the Colonies, "And what trouble has not been caused by the 'Declaratory Act' forbidding immigration or territorial extension of the Colonies westward of the Alleghenies?"

Unexpectedly Lord Middlebrook cut in. "I would say this Act was written for the benefit of important shareholders in the Hudson's Bay Company." He smiled thinly, "Among them number not a few illustrious members of the Government."

From the background Mr. Falconer's nasal voice added, "And certain Cabinet Ministers."

John Wilkes spoke so softly everyone strained to hear him. "True enough. Of course, the criminal stupidity of such a law lies in the fact that it cannot possibly be enforced.

"I believe Colonel Barré will bear me out that not even a great army could hope to restrain the steady flowing of settlers across the Allegheny Mountains into the Ohio country."

Lord Tilton snorted. "Oh, damme, ain't that overstating the case?"

Dr. Franklin's high-domed head swung slowly in his direction. "I fear not. The Declaratory Act is at once futile and a most dangerous move since it only prompts our Colonists to suspect — rightly or wrongly — that the British Crown intends to contain them along the coast while at the same time establishing beyond the mountains a *rival* economy more subservient to Parliament!"

Lord Middlebrook queried, "Tell me, Doctor, is it not true that American Colonial Assemblies are locally elected by persons very conscious of the power of their own purses?"

"Yes. As a rule that is so."

"Then in other words — do they not, because of this, object mightily to being required to pay salaries and upkeep for Royal governors and other Crown officials — all too often impoverished titled nonentities, rakes, bankrupts and discarded courtiers who, the Americans feel, are being foisted upon them?"

Benjamin Franklin heaved himself to his feet, stared into the coals. "Considerable truth lies in your observation, my lord. But that is only one of many grievances; for example, take the Sugar Act which forces us to buy sugar, rum and molasses *only* from the British West Indies and at a much higher price than that demanded in French, Dutch and Spanish possessions."

"Is there any present danger of rebellion?" queried someone.

To Jeremy's astonishment Dr. Franklin addressed his reply to him. "I believe, Mr. Brett, you are a native of New England and only recently arrived here; perhaps you will answer this question. Tell us, when you departed, what was the trend of public opinion in your region?"

"Distinguished sir, if the Crown's moves towards conciliation ain't quickly considered and speedily acted on, people in my part of the country are getting ready to take up arms."

Wilkes frowned, stroked his long, cleft chin. "Do these people really crave independence?"

"I don't believe so, sir. All they want is free trade and swift recognition of rights and liberties."

"And eef the Colonials elect to fight," queried the Chevalier smoothly, "what will 'appen then?"

Rasped Lord Tilton, "Bah, such a disordered and undisciplined rabble as they can field will be crushed by British Regulars like ants beneath a grenadier's boots."

Lord Middlebrook grinned at the way Jeremy flared right up. "Don't be too sure about that! If the Colonies combine and act together — I think Dr. Franklin already has expressed views on the advisability of united action — then American fighting power is not be despised!"

"Surely you exaggerate," snapped Lord Tilton.

Only by effort did Jeremy keep his voice level. "If you think so, sir, I invite you to remember what happened back in '45 when New Englanders combined and raised an army that captured the fortress of Louisburg."

"Where's that?" queried John Wilkes.

The Chevalier supplied, "Eet stood on Cape Breton Island."

Jeremy continued, "My father's ships served as transports for the expedition commanded by Sir William Pepperell. Two of my uncles died there."

"Louisburg?" Lord Tilton snorted. "Haw! Some insignificant wooden fort, I trow."

"*Non*, Milor'," instantly d'Éon cut in, painted features infinitely strained and sad. "Louisburg was one magneeficent fortress built of stone and designed by the great Vauban 'imself — like Verdun, Metz and Lille. Een France, Louisburg once was known as *le Gibraltar Américaine*."

"And what," prompted Mr. Falconer, "happened when this 'undisciplined rabble' of New Englanders besieged it?"

The Chevalier d'Éon recovered himself, head-bowed in Lord Tilton's direction. "Permeet me to eenform, m'sieur. *Hélas*, the Englees — 'Yankees' as the Indians name your countrymen," he smiled at Jeremy, "captured those great stone fortifications with no 'elp from 'Is Majesty's Regular troops. *Quelquechose d'extraordinaire!*"

"Haw!" huffed Viscount Tilton, pulpy nose going rich puce as he faced Dr. Franklin. "Is this Frog-eater — er, I mean this French gentleman, giving us an exact account?"

The balding head inclined. "My lord, he does not exaggerate. Unfortunately, no mention has been made that without the Royal

Navy's generous aid our Provincial troops could have accomplished very little."

Said Lord Middlebrook, "Ah, yes, naval power is the key to such campaigns — do the Colonies realize that?"

"They are beginning to appreciate it," Colonel Barré said and John Wilkes's narrow head inclined agreement.

For the first time Jeremy made bold to speak out. "Sirs, us New Englanders sure were disappointed when after we'd captured Louisburg at the cost of many lives and much treasure the King's Ministers soon *gave Louisburg back to the French,* who right away started sending Indian raids against us again and they fitted out privateers and pirates to plunder our ports and ravage our shipping."

For support he looked hard at Colonel Barré. "That went on till General Wolfe captured Louisburg again. This time, thank God, its fortifications were razed to the ground. Ask Dr. Franklin whether the memory of the Crown's return of Louisburg has been forgotten in New England."

Interpolated John Wilkes, "Surely, the Ministry must recognize this valid resentment and move to assuage it."

Towards the end of Jeremy's outburst Lord le Despencer's major-domo appeared to announce that a collation was ready. The guests promptly sought the refreshments and commenced to relax.

It was easy to tell where lay most of the guests' sympathies when several gentlemen followed Viscount Tilton to one end of the freshly replenished sideboard. Others accompanying the Chevalier and Mr. Falconer refilled glasses pointedly apart.

The Postmaster General of the North American Colonies carried his drink back to the fireplace and stood toasting a broad back. "Yes, Mr. Wilkes," he was heard to say, "I believe reconciliation can be effected *provided* the Colonies are not, through stupidity or greed on the part of certain Ministers, goaded into presenting a united front. Surely, the recent adoption of Non-Importation Agreements by Massachusetts, Virginia and New York must serve as an unmistakable warning signal?"

Lord Middlebrook broke away from discussion of a recent prize-fight and drew near, inquiring, "Heard of such — what do they mean? Maybe my cousin can explain."

"Why, they're a solemn agreement among Colonists to purchase no more goods made in the British Isles or imported in British bottoms until the unjust — and as we hold, illegal — import duties are lifted; the cost to both sides will be great."

"Rather imagine the pinch will be greater on the Colonists," ventured Colonel Barré.

"You are right there, sir," Jeremy stated. "Even before I left many merchants' shelves were empty, trade had started to stagnate, and many shipyards were idle for want of orders. Naturally, British merchants can't or won't deal with us so long as these Agreements remain in effect."

"True enough," said Colonel Barré. "British merchants are howling bloody murder."

Dr. Franklin turned to Lord Tilton. "Can you imagine the result if such Agreements spread to the other Colonies and there is a general embargo on British trade?"

"Hear! Hear!" cried Colonel Barré. Then he added in subtly meaningful tones, "Wouldn't it be *most* unfortunate if certain of the King's Friends chose this time to send troops to break such an embargo before it can be fully implemented?"

Lord Tilton scowled. "By that ambiguous statement, sir, I deduce you are averse to Parliamentary moves which might bring on a clash?"

"My lord," replied the Irishman evenly, "you are at liberty to interpret my remark as you please; such is the prerogative of any freeborn Englishman, home-grown or otherwise."

Uneasy silence was terminated when the Chevalier d'Éon addressed Jeremy. "Een the event of a rebellion, do you t'ink the Colonies weel be able to defend themselves on the sea?"

"We would make a damned good try at it!"

" 'Ow so? You 'ave no sheeps of war."

"We could build some — and we know how — having constructed many men-of-war for the Royal Navy."

Scattered laughter made the stiflingly hot library resound. "What! Blue-nosed Yankees challenge the Royal Navy?" "Absurd!" "In a few weeks their pitiable vessels would be swept from the seas — ain't that so, Doctor?"

Franklin was forced to nod.

Jeremy, big hands balled as if entering a ring, said stiffly, "Of course we couldn't hope to meet the world's mightiest fleet in battle but we sure could hurt English trade so badly they'd be ready to call quits before long. And don't imagine we don't know plenty about commerce raiding!" While speaking he became aware of the Chevalier's lustrous dark eyes fixed thoughtfully upon him.

John Wilkes and Colonel Barré were exhanging glances when Mr. Falconer drawled, "How so, friend Jerry?"

"As I've already told you — back in '45, we scraped together a Provincial navy of sorts to fight at Louisburg and in addition put to sea a swarm of armed merchantmen and privateers calculated to raise hob with French shipping along our coasts and overseas. Perhaps our friend the Chevalier recalls — ?"

"Oui, ver' well. But, Monsieur Brett, do the Colonies at present own many merchant vessels capable of being convert' eento private sheeps-of-war?"

"Not many," admitted the New Englander. "After all, sir, as a rule our yards don't turn out merchantmen with sufficient speed or canvas to cruise in wartime — they're mostly designed as roomy cargo carriers. Still, I reckon we soon could build a lot of fast merchantmen if we need to."

A sly smile appeared on Mr. Falconer's lean features and the Chevalier nodded almost imperceptibly. Lord Middlebrook noted both reactions. That the Chevalier d'Éon was an agent of Louis XV was an open secret about London, but what might lie behind Peregrine Falconer's evident interest?

Dr. Franklin pursed mobile pink lips and appeared thoughtful. Various other guests belched, yawned and excused themselves and drifted out of the library.

Soon only Sir Francis Dashwood, Lord Middlebrook and Jeremy Brett lingered, red-eyed and perspiring. Having partaken of hardly any liquor Jeremy yearned for rest.

While refilling his cognac glass for the twentieth time at least Sir Francis Dashwood seemed to read the Colonial's mind; he turned to Lord Middlebrook and said, "I say, George, 'tis indeed a pleasure to welcome your American cousin. Ain't I heard it bruited about that he's uncommon handy with his dukes? That so?"

"In my opinion, Boston Jerry — which incidentally is the name he fights under — is skilled so far above the average boxer I'm backing his chances rather heavily against Jemmy Twitcher's champion."

"How much?"

"Ten thousand pounds."

Jeremy could only blink.

37

Lady Frances Fane

⁓

FEELING SURPRISINGLY FRESH despite a surfeit of champagne followed by an enthusiastic tumble with a bold and charmingly persuasive but still unidentified gallant who, before dawn, had wandered into her room and bed, Lady Perdita Constable squirmed between damp and rumpled sheets away from her snoring husband who undoubtedly had not, straightaway, sought the connubial couch if the condition of his small clothing indicated anything.

Half out of her nightrail, Perdita sought the attiring closet, where her maid handed her a note. It was from Lady Frances Fane, a lazily voluptuous brunette beauty nearing early middle age. Early on, Fanny Fane had vouchsafed that her enormously wealthy and blasé husband was on a voyage to Bengal to conduct business with the East India Company.

Lady Frances, Perdita had decided, was hopelessly willful, lovely and useless as an orchid. She spoke in a deceptively simple and childish manner which, compounded by round and slightly vacant vivid blue eyes and full lips the color of ripe pomegranates, lent her a doll-like aspect.

Despite her disarming aspect, Lady Frances Fane, Perdita had heard, was presumed to have forgotten more about varied and complicated vices than many an accomplished French or Italian courtesan knew.

The note suggested that she and Lady Constable take breakfast in company. Mercy, something must be in the air when such a lady of *bon ton* composed a note at the deplorably unfashionable hour of ten!

When, an hour later, breakfast trays were being removed, Perdita, who'd waited in vain to discover what was on Lady Frances's mind, stifled a small yawn. "Well, Fanny, and how are we to amuse ourselves? Short of a catastrophe there won't be a gentleman upright till midday. I left Guy puffing like a whiskery grampus. I'm dying of boredom."

Archly, Lady Frances glanced out of the window. "Word has it you were well occupied late last night."

Hot color suffused Perdita's neck and almost completely exposed bosom. "Why, why, yes, but the — er, visitation was most unexpected ——"

"And therefore all the more exciting. Was he young? Virile?"

"Couldn't have been better served," Perdita laughed, then hurriedly changed the subject. "What have you in mind for this morning?"

Full and scarlet-painted mouth forming a lazy little *moue*, Lady Fane murmured, "Fearing an attack of *ennui*, I have conceived a project which should banish any trace of *accidia* by visiting the Brotherhood's seraglio better known as the 'Nunnery' or, less attractively, termed the 'Hen House'?"

"Nunnery?"

" 'Tis where the Club members put up females of the common sort till they are summoned to join in profligate pleasures.

"I propose we pay the place a visit. I'll summon my chariot and we can at our leisure inspect this haven of religious piety and harbor for sacrificial virgins."

Said Perdita after having recovered a measure of poise, "A very pretty notion, my dear Fanny, but first will you be a dear and tell me something? Guy's such a dreadful tease." To her annoyance she flushed. "Is it indeed so that, er — ladies of birth and rank who attend the revels go garbed like girls from the Nunnery?"

Lady Frances's ringleted, dark head inclined and she spoke lazily, "Aye, dear 'Dita. Therein lies half the fun. Each one of us 'Dollymops,' as we're called, will wear a nun's habit colored red as the flames of hell and a black half-mask which must *never be removed under any conditions*; an inviolable rule to be observed by the Friars and guests alike. I repeat: anyone entering the Caverns beneath St. Lawrence's obscene church must *never* remove their mask so there can be no telling for sure who really is who — or what!"

"I see. And what do we wear 'neath a nun's robe?"

Lady Frances giggled like a schoolgirl. "Nothing at all, dear simpleton, except the smooth skin in which you were born, with the exception of high-heeled slippers and silken hose gartered in colors of one's own choosing."

Perdita laughed a trifle nervously and relapsed into familiar accents. "Now I swan, it should rouse some lively sensations to sit at supper jay-naked 'neath a single robe."

Indolently Lady Frances directed a personal maid to comb her hair into a chignon and secure it in a net of dark-crimson thread. " 'Dita, does the prospect give you pause?"

"Not really. All this is so new and thrilling and I hanker for fresh excitement — truly I do." A deep breath raised and half-exposed full and symmetrical breasts into effective prominence.

"Then you're willing to join wholeheartedly in whatever — er, diversions lie in store?"

Once the tiring maid had disappeared Perdita leaned forward. "I will confide, dearest Fanny, that ever since Guy and I were bidden as guests of Lord Middlebrook I've anticipated this visit and am prepared to abandon myself to joining in the revels — no matter what their nature."

Lady Frances's round blue eyes glistened. "Would it make me a closer friend if I were to confess that I have taken the motto '*Fay ce que voudras*' very much to heart?"

Perdita nodded eagerly. "To what direction did your fancy guide you last night?"

"Being indisposed, I contented in calling in a handsome footman who was assigned to my suite." Again she emitted a schoolgirlish giggle.

"What do you make of Jeremy?" Perdita asked.

"All I can, darling. There's a real Hercules for you — plenty of

staying power I warrant so be warned, I intend to try his mettle ere we quit Wycombe Hall."

Perdita's gaze sought a lovely Aubusson beneath their feet. "Then good luck, Fanny dear; trust he won't disappoint you."

Lady Frances glanced out into the clear morning sunlight, murmured, "One doubts, 'Dita, you've yet drunk your fill from Pleasure's cup, so remember Sir Francis's motto and do whatever you wish.

"And Guy?" Lazily her gaze seemed to caress the smooth oval of Perdita's features, fresh and unlined beneath a hurried application of powder and rouge. "He's not yet fallen victim to *accidia*, has he?"

"No, but I'm not sure he's really cut out for a fashionable macaroni; at bottom he's but a sporting country squire."

Perdita lowered her voice. "Fanny, I feel I can rely on your discretion; Guy cannot much longer afford our *ménage* in London. God knows how deep he's mired in debt; this jaunt to West Wycombe may well prove our final fling. I intend to make the most of it."

Perdita arose amid fragrant swirls of her dressing gown. "Tell me, darling. When comes the Order's Grand Convocation in the Caverns?"

"Tomorrow night, Sir Francis tells me." Lady Frances smoothed her gown over sleek yet generous hips. "Tonight is held the Friars' New Pleasures Contest; would that females might attend."

"What is this 'New Pleasures Contest'?"

" 'Tis a competition in which Club members stage various skits or tableaux. A thousand pounds, I believe, is to be awarded to the Brother presenting the most original entertainment. Now, dearest 'Dita, I'll order a chariot readied within the hour."

At a smart trot a coachman wearing Lord le Despencer's sky-blue-and-white livery sent the graceful vehicle whirling along a white-pebbled drive wandering through pretty little spinneys and wooded nooks until it swerved close to the bank of a silvery, reed-bordered pond on the far side of which stood a little Grecian temple, dainty as a cameo, set against a background of green velvet. So artistically had it been sited amid a group of weeping willows that Perdita on impulse ordered the driver to pull up.

Inevitably, the shrine sheltered a piece of erotic statuary — in this case Mars and Venus entangled in the throes of ecstasy.

A gleaming white swan glided near, trailed by a brood of three bright-eyed and slate-gray cygnets. Farther out a huge cob swam in nervous circles until, great wings slowly flapping, he pattered over the surface until airborne. Vividly the flight reminded Perdita of a Canada honker departing a pond near Piscataqua.

Only mildly interested, Lady Fane queried, "What can have alarmed the bird? Ah! Someone's swimming out yonder."

From behind a clump of reeds appeared the head of a man cleaving the water with slow and powerful strokes which brought him nearer at a surprising rate.

Commenced Lady Fane, "Who could be so daft as to swim merely for pleasure?"

Perdita touched her arm. "Jerusha! 'Tis Dr. Franklin!"

"Can't be! No scholar would take exercise in so plebeian a fashion!" Lady Frances suddenly giggled when the swimmer drew near, powerful white body free of covering. "I'm wrong, 'Dita! Five pounds to you if yonder's not your fellow American."

"I recall hearing that when your eminent compatriot arrived, near-penniless, in London long years ago he for a time supplemented his earnings in the printing business by instructing sprigs of the rich and noble in the art of swimming."

Stringy brown hair eddying behind him Benjamin Franklin swam leisurely to within a few yards of the chariot then, grinning, waved a dripping hand, "Ladies, I can truthfully praise the water's temperature. Dismiss your carriage for a while and join me. In so secluded a place lovely naiads no more require bathing costumes than the goddesses of antiquity."

Perdita broke out laughing, recalled a few occasions when she'd slipped away with a few intimates to go swimming — "skinny dips," as the local phrase went — in a freshwater pond hidden in the heart of a pine forest at a safe distance from the Piscataqua's always icy waters.

"Hail to thee, Father Neptune!" Lady Frances's childish laughter rippled like a satin ribbon unrolling. "Alas, we are but poor, land-bound nymphs owning no skill in the deeps."

Benjamin Franklin's laughter rang across the still, bright waters so heartily that the swan quickly herded her offspring to safety among the rushes. "Off with your garments ladies and I'll soon remedy that; I am indeed a qualified instructor."

The merriment in his level gray eyes shifted to Perdita's. "Surely,

Lady Constable, you, American-born, must possess proficiency in the natatory art?"

Jeremy's sister blew a kiss towards that still-stalwart, pink-white figure so easily treading water. "Tomorrow, perhaps, Doctor. Right now we're on our way to the Nunnery of St. Lawrence."

The Philosopher offered a watery wink. "Then pray offer my humble service to those secluded neophytes and say I anticipate enjoying their elevating company."

In the act of turning away, Dr. Franklin called, "By the bye, Lady Constable, I met your brother last evening — a most interesting young man. Please invite him to drop in at my rooms for a chat.

"And now I fear, 'tis a case of *vale, vale, et si semper, indesemper vale, vale!*"

The Postmaster General for the North American Colonies, flashing ample buttocks, then dived and only surfaced a good fifty yards away.

Shortly before the chariot returned to the main approach to the Nunnery, a huge traveling coach rumbled into sight from the direction of West Wycombe Hall drawn by four matched grays and guided by white-wigged postilions in Sir Francis Dashwood's livery.

Drawled Lady Fane, "Now which of our fellow guests d'you suppose is being sent home in style?"

Curiosity became satisfied when the ponderous vehicle rolled by to disclose the sharply contrasting visages of Mr. John Wilkes and the Chevalier d'Éon; they blew kisses, called out extravagant compliments and lamented the cruel necessity of a premature departure.

Lady Frances settled gracefully back in the chariot's deep cushions and for once appeared thoughtful. "Let us pray dear Mr. Wilkes don't encounter Lord Sandwich along the London road. Once the closest of boon companions, they are now at daggers drawn — have been for years."

"Why the change?"

"Oh, the reasons are many but their real hatred commenced after Wilkes devised a famous practical joke which made Jemmy Twitcher the ignominious butt. If I remember right the occasion was when members of the Brimstone Club were known as the 'Monks of Medmenham' and convened in Medmenham Abbey instead of in the Caverns of St. Lawrence."

"And what was this jape?" queried Perdita tightening a kerchief securing wavy, gold-brown hair.

253

"In those days the Brotherhood practiced all manner of blasphemous rites, dabbled in sorcery and celebrated the Black Mass. 'Twas during one of these Black Masses that John Wilkes — he apparently never took a real interest in Satanism — felt prompted to play a clever joke on the Rape-Master General.

"At that time a Barbary ape was kept at Medmenham — Julian, my darling husband, said 'twas presented to the Club by one of the Van Sittarts. Well, quite secretly Wilkes ordered a devil's costume cut to fit this ape — scarlet doublet, cape, horned cap and all.

"Next he caused a secret compartment built directly behind the Abbey's sacrilegious altar.

"Once the Black Mass got into stride and Lord Sandwich and his fellow demon-worshippers were imploring Satan to appear, Johnny Wilkes jerked a cord to release the baboon which, screeching loudly, leapt onto the altar, knocked over a chalice abrim with some poor virgin's menstrual blood then, of all things, jumped squarely onto Jemmy Twitcher's shoulders!

"He, like most of the Friars, believed that His Satanic Majesty indeed had appeared! Sandwich, Julian told me, gibbered in terror, fell onto his knees, and groveled on the floor, all the while imploring Satan's mercy."

Skillfully shaped woods and broad lawns rolled by unnoticed while Perdita laughed more wholeheartedly than she had in weeks. "What then, Fanny dear?"

"Julian said the scarlet-caparisoned ape, chattering all the while, bounded about the Chapel and sent that congregation of hardened sinners into paroxysms of terror until finally it escaped through a window."

Assuming a distinctly unladylike attitude, Frances Fane braced satin slippered feet against drop-seats opposite and allowed the breeze to blow under prettily billowing frothy petticoats and up between wide-parted legs.

"For mercy's sake continue!"

"Wilkes, of course, was convulsed with merriment and so were a few other sensible worshippers but Sandwich and most of those obscene monks were livid with rage and shame. When in due course John Wilkes was found out, Jemmy swore never to pardon him and conceived for the Champion of Liberty a burning and undying hatred.

"Small wonder, then, our host speeds Mr. Wilkes on his way before Lord Sandwich can put in an appearance."

Once the chariot turned into a long, tree-lined avenue at the end of which loomed the Nunnery, Perdita shot a sidewise glance at her companion. "Why the thoughtful look? Haven't we only amusement in store?"

Lady Frances Fane laughed softly. "I was conjecturing on why the Chevalier d'Éon *also* should be departing and in Mr. Wilkes's company. Which presents another famous question — is the gallant Chevalier male or female?"

"No one knows for sure?"

"No although many, including a brother of mine called Robin, once dueled with the Chevalier for five thousand pounds against visual disclosure of his nature."

"Since nobody knows d'Éon's sex I must presume your brother lost?"

"Aye, Robin damn near lost his silly life for all he was one of the best épées in or about London. Broke his neck the next year, fox hunting, pity."

38

The Nunnery

AMID A JINGLE OF HARNESS the chariot's driver pulled up before the Nunnery entrance to have its passengers greeted with sedate formality by a patrician-appearing female. Mrs. Elizabeth Roach — actually keeper of one of the most fashionable brothels in London — also was appointed by Sir Francis to preside as "abbess" over the Nunnery and its lovely inmates.

Perdita was astounded how convincingly this tall, thin and ascetic-appearing purveyor of carnal pleasures counterfeited the role of a religious administrator.

Mrs. Roach curtsied deeply to the visitors and was mimicked in the background by Mrs. Stanhope, tricked out in the robes of a mock Mother Superior, snowy wimple, inverted gilt crucifix, diabolic rosary and all.

"My ladies," the Abbess declared in refined tones, " 'tis indeed an honor for this poor religious house to be called upon by such distinguished company. Is it too early to offer a refreshing dish of tea?"

Mrs. Stanhope's beady little eyes lingered speculatively on Perdita Constable. Coo! Here *was* a rarely handsome and well-formed number, with a fascinating and definitely passionate look about her mouth. Why should she be visiting Wycombe Hall at this time?

Airily, Lady Fane confessed desire to learn and understand certain terms, words and phrases likely to be employed during the impending revels.

While the Abbess poured tea with a sure hand the visitors learned that in this spacious and pleasantly sunny retreat the "guests" or inmates fell into three principal categories.

"First," explained Mrs. Roach, lifting a bony finger, "come the 'Dollymops,' also known to members of the Brimstone Club as 'Demi-reps' or *'Filles'* " — she pronounced it "fillies" — *"de joie de bon ton*. All are ladies of high social position, married and strict amateurs. Such 'Dollymops' attend banquets wearing black half-masks and nun's habits of gray-and-scarlet silk and are expected to enter into the — ahem — exercises to experience rare degrees of novelty and excitement" — Mrs. Roach smiled sadly — "and very often to escape the mechanical tedium of their marriage beds."

Eager not to be ignored, Mrs. Stanhope amplified, "Then we have 'Sisters' or 'Nuns,' smart prostitutes introduced by protectors or patrons. Such females are beautiful and quite as young as are our own well-taught nymphs. These also wear half-masks and their habits are scarlet to distinguish them from Dollymops."

Appearing more than a trifle annoyed over being interrupted by her colleague Mrs. Roach raised a third, claw-like finger. "Finally, there are the 'Does,' all very young girls, inexperienced and reputedly still in possession of their maidenheads. Fittingly, such buds of beauty are crowned with flowers, costumed in a single dazzling white robe and are forbidden the use of paint or jewelry. Usually their hair falls unbound down their backs in sweet, innocent fashion."

"Ah, so it's 'Dollymops,' 'Nuns' and 'Does,' eh?" remarked Frances Fane. "What picturesque designations!"

From the depths of this long, L-shaped, ivy-shrouded stone structure sounded occasional bursts of high-pitched feminine laughter. Following a particularly loud outburst of merriment Lady Frances raised a slender brow. "I say, what can be inspiring your charges to such wholehearted gaiety?"

Gray-and-white robes rustling, Mrs. Roach readjusted a well-starched and wide-winged coif. "It might amuse you, m'ladies, to discover for yourselves what may be taking place. Our neophytes are such bold and naughty creatures they may be up to anything."

Eagerly Lady Fane arose. "Why not? Coming, 'Dita?"

"Yes, but suppose I explore in another direction? Later we can exchange our findings."

Mrs. Stanhope, scenting an opportunity to further appraise the possibilities of this luscious young aristocrat, immediately suggested, "Come with me, m'lady, to the North Wing where we'll doubtless find many devout and dedicated ladies occupied" — the beldame winked — "in telling their beads! This way, m'lady." Habit billowing like gray sails, she headed for the staircase.

At a stately pace, the Abbess led Lady Fane in the opposite direction down a corridor off which opened a number of bedrooms tenanted by bright-eyed, half-naked young females occupied in altering and fitting nun's habits, coifs and wimples.

A few large and handsomely furnished bedrooms evidently had been allocated to pampered, high-class mistresses and courtesans. These females had a room to themselves or, probably through choice, shared it with another lovely of similar station. Invariably, these curtsied and viewed Lady Fane with envious curiosity.

In smaller rooms several amazingly pretty girls lounged, half-dressed, on couches or beds. Some occupied themselves with curling tongs heated over little charcoal braziers; others practiced songs or more or less mechanically rehearsed simple dance steps.

In a large chamber at the hallway's end Frances Fane caught her breath, for at one end of it the sinuous, pink-and-white forms of four quite naked girls were collected busily trying on exotic costumes.

Informed Mrs. Roach, pointing to a statuesque blonde young woman, "Yonder is Henneke, one of Betty Stanhope's more pleasing houris. She's been chosen to be captain of Lord Middlebrook's Corps of Valkyries."

" 'Lord Middlebrook's Corps of Valkyries'? What *can* dear George be up to?"

The ascetic-appearing Abbess dropped her gaze, looked uncomfortable. "Sorry, m'lady, I'm sworn to keep his purpose secret."

Color heated Lady Frances's smooth cheeks when these pretty creatures with pale rounded limbs agleam and breasts elevated placed on their heads helmets of silvered cardboard from either side of which flared glistening crows' wings.

Catching her breath, Sir Julian Fane's wife viewed this pattern of supple bodies bending, moving in unconscious grace while binding ribbons in crisscross patterns above buskins of white kid topped with snowy rabbit fur.

On perceiving the presence of Lady Fane the girl called Henneke smilingly ordered her three subordinates to attention, then employed a long-handled whip adorned with fluttering black ribbons to dress them into line before solemnly saluting the Abbess and the visitor.

"Girls, girls!" prompted Mrs. Roach, suddenly shrill. "Don shields and weapons, y' doxies."

Giggling, these graceful female "warriors" scattered briefly, then lined up again, firm rounded breasts aquiver; each now wore strapped to her left arm a small, round shield of gilded papier-mâché and with her right hand awkwardly saluted with whips similar to the one carried by their tall, blonde captain.

The Abbess then led Lady Fane to an adjacent room in which another quartet of nude Nuns were costuming themselves — this time as Amazons. Each girl already had donned a gilded mock-Grecian helmet of the Classic Age crested by bright green ostrich feathers. For footgear these feminine "warriors" wore knee-high cothurns of gilded leather and zones of the same material designed to afford scarce-needed support to erect and snowy bosoms.

Apparently care had been exercised in the selection of these antagonists-to-be. Quite as tall and lithe as Henneke was Gwen, captain of the Amazons, a handsome, raven-haired Welsh girl with a wide, red mouth and sparkling, dark-blue eyes.

Her companions, in Frances Fane's opinion, more or less accurately matched the build of the blonde Dutch girl's team.

At the Abbess's behest the Amazons paired up and faced off. Flourishing ribboned whips they closed in and, emitting bursts of high-pitched laughter, tentatively lashed out at one another. With helmets canting askew about glossy heads they ducked, danced about, and used make-believe shields to avert halfhearted swipes.

"Don't be misled, m'lady," muttered Mrs. Roach. "For all they're not aware of it, tomorrow night the girls won't attack each other with such toys."

At the moment Lady Fane wondered how far such simulated warfare would go towards winning for Lord Middlebrook Sir Francis Dashwood's grand prize.

On the floor above, Perdita was being less vividly but equally well entertained. In one room a pair of badly frightened Does of thirteen or fourteen, freshly scrubbed and toweled, were having their under-arms shaved.

A couple of the half-dozen Does, shamefully brazen and incredibly foul-mouthed, were strutting about patting meager breasts and boasting that despite slum origins they somehow had retained their maidenheads.

In a small, pleasant room at the far end of the corridor along which Mrs. Stanhope conducted her, Perdita found a really exquisite young girl with long, auburn hair busily stitching on a garment of very sheer white silk. Noting Mrs. Stanhope's massive figure in the doorway, this girl lowered dark-blue eyes, stopped her sewing and arose to curtsy gracefully once, twice and again.

"This, m'leddy," cackled the Mother Superior, "is Dolly Lawton, rather a pet of mine."

Perdita smiled warmly, wondering what was so very appealing about this winsome and modest-appearing maid. Was it because the Lawton girl was approximately of her own height — inches above the average — and of a remarkably similar build?

Evidently this girl was altering her costume after trying it on for, at the moment, she was clad only in shoes and a knee-length cotton undershift. Her cleanly modeled features were so regular and deli-cate Perdita decided she could pass amid any gathering of the so-cially elect; moreover, there was a sensitivity and intelligence about her large and lively eyes, becomingly fringed with long black lashes.

"Lady Constable, Dolly's been reserved for my Lord Sandwich's delectation. The gel's well-mannered, sweet-natured and is educated far above her station."

Abruptly Perdita Constable became aware of a searching expression in this Doe's eyes and was astonished to experience a burgeoning of interest in Dolly Lawton.

She stepped inside the room, reassured. "No need to stand in awe of me, Dolly. I'm from the North American Colonies and am titled only through marriage."

Dolly nodded imperceptibly and for the first time met her gaze squarely. "Thank you, my lady."

"How does yer costume fit, ducky?" Mrs. Stanhope queried.

" 'Tis too early to tell, ma'am," Dolly replied in rich undertones which quavered a little.

"Well, then, I'll be up later to see to yer fitting. Ye've got to look yer worth tomorrow night."

"I'll do my best, ma'am. You may be sure of that."

On impulse Perdita Constable assumed a suddenly formal manner and turned to Mrs. Stanhope. "Go seek out Lady Fane, say I will join her in the admittance office within a few moments."

"Yes, m'leddy. I'll inform her Leddyship instanter."

Once Dolly's preceptress, looking considerably nonplussed, had waddled out of the bedroom, Perdita seated herself on the bed, then slowly smoothed her skirts and peered so intently into the young girl's rosy-white features that, thanks to recent experiences, Dolly quite misinterpreted her motive. Blushing furiously, she caught up her Doe's costume to stand poised for retreat, clutching the garment before her.

Perdita's clear laughter rippled. "Oh, for God's sake, Dolly, don't fear; I've not yet succumbed to the wiles of naughty old Sappho of Greece!

"Dolly," she continued smoothly, "do I detect about you an air of refinement scarce to be expected in this highly spiritual retreat? Come, try on your sacrificial robe for me. Lord knows why I'm interested but perhaps 'tis because I notice that in general we somewhat resemble one another." She smiled encouragingly. "Might even be related; 'tis legend my grandsire — a lusty wencher if ever there was one — traveled far and wide about England."

For the first time alone with a lady of quality Dolly Lawton again blushed furiously, was at sixes and sevens about what to say or do; ended by mumbling, "Ye-yes, m'lady, perhaps you'll instruct me how best to — to make this — this garment fit?"

So saying, Dolly stepped smoothly out of her half-shift, then drew on the white robe but so swiftly she afforded only a glimpse of glistening, perfectly proportioned buttocks, back and limbs shining below her mane of auburn hair.

Perdita was thinking: better make sure my own habit fits as smartly as Fanny's or the rest of us Dollymops'.

For her part Dolly Lawton was experiencing uncertainty about the effect of this unexpected element on carefully worked-out plans.

Since her visitor remained seated and indolent she decided she'd perhaps misunderstood the motives behind this patrician young lady's implied offer of friendship?

Perdita, sitting up on the bed's edge, invited, "Is your virgin knot still tight?"

The small auburn head dipped shyly. " 'Fore God, m'lady, it still is — my only recommendation to fortune."

"And why have you determined on this course? Too good for menial work, is that it?"

Dolly's eyes flashed. "No, m'lady! I never have feared hard work. Ever since I can remember I've toiled and drudged about the parsonage. No, I don't shun hard work but it, well — it's come to seem a waste of time when perhaps I could better myself, live in comfort, travel and maybe play a part in high society."

Puzzled, Perdita said softly and without condescension, "Are you some great gentleman's by-blow?"

The pride evident in this young creature's manner as her big eyes filled was astonishing. "With all respect, ma'am, I'm no bastard child! I'm the daughter — one of too many — of a country parson. My father is well educated and a collegian, no less."

"I believe you, Dolly," said Perdita patting the girl's rosy cheek. "Is't indeed true you've been fetched here to string another pearl on a certain noble lecher's necklace?"

In a small, stifled voice Dolly informed, "Why, m'lady, I'm told my maidenhead has been reserved for Lord Sandwich."

"Not that horrible old goat, the Rape-Master General! But — but, this is monstrous!"

"No doubt, m'lady," Dolly admitted, then looked Perdita in the eye. "Since I must lose my virtue sometime, why not earn a great price for what many silly girls give away?"

Perdita burst out, "But Jemmy Twitcher's so riddled with the French pox he's but a walking cesspool!"

"An that be so," the Doe said nervously smoothing her fragile and shimmering white costume, "His Lordship will be made to pay ever most handsomely. Mrs. Stanhope will see to that. He is rich beyond belief."

"But if he ruins your health? There's not enough gold in the world to restore it!" Her voice hardened. "You cannot, you must not commit such a wicked folly."

Dolly's chin went out and, dropping her eyes, she said sullenly, "Beggars can't be choosers, m'lady. If I must part with my virtue for gain — and I've no choice — I intend the reward to be so great that if I do take the pox I can afford the finest physicians."

39

Wheels Within Wheels

B ENJAMIN FRANKLIN, LL.D., (Hon.), University of St. Andrews,
Fellow of the Royal Society and Postmaster General for the
North American Colonies, sat in a comfortable Louis XV chair in
the Caligula Suite and peered like a crystal-gazer into a coffee cup
held steaming under his nose. Parallel lines climbing his lofty forehead towards a receding hairline deepened.

Lord Middlebrook, for once clad in a simple but excellently tailored black coat and breeches, was saying crisply, "Good of you,
Doctor, to honor my chambers with your presence. I can only regret
that intelligences just received from London are not in the least encouraging."

"I believe," remarked the Philosopher, "you refer to news that Mr.
Wilkes has surrendered himself at King's Bench Prison demanding
to be jailed?"

"Oh, you have been informed?" Lord Middlebrook nodded to
himself. "Of course, of course. Then you must also be aware that
'King Mob' is beginning to stir and growl. God knows what the
effect will be upon North America when news of his jailing arrives
there."

Steadily, Benjamin Franklin regarded his host a long instant before shrugging almost imperceptibly. "It is about the effect here in

England, rather than at home, I am apprehensive. I mean, what will be the effect on the Ministry of Mr. Wilkes's astounding move? Surely, public outrage either will force the King's Friends to back down, cause John Wilkes to be pardoned and so abolish use of general warrants for good and all, or —"

"Or?" echoed Lord Middlebrook.

"Or the King's Ministers will attempt to coerce the Colonies through the use of force and so precipitate that armed resistance we spoke of last night."

"Then I'll inform you, Doctor, that the second alternative *already* has been decided upon," came the Marquess of Middlebrook's grim statement. "I have it on excellent authority that two reinforced battalions are being prepared for immediate transportation to Boston to enforce the tax laws." He smiled thinly. "Or have your agents already informed you?"

Benjamin Franklin made no comment, only looked highly disturbed while putting aside his cup. "Every effort must be made to prevent the troops' departure or any increase in the numbers of them. I shall fight this matter tooth and nail. May I count on your backing?"

"You may," said Lord Middlebrook. "Though I doubt 'twill count for much."

"What chiefly must interest men of good sense on both sides of the Atlantic is how so rash a move as this dispatch of troops will affect trade with America ——"

"Of course," interrupted Lord Middlebrook. "More of your Provincial Governments will be enraged into passing acts of non-intercourse which will strangle *all* trade between America and this country."

Benjamin Franklin shifted forward, gathered feet under him. "That will be inevitable I fear, and what will be the result in England?"

"Our merchants, bankers and Liberals will howl to high heaven over the prospect of losing invaluable commerce." Lord Middlebrook raised a brow. "And, Doctor, the effect on America will be — ?"

"Nothing short of disastrous! Most especially for our maritime interests. Shipments of masts, spars and other essential marine supplies to the Royal Navy will cease and our already struggling shipbuilding industry will face ruin."

He smiled gently. "However, should the Ministry wake up and realize the perils of the course upon which they are embarking most of these troubles will not come to pass."

"Doctor, what do you recommend for immediate steps?"

The big figure leaned forward. "Sufficient business to keep transatlantic trade alive till the Ministry moves towards conciliation as it surely must once the average Briton's common sense rises in wrath."

Tapping his chin, Lord Middlebrook treated the figure in simple gray to a lingering glance. "Curiously enough, my dear Doctor, I have been thinking along similar lines yet I fear not much can be accomplished till the peculations of my dear friend John Montagu and associates are threatened with exposure and disgrace."

Jeremy Brett strode in still breathing hard, his brown eyes bright and pink features aglow following a three-mile jog along West Wycombe Hall's network of bridle paths. Once he'd made his manners he disappeared to wipe off a film of sweat, then returned to learn what was transpiring.

"Cousin Jerry, Dr. Franklin and I have been discussing shipbuilding in North America. Be kind enough to give us your opinion as to its maximum capabilities at the present."

Relieved to find himself on sure ground, Jeremy spoke right up. "I hope, Dr. Franklin, you haven't credited awful lies spread by British shipwrights and contractors for Royal Navy that our New England vessels, 'plantation-built,' as they say here, are poorly found, ill-designed and constructed of inferior materials; these are shameless falsehoods calculated to rob us of contracts. On my word, gentlemen, there ain't a grain of truth in 'em!"

Lord Middlebrook said almost sharply, "I've already heard something to that effect so am prepared to credit your indignation. Tell us, Cousin Jerry" — Benjamin Franklin, bland of expression, did not fail to notice this second reference to relationship with his fellow countryman — "how many shipbuilders can you personally vouch for? I mean firms capable of turning out only first-class vessels?"

"I could give you a list longer than a day without bread."

"Pray spare us," interpolated Dr. Franklin. "Name a few of the best, if you please."

"Well, sir, at home, yards able to build ships of any tonnage are

Tom Westbrook's, Hunking Wentworth's, Sam Waldo's and, of course, my Pa's — I mean Father's.

"In Boston I can recommend Ben Holloway and Eli French's yards and Tom Coram's at Taunton, and there's Nat Meservey's yard in Kittery, and ——"

"Pray desist," smiled Lord Middlebrook, "else you'll have us replacing the entire Royal Navy in North America." His small, bright black eyes shifted to Franklin's powerful, impassive features. "Such being the case, I propose, my dear Doctor, at once to encourage the Commissioners of Naval Construction to allot contracts for a number of vessels to be built in North American yards while prices are low and threats of Non-Intercourse legislation remain, let us hope, a remote possibility."

"Amen to that!" Benjamin Franklin then recalled an engagement, for he finished his coffee and got to his feet. He said, "My dear Lord Middlebrook, since we appear to be allied in a determination to avoid a rebellion ruinous to both sides, shall we form — er — an unofficial compact? For my part I will undertake to keep you promptly informed concerning significant developments in America which might hinder our purpose; I trust you will be equally prompt about forwarding intelligence of any unwise legislation contemplated by the Ministry."

Manner altering, Franklin offered a broad brown hand. "And you, young sir, the best of luck to you in your bout with the Irish Ogre — which, alas, I cannot witness as I must depart these hospitable walls early tomorrow."

He bowed and moving lightly for so solid a figure quitted the Caligula Suite.

Lord Middlebrook's expression relaxed while he went over to tug on a bellpull. "I feel the time has come, dear Coz, for you to abandon your Spartan regime. From now on I wish you wholeheartedly to honor the motto of West Wycombe Hall — '*Fay ce que voudras.*'"

Jeremy gaped. "But, but — don't you want me to fight in the pink?"

George Liscard lowered his voice. "I did. Trouble is, you're in such good shape I can't get decent bets against you. As a matter of fact, " he added, "rumors are circulating that Jemmy Twitcher's man has been living too high of late and has contracted the French pox."

He patted Jeremy's shoulder. "Therefore you'll appreciate why I don't want you to enter the ring in excellent condition? Today and tomorrow you must be seen guzzling, carousing, indulging yourself in every possible manner." His expression tightened. "Only then can I command profitable odds."

Feeling like a puppy played with by small boys, Jeremy nodded and grinned. "Cousin George, it hasn't been fun to hold back, so here I go! By the way, what do I wear tonight — those funny monk's robes somebody's left in my bedroom?"

"No, they're not to be donned till tomorrow. Tonight's gathering is merely a convivial occasion to decide who'll win Lord le Despencer's prize for the most exotic entertainment."

40

Jemmy Twitcher

⟋⟍

FROM A WINDOW of his bedroom in the Caligula Suite Jeremy Dabney Brett, Esq., peered down at the white-pebbled driveway leading up to West Wycombe Hall's white-columned porte-cochere.

Ever since a rider had galloped up half an hour earlier to announce
the imminent arrival of John Montagu, Fourth Earl of Sandwich, Sir
Francis Dashwood's country seat had hummed like a gigantic disturbed beehive.

The weather being unusually fine for early autumn in Buckinghamshire Lord le Despencer's guests, gentlemen and ladies alike,
occupied themselves with such undemanding pastimes as archery.
bowling on the green or a fashionable new game called *"crochet"* or
more commonly "croquet" recently imported from France.

A few moments earlier Lord Middlebrook, while being assisted by
Jervis into a long-skirted coat of peacock-blue, had treated his pink-
faced American cousin to a lingering regard. "Boston Jerry, we shall
shortly descend to greet John Montagu, my very dear old friend and
fellow Friar. Please linger in the background but for God's sake use
your eyes and ears."

When word spread that Lord Sandwich — Postmaster General of
the Realm and Vice-Secretary of State — was about to arrive guests,

brilliant as so many butterflies, converged on the white-pillared entrance.

Preceded by jackbooted outriders a massive, elaborately carved and gilded coach rumbled up the statue-lined drive. Drawn by six bays in glittering harness and guided by a trio of mounted postilions, the imposing equipage rolled to a halt before the entrance.

Lord le Despencer, resplendent in a velvet coat of burnt-orange trimmed in Lincoln green, descended broad front steps and sauntered indolently towards a tall, grossly corpulent figure being assisted to alight. His weight caused the ponderous coach to sway like a ship in a seaway.

"Ah, there, Jack! 'Tis much too long since last you graced these portals."

Lord Middlebrook, standing among the foremost greeters, noted that the Fourth Earl of Sandwich's looks hadn't improved of late: same long face and nose, same bloated and mottled complexion, thin lips and supercilious manner. It proved difficult to believe that at college John Montagu had been a brilliant athlete.

At once it became apparent that the Postmaster General must be far gone in drink; his oddly shaped little eyes wandered vaguely about till, with a grunt, he recognized his host and weaved forward; pumps equipped with excessively high red heels accomplished nothing towards steadying his progress. A huge wig's curls swayed forward when he extended gem-covered hands.

Smiling broadly, Sir Francis Dashwood warmly embraced his guest of honor. Why not? Hadn't they been roistering together since 1752 when the Brimstone Club had celebrated its blasphemous rites at Medmenham Abbey — only since 1763 had the Friars held convocations in the Caverns of St. Lawrence.

Lady Perdita Constable, standing beside her husband on an upper step of Wycombe Hall's grand staircase, was able to obtain a clear view of this most notoriously depraved, yet intelligent and in many directions extremely capable nobleman.

Sir Guy observed, "Here comes the Rape-Master General. God above, hope I'll be in better shape than he at his age."

Perdita, staring, said clearly, "What a perfectly loathsome caricature of a Minister."

Sir Guy gripped her elbow. "For Christ's sake, lower your voice.

While he mayn't be an Adonis never forget that he can break or make most people present."

By tilting on tiptoes Silas Brett's stately, golden-haired daughter became able to peer over powdered heads and watched Lord Sandwich, steadied by his host's arm, advance towards the Tapestry Room through a passage lined by bowing men and curtsying ladies.

Both Constables got sharp impressions of John Montagu's long, straight nose, rose-red and swollen by countless cups, and pointed chin jutting boldly out of a broad and deeply suffused face.

His scar-thin lips remained fixed in a sneering, meaningless smile. What especially attracted Perdita's attention were the man's eyes; the color of turquoises, they were piercing, cold and fairly large. The Cabinet Minister's voice didn't please her in the least; it sounded hoarse, affected and blurred.

" 'Pon my soul, Francis," she heard Sandwich say. "Damn decent of you to spare me sight of that scurrilous outlaw and former friend, John Wilkes."

Sir Francis Dashwood said instantly, "Come now, Jack, haven't I ever been the peacemaker, eager to spread oil on troubled waters? However, I fancy 'Liberty Jack' returns your dislike with interest."

Sandwich halted, shiny, purplish cheeks aglow."By God, Francis, I'll not rest till I see that treacherous demagogue behind bars for life — if he can't be hanged on Tyburn Tree."

Lord le Despencer passed an arm through Sandwich's, gently propelled him onwards, murmuring, "We'll talk about that later — if you insist — but now, my dear fellow, I wish to present guests who may be unknown to you."

Mercurially Lord Sandwich's manner changed. Although still swaying noticeably on thick and powerful legs he suddenly exuded convincing affability, adopted the affected drawl of the day, greeted acquaintances. " 'Pon my word, Tilton, 'tis indeed a pleasure to see you again and on an occasion so pregnant with stimulating entertainment.

"Ah, there, Lady Fane," he croaked, "trust to see more, much more of you ere this convocation ends."

He remained cordial while acknowledging Mr. Peregrine Falconer's almost obsequious salutation.

His odd-colored eyes lingered on Perdita, who, curiosity having got the better of her, had descended to the ground floor. He leered so openly she felt as if stripped bare and a small shiver rippled down her spine while she offered that bloated, glittering figure a faultless Court curtsy.

As he entered the Tapestry Room, the Fourth Earl of Sandwich's strong chin elevated itself while he glanced about. Smile more supercilious than ever, he indicated to his host a group lingering about a French door at the great room's far side. "Damme, Francis, ain't that fellow in brown rat-catchers Dr. Franklin, the homespun philosopher one hears about?"

John Montagu had no need to inquire; he'd encountered Benjamin Franklin at Court on several occasions.

"None other," Dashwood replied, a touch of asperity in his tone. "Dr. Franklin is a distinguished guest who on several previous occasions has honored this roof."

"Indeed," drawled the magnificent figure at Lord le Despencer's side, "I'd not thought it possible a rustic Provincial could appreciate the intricacies of our *recherché* amusements."

A titter subsided when the host said coldly, "My dear Jack, don't disquiet yourself. Your fellow Postmaster General's inventiveness runs in many directions — has earned deserved recognition. For example, he and I at the moment are collaborating on a revision of the Book of Common Prayer."

Lord Sandwich rolled eyes, dramatically raised his arms. "What! This passes the unbelief of Satan! An unlettered Colonial and you, the ultimate blasphemer and lecher, revising the Prayer Book! God's wounds! This is too rich!"

"I've changed somewhat, Jack, since our pranking in Medmenham Abbey."

"Ah, yes. Suspect 'tis another case of 'When the Devil was young, a devil was he; but when the Devil grew old, a saint he'd be.' Oh, Francis," guffawed John Montagu, "I'll *never* credit this!"

"Think as you please, but here comes my *dear*" — verbally he underlined the adjective — "American friend."

The Postmaster General of the North American Colonies, squarish features composed, was drawing near, outwardly unruffled. He began in soft yet compelling accents, "Your servant, my lord," and offered a half-bow acknowledged by the other with a careless nod.

"Pleasure, Dr. Franklin," he murmured. "Everywhere one hears talk of your great achievements in the scientific world. Is't true you've invented a wonderfully efficient new stove and have opened up new avenues of thought about that demmed mysterious force called 'electricity'?"

Quite equably, Franklin stated, "My lord, I will admit to some small success in that science."

"Ah! Next I presume you'll devise some way of causin' the sun to rise in the west?"

Benjamin Franklin's trangular upper lip flattened while his clear, light-gray eyes considered Sir Francis's companion with an unwavering regard. "No, my lord." He smiled. "I now direct my attention towards zoology, beginning, of course, with primates, especially the apes, which, as *you*" — ever so slightly he emphasized that pronoun — undoubtedly are aware, possess the highest intelligence of any species after *homo sapiens*."

At the word "apes" smothered gasps arose. Hastily, Sir Francis interposed. "Possibly, Doctor, before you depart you might condescend to afford my friend a demonstration of your scientific knowledge?"

Sir Francis's pacific effort failed to dispel fury in the Cabinet minister's turquoise-hued eyes but Lord Sandwich controlled himself and turned aside to greet Lord Tilton with a degree of warmness which startled that sturdy individual. "Well, Geoffrey! 'Twould appear in Parliament my predictions are about to be fulfilled."

"Predictions?" broke in Colonel Barré. "Which in particular? As I recall you have made several, my lord."

The Cabinet minister glared. "Why, that those rascally so-called 'Sons of Liberty' will go too far! Damme, I *must* be clairvoyant!"

Guests came crowding in to listen.

Lord Sandwich's clouded gaze switched from Lord Tilton to Isaac Barré and came to rest on Mr. Falconer when he inquired, "Too far, my lord?"

His attention returned to Viscount Tilton. "Word has been received that not long ago would-be rebels in Boston have attempted to land duty-free a cargo of Madeira wine imported by John Hancock — one of the most intemperate troublemakers in our disloyal Colony of Massachusetts Bay!"

Angrily Lord Sandwich snatched a glass from a tray offered by a footman. "Not only that, but those damned rebels dared to confine several of His Majesty's Customs officers and freed them only when

H.M.S. *Romney* sailed in and ordered the Yankees to anchor under her guns."

The speaker glared about him, fiddled with an enormous ruby glowing on his watch fob. "Imagine it! Those rabble-rousers, Sam Adams, John Hancock, James Otis and others, so incited the mob they chased His Majesty's Customs officers to their homes and threatened them with all manner of bodily harm till they sought sanctuary on some islands in Boston Harbor held by British Regulars."

Coldly he regarded Benjamin Franklin's solid, brown-clad figure. "And you, in your infinite wisdom what do you say to that?"

"My lord, I can only hold that theirs was a most reprehensible course. I have always deprecated illegal actions — especially when accompanied by violence."

Lord Sandwich drained his brandy at a single gulp. "Trust you're sincere in that, Doctor, because two regiments of the line, the Fourteenth and Twenty-fourth, plus artillery, already are in Boston to remind our rebellious subjects that His Majesty's Government will enforce the law — whatever the cost."

41

Dr. Franklin and the River Styx

M R. PEREGRINE FALCONER met Jeremy at the door to his Acteon Suite. Using a handkerchief edged with Bruges lace he was mopping eyes still moist with amusement. "Come in, Jerry, m'friend, whilst I confide how old Jemmy Twitcher attempted to confound Dr. Franklin by inviting him, in that sneering way of his, to afford practical proof of his supposed scientific knowledge."

Once they had settled themselves Jeremy, poising a flaming paper spill above his pipe, inquired: "You witnessed this — this test?"

"Wouldn't have missed it for rubies or fine gold! If only you, a compatriot, had been on hand for the Rape-Master General's undoing it would have been all the more perfect."

"What happened?"

Mr. Falconer chuckled, then burst out laughing. "Once Lord Sandwich loudly demanded a demonstration of Dr. Franklin's scientific knowledge, your countryman, nothing loath, proposed that he and his challenger proceed to the Caverns of St. Lawrence — where the Friars will convene tonight."

Long and pallid greyhound's face outthrust. Peregrine Falconer continued, "Aside from Dr. Franklin and Jemmy Twitcher, Sir Francis and Lord Middlebrook, only a few important others were invited to come along.

"In short order we all crossed the Wye — as you know, the river skirts the base of chalk cliffs at that point — and passed under a scroll chiseled out of the rock reading the inevitable '*Fay ce que voudras.*'

"Since you'll soon visit the Caverns I'll not weary you with a description of an amazin' series of tunnels and passages the walls of which are liberally sculptured with wonderfully weird, obscene and blasphemous subjects. Couldn't see too much; 'twas blacker than Satan's belly in there and we were being lighted by only a few lanterns and flambeaux.

"Wielding a long walking staff topped by a big gold knob, Dr. Franklin stumped along. We straggled behind him and Sandwich till we reached the brink of a small black stream which Sir Francis long ago had dubbed the 'River Styx.' Doctor Franklin suggested we halt.

" 'Is it here, my Provincial scientist,' queries Lord Sandwich with more than usual arrogance, 'you intend to demonstrate the depths of your knowledge?'

"At my lord's pompous and disdainful manner, Dr. Franklin almost snickered; 'Yes, my lord,' says he. 'I invite you to observe' — he pointed with his staff — 'how troubled and agitated flows this dark stream along its course.' "

Again Peregrine Falconer lapsed into silent merriment. "Friend Jerry, the water indeed was licking and lapping most angrily at the rock walls.

" 'Well, my lord,' says Franklin, 'for your edification I now propose to calm its frenzy and cause this stream to flow as peacefully as any meadow brook.'

" 'Now do you indeed?' Sandwich guffawed — you know what a noisy swine he can be. 'Which of you present will hazard one hundred guineas that this Provincial pundit fails in his promise?'

"Several present, no doubt courting Jemmy Twitcher's good opinion, took up portions of his wager. Sir Francis, looking most uncomfortable, invited his old friend to proceed.

"Dr. Franklin then declared, 'Gentlemen, I propose to still these waters by making certain cabalistic signs above them while intoning an ancient and secret incantation confided to me by a learned shaman — or sorcerer — of the Catawba tribe of American Indians.' "

Jeremy queried breathlessly, "What chanced then?"

Peregrine Falconer laughed. "After making several wonderfully complicated passes over the stream with a cane which wears a huge gold knob at its top Dr. Franklin chanted, '*Bub-eye, sus-tut-iyi-lul-lul, yak-eye, wow-aya-tut-eye-rur-sus!*'

"All the while he kept the staff circling in the water — generally upstream and against the current I noted. Well, may I roast in Hell forever, which most likely I will, if the Styx's waters *didn't* stop rushing and splashing! Before long the surface had grown smooth as any maiden's rump and flowed tranquilly."

Jeremy shook his head. "Surely, Perry, you're funning me!"

"Dammit, I'm not! 'Tis God's own truth — saw it with my own eyes! Imagine the tumult over your compatriot's miraculous performance."

"How did that incantation go?"

Peregrine Falconer produced a slip of paper. "Here 'tis. At my earnest solicitation the worthy Doctor later on kindly dictated it."

After reading, then rereading the scrawl, Jeremy hugged himself and burst into roars of laughter. He started to explain the nature of Benjamin Franklin's weird incantation but thought better of it; recently, he'd learned the wisdom of guarding potentially useful knowledge.

Later, when he and his sister contrived to find a few moments in private he recounted Dr. Franklin's feat. Delighted at Lord Sandwich's discomfiture, Perdita, eyes a-twinkle, prompted, "Now about that Catawba shaman's incantation?"

Jeremy grinned. " 'Catawba,' my cat's left hind foot! All the dear Doctor did was to speak in 'Tuttannee.' "

" 'Tuttannee'? That's a tribe I've never heard of."

"And you never will. Ain't no such a tribe. Oh, come now, Sis. Can't you remember how when we were children we used Tuttannee to mystify playmates?"

Lady Constable brightened, actually snapped fingers. "Of course! You used it in that wigwam you boys built on the edge of the woods where we used to play Settlers and Injuns."

A hand shading her eyes she tilted back her striking, golden-brown head. "Let me think. To speak Tuttannee we'd spell out our message in English but used only initials."

She glanced at Peregrine Falconer's scrap of paper. " '*Bub-eye,*' of course, stands for 'B' and 'E,' which equals 'be.' '*Sus*' stands for 'S'; '*tut* is 'T' '*iyi*' is 'I'; '*lul-lul*' is 'LL'; which spells out 'still' —"

"Correct. The rest of its goes, *'yak-eye, wow-aya-tut-eye-rur-sus,'* which means Dr. Franklin's incantation was simply, 'Be still, ye waters.'

"Anyhow, the Philosopher's jape won our host and your adoring husband sums which should come in handy before we quit these gilded halls of vice."

Only long afterwards did the true nature of Dr. Franklin's "miracle" become known, its explanation laughably simple: the great, golden knob topping the Provincial Philosopher's staff had contained a supply of a heavy oil which, when mixed with water, immediately calmed that element.

The learned Doctor, however, discreetly kept the true nature of his oil a secret to his dying day.

42

The Masques of St. Priapus I

—————⌣—————

Hampered by a splitting headache which refused to abate Jeremy Brett lingered abed recalling what he could of the previous night's revelry. Along with other guests evidently not considered of sufficient importance to attend the Masques of St. Priapus he'd gamed with moderate success until too drunk to make sense.

It was then that a footman had touched his sleeve and said, "Sir, a certain lady wants a word with you," and led him to a suite occupied by a dashing blonde Dollymop he had had no difficulty in recognizing as Lady Frances Fane.

Jeremy pressed palms to throbbing temples. How many times had they made love? Twice at least, possibly thrice? No matter. Their transports had been sufficiently ardent to leave him drained and inert.

He licked bone-dry lips. One consolation — if Cousin George really wished him to enter the ring in disreputable shape there'd now be no necessity of playing a part.

Listening to voices in the corridor he wished he dared risk reaching for the bellpull; milk and a plate of rolls might diminish the constant threat of nausea.

The valet assigned by Sir Francis knocked on his door. He had come, that imperturbable servant explained, bringing a cordial recommended by His Lordship as an infallible antidote for the megrims.

Jeremy, prepared to try anything to make the hammers of hell quit beating on his skull, hurriedly held out a quivering hand. Once he'd downed a half-tumbler of a thick, sweetish-sour yellow liquid he felt better with miraculous speed, so much so that ere long he rang for the valet to fetch razor, soap and hot towels; but the violence with which his hand still shook precluded any attempt at shaving himself.

While gradually his head cleared, one unanswered question continued to plague him. Did Cousin George's motive in encouraging dissipation consist simply in a confirmed gambler's ambition to secure better odds? — Or was some other motive lurking at the back of Lord Middlebrook's mind?

Responding to a summons from his sister delivered shortly before noon, Jeremy Brett, still more than a trifle resentful over not having been invited to attend the Masques of St. Priapus, stalked stiffly out to the "Bower of Ganymede," a small, pseudo-Greek marble shrine occupying a dell at no great distance from West Wycombe Hall.

In it he discovered Perdita, Sir Guy and Peregrine Falconer languidly finishing a breakfast served on basket-edged trays.

As his wife pointed out with some acidity Sir Guy, although sipping stiff brandy eggnog, looked as if last night he'd been dragged backwards through a knothole. Both Falconer and Constable were haggard, unshaven and wearing night turbans and Turkish bedroom slippers. Banyans ineffectively concealed their nakedness.

Perdita, on the other hand, Jeremy decided, had never appeared more delicately sensual in a dainty green-and-pink shepherdess's costume which set off abundant golden-brown tresses.

Screaming, a bronze-plumed cock pheasant came slanting down past the Bower of Ganymede, set wings, then executed a graceful running landing which carried him past a marble statue of Leda being vigorously ravished by Jupiter in the guise of a swan then strutted up to a trio of dun-colored pheasant hens demurely exploring a dew-spangled stretch of lawn.

Peregrine Falconer, aside from an increase in his natural pallor, appeared relatively unaffected by the previous night's debauch. Sighing, he extended skinny, black-haired legs while draining the last of his flip and considering the cock pheasant's amorous advances.

Eyes flashing, Perdita suddenly burst out, "Damn you both for surly clots! Speak up! What chanced in the Caverns? I'm fair perishing to hear!"

"*Touché*, my dear girl," smiled Falconer. "Guy and I will take turns in describing that most entertaining competition for Sir Francis's prize — a mere thousand guineas — for the most original act."

Peregrine Falconer began by describing how, just as the sun was setting over Wycombe House, "we joined Sir Francis, Lord Sandwich and Lord Middlebrook on the banks of the Wye and, headed by the Club's secretary, the Honorable Paul Whitehead, we made our way towards the entrance to the Caverns of St. Lawrence."

Jeremy queried, "Who else was there?"

"Why, Will Hogarth — the celebrated painter and cartoonist — must confess I was astonished to learn he's been a Friar for years. Then there was a van Sittart — didn't then know which one — Viscount Tilton and, among others *mirabile dictu*, Dr. Benjamin Franklin, all abrim with cheer and rising concupiscence."

Pettishly, Perdita brushed biscuit crumbs from her lap. "Oh, Perry, do get to the nub of your tale."

Falconer grinned. "Patience, dear girl, patience; don't force me to slight details.

"In addition there were a couple of young Friars who've just arrived — dreadful macaronis."

Perdita's slim, winged brows rose. "Who are these carpet knights?"

"One's called Peter Villiers, a fop who emits the silliest schoolgirl giggles I've ever heard; the other's called Snowdon — a precious fellow if ever there was one — uses green face powder and minces about carrying an ermine muff.

"Well, we crossed a footbridge over the Wye and old Paul Whitehead, as presiding Abbot, stopped before an iron grille decorated with all manner of naughty designs to chant some sort of mumbo-jumbo — in Pig Latin I suspect.

"Next we shuffled into a dank-smelling high-roofed tunnel lined with flaring torches stuck in sconces; we advanced into the cliff near two hundred feet along a narrow black carpet — 'twas about that far, eh, Guy?"

Gingerly, Perdita's husband's head inclined. "Or thereabouts, ain't sure. I was too busy admiring the sculptures — very juicy, all of 'em."

Smiled his wife, settling languidly on her cushion-covered settee, "I'll bet. Hear decorations in there are extraordinary. What happened next?"

"Plagued by damned, eye-stinging torch smoke we reached a sizable cave called the 'Robing Room.' Here we one and all stripped down to breeches, shoes and hose, taking care not to disarrange cosmetics and wigs while we garbed ourselves in black monastic robes set off with hoods of what Sir Francis calls 'vaginal pink.'" He smiled at Lady Constable. "A pretty conceit.

"I really was shaken to perceive how the skin of so many Friars showed red buboes and yellow pustules; the worst afflicted was Lord Sandwich. My God! He's fairly speckled with pox sores."

A harsh laugh escaped Peregrine Falconer. " 'Tis utterly appalling that someday so decadent a creature may well become Prime Minister; should Jemmy Twitcher come to power God help Great Britain."

The raconteur straightened the cloth-of-gold turban on his close-shaven head before describing the Hall of St. Priapus as a large, oval-shaped banqueting chamber off which opened several small rooms called "cells," furnished only with a washstand and stool in addition to a hard and narrow cot.

Intently, Lady Constable and her brother listened. "Once the Abbot had amused himself by pretending to lose his way in a labyrinth we reached the Hall of St. Priapus which is hewn out of the chalk rock in the shape of an enormous swollen womb. In the middle of the hall stood several oval tables set for supper.

"I say, Guy, suppose you take up the burden of this tale?"

Perdita's husband took another swallow of brandy flip. "Till one's been there one simply can't imagine the effect of the dim and lofty dome, sculptured walls, flaring torches and dozens of tapers burning dimly in a damp atmosphere reeking of stale incense, wine and food odors. All viands, incidentally, are prepared up in the Great House and merely kept warm in the Caverns' buttery."

Perdita sat up. "And what was served?"

"Damned if I really know," admitted Jeremy's brother-in-law. "The dishes all were delicious and called by such erotic names as *'Roti des Poitrines de Vénus'* — roasted Venus's breasts. Near as I could tell they really were squabs with a cherry centered on each breast.

"Another offering was 'Devil's Loins' — a roast of beef carved in the shape of human buttocks; and how the drinks were named!"

"Such as?" prompted Jeremy's sister, eyes shining. "Go on, I die of curiosity."

"To name a few: 'Roll-me-over,' 'Strip-me-naked,' 'Gin and Sin,' 'Gin and Fanny' and 'Brimstone punch,' the headiest of all. As for me, I stuck with 'Strip-me-nakeds' and a few ——"

The harsh screeching of a peacock flying over the temple interrupted Constable's dissertation.

"For Heaven's name get to the point!" Perdita pleaded. "What entertainments were offered? Which earned Lord le Despencer's prize?"

43

The Masques of St. Priapus II

LAZILY, Peregrine Falconer lifted a brow in Sir Guy's direction. "Will you describe the opening skit — or shall I?"

"You, an it please you, friend Perry."

"The first act was sponsored by Lord Lawrence van Sittart, fresh-returned from a high diplomatic mission to the Sublime Porte of Constantinople.

"Oh, bother! 'Dita dear, I forgot to mention that at one end of the Hall of St. Priapus lies a smallish stage with a little dressing room behind it.

"Creating a considerable hubbub, we all rearranged our chairs to insure a good view of what was about to happen while servants lit candles before the footlights — a row of polished tin reflectors.

"Once a degree of silence had been obtained Larry van Sittart announced the name of his skit as 'The Odalisque and the Turkish Tripod' and ordered the curtains drawn.

"In the stage's center stood a tripod consisting of three slender poles about ten feet long striped in red-and-gold and secured together at the apex.

"At either end of the platform with arms folded and mighty solemn expression, stood a pair of giant half-naked Negroes in great white turbans and baggy yellow pantaloons."

Falconer snickered. "From the summit of this tripod was suspended a round wicker basket, upholstered in pink satin and trimmed with ribbons and other gewgaws. 'Twas a fetching nest for one of my favorite bawds — a slim, young wench called Janine."

"Damme, 'twasn't little Janine from Mother Stanhope's whorehouse?"

"Oh, you uncouth Colonials! 'Bordello' and 'bagnio' are more stylish terms for such pleasurable haunts. Anyway, Janine was ushered in nude as Eve by a third blackamoor.

"Solemn as a boiled owl, Larry van Sittart announced, 'What I now offer is a favored method of provoking enjoyment of *houris* by members of the Sultan's Court.' "

Color mounting, Perdita leaned forward, great dark eyes widening in anticipation. "What next?"

"On signal the blackamoors tilted forward the basket so all could view a round hole some five or six inches across let into its bottom.

"When the basket had been restored to its hanging position beneath the tripod, Janine, who has the blackest hair and creamiest of skins, was placed, cross-legged, in the basket with her bottom precisely above the aperture."

Jeremy moistened lips, kept his gaze on the raconteur.

"Once little Janine had been comfortably settled the blackamoors commenced revolving the basket till knots formed in the sustaining cords and gradually lifted the whole contrivance a foot or so above a low settle shoved directly beneath the basket and its delicious burden.

"At once appeared a huge Turk naked save for silver bracelets and upturned slippers. His equipment — !" Falconer leered, enjoying Perdita's quickening breathing.

"Go on! What next?"

"Why, the Infidel merely improved his position beneath the basket by tucking a bolster 'neath his rump then signaled for the basket to be released. At once it commenced to revolve fast, faster as the cord unwound and tension knots in it disappeared the whirling basket became lowered upon the Turk's monstrous upright member until it could spin no more while Janine fairly screamed with pain and pleasure."

"God's love!" burst out Perdita. "What a pretty invention."

"Aye. Ingenious, to say the least," commented Sir Guy. "Must try it some time, eh, Perry? You game, 'Dita?"

Perdita's slim fingers worked at the watered silk covering her lap. "Yes, but not with a greasy Turk, damn you!"

The raconteur went over to select a pomegranate from a dish and, turning, manufactured a smile which didn't uncover his teeth. "I might add, friend Jerry, that among those most entertained by this fantasy was your compatriot, Dr. Franklin; he fairly drooled."

44

Fair "Gladiators" I

⌒

BECAUSE THE DRESSING ROOM behind the stage in the Hall of St. Priapus was quite small, participants of the next and ultimate presentation of the evening assembled in the Robing Room close to the Caverns' entrance.

With other Does, Dolly Lawton made last-minute adjustments to costumes of the four lively young Nuns about to portray Valkyries.

Deeply stimulated, Parson Lottimore's auburn-haired daughter remained unobtrusively observant of what took place while devoting special attention to Henneke.

The Danish girl cast as Brünnhilde, Wotan's daughter, stood half-a-head taller than her three flushed and bright-eyed companions, presented the only muscular figure on her team; the rest, naked save for chitons, greaves and buskins, were softly rounded and essentially feminine in aspect.

Like her companions Henneke was wearing a winged helmet of gilded papier-mâché and nothing at all under a knee-length topaz-yellow chiton of silken gauze so cut as to leave the left breast exposed. The brief garment was so transparent it revealed rather than concealed the least details of a supple pink-and-white body. Cornsilk-hued hair flowed freely over Henneke's shoulders, fell down her back, and undulated effectively whenever she moved.

The Valkyrie maidens chattered while yellow ribbons were used to tie shields of gilded tin to their left arms.

At the Robing Room's far end girls composing the Amazon team likewise were being readied. These experienced but still beauteous harlots went nude under sleeveless smocks of sky-blue voile.

They were to be led into battle by the Welsh girl, Gwen, which tawny-skinned beauty had been cast as Hippolyta, Queen of the Amazons. She alone approximated Henneke in height and muscular development.

Air had grown so heavy with perfume and feminine body odors that candles smoked and burned low.

Along a low, vaulted corridor carved from chalk rock beat bursts of music punctuated by sudden gales of deep-toned masculine laughter.

After loud rapping on the Robing Room's door in minced M. Beauchamps, Lord le Despencer's faun-featured French major-domo wearing more than a hint of rouge on lips and cheeks. With almost reptilian speed his small, jet eyes darted over the Nuns.

"*Alors! Tranquille!* Be quiet, everyone!" Pettishly M. Beauchamps thrice struck the floor with a tall, silver-headed walking stick.

The babbling Nuns stared and fell silent.

"*You, la Capitaine* of the Valkyries," he directed tired eyes at Henneke, "in order that you shall use your whips in earnest, Milor' 'as wagered much monies, that *la Capitaine* Brünnhilde and her warrior girls soon will lash the Amazons into weeping submission."

Deliberately the Frenchman produced a monocle and through it viewed the Amazons, armed like the Valkyries except that their helmets were of ancient Grecian design topped by crests of emerald-green feathers.

Dolly had retreated unobtrusively into a corner and, breathless, watched from eyes bright as beacons.

"In order that you shall not spare yourselves or your enemies, *les Frères Religieux du Brimstone Club* 'ave made up a purse; so, no matter what 'appens, each of you will be paid ten guineas!"

Laughed a sprightly Amazon, "Lor' love a duck, *ten* guineas! A pretty fee even if I do get me backside tanned."

M. Beauchamps clucked like an angry hen. "*Taisez-vous!* Lest you be tempted to slacken, ten extra guineas will be given the winning team and yet another ten to the last 'gladiator' on 'er feet.

"Imagine! One of you *poules* can earn twenty gold guineas for suffering fewer stripes and bruises than an angry pimp might deal you!"

Wide-eyed, Dolly watched M. Beauchamps beckon a brawny, white-wigged footman who carried in an armful of cane whips slender, terribly supple and nearly four feet long. All were bound in vari-colored satin ribbons and suggested pretty wands until one noted that, from the tip of each rod, dangled three thrice-knotted thongs the sinister outlines of which failed to be disguised by a coating of gilt paint. However, in Dolly's inexperience, these lashes didn't appear really dangerous or cruel.

The dark-haired Queen of the Amazons, on receiving her whip, bowed it several times above her crested helmet much as a fencer tests the temper of a foil prior to engaging. She ended by swinging the whip about her head in hissing arcs then shook it at her rival captain.

"Look and tremble, dearie!" cried Gwen. "You'll taste this often enough to forget all about prizes and beg for mercy."

Henneke bared gleaming teeth. "Bah! 'Tis you, you soft-bottomed bitch, who'd better look out if my blood gets heated!"

Save for the two captains, Dolly decided, these dimpled, carefully coiffured, painted, powdered and soft-bodied "gladiators" didn't look as if they could administer or endure much punishment — no matter what the inducements.

Down the rock-hewn passage sounded the strident blast of a trumpet.

Hands fluttering, M. Beauchamps backed out into the passageway illumined by a line of torches creating a diabolical reddish glare and clapped hands. "*Allons, mes braves fillettes. Au combat!* Stop giggling, adjust your gear and attempt to present a warlike air."

Amid a miasma of perfumes and candle smoke the Nuns straggled out into the corridor and, suddenly silent, moved off towards the sources of a bacchanalian tumult. A string orchestra struck up "The March of the Gladiators," composed in honor of the occasion by Mr. Paul Whitehead, the Brimstone Club's satyr-like permanent secretary.

Dr. Benjamin Franklin rubbed eyes smarting from torch and candle smoke then peered hopefully at the cramped little stage. Although blasé through years of association with high society he was experiencing a definite sense of anticipation. What next would take place in this den of refined debauchery?

Absently, the Postmaster General for the North American Colonies waved aside a steaming mug of Brimstone punch and fixed his attention on the eight female gladiators who, holding whips at the ready, were marching up to the footlights amid drunken cheers and thunderous applause.

45

Fair "Gladiators" II

SIR FRANCIS DASHWOOD, Abbot of the Friars of St. Lawrence, meditatively stroked a squab-plump and prominent chin while sur-
veying the rank of yellow-clad Valkyries looking absurdly frail, awkward and unmartial in greaves, shields and winged helmets; nor did
he find the Amazons in transparent blue smocks any more warlike.

He bellowed over the din, "Fair Daughters of Bellona, when I
flourish this handkerchief you will commence to battle for fame and
fortune!"

Once his lace-edged square of cambric had fluttered the contestants, with the exception of the captains, shrilled cries and threats
and uncertainly flourished lash-tipped weapons, raised shields and
pranced forward, making timid striking motions.

However, Henneke and Gwen, seen by the murky half-light,
lashed out with such abundant vigor that thin screeches and wails of
pain stirred the disheveled audience to chorus obscene advice and
encouragements.

"Twenty guineas on the Yellow!" yelled a wild-eyed rake from the
background.

Young Villiers without diverting his gaze, called, "Done! The
Blues will win."

Beyond the footlights action dissolved into a confused pattern of flashing white limbs, flying hair, swirling colors, gilded equipment and whirling lashes. Anguished shrill cries of pain soon dominated the din reverberating in the vaulted Hall of St. Priapus.

Prompted to action by hopes of glittering rewards the "gladiators" laid about effectively enough to reduce each other's costumes to shimmering tatters and then draw red parallel streaks across nacreous torsos, arms and thighs.

Whenever a lash struck some girl's breast her screams dominated the high-pitched tumult and roused the audience to pandemonium. Soon combatants lost their helmets and hair was freed to stream like battle-tossed gonfalons.

Before long the smaller, less strongly built girls ran out of strength and spirit and, sobbing, dropped whips and ran to cower weeping on the fringes of the fight. Panic-stricken, most dropped their shields and were forced to ward off random blows with hands and arms.

Soon only shreds remained of the gladiators' gay and colorful smocks and chitons and did little to conceal vivid scarlet streaks marking palpitating bodies.

One of Henneke's remaining companions, a chubby, young blonde, lost her winged helmet and when she stooped to retrieve it Gwen caught her such a stinging swipe across the buttocks that the Valkyrie uttered a piercing scream, dropped her whip and sank to her knees wailing for mercy.

"Fifteen on the Blues!" instantly shouted Sir Peter Villiers.

"Done!" yelled Lord Middlebrook. "Come on, Henneke! Strike harder, damn you. That's no powder puff you're handling!"

Henneke heard, dashed drops of blood from her cheek, then, bright blue eyes ablaze and breasts heaving, leaped to center stage, panting, "Come on, you damn Welsh hussy, for the beating of your life!"

Having staked a small fortune on Lord Middlebrook's Yellows, Falconer leaped up shouting through cupped hands, "Use the butt of that whip, Henneke! There's real weight in it!"

"*Har-r, yutch! Yutch!*" Henneke raised that Viking warcry which ever centuries had chilled British and Irish hearts. Immediately she reversed her weapon and used its butt to swing at the Amazon's head and sent her helmet flying across the stage. The blow caused Gwen's nose to bleed and spatter sweat-brightened breasts and the remnants of her smock.

Amid roars of excitement Henneke ripped off her helmet; her supple figure, red-striped and bleeding a little, bent in time to avoid Gwen's savage return slash. In order to wield her whip with both hands Henneke, cursing in Danish, ripped off her shield at the cost of suffering a pair of whistling lashes shrewd enough to make her gasp and bare strong white teeth in anguish. Then she went into a crouch with whip shank held vertically before her in a quarter-staff fighter's "on-guard" position.

Lips compressed and quivering, Dr. Franklin decided that here was a scene never to be forgotten. Conquered, red-streaked and hysterical gladiators cowered about the littered stage while the two captains, almost evenly matched, disheveled and nearly naked, circled about still striking strongly but obviously tiring.

Suddenly the Danish girl bent under a hissing swipe and, gripping the reversed whip in both hands, with vicious force drove its butt upward into the base of Gwen's belly.

Uttering a piercing scream the Amazon leader doubled over, clutching the junction of her legs. Immediately the stock of Henneke's weapon descended on the nape of her rival's neck and to a chorus of animal noises raised by the onlookers dropped her, shuddering and semi-conscious, onto the stage.

"*Har-r! Yutch! Yutch!*" The victrix, crimson trickles slowly descending her body, planted the sole of a half-tied golden buskin on her adversary's neck and pointed her weapon at Sir Francis Dashwood in ludicrous mimicry of a winning gladiator's plea for a signal to determine whether a vanquished adversary should be spared.

In a fury, John Montagu held out a glittering hand with thumb downturned. "Flay that wretched baggage to ribbons!"

However, Lord Middlebrook, Sir Francis Dashwood and most of the drunken, wild-eyed company held out hands thumb upward.

46

Fay Ce Que Voudras

Around nine of the evening, bells in St. Lawrence's grotesque steeple commenced to clang sonorously whereupon in West Wycombe Hall's glittering ballroom the Friars of St. Lawrence and guests collected in no great haste. They formed in a sandled column of twos, disguised by black half-masks and wearing nothing beyond pearl-gray monastic habits with contrasting scarlet cowls.

Jeremy estimated the robed figures might number around thirty. A curious tension continued to quiet all save a few hopelessly inebriated Friars. Of these Lord Sandwich proved the most obnoxious; he kept talking at the top of his voice and lurching clumsily about.

Lord Middlebrook as Jeremy's sponsor remarked acidly, "Ah me! The Rape-Master General's in his usual endearing form."

Jeremy, uncomfortable in heelless sandals, felt his legs and lower body become chilled by a breeze beating strongly through wide-flung portals. What expensive mumbo-jumbo! Half this waste could finance construction of three good-sized coasters and cargoes for them to boot.

Sir Francis Dashwood, as Abbot, took his place at the head of the column and raised arms stilling the company long enough to call loudly, "Brothers! We will now proceed to the Caverns of St. Lawrence. On the way, *in nomen Sanctus Satanus,* conduct yourselves with decorum befitting this pious Order."

As each pair of Friars neared the front door a footman passed each red-hooded figure a taper already lit. Fortunately for men unaccustomed to scant covering the night proved fairly warm with stars bright as might be expected during early October.

Long since, Dollymops to the number of six had been driven to the Caverns and now waited beside the River Wye watching a column of glowing candle flames come meandering down from West Wycombe Hall.

Lady Wollcott, half-sister to Sir Francis Dashwood, readjusted her mask before turning to Lady Frances Fane. "And who, my love, is to be your lucky fellow worshipper at the Shrine of St. Priapus?"

"Geoff Tilton, I believe — to begin with, at least. And you?"

"Guy Constable. Only this afternoon his wife commended his capabilities. And with whom will you be sharing devotions?" She turned to Perdita, oddly exhilarated by realizing that under her silken habit, scarlet with a pearl-gray hood, her smooth body was covered by not a stitch.

A half-smothered little laugh escaped her. "Believe it or not, 'twill be none other than Jeremy Brett."

Chuckled Lady Wollcott, "A touch of incest, eh? Naughty, naughty!"

Following the procession's solemn cntry into the banqueting cavern, Brethren and their companions reclined on places indicated at three *triclinia* — Roman dining couches brilliantly illumined and heaped with all manner of delicacies.

Once the Friars had found their stations the Abbot held up arms as in an invocation. "Fellow Friars, as many of us are aware and our guests can readily perceive, there are at hand a number of cells opening off this sacred hall.

"Six special chambers are reserved for those of our membership who will, when the feasting ends, pay homage to our Patron Saint by performing the hallowed rite of defloration!"

"Hear! Hear!" Hearty voices called from the dining couches.

"Please note that on the keystone above each sacrificial cell is graven a symbol."

Briefly the masked, robed and hooded figure referred to a list.

"Brother John Montagu, you will occupy the cell bearing on its keystone the mask of a goat."

A roar of laughter made the vaulted ceiling resound.

"Brother Geoffrey Tilton occupies the retreat bearing a bull's head; Saintly Brother van Sittart, that of the boar; Brother Perry Falconer, that of the monkey."

Sir Francis Dashwood's eyes glittered behind his half-mask as he bowed decorously. "Brother George Liscard will sacrifice under the sign of the fightingcock —"

Applause and derisive laughter greeted this announcement.

"Whilst your humble Abbot will seek a priceless pearl in an apartment distinguished by the sign of the rabbit."

"What about us poor neophytes?" demanded a burly masked Friar.

"Be patient, Brother. In a trice succulent Dollymops and entrancing Nuns will join us. If you ain't already bespoken one, take your pick."

Once again Jeremy's head commenced to throb so painfully that only by masterful efforts could he focus his eyes sufficiently to witness the entrance of a procession of gray-and-scarlet-clad Dollymops and Nuns wearing all-red habits.

Jeremy was too muzzy to recognize the uncommonly tall and graceful Dollymop who sidled up to his *triclinium* and seated herself beside him.

At long last the banquet was nearing a boisterous and disorderly conclusion when Perdita whispered. "Don't be afeared, little brother. Sister is watching over you."

Stupidly he grinned, loosely straighted his mask and raised a hand to his companion's face. "Damn my soul, if 'tain't the righteous 'Dita! Real white of you! Doubt if I can navigate much longer."

"You won't if you drink any more."

On nearby couches robed figures were merging in movements of increasing shamelessness.

"Lie quiet, darling. How bad do you feel?"

"Be all right could I rest somewhere; ready to get sick."

"Take it easy, Jerry — let me tend to you."

In the low vaulted banquet hall the atmosphere grew heavier, less vital; in vain he tried to focus his vision. Criminently! Why wouldn't the deck of this ship quit heaving?

Perdita's cool fingers closed over his wrist. "Come, lad, let's lie down awhile, or d'you need to vomit first?"

"Yes," he said thickly, "Tha's what — then come back — join the fun."

"That's being sensible, Jerry. I'll amuse myself till you rouse."

Once he'd visited a Roman *vomitorium* and emerged, sweating and pale, Perdita, setting her mask straight, guided him to a cell in a far corner.

Soothingly, her voice sounded as from a great distance. "Jerry, you need to lie down; if you have to puke use this urn. You'll soon feel better."

Perdita on returning to her *triclinium* found it occupied by a masked, solid-looking figure. When he offered ribald invitations she found no difficulty in identifying the Third Marquess of Middlebrook.

Although George Liscard was pretending to be roaring drunk she knew he wasn't; while pulling her onto the couch and bestowing slobbering kisses he said clearly, "My dear, it is of the utmost consequence for your brother — and to myself for that matter — that you listen carefully.

"Since I've just watched you steer Boston Jerry to that corner cell," he said, "I know you ain't even half-jingled."

Exhaling brandy fumes he kissed her hard, lasciviously. "Curse of Satan! Wish I'd no other duty than to squire you, but I needs must win another pearl if I'm to compete with Jemmy Twitcher."

Although perspiration was now coursing beneath her mask she said steadily enough, "Pity. I've often wondered how much your gallantries are based on fact." She pulled back her head. "And now, sir, what do you expect of me?"

"In around an hour the Abbot will proclaim the rites of defloration. Only then must you seek that old bawd, Mother Stanhope, masquerading as Mother Superior."

"I've already met her."

"Good." His voice hardened. "Tell her as she values my patronage she must arrange for you to lead a Doe named Dolly straight to Lord Sandwich — he occupies a cell marked with a goat's head. See that Dolly enters, then close the door and guard it till you're sure the old devil really has her in his clutches."

Once the rites of St. Priapus had been announced, Perdita, mightily perplexed as to what this had to do with Jeremy, avoided clutching hands and obscene invitations to make her way through lurching, staggering groups of half-clad revelers to the Robing Room where she found the Mother Superior and the Abbess in a antechamber guarding six flower-crowned, white-clad and very young girls.

A masked figure brushed by to mutter under Mrs. Roach's wimple, "Which one is Mr. Falconer's fancy?"

"Daisey, yonder." She seized by the wrist a frail, golden-haired child of thirteen who whimpered and tried to hold back.

All at once Perdita was reminded of an afternoon back home when Pa's cook had gone out to select a fowl from a coop of white hens. After looking them over the fat old woman had decided on a snow-white pullet which she had carried, screaming, off to the chopping block.

Perdita drew a deep, deep breath of smoke-tinctured air and thought swiftly as she approached Dolly Lawton. She cast the girl a sympathetic glance. How very lovely she looked with abundant chestnut curls cascading over her shimmering white gown. A meaningless smile was stamped rather than formed on Dolly's sweetly dimpled features. She wasn't trembling as she stood stiffly erect and staring fixedly before her.

Of course amid such confusion she hadn't recognized Lady Constable behind her mask.

"Keep Dolly ready for a few moments," Perdita ordered the Mother Superior. "I must be sure His Lordship is ready to enjoy his pearl."

Lady Constable soon returned with an impression of Lord Sandwich sprawled half-naked on his couch snoring stertorously and with a pool of vomit on the floor beside him creating an acid stench.

Said she briskly, "The Rape-Master General awaits you. Come along Dolly but for pity's sake brighten up; think on the fortune you're about to earn!"

47

Hazardous Gambit

WITH AN ARM about Dolly's shuddering shoulders Lady Constable kept her charge in an alcove until the Hall of Priapus became deserted but for couples too drunk or too brazen to seek privacy.

Once in a while thin shrieks and pitiful treble pleas for mercy sounded in chambers behind sculptured keystones; gradually silence descended. Most candles were guttering by now and lamps either had gone out or burned low in the Hall of St. Priapus.

Numbed, Dolly Lawton responded only mechanically when the tall Dollymop whispered, "Come along; don't make a sound."

Gloom in the dining hall was so deep Perdita Constable had difficulty in finding the cell to which she'd guided Jeremy, but then she stepped inside tugging the small, flower-crowned figure after her. When she drew a heavy curtain it grew so dark only the shadowy outline of a man's figure sprawled on the bed could be seen.

"My lord," she muttered very softly, "here is the new pearl for your necklace — compliments of George Liscard."

Heart hammering, Lady Constable then drew the curtain and hurried away allowing subsequent events to take their course.

Better than half-sobered, Jeremy shook his head to clear it of lingering fumes but didn't open his eyes. What the hell? That voice just now had sounded faintly familiar. What had the woman said? Couldn't remember anything except "compliments of George Liscard."

He grinned in the dark. Dear Cousin George! How damn typical of him. Sitting up, he rubbed his eyes. Criminently! It was so dark in here that if the girl waiting submissively beside his cot hadn't been dressed in white he'd have missed seeing her.

Freed of nausea he stood up, flung arms about the pliant figure and hugged its softness to him. Too hellish black to tell what she looked like but he knew she was slim and smelled fresh and sweet as a new-mowed clover field.

Her arms slipped up about his neck and before she kissed him she whispered, "Please, my lord, be gentle with a poor virgin and then be generous."

Only briefly did the words "my lord" linger in Jeremy's fevered mind while he ripped off her garment. With a single swoop he lifted her off the floor then lowered her, limbs quivering violently, onto the cot. Stimulated by ineffectual struggles and frightened moans urgent, fiery currents shot through his body before he became engulfed in a delicious maelstrom of sensuality.

Emitting a single, breathless little scream Lord Middlebrook's gift then ardently blended her body with his and they loved furiously among shimmering mists of ecstasy till they fell asleep. Neither stirred until shortly before dawn a servant slid aside the curtain long enough to place a chimneyed candle on a stand just within the cell's entrance.

When groggily Jeremy finished knuckling his eyes he realized his bedmate had risen with auburn ringlets flowing in wild confusion over pallid shoulders and with a bewildered expression on flushed and lovely features.

Understandably he failed immediately to recognize this disheveled beauty clutching a red-marked white robe before her breasts; after all, he'd only seen her once — in the library of Middlebrook House.

Dolly Lawton then cried softly, incredulously, "But — but you're not Lord S-S-Sandwich! Why — why, you're Adonis!"

Although he understood the significance of that reference to "Lord Sandwich" the term "Adonis" made no impact on the whirling mind he was attempting to lash back into some semblance of order.

Hurriedly he dipped a rag into a ewer standing at the bedside, then by candlelight wiped his and his companion's heated features. "Good God, what mischance is this?"

"If only I knew," Dolly whispered thoughts struggling like a kitten entangled in a skein of knitting wool. Her prevailing sensation was one of relief; at long last that precious, pestiferous virgin knot had been untied and by the one person she willingly would have accorded the privilege.

Visions of sudden ease and affluence evaporating like a mirage, Dolly dropped her covering, surged forward to crush herself against his broad and naked chest, panting, "Oh, oh, Boston Jerry! Can this *really* be you?"

"Yes, and you're Dolly, the same girl Mother Stanhope fetched to Middlebrook House a good while back."

He held her close till returning hardheadedness caused him to release her. Damn! Disaster, complete and irretrievable, was staring him in the face! What mightn't happen if Cousin George discovered that Jeremy Brett had robbed John Montagu of such a costly gift?

As if a sluice gate abruptly had been opened, a cold stream of thought steadied him, made him aware that everything now depended on whether Lord Sandwich still was wallowing in drunken slumber or whether he'd recovered sufficiently to search for another companion.

"Wait here and stay quiet," he whispered. "No! *Don't* start tidying yourself! Be back very soon."

Silently as if stalking game in the backwoods, Jeremy, although stung on occasion by splinters of shattered glass on his bare feet, picked a course across the wildly disordered banquet hall.

For a wonder, he was able to recall that, almost certainly, the Abbot had assigned Lord Sandwich a cell distinguished by a goat's head on its lintel.

Several times he blended with shadows when muffled voices sounded nearby. His chief concern remained with an aged manservant engaged in discreetly placing night lights in various cells and chambers.

Finally a door beneath a sculptured goat's head became discernible; heart in mouth he listened an eternal moment before putting a

shoulder to the portal. He shoved gently and when it gave without sound immediately stepped inside.

Apparently efforts must have been made to cleanse the floor of vomit but the Earl of Sandwich lay on his back grunting and snuffling like some sleeping boar-hog; otherwise the chamber was untenanted.

On scratched and bleeding feet Jeremy regained his cell almost before he knew it and was whispering, "Trust me and do exactly what I say. Mother Stanhope taught you some arts in make-believe?"

"To dissimulate? Oh yes, sir. What shall I do?"

Holding her by marble-smooth shoulders he peered earnestly into her face, only half-seen by the night light's gentle radiance. "We're headed for Lord Sandwich's couch. You'll join him on it."

"What then?"

"Lie down, gently embrace him and wait for His Hogship to wake up."

Meekly, "I can do that."

"When he wakes, sob and carry on; everything depends on convincing him that although he was drunk as a fiddler's bitch he did a masterly job while ridding you of your maidenhead."

"Oh-h, dear Adonis, that will be easy — I've heard such patter a dozen times."

"Good. Sting the old lecher for every penny you can wring out of him then when it's safe let me know your whereabouts at Middle-brook House — hope I'll still be there."

"I will do that, dearest heart. Never doubt it!"

So much silly adoration was in her expression he kissed her a long moment before gathering up and carrying the disheveled young creature, red-stained robe and all, to her destination. Silently he opened John Montagu's door, set Dolly down, patted her buttocks reassuringly, and pushed her into the dim interior.

48

Irish Ogre I

To DESCRIBE Jeremy Brett's condition as poor would have been inadequate. Recognizing this fact he set out on a long, brisk walk about the estate to shake off mordant doubts as to whether his ploy in the Caverns had come off. Should Lord Sandwich have failed to be taken in God only knew what would happen!

As he jogged along breathing deeply he realized another critical problem loomed ahead: what would happen this afternoon when, at long last, he'd square off against the Irish Ogre? It didn't help a bit that he'd heard little if anything useful or reliable concerning his opponent or about that savage Irishman's ring tactics and style of fighting.

Disgust with himself filled him. Definitely his step wasn't springy right now; on the contrary, his feet went down solidly, as if at the end of a long day's tramp. Then, too, his nerves were so badly frayed that when a deer suddenly darted out of a thicket and dashed by a few feet before him he flinched, heart hammering wildly.

Even yet he'd failed to comprehend Cousin George's insistence upon the dissipation in which he'd been indulging — perhaps too wholeheartedly. Still, His Lordship, so he'd heard, had secured mounting odds against his winning. His best chances lay in the fact that, reportedly, the Ogre was being equally reckless about his condition.

He regained the Manor House to find a good many pouched-eyed and bleary-looking fellow guests congregated in the Billiard Room, and drinking with reckless enthusiasm.

It soon turned out that a Friar, the Viscount Ormond Dalrymple, had just arrived from Ireland, obscenely furious over having been detained by highwaymen long enough to prevent his attending the Banquet of St. Priapus. Nearing forty, this tall, lank and blue-jawed gentleman was landlord of enormous holdings in County Wicklow.

A quick look about informed Jeremy that neither of the two men he felt most anxious to observe had as yet put in an appearance.

It was most unfortunate that he couldn't be aware that, at that moment Lord Sandwich and Lord Middlebrook were lounging in the former's suite, bloated about face and eyes, with heads swathed in cloths servants kept saturating with icewater.

The Fourth Earl of Sandwich, corpulent figure enveloped in a liberally ruffled yellow silk dressing gown, vented a long-drawn sigh and fixed bloodshot, turquoise-blue eyes upon his companion. "Simply can't tell you, old friend and fellow Friar," rumbled John Montagu, "how deeply sensible I am about your most generous gesture of last night. Curs'd if I can."

"You found the wench really a virgin?"

"Must have been; there was gore aplenty as supportin' evidence, but I was so blasted fuddled I fear that though I took her maidenhead right enough I failed to enjoy your generosity to the fullest. Pity!"

A bleak smile flitted over George Liscard's haggard features while he pulled a little gold pillbox from his banyan's pocket. "In that case, my dear fellow, allow an old friend to offer a slight souvenir of the occasion." A large, iridescent pearl lay in the palm of his outstretched hand.

"Damme, George! Can't readily recall a more delicate compliment. This is sheer inspiration. Trust some day to repay so costly a piece of sentiment. No, shan't forget this, damned if I do!"

"And what does this trifle count on your necklace?"

"Eighty-one. Easily should score a hundred before the year's out. And you?"

"But seventy-seven, though to keep in the running I, too, added a bead to my rosary last night. Gad, I'm weary. For my age I've been covering a bit too much turf lately."

They chatted affably until Lord Sandwich, picking at his long, red nose, drawled, "What about the bout this afternoon? Not sure I ain't been taking advantage of you. I really believe your man is worth nearer five-to-seven rather than eight-to-six. Your man's been wenching and drenching till all hours — rather like a founding father of this sacred Order."

"Generous of you, Jack, but suppose we allow that five thousand to stand on the original odds?" He didn't miss the greedy glint in those blurred eyes peering wearily from beneath that turban-like ice-pack.

John Montagu poured a spoonful of some restorative and made a face as he swallowed it. "Best get some rest, old friend. Fight's slated for four o'clock."

"Where?"

"In a wooded paddock beyond the stables — you know the place; 'tis where the cockpits usually are set up. Thank God the weather promises fair."

Downstairs Jeremy was trying to forget ever-increasing uneasiness by crowding in to listen to Viscount Dalrymple's discourse.

Said he, amiably sloshing his drink around in a silver stirrup cup shaped like a fox head, "Life, y'know, can grow pretty dull in the huntin' county south o' Dublin; 'specially after Twelfth Night, so some playful neighbors and I ha' invented a new and fascinatin' sport — call ourselves the 'County Wicklow Wench Hunt.' "

" 'Wench Hunt'? Why? Don't you chase foxes?"

The new arrival's heavy eyelids lifted, lazily swung to the speaker. "God love ye, no, my friend. After the New Year we're fed to the teeth with chasin' Reynard."

The babble of voices subsided; everybody listened.

"Must ha' heard tell of wild, untamed Irish who, landless, master-less and lawless, range the bogs and fens like savage beasts. Cunning they are, and desperate to the last man, woman or child of 'em —"

A voice called, "Aye! And that's puttin' it mild-like!"

"Well, Terry Auchinlech and I invented the sport last winter — commissioned our bailiffs to round up and cage around a dozen o' the best-lookin' wild girls they could capture."

A babble of excitement arose. "And then what?"

" 'Twas simple. We mounted up, fetched out our bitch pack, and rode to the meetin' place. The huntsmen then stripped a colleen stark naked. God, ye should ha' seen the way that shaggy beauty kept cursin', hissin' and spittin' whilst her rags were bein' ripped off. After they'd rubbed the wild girl's feet with oil of aniseed they turned her loose. We granted her a half-hour's start on the edge of a rugged cover before we loosed the hounds.

"Then we took up the chase hallooing, 'Harkaway! Yoicks! Wench! Wench!' " The Viscount paused to drain his stirrup cup.

"And then what?"

"First gent who rides up after the wench is brought to bay can claim her and use her to suit himself."

Lord Tilton drawled, "Sounds like rare fine sport."

"Very often — 'specially when the quarry is long-legged, as most o' those wild colleens are — they're swift and nimble as deer. Come over and hunt with us next winter — fancy you'll find wench huntin' a welcome escape from *accidia*."

Long since, it had become evident that the Earl of Sandwich effectively had been keeping the Ogre "under wraps"; not only had he quartered his bruiser in a gamekeeper's lodge on the extreme east side of the estate but also had hired a squad of toughs to keep the curious at a distance.

Therefore when the Irish Ogre descended from a trap and promptly disappeared into one of the two blue-and-white-striped tents serving as dressing rooms his frightening appearance came as a shock to ever-increasing throngs of onlookers.

Some thirty minutes before the bout was scheduled to commence, Jeremy Brett and his professional handler, a hard but cheerful-looking individual named Harris, entered the small pavilion reserved for his use. Striving for calm, he squatted on a three-legged stool to allow his handler to strip him down to small clothes.

It didn't seem real. Of course, he was going to win. He had to. Last night, Cousin George had plainly indicated his patronage and all it meant lay on the line.

How fine to feel the handler expertly massaging his torso and limbs with a pleasant-smelling oil. While relaxing, he gradually drew a long series of deep breaths and arrived at the conclusion that although far from his best he was feeling more fit than he had on awakening; still, he could wish his stomach less queasy and his head not so thick.

Without looking up, Harris queried, "Seen yer hopponent yet, sir?"

"No, which bothers me considerably. Can you tell me anything I need to know. What's the fellow like?"

"'E Ogre looks powerful as a ox and uglier nor original sin."

"About how old?"

"'Is fyce being that battered, sir, 'tis 'ard to sye. Venture 'e's scarce over thirty."

"What's his build?"

"Broad-chested and bandy-legged, sir." Anxiety entered the handler's tone. "I'd sye wot ye'll chiefly 'ave to watch out for are them extry long arms on 'im; 'ang right down to 'is knees, they do; ye'd best keep close inside 'is reach so ye can pound 'im w'out getting 'urt with no chance for reply."

The afternoon had turned warm, sunny and humid following a brief but intense shower which had drenched West Wycombe Park just after midday.

For the first time Jeremy noticed the steadily mounting babble of voices. "Our bicker seems to be well attended," Jeremy remarked after casting a quick glance through the tent's fly.

"Aye, sir. Please relax them muscles — they're that tight I scarce can dent 'em," pleaded Harris and set about kneading neck and shoulders. "Nigh 'arf the neighborhood's 'ere or on their wye."

This proved no exaggeration; on a grassy circle of low mounds enclosing a natural depression in which the ring had been pitched was gathering a motley throng of local gentry, farmers, grooms, gamekeepers, house servants and other employees.

For the convenience of Lord le Despencer and his guests, along one side stood a long double row of armchairs with their backs turned to the sun.

To his dismay Jeremy's stomach suddenly started to feel unsettled again. Damn! Why *had* he so faithfully respected Cousin George's admonition to break training?

Fairly soon the thudding of hooves and a sound of wheels announced the arrival of guests from West Wycombe Hall.

Briefly, he wondered how Perdita, Sir Guy and Peregrine Falconer were placing bets. No telling; sentiment found no place in the smart gambler's lexicon.

A professional bookmaker set up his table nearby and just as if taking bets at Newmarket chanted: "Offerin' eight-to-six on the Ogre! Thank ye, sir! And you, sir, how much at eight-to-six?"

Jeremy's mouth tightened — eight-to-six against him! Well, at least he'd accomplished that much for Cousin George who entered into the pavilion with Peregrine Falconer.

Although the Third Marquess of Middlebrook remained red-eyed and more flushed than usual, otherwise he seemed in high good spirits. "Well, m'lad," said he, clapping the Colonial on his shoulder, "how do you feel? Fit as a fiddle I daresay."

Grinning, Jeremy flexed first his knees then his arms and shadow-boxed on stockinged feet about the springy turf. "Cousin George, I'm confident I'll do all right." Silently he added, and I'd do a damn sight better if I'd a sound night's sleep instead of robbing a wretched child of her maidenhead.

He became conscious of Lord Middlebrook's small black eyes intently boring into his features. "Boston Jerry," he whispered, "this is important! You must put the Ogre away *not later* than the end of the fourth round!"

"Out to win a pool on which round finishes Jemmy's boy," explained Peregrine Falconer.

"I'll do my best," Jeremy attempted to sound confident but must have failed. Lord Middlebrook quietly pulled a small bottle from a coat pocket.

Said he in an unfamiliar flat voice, "Better take some of this elixir which speeded your recovery the other day. You recall?"

"Of course. Its effect was — well, 'twas near magical."

From a plain wooden table the Marquess of Middlebrook selected a tumbler and filled it with that bitter yellow liquid he remembered.

Falconer bent, said softly, urgently, "Good luck, Jerry. Put him away in the fourth and things will go well for all of us."

49

Irish Ogre II

THE CLANGING of a brass handbell partially silenced the crowd when Lord van Sittart, no mean boxer on his own account, parted the ropes and stepped into a ring, supported at each corner by sturdy posts.

Cupping hands and throwing back his head he announced in clear, far-carrying tones: "Gentlemen and ladies! Through the generosity of our distinguished host," he made a semi-derisive "leg" at Sir Francis lolling in his armchair. "We are about to witness a fight to the finish between the Irish Ogre, backed by Lord Sandwich, and Boston Jerry, sponsored by the Marquess of Middlebrook!"

A ringing shout went up when Jeremy ran out of his pavilion closely followed by Harris carrying a sponge, a water bucket and a towel.

Lady Perdita Constable, seated between Peregrine Falconer and Lord Tilton, experienced a lifting sensation in her breast. Till now she'd never fully appreciated the magnificent proportions of her brother's physique; unlike most people Jeremy looked larger out of his clothes than in them.

His mane of strong brown hair had been pulled back and bound tight over the nape of his neck. To her relief her brother's color looked fine and his step lithe when, clad only in linen knee-breeches and heavy cotton thread stockings gartered above the knee, he climbed through the ropes and danced to the ring's center. She could have wished, however, he didn't appear so tense.

The women in the crowd kept exclaiming over Boston Jerry's muscles swelling on his arms and torso already agleam with perspiration.

He bowed perfunctorily first to the referee, Lord van Sittart, then in George Liscard's direction.

"And now," shouted van Sittart, "I present Lord Sandwich's fancy, the Irish Ogre!"

The crowd, as if startled by what they saw, created a deafening tumult when the Irishman, black hair tossing, ducked through the ropes and stood, grinning and touching huge fists above his head.

Gasped Perdita to Lord Tilton seated at her left, "God's love! Can that creature be human or is it an ape of some sort?"

A reassuring calm gripped Jeremy on discovering himself unshaken by his opponent's ferocious aspect. As Harris had warned, this Irishman's arms were preternaturally long, his hairy body was massive and his short legs greatly bowed.

Once the Ogre shuffled near Jeremy noticed that all the fellow's upper front teeth had been knocked out; that his nose was twisted and flattened and his ears had been mangled into shapeless lumps of dead-white cartilage.

Cavernous bright-blue eyes glared from beneath shaggy, sable brows. Not only the Ogre's chest but also his upper arms, shoulders and back were covered by a matting of thick black hair.

The two boxers peered curiously at one another till the bell clanged.

"Here we have a fight to a finish," announced the referee, "Five-minute rounds, two minutes between. Give it all you've got, boys, and may the best man win."

Breathless, Perdita watched the Irish Ogre go into a crouch and settle a bullet head low between such massive shoulders he appeared to have no neck at all.

Grimacing, the Ogre shuffled forward on bowed legs. Jeremy, fists balled, offered to touch hands but the Ogre only snarled, shook his shaggy head, fell back, braced legs and raised fists before him in the conventional stance.

While quitting the ring, Lord van Sittart coldly remarked to John

Montagu, "A discourteous rogue, your man. Hope he gets what's left of his ears ripped off."

Called young Villiers excitedly, "My lord, I'll bet a hundred guineas on your man!"

"I do and be damned to you!" rasped Lord van Sittart seating himself behind a bench supporting a small brass mantel clock. "Time!" he shouted, ringing his hand bell. "Round One coming up!"

Years later Jeremy could recall a sudden feeling of confidence: strength and mental clarity were returning so fast Cousin George's elixir must be taking effect; sinews, reflexes were responding as they should, his feet felt sure and light as of yore.

For a few seconds the boxers circled, testing their footing and estimating the other's probable tactics.

Jeremy went on the defensive; not yet time to close in. Easily he ducked under long, looping blows delivered by those amazingly long and sinewy arms. Twice his knuckles impacted hard against the other's midriff but a little high; his punches produced no discernible effect. It was like hitting a side of beef.

He took a glancing blow in the left cheek which barely jarred him. He danced lightly aside, weaving and bobbing out of range. The Irishman roared unintelligible obscenities, then rushed in, arms flailing.

Lady Constable wasn't conscious of a warm sickish-sweet fluid flooding her mouth; didn't yet realize she'd bitten her lip during a furious slugging match which demonstrated beyond a doubt that the Ogre was by no means as slow or heavy-footed as the yammering crowd had deemed him.

Round One ended with neither boxer seriously marked; nevertheless, odds barked by the brazen-voiced bookmaker changed slightly in Boston Jerry's favor.

" 'Ow d'yer feel, sir?" muttered Harris.

"Well enough," Jeremy panted, "but he's a sight faster than you'd think."

"Keep out of reach, sir. Just keep *out of reach* for the next few rounds, then mark my words, them short legs of 'is will slow 'im. Then ye close in fer a kill."

The second round was very much like the first, Lord Middlebrook decided with a bleak smile, hands tightened on the arms of his chair.

The wildly excited crowd kept clamoring, pleading with Boston Jerry to win by a quick knockout.

In the third round came the first break. Jeremy, with a lightning left, hit the Ogre's nose so hard bright scarlet blood spurted then dribbled over his chin onto the matted black hair below.

Stung, the Ogre vented an infuriated roar, charged, and caught Jeremy two savage blows on the short ribs. A handsbreadth to the left the Irishman's fist would have smashed into the Colonial's solar plexus and ended the fight. As it was, Jeremy danced out of range, then closed for a quick flurry of blows.

How amazing he remained feeling so strong, clear-headed and well coordinated.

"Even money on Boston Jerry!" "Hurrah for Jerry!" Shouts made the crowded paddock resound and tethered carriage horses snort and plunge. Panting lightly, he sought his corner well-aware that the all-important fourth round was about to come up.

Well, he reckoned, it was beginning to look like he had a damned good chance of carrying out Cousin George's orders; for when the Irish Ogre gargled he spat bright scarlet water and was drawing breath in great, whooping gasps.

He forced himself to relax on the stool and make the most of Harris's furious rubbing at the nape of his neck.

Immediately the timekeeper's warning bell clashed. Jeremy sprang up, grinning. But even as the Ogre was leaving his stool the earth shifted just a little beneath Boston Jerry's grass-stained stockings.

Impatiently, the Colonial shook his head as if to rid it of so impossible a phenomenon then started forward but, strangely, his feet didn't respond as smartly as they had.

Blinking, Jeremy barely avoided a vicious punch aimed at his head and, unable to counter, tried to clinch. Inexplicably that bloodied head bobbing before his blurring eyesight began to swing like a clock's pendulum and his counter-punch missed by so wide a margin the crowd groaned.

Panic seized him. Covering up, the Colonial retreated an uncertain few steps amid jeers and howls. By now he couldn't even focus his eyes and a queer lassitude was relaxing his muscles.

In bemused desperation he attempted a rally, lurched forward and swung clumsily a split second before the Irishman's enormous fist impacted savagely upon his sternum and made the world explode into a sun-burst of blinding white agony.

While her brother's slowly writhing figure was being lugged out of the ring, Perdita, eyes wild, clutched Falconer's arm. "Perry, for Christ's sake find Guy and go to him. He's bad hurt!"

They arrived barely in time to witness a most extraordinary spectacle. The Marquess of Middlebrook apparently had gone insane with fury. His complexion had turned a deep shade of crimson and his small black eyes were bulging like grapes of wrath.

He spat on the unconscious figure stretched on the grass. "You blasted, double-damned Colonial! Beelzebub's balls! You've cost me a fortune! After all I've done for you, how dare you fail me, you ungrateful whoreson?"

People crowding about the pavilion could hear his every furious word.

"You worthless bastard, you've cost me above ten thousand pounds!" He whirled on Peregrine Falconer, roaring, "Get this dog out of my sight and never let me hear his name again!"

50

Dolly Lawton's Diary Resumed I

WASN'T ALL THIS TOO BEAUTIFUL TO BE REAL? Dolly Lawton considered the large and pleasant bedroom so much at variance with her accommodation in Mrs. Stanhope's brothel. How tastefully everything was arranged; how comfortable and pleasing to the eye were its appointments.

Dolly considered the huge canopied four-poster in which she'd spent the last three nights, then brought out and unlocked her diary. After brief deliberation she dipped her goose quill.

Seems Incredible this Change in my Prospeckts really has Occur'd so soon after we departed that Haunt of pleasing Horror called West Wycombe. Never shall I Forget what Chanc'd there!

I was terrified over my Future when a Message arriv'd at the Nunnery on the Morning after my suppos'd Ravishm't Commanding Me to an immediate Attendance on His Lordship, the Earl of Sandwich.

Expeckting the Worst, I trembl'd like a leaf on obtaining a first clear View of this powerfull Nobleman and perceiv'd how ravag'd he is through Dissipation and Debauchery.

He view'd me with Care then fetch'd a gusty Sigh saying, "What a vast Fool I was to get so Bottl'd at the Banquette I could not Enjoy

to the Fullest breaking your Maidenhead for you Indeed are an uncommon lovely little Doe."

My Heart sank when he added, "Would it were Possible to offer you Continu'd Protecktion but Mistress Raye is so Fiendish Jealous I dare not risk Affronting that dear Creature. By the bye, Child, how are you call'd?" He wrote the Name I gave on a Bank Draught and My Heart leapt like a hunted Stag when I saw the Sum nam'd was Five Hundred Guineas!

Again he chuck'd me under the Chin, kiss'd me which near to Sicken'd me with the Foullest Breath one can Imagine.

Dolly straightened on her chair and stretched arms slowly, luxuriously. How wonderful to be in Constable House, befriended and secure for the time being at least.

As yesterday, she heard crowds clamoring in the distance so sought a window. Peering down into Deane Street she noticed knots of roughly-dressed fellows tramping in the direction of Broad St. Giles' Street. She didn't like the look of them at all.

Forgive me, Dear Diary, for having Neglecked you so long. During our Stay at West Wycombe there was small Opportunity to write and Since then, Events for me have march'd at so Furious a Pace there has been no Time to record either Thoughts or Experiences.

Suffice it that once we had Return'd to London Mrs. Stanhope press'd me to Continue in her Service but This I stoutly refus'd to do. I have no Wish to suffer the Fate of too many thoughtless Wenches who have Remain'd under that Roof.

To my Surprize Mrs. S. remain'd Good-humour'd, saying, "Dolly, I deem you to be Clever and Ambitious above young females, much too Smart to remain a Publick Whore. Therefore whilst you are making your Boxes, I will go cash my Lord's Draught at Mr. Coutts's Bank."

The old Strumpet then kiss'd me on the Forehead and patted my Shoulder saying, "In Transactions of this Sort I generally take Half the Sum earned by a girl of Mine as Commission. However, you so put me in Mind of Myself long ago, in your Case I will take out but a Third instead of a Half of your Fee, that You may make your Way towards Real Riches with better Advantage."

So overwhelmed was I with Gratitude I burst out blubbering like a spank'd Child.

Finally Mrs. S. ask'd kindly enough, "Have you any Friends?"

I told her no respecktable ones saving a kindly Lady I first encounter'd in the Nunnery and who had not only preserv'd me from Lord Sandwich but all Unknowing deliver'd me into the Arms of Boston Jerry, my dear Adonis who is a close friend to Lord Middlebrook. "Alack," I cried, "that I do not know that Kind Lady's Name."

"I do," vouchsafes Mrs. S. "She is Lady Constable and Sister to that manly young Fellow who so Enchanted you the Night of Mr. Treymane's Frolicks."

I soon learn'd the Lady and her Husband, Sir Guy, occupy'd a fine Town House lying at no great Distance from Mrs. S.'s establishm't.

I therefore Screw'd up my Courage, call'd at Constable House and left a Note Soliciting that Kind Lady's Advice. To my unbounded Astonishment and Delight Lady C. sent Word that for the moment a Guest Room was vacant in Constable House which I was free to Occupy till I could arrive at a Plan for my Future.

Again she raised her pen, listened to the singsong chant of a street vendor.

"Fresh China Oranges! Hot, Spiced, Gingerbread, Hot! Oh!

"Buy my China Oranges! Hot, Spiced, Gingerbread, Hot! Oh!"

Beneath her dressing gown of fine lawn, Dolly shivered; this day was growing chilly.

Soon I Discover'd to my Inexpressible Delight that my Belov'd Adonis, after Stormy Dismissal by Lord Middlebrook, also was Sheltering under this Hospitable Roof. I find Lady Constable is not without real Sensibility for she vows her Brother is much Stricken with Remorse over having Robb'd me of my Innocence.

She nibbled the tip of her quill and stared unseeingly before her. Could any other man even begin to possess such charming ways, such manly good looks and so splendidly-proportioned a body? Her pulses quickened and she fetched a resounding sigh.

*The Goddess of Fortune indeed has smiled for Things to fall out
as they have for Parson Lottimore's runaway Child — and in so brief
a Span! Here I am Possess'd of a modest fortune and under the
very same Roof as my Heart's Desire! Best of All, my Adonis protests
he has Conceiv'd an ever-deepening attachment for me and is Determin'd I shall never become an Abandon'd Female.*

*He speaks glowingly of the simplicity of Life amid the natural
Beauties of his Homeland. 'Tis all I can do to Contain myself when
he Caresses me and talks in such a Vein.*

*Lady Constable and her Husband seem both pleas'd and Amus'd
over any display of our Mutual Passion. Altho' my Beloved has not
yet suggested the Possibility of Marriage I am entirely Confident
that ere Long the Depth of his Attachment will persuade him to so
blissfull a Course.*

*I trust I have Further'd my Cause by welcoming him to my Bed
after the House has quieted. What incredible Transports of Delight
do we not indulge in!*

A light rap on the door preceded the entrance of Perdita Constable clad in a well-beribboned house cap and a pale yellow satin
negligée. Smiling, she patted Dolly's cheek and cast an amused
glance at the rumpled four-poster, then bade her resume her seat.

She glanced through the window at low-flying, lead-hued clouds
which already had begun to loose delicate snow flurries to conceal
London's grime. "Ah me, judging by that, drear winter will soon be
upon us."

Amid a swirl of silk the lady of the house seated herself, indolently
crossed long and lovely legs. "Yes, I dread to find winter closing in,
although winters here in England are nothing compared to the furious, icy, sometimes week-long blizzards we have to endure back
home."

She made a pretense of shivering. "Raging, frigid blasts penetrate
even into the best-built dwellings, of which, alas, there are not very
many in New England. It seems as if, back in Piscataqua, I spent
hours tending fires."

Dolly's eyes rounded themselves. "*You,* Lady Constable, tending
fires! Surely you jest? There must have been servants to ——"

"No, my dear. I'm quite serious; there are very few real servants in
America. Even wealthy families do without them for, all too often,

hired help is stupid, unmannerly and independent as pigs on ice. Have you ever tended fires?"

"Oh yes, m'lady, at the parsonage." Dolly frowned. "That was not the least of many tasks."

"I gather your early life cannot have been easy. I've no wish to pry, but tell me about it an you care to."

She reached out, selected a bonbon from a crystal dish, and, nibbling delicately, prepared to listen.

For the first time since running away to London, Dorothy Lottimore, overwhelmed with gratitude, raised the floodgates of memory and described in vivid detail life in the cramped, bleak and always damp old parsonage. Young face hardening, she described endless rounds of drudgery, bitter bickerings caused by overcrowding — imagine two adults and seven children — of which she was the oldest — packed into a tiny three-room cottage!

Effectively she dwelt on the misery and monotony of the only life she ever had known. Only through reading books that the Reverend Mr. Lottimore hadn't approved of had she learned about a different way of life — a life of comfort in which beauty, graciousness and joyousness had their place.

"Poor Dolly. Small wonder you ran away!" Perdita summoned a smile of understanding.

"However, you must not imagine that conditions across the Atlantic for most people is much different. In your home you may have been miserably uncomfortable, but at least you'd no fear of being torn apart and eaten by prowling wolves, or of hearing terrifying Indian war whoops in the dead of night or of listening to dying shrieks and sometimes even having to watch relatives and friends having their scalps sliced off by some painted demon's skinning knife."

"But surely," gasped Dolly, "wolves and savages would never dare to venture near civilization?"

Grimly, Jeremy's golden-haired sister shook her head. "Such happened a few years ago in a settlement not three miles from my father's doorstep."

"Near big town and cities?"

"My dear child, in North America you'll find no cities in the European sense and precious few sizable towns scattered along the coast. Ours is a rich and beautiful country, but vast, lonely and very scantily inhabited.

"Once one counts Boston, New York, Philadelphia and Charlestown — which lies far to the south of the other three — you find the sum of our so-called great towns. On the other hand the Colonies are prospering and growing fast. Mere crossroad hamlets swiftly increase into sizable villages; villages become towns often within a few years.

"Yes. The future *is* bright for us if only George III and his Ministers don't attempt to crush us."

"They can, can't they?"

Lady Perdita Constable stiffened on her chair, cast her amazed guest a hard look and her voice no longer held the affected accents of the realm's high society. "They can't! Our country's too vast, our people are tough and demand their rights as freeborn British subjects! Pushed too far, the Colonies will revolt and fight to the bitter end the sort of war they understand and that European soldiers don't know anything about.

"Dear Dolly, I fear I've got carried away. America is not all *that* grim." She then described local sports and entertainments; hospitality — crude, she admitted, but as generous as circumstances permitted.

Perdita concluded with studied casualness. "Sometime soon you must visit New England. You'll find people there plainly dressed but friendly, straightforward and sturdy. Ere long, I venture, there will appear families owning considerable wealth — but of course nothing to compare with what we see every day in Britain."

Dolly sat still a moment, queried, "Then there are no great estates in America, no landed gentry, no great families of title?"

"Not as yet, my dear. We still have to make our way." Perdita was startled to find herself saying "we." "What few titled personages exist amongst us are generally unimportant men serving King George III in some capacity. American-born nobles can be counted on your fingers."

51

King Mob

⌢

A FTER A WEEK in Constable House the reflection in Jeremy's Brett's shaving mirror became less depressing; last traces of cuts and bruises had faded; pouches had disappeared from beneath eyes no longer laced by tiny red veins.

Although his expression was neither happy nor confident, it wasn't near as grim and haggard as it had been. Perhaps this was because he was adjusting to the fact that to Society he now was a pariah, stripped of friends and fortune.

Several times when out of restlessness he'd gone walking and had encountered acquaintances they'd looked through him as if he were a pane of glass.

That ghastly day at West Wycombe Park! He'd never forget that moment he'd heard Sir Guy Constable drawl, "You're not really hurt, so I need only say I made a huge mistake by marrying into your family." Derisively, he'd added, "Your Servant, sir."

Peregrine Falconer, however, had treated him to half-sympathetic looks. "Trust you've now learned how absurd it is for a minnow to try to swim amid a pod of whales. Good luck, Boston Jerry, and fare-well." So saying he'd followed Sir Guy out of the pavilion.

While wiping his razor Jeremy recalled his banishment from West Wycombe Hall; being sent away in a manure cart seated on half-packed baggage. He'd been crushed but defiant, for, by Jesus, he'd fought his best as long as possible!

Once past the gatehouse, however, his spirits had sagged to their nadir, had floundered in bewildered hopelessness.

The first hint that life was not of unrelieved gloom had come when a few miles out of West Wycombe a groom in Sir Guy's familiar blue-and-white livery coach had galloped up, signaling the malodorous wagon to a halt.

"For Mr. Brett, sir." The groom had touched his hat before passing over an envelope bearing Perdita's handwriting; the message was terse:

My poor Bro. Make your way direckt to Constable House. We both are Bretts come what may.   There is more to this business than meets the Eye.

In great Haste,
P.B.C.

For the first time since childhood Jeremy had wept from the very depths of his being — not like a woman who weeps only with eyes and mouth.

During his first days at the Constables' he'd sulked in his room but, tactfully, was left alone to brood over the certainty that Lord Middlebrook had canceled not only his charter of the *Pelican*, a merchant brig, but also the cargo for Boston he'd underwritten.

Once more he was stony broke save for a few pounds in his pockets — less than he'd landed with half a lifetime ago.

Nor was it encouraging to learn when, finally, he sought out his sister that it was being bruited about fashionable clubs and coffeehouses that Boston Jerry had "taken a dive" thanks to a bribe paid by the Earl of Sandwich's agents.

This calumny had rankled worst of all till Guy Constable put him straight and confessed that his disavowal in the pavilion had been spoken for the benefit of Lord Middlebrook's hangers-on.

" 'Twas sheer poppycock!" declared Perdita's husband. "But Middlebrook lost so great a sum that libel like that was bound to arise."

Seemed curious that the Marquess of Middlebrook had so abruptly invited him to carouse. Jeremy recalled George Liscard's visit to the pavilion and the elixir pressed upon him.

Perry had been right. He *was* but a raw Colonial blundering in a web of intrigue.

On the third day of his stay Perdita sauntered into his bedchamber, beautiful and *insouciante*. "Now that you ain't sore as a bee-stung bear any more, maybe you'd welcome a bit of news.

"As you may have guessed, Guy doesn't believe there wasn't hanky-panky about that fight, nor does your boon companion, Perry Falconer. By the bye, Perry's stopped by twice to inquire how you're faring."

Jeremy's resentment flared. "Has he now? Don't believe it! Nobody in this goddamned rotten town has the decency of a starving wolverine! Surprised he's even recalled my existence."

"Oh, he does; Mr. Falconer's truly fond of you in his odd way — perhaps for a reason."

"Damn it, 'Dita, what's your meaning? Speak up — I'm fed to the teeth with mystery."

Perdita laughed lazily. "Why, 'tis simple as this: Dolly Lawton, the lass you ravished in Jemmy Twitcher's place, sought my protection. 'Tis only fitting I should take her in here since 'twas *I* who guided her to you."

"You! She's *here?*"

"Aye. The pretty thing seems resolved not to enter a life of shame. She tells me Jemmy Twitcher presented her with a round sum under the impression 'twas he who ravished her — thank God for that!"

For the first time in days Jeremy's laugh really rang out. "Rich! Uncommon rich!"

"And so Dolly called to solicit my advice. Things standing as they do —" her bright eyes twinkled — "now *that's* an apt verb, eh what? I fancied you'd not be averse to having your 'victim' convenient.

"I declare, Jeremy, this Dolly truly is mad for you. At the very mention of your name stars show in her eyes."

"You mentioned Peregrine Falconer?"

"Seems since he's learned she's here he's called and has paid her, for him, polite attention."

"Small wonder. He, like I, was present when Mrs. Stanhope made Dolly strip before Cousin — no, damn it! — before Lord Middlebrook. Well, what of this?"

"Nothing, save I noticed Perry's interest and have told you about it."

She went over and, stroking his head, added, "Guy last night being in a mellow mood vouchsafed he may be able to secure a contract for Pa. 'Tain't much, Bro, he says, still it might be sufficient to keep your yard going but he fears it may require time to arrange the matter."

"Time! Time's just the thing we can't afford! Within a matter of weeks our creditors will close in like hungry wolves."

Quite without being aware of it he completed shaving — thank God he could do without help from some fancy foreign barber.

A footman rapped and informed, "Mr. Brett, sir, there is a Mr. Pocock below who has fetched this letter the now. Sir, he earnestly invites you read it and return a reply instanter."

The message read:

My Dear Mr. Brett:
Mutual Friends have Brought to my Attention Matters which may prove of Interest to us Both. I trust you will call at my Residence in Craven Street. I sincerely hope that Three o'Clock of this Afternoon will prove Feasible.

Y'r Humble, Obed't Servant,
Benjn Franklin

For several minutes Jeremy debated his decision. The salient factor was Dr. Franklin's reference to "mutual friends." He hadn't any friends he was aware of beyond Sir Guy Constable.

A discreet cough recalled him to immediate considerations. On a sheet of Perdita's stationery he scribbled:

Learned Sir:
Will be Honor'd to comply.

Y'r Humble, Obed't Servant,
J. Brett

He felt an impulse to see Mr. Pocock but foresaw that that astute individual in all probability would impart no information of significance.

He completed his toilet and while thinking of Dolly the room seemed to brighten.

What an amazing creature, this lovely auburn-haired child — sixteen. A puzzling mixture: pathetically appealing, trusting and naïve; yet with a practical and perceptive streak in her.

Humming, Jeremy knotted his cravat, was aware of a lifting sensation. Criminently! He'd never been in love, beyond a few fits of puppy-love which had left him unaffected.

He stretched; good to feel his muscles respond smoothly, powerfully. Jesus God! What a wonderfully passionate creature! Despite Dolly Lawton's eagerness there was nothing lewd about the way she made love — she seemed only ready to give. In bed they were as perfectly matched as two humans might be. Without shame Dolly reveled in wondrous raptures attained through contact with his hard body.

What sort of wife would she make for a struggling young shipbuilder? How seriously would these parlous times delay recovery of the shipyard? How vividly would she recall her misery in the parsonage? She'd forget that in a hurry once the radiant perfection of their love blossomed. Didn't poets proclaim good marriages are made in Heaven?

He took a turn around the bedroom. What the devil lay behind this summons from the Postmaster General for the North American Colonies?

Craven Street, he learned from the butler, Thompson, lay distant by a good half-hour's walk. To Thompson's offer of a saddle horse he said, "The day's pleasant, since I've time to spare I'll go afoot — need exercise."

Thompson looked grave. "Please, sir, might I advise you not to go abroad afoot? Lawless men and gangs of the common sort are tramping the streets telling their betters to cheer for 'Wilkes and Liberty'."

"Thank you, Thompson, but I believe I'll walk — with a stout walking stick."

"Yes, sir. I'll fetch your hat and stick directly, sir."

When the butler reappeared he was carrying in addition a cockade made up of pale-blue ribbon.

"What in the world is that?"

"These, sir," explained the butler quietly, "are Mr. Wilkes's party's colors. Well displayed, they should avert insult and attack by guttersnipes, hoodlums and such other alley scrapings as you may encounter, sir."

Laughing, Jeremy slipped the cockade into his pocket. "Don't imagine I'll require such protection but thank you, Thompson."

"I trust not, sir, but hourly the mobs grow more inflamed over Mr. Wilkes's continued imprisonment. God knows what may chance an he's not quickly released."

To Jeremy's surprise he found Deane Street almost deserted but in the direction of High Holbourne sounded angry clamorings which ebbed and flowed like combers on a distant shore.

Increasing numbers of shaggy, savage-appearing characters clad in noisome rags slouched by. A few cast the Colonial hard, inquisitive stares but since his clothing was of the plainest and he was powerfully set up and carrying a heavy cane they made no move in his direction.

Unfortunately his course towards Craven Street required him to proceed towards the origins of a steadily increasing tumult. Gangs of roughly dressed characters appeared out of side streets; most were wearing light-blue bows or streamers bound about their upper arms.

Not inclined to become embroiled in a free-for-all in view of his appointment, Jeremy stepped into the recessed doorway of a bootmaker's shop long enough to pin Thompson's cockade on his left lapel.

While he did so a tough swaggered up and chalked "45! Up! John Wilkes!" across the shop's shutters.

Disheveled and evil-smelling rascals raised strident yells when into the narrow street turned a glittering carriage with sunlight flashing on plate-glass windows and gilded scrollwork.

Out from an alley swarmed jeering ragamuffins shaking sticks and cudgels or gripping bricks and cobblestones. To Jeremy's surprise there were not a few respectable-looking tradesmen, mechanics and clerks among the rabble.

Quickly, shouting swelled to a blood-chilling roar, then ruffians ran up to seize holding bars set beneath the horses' bits and halt them. The coachman, bellowing curses, lashed frantically about till dragged from his box to disappear under flailing fists and terrible kicks.

Bestial yells made this crooked little street resound. Pressed flat against a doorway and gripping his stick, Jeremy braced himself, then recognized screeched slogans: "Wilkes and Liberty!" "Up the North American Rebels and their Rights!" "Long life to their Sons of Liberty!" "Huzza for Otis, Adams and Hancock!" "Devil take all Despots!" "Down with the King's Friends!"

The carriage horses reared and, pawing frantically with their forefeet, knocked down several of the mob. All the same, the vehicle commenced to rock like a small boat struck by a squall. Stones shattered one of its windows, then a door was wrenched open and a dignified old man in black was hauled out, white as chalk and apparently confused.

"Raise a cheer for Wilkes, ye bloody nob!" commanded a beetle-browed bully. "Sing out loud if yer wants to keep yer balls!"

The old man quavered, "Huzza for John Wilkes."

"— And Liberty," prompted the mob leader.

"— And Liberty."

"Again! Louder yet!"

Suddenly the frail, black-clad figure stiffened and his eyes blazed. "Damned if I will! I'll see you hanged for this, you filthy scum!"

Murder might have been committed had not a platoon of kilted Scottish soldiers, probably on their way to relieve troops on duty around King's Bench Prison, at that moment come tramping into sight.

Jeremy heard the sergeant in command halt his men then briskly order them to lock on bayonets. Emboldened by yonder flashing steel and his blue cockade, Jeremy ran out into the street waving his staff and bawling, "Run for your lives! King's troops are here! Follow me!"

An eternal instant the mob milled uncertainly but when Jeremy yelled, "Come along and I'll show you where we really can accomplish something for our cause! This way!"

All required to accomplish his purpose was the rhythmic cadence of military boots advancing. Cursing the Scots for foreign hirelings the mob wavered, then pelted along in Jeremy's wake leaving the shattered carriage, wild-eyed horses and the straight-backed figure in black surrounded by the somber tartans of the Black Watch.

With the mob roaring in his wake the Colonial at a brisk trot resumed his course towards High Holbourne. Very soon the mob collided with another gang and it became a simple matter to work his way to the edge of the confusion and at a sedate walk continue on his way to Craven Street.

52

The House in Craven Street

WITH NOISES of disorder sounding fainter in the distance Jeremy Brett, Esq., used a well-polished brass door knocker and promptly was shown into the modest brick residence of Dr. Benjamin Franklin.

The housekeeper, a handsome, middle-aged female, quickly conducted him up to the Philosopher's study, where he experienced the shock of his life; for, aside from Dr. Franklin's tall figure advancing with hands cordially outstretched were Sir Guy Constable and the Third Marquess of Middlebrook!

He stood rooted while George Liscard offered both jeweled hands with a huge grin expanding his heavy mouth. "Cousin Jerry! Ah, dear boy, how impatiently I have awaited this moment!"

When Jeremy made no move to accept his greeting the nobleman actually reached out to seize his hand. "Come, come! This is a difficult moment for us all." Small black eyes twinkled and the familiar, wine-red features relaxed, albeit slowly.

"Must hasten to explain my recent unpleasant behavior. 'Twas far from genuine and inspired only through sheer necessity. When you've heard the rights of the matter I trust you'll find it in your heart to forgive your Cousin George."

Sir Guy then gripped Jeremy's fist. "Dear Jerry, never believed I could dissimulate as well as I did at West Wycombe — never have shone at dramatics — but for some time I've been party to George Liscard's machinations."

Jeremy began to get angry. "Just what the hell are you two trying to say? Talk plain, damn you, and quit treating me like a carnival clown's puppet!"

Dr. Franklin raised a placating hand. "Gently, gently, friend Brett. Perhaps Lord Middlebrook has been a trifle late in explaining this business. Let us seat ourselves, and whilst we sip Madeira, possibly I, in my unpolished way, can explain the situation."

Still resentful, Jeremy sank into a chair across the desk from the Postmaster General; the two noblemen resumed the seats they'd been occupying when he'd entered.

"I shall endeavor to be brief," announced Dr. Franklin, removing square-lensed and steel-rimmed spectacles to polish them. "What has been done, no matter how callous in appearance, has been done *only* with intent to thwart the present Ministry's dangerous policies.

"My good friend, Lord Middlebrook, along with certain others, has been long aware that the Earl of Sandwich and intimates are at the bottom of appalling, intolerable and ruinous corruption in many branches of the Government.

"Utterly conscienceless, these noble rascals undermine the strength and efficiency of the realm's Armed Forces — especially the Royal Navy." Dr. Franklin's clear, light-gray eyes shifted to Jeremy. "Mr. Brett, they goad our fellow countrymen to desperation, to the point of a revolt which must prove ruinous to both parties.

"Sir Guy has been overly modest about his duties at the Admiralty and has played the part of a vaporing macaroni with such success everybody considers him a trifler devoid of intelligence — or worse, of influence. And how do you plead to that, Sir Guy?"

Grinning, Jeremy's brother-in-law stood up, offered a mock bow. "Guilty as charged, your Worship."

"Hear! Hear!" murmured Lord Middlebrook. "In other words, with Mr. Wilkes ineffective for the moment, it remains my party's intent, nevertheless, to put a stop to this corruption employed by Lord Sandwich and others among the King's Friends. To accomplish their ruin we must secure indisputable evidence of guilt.

"I could continue in this vein all day but will only say that an opportunity has presented itself; Sir Guy recently has become aware of the Navy Board's having secured a sizable appropriation from Parliament for construction of replacement supply ships which are to be 'plantation-built' in North America."

Constable's gaze sought Jeremy. "I've learned that while high prices are to be paid for specified first-class designs, materials and workmanship, what actually will go into 'plantation-built' vessels are inferior materials and indifferent workmanship." He summoned a mirthless smile, "The difference, of course, will disappear among the King's Friends and associated thieves."

Smiling faintly, Dr. Franklin nodded several times. "Lord Middlebrook, will you inform Mr. Brett what happened as a result of that memorable Convocation at West Wycombe Hall?"

The Marquess of Middlebrook broke into a laugh. "I would to God, Cousin Jerry, you'd been present when, mournfully but with seeming good grace, I paid Lord Sandwich my losses on your bout! Pah!" The solid, red-faced figure almost spat. "My dear friend Sandwich fairly oozed gratitude over that and for my having supplied a new pearl for his necklace. He couldn't have been more sympathetic over your defeat and ——"

Jeremy surged to his feet, face flaming. "Damn it, sir, I did the best I could!"

"Never have doubted that for an instant," the Marquess of Middlebrook stated equably. "I remain convinced you could have beaten the fellow handily but for a certain elixir I gave you — it contained not exactly the same ingredients as the earlier one."

Jeremy started up in a fury. "How dared you trick a trusting friend so shamefully?"

Sir Guy broke in, fine features taut and bright-blue eyes hard. "Easy on, Jerry! Easy on, for God's sake. You were victimized *only* so that you may win what you seek — and then some, shouldn't wonder. Thanks to your defeat, Jemmy Twitcher in an expression of gratitude has fallen squarely into a trap."

Jeremy grunted, "You talk riddles again."

"Lord Sandwich has delivered those cheating ship contracts into Lord Middlebrook's hands for disposal among his friends."

The Marquess of Middlebrook spoke succinctly, "Among those North American contracts we have discovered evidence needed to prove outrageous dishonesty. At the right time I will threaten Lord

Sandwich with exposure unless new and honest commissions are placed in my own hands.

"In due course, Cousin Jerry," continued George Liscard, "I will see to it your family shipyard is awarded orders for two of the larger supply ships — possibly with more to follow. There is only one drawback — time will be required to accomplish this matter."

"Time," Jeremy informed grimly, "is just what Brett & Son can't afford. Pa's just written that our creditors intend to foreclose come the New Year."

Dr. Franklin, honorary LL.D., St. Andrews University and Member of the Royal Society, raised a quieting hand. "Pray control yourself, young sir, control and listen! Sir Guy already has informed Lord Middlebrook about your unhappy tidings from New Hampshire; already he has taken steps to avert your firm's bankruptcy."

Infinitely puzzled, Jeremy stared at the Marquess of Middlebrook. "What steps, may I ask?"

"Why, Cousin Jeremy, I never have canceled my charter for the *Pelican*. At this moment she lies in London pool with cargo stowed, crew aboard and papers cleared for Boston. She can sail within a matter of hours, should that become advisable."

Jeremy's head spun; too much was coming about too rapidly. Right now, he simply was unable to grasp the full implications of this astounding situation.

"I appreciate," Lord Middlebrook resumed, "that a departure by the *Pelican* by no means solves your problems — as I've said, several months must pass before you can hope to sight payment for the supply ship. I have explained this fact to Dr. Franklin, who has, I believe, come up with a solution which may well bridge this financial gap." The Marquess of Middlebrook's tone deepened.

"As loyal subjects of His Majesty, King George III, Sir Guy and I feel it — er, unadvisable to be present when Dr. Franklin's solution is explained."

Following a round of mellow sherries Lord Middlebrook and Sir Guy offered their excuses to the host, clapped Jeremy's shoulder in friendliest fashion, then disappeared.

Once Lord Middlebrook and Sir Guy Constable had departed Dr. Franklin said pleasantly, "Is it not apparent, Mr. Brett, that American rights have to be won in London as much as in Boston or Philadelphia? I cling firmly to the belief that revolt and a war for American independence is neither necessary nor inevitable. Surely, there must be enough men of reason on both sides of the Atlantic to prevent so disastrous a course?

"Of course —" Benjamin Franklin broke off when his housekeeper, the handsome and lively Mrs. Stevenson, announced two gentlemen seeking a word with him.

"I hazard, Mr. Brett," Franklin remarked, "you may be astonished at the identity of these gentlemen. One, I might add, declares himself to be a close friend — Ah, here he is. Mr. Falconer, be most welcome! And you no less, *mon cher Chevalier!*" Then in flawless French, "And how do you carry yourself today?"

The Chevalier d'Éon, graceful and dainty as a ballet dancer, treated his host and then Jeremy to formal bows and declared himself enchanted to renew their acquaintance.

Peregrine Falconer, long greyhound's features losing their habitual mournful expression, strode forward and flung arms about the Colonial. "Dear Boston Jerry! How impatient I've been for this moment! 'Twas especially difficult to postpone explanations when calling at Constable House and knowing you were under the same roof. Please believe that for me the pretense of despising you has been a sad if necessary experience."

"You amaze me," Jeremy said uncertainly. "Indeed you do."

"Come on, man, smile! The Rape-Master General really was taken in while you had all the fun; there's the cream of the jest."

This time it was Jeremy who hugged his playfellow.

Dr. Franklin's clear voice suggested, "And now, gentlemen, shall we get down to practicalities? The Chevalier may have a few words of interest."

The Frenchman, exquisitely made up and elegant to the last detail, managed a walking sword and primly seated himself on a huge wing chair. "One 'as discover' that een dealing weeth natives of North America eet ees wise to avoid nuances.

"Therefore I weel merely venture that my master, Hees Most Christian Majesty, Louis XV, recently 'as conceived admiration for the American Colonies and their struggles to obtain their rights.

"'Owever, at thees point, he cannot now admeet such admiration and must move with caution of the most extreme. I weel now re-

333

quest my colleague, Monsieur Falconer, to explain what ees contemplate."

Succinctly Mr. Peregrine Falconer admitted that like many other Englishmen he was deeply involved in trade with North America, so could only contemplate with despair the effects of Non-Intercourse Agreements among the Colonies.

"Means must be found to keep trade with America in a healthy state," said he, losing his customary affected drawl. "Among other things the deplorable state of the Colonial shipbuilding industry must be remedied through swift construction of a number of American-owned merchant vessels capable of —" he shot a glance first at Benjamin Franklin then at the Chevalier d'Éon — "being quickly converted into private ships-of-war."

The Chevalier d'Éon's smile was a trifle smug. "But yes. One 'opes eet weel not 'appen, but should the Colonials be force' to defend themselves would eet not be wise for them to own a certain number of vessels capable of mounting cannon which een short might form beginnings for a navy — 'owever feeble?"

Peregrine Falconer briskly interrupted, "In other words, friend Jerry, business associates and I have been promised credit, courtesy of the Chevalier, to order the *immediate* commencement of construction of vessels designed for the purpose just described.

"Tomorrow, if you agree, you will receive orders for two swift schooners to be laid down immediately you return to your native shores."

Jeremy shook his head. "Sorry, Perry; we can't do much till our winter's over and the ice goes out, which usually is round the end of March."

"Pity," came Falconer's equable reply. "Nevertheless, you will receive funds with which to start work at the earliest practicable moment. Let us hope our vessels will be completed before you start work on the Royal Navy contract."

53

Dolly Lawton's Diary Resumed II

—————⌣—————

Slowly Dolly Lawton's gaze traveled about the big, bright bed-chamber, noted her two traveling boxes had been well corded and that three bundles containing linen had been protected by light, waterproof tarpaulins. Otherwise, her bedchamber looked pretty much as it had when she'd first arrived in Constable House.

A warm, dark-gray hooded coaching cloak lay across the foot of that four-poster she'd never forget. A stout leather reticule reposed alongside a handsome traveling desk Lady Constable had made her the compliment of just before departing for Bath.

A glance at a brass mantel clock showed the hour of ten. Silly of her to have so rushed preparations for departure, especially since Sir Guy's town carriage, placed at her disposal, wasn't to appear before eleven o'clock.

The parson's daughter fought to control rising uncertainty. *What* lay ahead? Fingers trembling, she opened the traveling desk, got out her diary, and nervously plunged a quill into a small, lead-stoppered ink bottle.

Thus arrives the Greatest Day of My Life, one which should prove the Happiest of All were I able Surely and Wisely to determine on the Course I must adopt.

335

Yesterday My Adonis, with his Belongings went on board the Pelican, *a Merchantman charter'd in his Interest by none other than Lord Middlebrook. How strange that His Lordship's Patronage has been so Unaccountably and so Generously restor'd.*

I would not, at this Fatefull Moment, be so rack'd by Anxiety were it not for Something which Chanc'd only Yesterday. Mr. Peregrine Falconer, who has prov'd Markedly Attentive during my Stay in this beautifull Home, press'd me to Accompany him for a Drive about in Hyde Park and then to take a Dish of Tea in Covent Garden.

Being of Two Minds I pos'd the Question to Lady C. She laugh'd and declar'd no Harm likely would come of it should I accept Mr. F.'s Invitation.

Imagine my Astonishment when once we were in Mr. F.'s Carriage, he says, quite Serious, "My Dear Dolly, you may have notic'd how deeply I Esteem your Beauty, your Winning Ways and Chearfull Manner?"

I reply'd that I had indeed and could only wish my Heart were not already pledg'd to my Adonis. (He swears we are to be Marry'd by the Ship's Captain once sail is set for North America.)

He nodded. "My sweet, young Goddess, my Ears have grown weary'd by hearkening to my dear Friend's constant Protestations of Love and Devotion towards You. Indeed, Dolly, I truly believe you would be very Happy with Jeremy — save for two Reasons."

I Implor'd Mr. F. to tell me what these might be.

Says he, sadly, "Poor Jeremy is Penny-less and it will be a Long Time before he can provide you with even the most Ordinary Comfort."

This came like an Icy Shock for I had Conceiv'd that, with his Return to Lord Middlebrook's Favour, my Adonis must be at least Moderately Well off.

"I don't care," I burst out. "I would liefer live with my Love in a Hovel than in a Palace with any Other."

Mr. Falconer only smil'd, then query'd gently, "Have you, sweet and tender maiden, heard aught concerning the Life you must lead in the Colonies?"

Mr. F. then describ'd how very Rude and Simple are most of the Habitations in North America; how Uncouth and Ignorant and

Violent are most of its Inhabitants. Then he dwelt on Terrible Discomforts resulting from the extremes of Climate in New England.

I thought lovingly of my Adonis and though I earnestly begg'd him to desist I could not but recall Lady C.'s mention of Wolves and Cruel Savages ever Prepar'd to pounce upon the Unwary and her Talk about the rough Fare to which the Colonists are Accustom'd.

Mr. F. then confided, 'tis quite possible a Rebellion soon will be rais'd, first of all in the Massachusetts Bay Colony, in which Case, he warn'd, American Merchants and Shipmasters must surely suffer Ruin.

He spoke so softly he reminded me of my Father in his Kinder Moments. "My Dear Dolly, you must approach your Situation with Eyes wide Open. I would be sadden'd to see you make a Mistake in Judgment which may could Ruin the Rest of your Life."

Next he took my Hand between his and gaz'd most earnestly upon me. "Pray attend What I am about to say with the Greatest Attention."

Mr. F. then offer'd me a spacious, eight-room House in Carnaby Square which has a little Garden belonging to it. He promis'd to Convey the Title to it under my own Name! Further, said he, I would have Servants to ensure my Comfort: a Cook, Chambermaid, Footman and a Groom, the last to care for, and Drive a pretty Chariot, already Selected, with a Pair of spirited Horses to draw it. In Addition Mr. F. promis'd me a most Lavish Dressing Allowance.

When I demurr'd and protested my Determination to sail with my own True Love and would marry him and dedicate my Life to his Happy-ness he reach'd over and kiss'd me on the Cheek saying, "As you know, I remain a Bachelor so — who can tell? If we get on as well as I expeckt, 'tis not impossible you may someday Discover a Golden Band upon your Fourth Finger!"

I tried to Upbraid him for a False Friend to my Own True Love but fell Silent, whereat he encircles my Waist.

"Should you feel inclin'd to accept my Friendship know that my Coach will be waiting in the Stableyard of the Bull and Bush Hotel, which lies in Great Russell Street, from Half-after-Eleven till One o'Clock. You have no more to do than come to the Bull and Bush and step from one Conveyance into Another.

"And now, my dearest Dolly, adieu," says he earnestly. *"I trust good Common sense will Decide you on the Wiser Course."*

The parson's daughter broke off, stared blankly at pallid winter sunlight streaming through the window.

Oh, Jerry, my true Love. Why are you not here to Support me in this my most Cruel Dilemma?

She started when a footman rapped and entered to carry her baggage below.

With quivering hands Dorothy Lottimore knotted the traveling cloak about her, agitatedly settled its hood over luxuriant auburn locks, then, taking up her reticule heavy with golden guineas, drew a sobbing breath. Eyes swimming, she groped her way below and out to the Constables' town carriage in which her boxes were being stowed beneath the boot's leather cover.

Although she'd already tipped the house servants she pressed a red-gold guinea into the delighted footman's hand.

" 'Ave a good trip, mum. And where shall I tell 'e coachman to drive yer, mum?"

Without making reply, Dorothy Lottimore entered the carriage and waited till the door was locked before she lowered its window. "James, I will give the driver directions just as soon as I make up my mind."

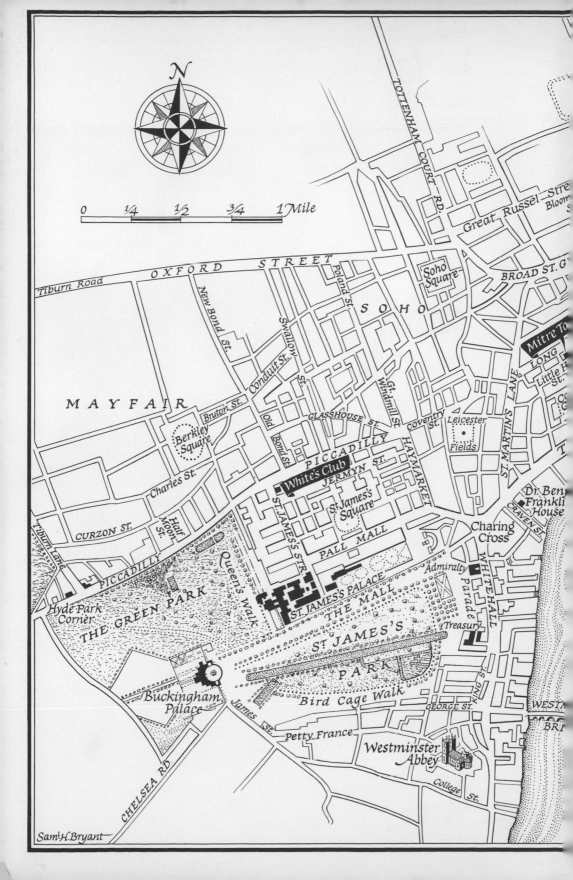

N

0   ¼   ½   ¾   1 Mile

Tiburn Road   OXFORD   STREET

MAYFAIR

SOHO

Soho Square

Great Russel Stre   Bloom

BROAD ST. G

TOTTENHAM COURT RD.

New Bond St.

Swallow St.

Poland St.

Conduit St.

Bruton St.

Berkley Square

Gt. Windmill St.

GLASSHOUSE ST.

Coventry St.

Leicester Fields

ST. MARTIN'S LANE

Mitre To

LONG

Little H
St.

Charles St.

Old Bond St.

PICCADILLY

White's Club

JERMYN ST.

St. James's Square

HAYMARKET

Dr. Ben
Frankli
House

Charing Cross

CRAVEN'S

CURZON ST.

Half Moon St.

PICCADILLY

Tiburn Lane

Hyde Park Corner

THE GREEN PARK

Queen's Walk

ST. JAMES'S STR.

PALL MALL

Admiralty

Parade

WHITEHALL

St. James's Palace

THE MALL

Treasury

ST. JAMES'S

Buckingham Palace

James St.

Bird Cage Walk

PARK

KING ST.

GEORGE ST.

WEST

BRI

CHELSEA RD.

Petty France

Westminster Abbey

College St.

Sam'l H. Bryant